GIFT OF THE HEART

"I beg your pardon, Miss Ashely," murmured the marquess. "It was not my intent to startle you."

"No, of course it was not. How silly," she gasped, placing a hand to her heaving breast. "I-I'm afraid I did not hear you come up behind me."

"No, how could you? You were intent on that bonnet. As well you might be. It is a fetching piece."

"Yes, but frivolous, don't you think?"

"Oh, absolutely," he agreed, smiling. "Which is why you shall try it on."

"Oh, no, I-I couldn't," Jane gasped in consternation as the nobleman reached to undo the bow beneath her chin. "Indeed, I don't want to . . ."

"But of course you can and do. And why should you not? It is traditional, is it not?"

"Traditional, my lord?" queried Jane.

"Easter," he explained, straight-faced. "Flowers stand for love, a deer for good health, the sun for good luck, the rooster for wishes that will come true, and a new Easter bonnet. . . ."

"For good fortune in love," Jane finished for him.

* * *

ZEBRA'S REGENCY ROMANCES
DAZZLE AND DELIGHT

A BEGUILING INTRIGUE   (4441, $3.99)
by Olivia Sumner

Pretty as a picture Justine Riggs cared nothing for propriety. She dressed as a boy, sat on her horse like a jockey, and pondered the stars like a scientist. But when she tried to best the handsome Quenton Fletcher, Marquess of Devon, by proving that she was the better equestrian, he would try to prove Justine's antics were pure folly. The game he had in mind was seduction — never imagining that he might lose his heart in the process!

AN INCONVENIENT ENGAGEMENT   (4442, $3.99)
by Joy Reed

Rebecca Wentworth was furious when she saw her betrothed waltzing with another. So she decides to make him jealous by flirting with the handsomest man at the ball, John Collinwood, Earl of Stanford. The "wicked" nobleman knew exactly what the enticing miss was up to — and he was only too happy to play along. But as Rebecca gazed into his magnificent eyes, her errant fiancé was soon utterly forgotten!

SCANDAL'S LADY   (4472, $3.99)
by Mary Kingsley

Cassandra was shocked to learn that the new Earl of Lynton was her childhood friend, Nicholas St. John. After years at sea and mixed feelings Nicholas had come home to take the family title. And although Cassandra knew her place as a governess, she could not help the thrill that went through her each time he was near. Nicholas was pleased to find that his old friend Cassandra was his new next door neighbor, but after being near her, he wondered if mere friendship would be enough . . .

HIS LORDSHIP'S REWARD   (4473, $3.99)
by Carola Dunn

As the daughter of a seasoned soldier, Fanny Ingram was accustomed to the vagaries of military life and cared not a whit about matters of rank and social standing. So she certainly never foresaw her *tendre* for handsome Viscount Roworth of Kent with whom she was forced to share lodgings, while he carried out his clandestine activities on behalf of the British Army. And though good sense told Roworth to keep his distance, he couldn't stop from taking Fanny in his arms for a kiss that made all hearts equal!

Available wherever paperbacks are sold, or order direct from the Publisher. Send cover price plus 50¢ per copy for mailing and handling to Penguin USA, P.O. Box 999, c/o Dept. 17109, Bergenfield, NJ 07621. Residents of New York and Tennessee must include sales tax. DO NOT SEND CASH.

An Easter Courtship

Sara Blayne

ZEBRA BOOKS
KENSINGTON PUBLISHING CORP.

ZEBRA BOOKS are published by

Kensington Publishing Corp.
850 Third Avenue
New York, NY 10022

First Printing: March, 1995

Printed in the United States of America

To Jack, Tracy, Bob, and Rick, my dearest friends and fellows. And to Steve, Caleb, and Kathryn, my marvelously patient family.

One

"I do wish you would reconsider, dearest Jane, and come with us," said the Countess of Melcourt, bending forward to peer into the ormolu looking glass. Giving a final pat to the brown curls peeping out from beneath her sealskin hat, she straightened the black Cardinal mantle, lined in ermine, over slim shoulders and pulled on black kid gloves before turning to look earnestly once more at her sister-in-law. "At least for the Easter festivities. With Easter coming at the end of April, the Easter Ball will be at the height of the Season. And you, after all, have sequestered yourself in the country for nearly seven years. Don't you think it is time you indulged yourself just a little?"

"Really, Mina," Lady Jane laughed, as she gazed fondly on her sister-in-law, "you make my existence sound positively bleak, when you know very well I am perfectly comfortable here, away from the city."

"And you, my dear, are in danger of sounding very much like an old maid firmly fixed in her ways," retorted the countess. "You are only five and twenty. You should be spending your days shopping in Bond Street. When was the last time you bought a new dress?" she added, eyeing with distaste the younger woman's gray silk round gown, which, though exceedingly attractive and perfectly in taste, was yet, in Mina's opinion, better suited to a matron of advanced years. "And your nights dancing with eligible young men."

Lady Jane only just managed to suppress a sigh. Ah, so
here it was, she thought to herself. And, in truth, she had
been waiting since Mina's unheralded arrival at the unthink-
able hour of eight for her sister-in-law to broach her real
purpose in coming there.

"Really, Mina," she said, shaking her bright curls in gentle
reproval at the indefatigable matchmaker, "you must know
that is the very last thing I should wish. Indeed, I should be
worn to the nub with an endless array of routs, balls, and
soirees. Nor have I the least desire to reenter my name in
the lists of marriageable females. My dear, I have had my
come-out once, and once was quite enough, thank you."

Mina observed the stubborn tilt of her sister-in-law's chin
with a mingling of regret and exasperation. Still, she could
not deny that Lady Jane's come-out had been one to discour-
age many a young female from ever wishing an encore. Not
that the girl had not taken, for she had. And, indeed, possessed
of a more than sizable fortune of her own and blessed with
hair the color of gold guineas, violet blue eyes, and a face
and form that had made the other young beauties pale before
her, how could she not? Almost from the very first moment
she had set foot in London, she had been surrounded by a
veritable host of eligible young bachelors, not the least of
whom had been Geoffrey Charles Bartlett, Viscount Castlebridge. Handsome, titled, and immensely wealthy, the viscount
had wasted little time in winning the heart of the young heiress, only to succumb to a fatal inflammation of the lungs
barely a week before the wedding was to have taken place.

Oh, it did not bear thinking on. And yet how like Geoffrey
to fling everything away! Doubtless Lady Jane was better off
without him, for she doubted that marriage would have
changed him one whit. He would still have been the same
ne'er-do-well who had dared a senseless carriage race in the
middle of a snowstorm and all for a wager! Not that his

bereaved intended could ever be convinced of that. Indeed, it seemed that the girl was set on wearing the willow for him forever.

Ah, well. Rightfully deeming there was nothing she could do to alter the situation at present, the countess gave Jane a fond buss on the cheek and stepped through the door.

Hastily she clasped her cloak more firmly around her as a cold blast of wind whipped at her skirts.

"It seems that dear Wilfred was right," she exclaimed. "For if you must know he said it would snow before tomorrow morning. Which is why he would allow me only a bare half hour for this visit. Were I you, I should remain close to the house for the next day or two, Jane. Your brother is positively uncanny when it comes to predicting the weather."

"Then perhaps the same advice should apply to you, Mina," Lady Jane answered, her eye anxious on the gathering gray bulge of clouds. "A spring snow does not usually last very long, but it can be fierce. Would it not be better to wait a day or two before setting out for London?"

"Nonsense. We shall be off before nuncheon and in Luton before dark. From there it is only a hop and a skip to Town. You needn't trouble yourself about us. We shall be fine. But I do worry about you, Jane. Life is far too short to simply let it pass you by."

"Then I promise I shall fill every hour to the brim while you are gone," said Lady Jane gravely, though there was a decided twinkle in her lovely eyes. "I shall take long walks along the river and tend to my garden. I might even bring myself to make a call or two. So you see, my life promises to be a veritable whirlwind of events. Now you had better go before Wilfred comes looking for you. And know that I wish you both a safe and uneventful journey."

"Well, I, on the other hand, shall wish you no such thing," declared her sister-in-law, frowning reprovingly. "On the contrary, I hope that something terribly upsetting and marvelously exciting occurs to you that will change your life forever. There! I have said it, and I don't regret it in the least."

Abruptly hugging the other woman close, the countess fled down the steps to her waiting carriage.

Startled, Lady Jane stared after her. A smile half of amusement and the other half wry curved her lips. Waving farewell, she braved the cold long enough to watch the carriage sweep around the bend in the road before she went back inside. Hastily shutting out the wind, she leaned for a moment with her back against the door, strangely troubled.

How empty the house seemed! Indeed, in spite of the bright walls with their ivory wall hangings, the caffoy-covered settee and matching chairs ranged cozily before the fireplace, and the fire, crackling merrily in the grate, she could not quite dispel the odd, uneasy feeling Mina's words of warning had aroused or the memory of the slight shiver she had experienced at the countess's final wish for her. They seemed even now to hang in the air, like some foreboding of mischance.

Not since she had left Oaks, the ancestral home of the earls of Melcourt, to take up residence with her mother in the Dowager's House, had she known anything but a quiet contentment with her peaceful, if somewhat uneventful, existence. That had been nearly six years before, and she had grown quite accustomed to filling her hours with long rides on Nesta, her spirited bay mare, tending her garden, making her appearance at the occasional social functions in the country, and serving as a companion to her mother, until finally the sharp edge of anguish she had suffered at Geoffrey's passing had receded to a dull ache she hardly regarded anymore. And if the nights seemed rather long at times and if she suffered a small pang at the sounds of children playing, she never let herself think that perhaps her life was not quite complete.

She was content, and that was far better than the terrible hurt of which she had thought never to be free.

Little wonder, then, that she should be disconcerted to discover some of the old feelings of restlessness stirring within. But how absurd, she told herself firmly, pushing away from the door. If the house seemed somewhat emptier than usual, it was only because her mother was away to Oxford for three weeks to visit Aunt Biddel. Save for Bixley, her mother's aged butler, Mrs. Bledsoe, the housekeeper, the cook and the kitchen staff, Jenny, her abigail, Daisy, the upstairs maid, and Jeremy, of course, the stable lad, she had the house all to herself, and she meant to take full advantage of it.

Resolutely dispelling any such notions of portents and warnings, she made her way to the sitting room where a seeming multitude of samples of wall hangings and upholstery fabrics awaited her inspection. She had wanted to redo the sitting room for a very long time, but had put it off out of deference to her mother's aversion to having her peace and quiet cut up. Now, however, there was nothing to stop her, and she meant to see the thing done before the fortnight was up.

The morning passed quietly enough, and with a cold nuncheon of chilled asparagus, paper-thin slices of ham, and freshly baked apple tarts behind her, she was immersed in choosing between powder blue plush or camel-colored tapestry upholstery for the divan, when the first snowflakes began to fall.

It was mid-March, hardly too late for a snowstorm in Northamptonshire, and she paused to stare out the window at the thickening flurries. It promised to be a full-blown blizzard by nightfall, and a frown creased her brow at the thought of Mina and Wilfred on the road to London. Immediately, however, she chided herself for being a silly pea-goose. Had her brother and his wife gotten away by midmorning as they had planned, they should be well on their way to Luton by now. Besides, she knew her brother to be a top-of-the-trees sawyer. Firmly telling herself there was nothing to worry about, she returned to her pile of samples.

It was not until late afternoon, when Mrs. Bledsoe came in to light the lamps, that she became aware that the storm had worsened, blocking out the sun and bringing on an early dusk.

"We can be thankful to have a roof over our heads this day, Miss Jane," grunted the housekeeper as she knelt to place a fresh log on the fire. "Mr. Bledsoe, may God rest his soul, was used to say as how a spring storm was like to catch more than the budding roses unawares. But you needn't worry none. I made sure Jeremy filled the wood boxes, and Cook has oxtail soup simmering on the stove whenever you're of a mind to sup."

"Whatever should I do without you, Mrs. Bledsoe?" chuckled Lady Jane, a smile bringing out the dimples in her cheeks. "I shall take just a moment to put these things away, and then I shall have a tray in here by the fire, if it is not too much trouble."

The cozy supper she had visualized, however, was not to be. Both women started at the sudden clamor of the door knocker, which was pounded with an almost frenetic insistence.

"Now, whoever can that be?" Mrs. Bledsoe exclaimed.

Lady Jane, whose thoughts immediately turned to Wilfred and Mina, felt her stomach clench. Indeed, it was all she could do to wait with at least the semblance of calm for Bixley's staid steps to cross the foyer. There was the sound of the door opening, followed by the muffled exchange of voices, and then silence. Strangely, Lady Jane had the feeling that it was the silence before mayhem, when Bixley knocked on the sitting-room door.

"Yes, Bixley. What is it?" she called, vaguely surprised that her voice should sound as unruffled as ever.

"Begging your pardon, m'lady," intoned the butler upon entering, "but there is a—er—young person desirous of seeing you. A Miss Winter," he added, in tones that left little doubt as to his disapproval of the caller. "She claims there has been some sort of accident."

Lady Jane felt her heart skip a beat.

"But then, you must bring her here at once. No, wait, I shall come with you."

Lady Jane started forward, only to halt in her tracks as a bedraggled figure slipped past the butler into the room.

"I-I beg your pardon, my lady, for this intrusion," came a husky voice. "But you must see that I could not wait. It-it is Freddy—Fredrick William Bartholomew the Fourth, that is. My—er—cousin. Oh, please. He lay so still when I left him. Will you not send someone at once?"

The girl's white gown and pelisse, which were better suited to a ride in Hyde Park than to a foray through a raging blizzard, besides being soiled, looked rather as if they had been mauled by a wild beast of some sort, and her curls, of a blue-black, hung wet and disheveled about her face. Nevertheless, in spite of her unprepossessing appearance, she was obviously a female of gentle birth. Lady Jane needed only a single look at the lovely face, deathly pale and pinched with fear, to send her instantly across the room to the girl.

"Why, you poor child," she exclaimed softly, pulling her visitor to the fireplace. "You must be half frozen. Of course we shall send someone, but first you must tell us where Freddy is and how we may help him."

She was awarded a grateful look from startlingly green eyes.

"You are very kind, my lady . . ."

"Jane, my dear. You must call me Jane," kindly interrupted her hostess, putting the girl at ease with her warm smile. "And you are . . . ?"

"Ethne. Ethne Winter. Oh, Miss Jane, it was horrible. Something frightened the horses. They bolted, and the carriage overturned. It was not far from here, though it seemed like miles. Just at the bend in the road." Nervously she paced two steps and came back again, wringing her small hands. "I told Freddy to be careful. But he insisted he could handle Dan—er—the cattle. Oh, *why* did I not make him listen to me! I was thrown clear, but Freddy must have hit his head. There was bl-blood. I covered him with the carriage rug. Then I came toward your lights. You must see I had to leave him. Oh, please, can we not go now? He lay so dreadfully still, I'm afraid he may be . . ."

She could not go on, but, covering her face with her hands, gave in at last to the tears that she had been gamely holding in check until then.

"Yes, of course someone must go at once, but not you, my dear," said Lady Jane, hugging the girl to her. "You will remain here. Mrs. Bledsoe will prepare you a hot bath and a change of clothes. Bixley, you will instruct Jeremy to saddle Nesta and bring two lanterns to the house. I shall need only a moment to change."

"But, Miss Jane, surely *you* are not going!"

Lady Jane was quick to silence the housekeeper's horrified outburst with a quelling look.

"But of course I am going," she declared calmly, as if she were proposing nothing more out of the ordinary than a quiet stroll in the garden, she thought half hysterically to herself. "Surely you do not expect me to order Bixley out in such a storm."

She was considerably less sure of herself when, some ten minutes later, she found herself trudging with Jeremy through knee-high snowdrifts in the face of a raging wind. In spite of her Witzchoura mantle lined with ermine, the hood tied firmly beneath her chin, and her "High Shoes," laced firmly across the front, she was nearly frozen before they had gone half the distance to the bend in the road, which was, in actuality, little more than a quarter of a mile. Indeed, she was heartily wishing her unlooked-for guests to the devil when Nesta abruptly reared her head, nearly dragging her mistress off her feet, and let out a resounding whinny.

"It's the cattle, Lady Jane," Jeremy shouted, pointing toward a pair of prime bloods standing, heads down, a few yards away. "Tangled in their traces, they be, less'n I miss my guess."

"I fear you are right," Lady Jane shouted back. "You must go and see if you can free them. Then lead them home while I go on. They will most assuredly perish left out here on their own."

Without waiting for an answer, Lady Jane pushed on. After all, Jeremy was a sizable lad, almost a man, and an old hand with horses. He hardly needed her help in dealing with the cattle, but presumably Fredrick William Bartholomew the Fourth did need her somewhere close by.

Once again it was Nesta who gave the alarm when, some time later, a dark shape reared up before them out of the gloom. It took only a single glance for Lady Jane to realize it was the carriage, resting on its side, and beside it, almost covered with snow, a prone figure, lying very still.

Unexpectedly, she experienced a painful wrench in the vicinity of her breastbone. How very like this must have been that other carriage accident so long ago—the wind and cold, the overturned curricle, the still figure in the snow. Only Geoffrey had not been so fortunate as to have someone to go for help.

Resolutely shaking off the somber mood that threatened to engulf her, she dropped to her knees beside that ominously quiet shape. With hands that trembled, she pulled back the fur rug.

Fredrick Bartholomew was handsome and very young, probably no more than one and twenty. Furthermore, the fur had evidently done very well to keep the cold from him, she was relieved to discover, as she felt for a pulse at the base of the neck. The beat was strong and steady, and his skin felt warm to her touch. Nor could she discover any injuries other than a nasty gash on the forehead below a brown cluster of curls. Still, he would no doubt do a great deal better in bed with a bowl of Cook's sustaining oxtail soup in his belly, she decided, reaching for the smelling salts she had had the foresight to bring with her.

"What . . . ?" moaned the youth, turning his head away from the pungent fumes. "Who . . . ? Where am I?"

"Rest easy, Mr. Bartholomew," Lady Jane soothed. "I am Lady Jane Ashely, and you are a short distance from Melcourt's Oaks. You have been in a carriage accident."

"Carriage accident!" Mr. Bartholomew exclaimed, bolting upright into a sitting position. "Good God, the cattle!" Instantly his face went an alarming white, and, clutching his head, he sank down once more. "Oh-h, my head. It feels as if I had gone a round with Mendoza."

Lady Jane hid a smile. How like a gentleman to think more of his cattle than himself, even very young gentlemen.

"You have sustained a small concussion," she kindly informed him. "And very likely you will suffer the headache for a day or two. But I think there is no great harm done. Nevertheless, you will no doubt do better with dry clothes and a warm fire. Do you think you can stand, Mr. Bartholomew?"

"Certainly," asserted the youth, his boyish pride stung to the quick. "I have experienced a deal worse and lived to tell of it. I—I was only taken by surprise."

"Of course you were," Lady Jane agreed smoothly, only

to be startled as the gentleman gave a sudden violent start, followed by an unmistakable yelp of alarm.

"Good God! Ethne!" he cried, his face gone even whiter than before. "I completely forgot." Earnestly he looked at her, his hand clutching at her mantle. "There was a young lady with me. A—a Miss Winter. Please tell me if . . ."

"Now, now," Lady Jane crooned, hard put to hide her amusement at his peculiar lapse. "Miss Winter is safe and sound. It was she who brought word to us of your predicament. And now, if you are not to catch your death, let alone mine, I suggest you try and see if we can get you on your feet."

Mr. Bartholomew, thus brought to the uncomfortable awareness not only that his rescuer had gone to a great deal of trouble on his behalf, but that she must very likely be chilled nearly to the bone because of him, blushed.

"Yes, of course. How very thoughtless of me," he stammered. "I-I fear I was thinking only of myself."

Apparently having learned his lesson well, he cautiously shoved himself up and, with Lady Jane's help, was even able to climb somewhat unsteadily to his feet. Nor did he object when Lady Jane ordered him to remain where he was, leaning against the carriage wheel, while she went to lead Nesta forward. It was not until it became obvious that Lady Jane meant for him to ride while she walked that a protest at last sprang to his lips.

Lady Jane, in no mood for an argument, firmly cut him off before he could utter it.

"No, no, Mr. Bartholomew. Not a word. Clearly you are in no case to be walking, while I, on the other hand, am a great deal hardier than I may look. Just this once you will forget your notions of gallantry and do what is sensible. Now, let us see if you can mount."

It reflected well on the youth that he was able to swallow

his pride enough to do as he was bidden without further argument. Though Lady Jane could see that it did not sit at all well with him to find himself mounted and clinging to the mane while she took the reins, he gamely held on. Obviously Fredrick Bartholomew had both the good instincts and the manners of a properly brought-up young gentleman. Furthermore, from the looks of his clothes, he came from a well-to-do family. What, then, was he doing driving a young, unescorted lady of quality on the road north from London?

She very much feared that she knew the answer to that most disturbing question. In spite of Miss Winter's avowal that the youth was her cousin, Lady Jane had not failed to note the slight blush that had attended her words or the manner in which the girl's glance had slid self-consciously away. It seemed all too likely that her young guest had not been telling her the truth. In fact, Lady Jane greatly suspected that she had been made the unwitting party to an elopement!

The thought was not one conducive to comfort. Indeed, if such were the case, the young couple had placed her in a most untenable position, for far from being a blood relation to either one of them, she was instead a complete stranger. One, moreover, without the least authority to forbid what must be a very unwise course of action. Thus while in all conscience she could neither condone nor abet what was very likely to bring ruination to them both, she did not see how, short of locking them in the attic, she could stop them.

Indeed, if what she suspected were true, she was very likely in for a very trying night, thought Lady Jane. But almost immediately she caught herself. Though things seemed at a sad pass at present, no doubt everything would look brighter once she and her young charge were safely delivered from the storm. At least, she consoled herself, it could not possibly get any worse.

No sooner had that thought crossed her mind than Nesta

gave a wild whinny and, rearing up on hind feet, dragged the reins from her mistress's hands. Before Lady Jane could do anything to stop it, the mare had bolted. The next instant a great black shape hurtled out of the darkness straight at her.

Lady Jane froze, a scream welling up in her throat.

"Hellsfire!" The curse rent the air from somewhere above her head. Then an iron arm dragged the stallion—for so it was—to one side. Too late.

Lady Jane, struck a glancing blow by the powerful shoulders, crumpled, senseless, to the ground.

Two

Lady Jane came awake to the gentle touch of strong fingers searching for broken bones. Blinking, she opened her eyes to discover a man bending over her. In no little bewilderment, she stared at the lean profile limned against the light of the lantern sitting beside her in the snow.

Though the curly brimmed beaver, pulled down low on the forehead, hid the eyes in shadow, the nose stood out in bold relief, stubborn and distinctly aquiline, and the mouth above an uncompromising jaw was thin-lipped and stern, giving the whole an unmistakably cynical cast. Somewhere in his early thirties, he was not handsome in the strictest sense, at least, that is, not in the way of a Lord Byron, or of a Geoffrey Charles Bartlett, for that matter. The lines about the mouth were rather too harsh, and there was something disconcerting in the chiseled hardness of the jaw and high-boned cheeks. No doubt not a few would find him daunting, though she, surprisingly did not. But then, *she* could not mistake the sensitivity of his touch or the great care with which he straightened her limbs so as not to do her any hurt. Obviously, he was not an *unfeeling* man, something, which she strongly suspected he was at great pains to keep hidden from the rest of the world, she decided, observing the cold impassivity of his expression. He appeared a strong-willed man with a reckless nature, arrogant and proud.

But who was he? she wondered, and, more importantly,

what was she doing lying on her back in the snow with a complete stranger bending over her?

Then all at once everything came rushing back to her.

"Oh, dear!" she exclaimed, struggling to sit upright. "Nesta and poor Mr. Bar . . . !"

"*Softly*, little fool," growled the gentleman, grasping her by the shoulders and gently shoving her down again. "While I think you have suffered no broken bones, it would hardly do to chance bringing on another swoon."

Lady Jane, unaccustomed to being called a fool by anyone, much less by an uncivil stranger, lifted her eyebrows ever so slightly.

"No doubt I am grateful for your concern," she replied wryly, little knowing whether to laugh or be angry at his abrupt manner. "However, I am not such a poor creature. Indeed, I am far more likely to succumb to the cold than I am to a swoon. Therefore, if it would not be too much trouble, perhaps you would be so kind as to help me up. Doubtless you are as anxious as I to be on your way."

"You, my girl, have already caused me a deal of trouble," he answered darkly. Without warning, he slipped his hands beneath her shoulders and knees, and, lifting her in his arms, rose with her as easily as if she were no more than a child. "And promise a great deal more," he added baldly.

Lady Jane, startled into uttering an unladylike squeal, had little choice but to clasp him about the neck. At first she was rendered speechless at finding herself in the arms of a complete stranger, but at last an awareness of the very impropriety of her position unloosed her tongue.

"Oh, this is not at all necessary!" she exclaimed, a blush staining her cheeks. "Indeed, sir, I must ask you to put me down at once!"

The gentleman never faltered in his step.

"And I, regrettably, must refuse," he had the temerity to

answer her. "I did not ask to have you rear up out of nowhere beneath my horse's hooves. But since you *were* where you had no business to be, it is now incumbent on me to see you safely to your destination. Tell me. Just what the devil were you doing wandering along a country road at night in the middle of a snowstorm?"

Lady Jane, considerably taken aback at this further demonstration of his rudeness, did more than lift her eyebrows.

"I beg your pardon," she said in tones meant to freeze his very soul. "I cannot see that that is any business of yours. Furthermore, I was not 'wandering.' As it happens, I was on my way home when you came tearing heedlessly out of nowhere and frightened my mare away. Tell me, is it your usual practice to employ language better suited to the stables, or are you trying deliberately to test my sensibilities?"

She was startled to see the sardonic flash of white teeth against the darker background of his face.

"That has given me back some of my own, has it not?" he queried cynically, immediately dispelling any such erroneous illusions. "I am not, however, noted for my civility. Nor is it your sensibilities that concern me at present. You, my dear, are in danger of contracting a fatal inflammation of the lungs. I suggest, therefore, that you cease to yammer at me and instead point me in the direction of this home of yours."

Lady Jane, who was quite certain she had never before met anyone so ungracious, was sorely tempted to tell him *exactly* where he might go. Nor did it help in the least to know that he was odiously in the right of it. Not only were her limbs gone quite numb from the cold, but she could not stop herself from shivering. Furthermore, while she was reasonably sure Nesta had bolted for the warmth of her stable, she could not be equally as certain that Freddy had managed to accompany her there. It was imperative that she discover as soon as possible if he were lying somewhere unconscious in the snow.

The thought came to her to enlist the aid of the gentleman on Freddy's behalf only to be reluctantly discarded. After all, if it was an elopement on to which she had stumbled, the fewer who knew of it the better. No, the best thing she could do for Freddy was to reach home as quickly as ever she could.

"Oh, very well," she said grudgingly, having come at last to a decision. "It is over there. If you look closely, you can just see the lights. And I shall thank you not to call me your 'dear,' since that is quite possibly the last thing I should ever wish to be. To you, I am Miss Ashely."

"Ashely!" She almost jumped with the unexpected vehemence of that exclamation. "Not a relation of Melcourt's, are you?"

"I am. As a matter of fact, I am Jane Ashely, his sister." She could not mistake the sudden tightening of his arms or the exceedingly strange manner in which he looked at her then. Lifting her head, she peered curiously up at the shadowed countenance. "Are you acquainted with my brother, sir?"

"I have not the pleasure," he said disappointingly and, having come to his waiting mount, set her without round-aboutation on her feet. Just then a fist of wind came out of nowhere, frightening the stallion. Showing the whites of its eyes, it reared back. "Steady, Brutus," growled the stranger. A steely hand reached for the reins.

Left to herself, Lady Jane discovered, to her dismay, that her numbed limbs were incapable of supporting her. She swayed and felt herself falling. A blistering curse rent the air just before iron fingers clamped about her tiny waist and thrusted her, reeling, into the saddle. She was vaguely irritated that somehow she could not summon the voice to object either to the gentleman's unseemly choice of words or his ungentle treatment of her. Then to her further annoyance, she found that she was not at all averse to have a strong pair of arms go around her as he vaulted swiftly behind her to the saddle. Indeed, feeling the comforting warmth of a hard masculine chest next to her, she decided she liked it very well where she was.

The next instant he had lifted the reins to set the stallion in motion.

The steed was possessed of a smooth, easy gait, and it was not long before Lady Jane found herself going peacefully adrift.

An odiously insistent voice broke through the spell.

"You still have not told me what you were doing out in the middle of the night."

Annoyed in spite of herself, Lady Jane aroused herself to render some sort of answer.

"I-I beg your pardon?"

"Oh, come now. It is a simple enough question. No doubt you will pardon what is a natural curiosity. Or is it the earl's usual practice to allow his sister the freedom to roam the countryside unescorted and at night?"

Lady Jane stiffened in indignation.

"You must know very well that it is not," she retorted, little caring at the petulance in her voice. "And I was not 'roaming.' Indeed, I cannot see why you insist on laying the blame on me for what was clearly not my fault."

"From which I must deduce that the fault is all mine," he came back at her in such a manner as left little doubt that he did not in the least adhere to such an interpretation of the events.

Lady Jane was hard put to stifle a gasp at such gross incivility. It was on her tongue to tell him that if the shoe fit, he must just wear it. Her innate sense of fairness, however, would not let her.

"Oh, you really are the most provoking man," she said, her voice colored with a tremor of rueful laughter. "You must be as aware as I that it was naught but an unfortunate accident for which no one can be blamed. Nor can I allow you to think ill of poor Wilfred. No doubt he would be as disapproving as you to discover his sister in such circumstances. It does not signify, however, for though I do try and regard his probable wishes in most things, I am independent of his purse strings and well of an age to determine my own life."

"For which you no doubt think to be congratulated," he offered in tones best calculated to rouse her temper, which, had she stopped to think about it, must certainly have been his intent all along. The immediate effect of his barbed remarks had been to jar her out of the stupor that had by degrees been creeping over her and to cause her heart to fairly pound with indignation at his boorish treatment of her. With the result that not only were her senses now thoroughly aroused, but the blood rushed furiously through her veins, imbuing her throughout her entire length with something approaching warmth.

"Never," she exclaimed roundly, "in my entire acquaintance have I known anyone as rude as you. But then, fortunately, I cannot account you as one of my acquaintanceship, can I?—not having the dubious pleasure of your name."

She was startled by his harsh bark of laughter.

"Oh, you are quite right to fault me for that," he replied maddeningly. "An omission that I shall immediately set to rights. I am Danforth, Miss Ashely, and pleased, no doubt, to make your acquaintance."

For an instant it seemed that the whole world had gone suddenly topsy-turvy, leaving her head spinning. Indeed, had he claimed to be the Prince Regent himself, she could not have been more unsettled.

"Danforth!" she breathed in accents of bitter loathing.

"Even so," drawled the gentleman imperturbably. "It would

seem almost providential, would it not, that we should meet at last under such ironic circumstances."

Lady Jane, who would have preferred never to meet the gentleman under these or any other circumstances, could not but take exception to the fate that had brought them together. How could the powers that be have been so unkind as to place her in the arms of the one man to whom she must least have wished to be in any way beholden? Danforth, she thought, who had robbed her of her happiness! Indeed, Danforth, whose wager had taken Geoffrey forever from her!

"You will pardon me, my lord marquess," she uttered in a voice that sounded cold and pinched even in her own ears, "if I cannot view it in the same light as you apparently do. Far from providential, it can only be a cruel twist of fate that has thrown us together, one that can occasion neither of us any good. Indeed, I cannot but wonder what ill chance should have brought you so far from your usual London haunts."

"You might well ask, Miss Ashely," he said as, abruptly, he reined the stallion to a halt. A glad cry rang out.

"Lady Jane! It's Lady Jane, Mrs. Bledsoe. A gentleman's brought her home!"

In the back of her mind, Lady Jane recognized Jeremy's shout, but she did not look to see the lad running eagerly toward them. Her entire attention was focused on the nobleman. Slowly, as if compelled, she at last turned her eyes in the direction in which he was staring with such grim certainty.

"Oh, Lord," she breathed upon seeing the slender figure of Miss Winter, limned in the doorway, her eyes on the marquess peculiarly stricken, and behind her, Freddy Bartholomew, his face exceedingly pale. "I might have known!"

"Indeed you might," growled the gentleman. "In truth, since you have seen fit to extend your hospitality to my half-sister and the young whelp who has foolishly let himself be drawn into her toil, I must assume you knew very well not only *who* would be riding *ventre a terre* on the road north from London, but *why* he should have done it."

Lady Jane, quite naturally incensed at so erroneous a supposition on his part, drew a sharp breath.

"Then, my lord," she replied coldly, "you would be seriously mistaken. Miss Winter turned up on my doorstep considerably shaken and pleading for help. I had not the least notion that she was in any way related to you. Nor was there time to exchange amenities. In the circumstances, I deemed it advisable to go in search at once for Mr. Bartholomew."

"You went in search of him! Why the devil should you do anything so patently lack-witted?"

"Pray tell what else would you have me do when I was told that a gentleman had been injured in a carriage accident and left unconscious in the snow?'

A telling silence fell over them. Then, grim-voiced, he said, "Just as one other gentleman—one very dear to you—was left in similar circumstances?"

"Yes," she answered simply. He looked at her so strangely then that she dropped her eyes in sudden confusion. Immediately, however, she lifted them again to gaze earnestly up at him. "Only, fortunately, this time help arrived before it was too late. They are very young, my lord. And while I cannot know the facts surrounding what one might suppose to be a very unwise course of action, I can only hope that older, wiser heads will prevail to ensure they are brought to no greater harm."

A harsh bark of laughter seemed forced from him. Nor did it seem he would render any farther answer as he continued to stare at her with those singularly penetrating orbs. At last, however, apparently having become aware of Jeremy, standing self-consciously at the stallion's head, he dismounted and, lifting his arms to clasp her about the waist, looked once more into her face.

"I congratulate you, Miss Ashely. It is not often that I am surprised by anyone," he drawled with just a flicker of bafflement in the harsh features. "You are not at all as I had supposed you to be. As to the probable fates of my sister and her moon-stricken cub, you need not concern yourself further. You have done enough." The protest that rose instinctively to her lips was cut off as he lowered her without warning from the saddle and set her on the ground. "Rest assured, however, that I shall keep what you have said in mind."

The next instant he had swooped her into his arms. Issuing a curt command over his shoulder for Jeremy to see to his horse, he carried her toward the house.

"I am fine, Mrs. Bledsoe. Really," Lady Jane insisted, as the marquess bore her into the foyer against her embarrassed protests. "There is nothing wrong with me that a bowl of Cook's soup will not soon set to rights."

"On the contrary, Mrs. Bledsoe," coolly interjected the nobleman, "your mistress is a good deal more shaken up than she would have you to believe. I suggest, therefore, that you direct me to her bedroom. After which, you will prepare her a hot bath and provide her a tray in bed. Under no circumstances is she to be disturbed before morning, is that understood?"

"I beg your pardon," declared Lady Jane, who, in spite of the fact that she had been wishing for that very thing, quite naturally took exception to his lordship's high-handed manner of intervening in her affairs. "I should be a very poor hostess were I to abandon my guests in such a manner. I wish you will please put me down, my lord. I assure you I am very much recovered and am quite capable of standing on my own."

"Yes, so you have repeatedly informed me," answered his lordship, making no discernible effort to carry out her request. "In this one instance, however, you will oblige me. And while I must indeed impose upon your generosity insofar as my troublesome little sister is concerned, Mr. Bartholomew and I shall be leaving directly. So you need not concern yourself as regards the responsibilities of a hostess."

"Leaving! But you cannot. Freddy is not fit to travel!"

This, coming as it did from Miss Winter, won a quelling lift of an eyebrow from the marquess and a blush from Mr. Bartholomew.

"My dearest Ethne," drawled his lordship, "Freddy has seen fit to hazard your good name and his, and, further, has committed the supreme folly of having been caught. He not only is *able* to travel, but will most certainly do so within the hour. Just as a matter of curiosity. Was it his lack-witted notion or yours to make use of my curricle and pair for this ill-considered scheme of yours?"

"You must not blame, Ethne, Cousin Nicholas," spoke up Freddy manfully, coming to attention. "It was all my idea."

"Oh, quiet, Freddy," sulked the young lady. "Nick must know very well it was not."

"Cousin?" Lady Jane exclaimed. "But then, Miss Winter was telling the truth when she so claimed him to be."

"Oh, did she then," murmured his lordship. "Yes, she would no doubt. Freddy, however, is *my* cousin, being the son of my father's sister. He does not share a similar kinship to my half-sister, whose father was Lord Winter. Still, I offer you my congratulations, dearest sister, on seeking to wrap the whole in clean linen. I would suggest, nevertheless, that were I in your place, I should keep my tongue between my teeth in order not to draw undue notice to myself. You are very close to finding yourself transported to your Aunt Aberdeen's in Devon until you are of a very advanced age."

Instantly, Miss Winter's chin came up, her green eyes flashing defiance.

"Naturally," she retorted disparagingly. "You would like that very well, would you not? I might as well be dead for all the attention you pay me. Indeed, I cannot see why you came after me, when you so plainly wish me out of your hair. And do not bother to deny it. It is true, you know very well that it is."

"But I have no intention of denying it," replied his lordship with maddening imperturbability. "On the contrary, the notion has never entertained greater appeal than at this very moment. I have been disposed in the past to deal leniently with you, my girl. However, if it is my *attention* you want, you shall have it."

Lady Jane, observing Miss Winter's face go pearly white at this promised treat, and keenly cognizant of the fact that she herself still resided in his lordship's embrace, chose at that moment to intervene.

"I beg you will desist from this demonstration, my lord," she said, hard put to keep the impatience from her voice. "Indeed, I am quite sure I do not know which of you is behaving more childishly, though it is obvious which of you has the least excuse to do so."

"Devil!" said his lordship with obvious feeling.

Lady Jane ignored him.

"Clearly Miss Winter," she continued, "is on the verge of exhaustion, else she would not choose to speak in a manner so unbefitting a young lady of refinement." Satisfied, upon seeing the girl blush as red as she had been pale only a moment before, that Miss Winter was not the shameless hoyden she had thus far presented herself to be, Lady Jane next turned her attention, tellingly, back to his lordship. "Quite naturally I cannot allow you and Mr. Bartholomew to set forth in the middle of a snowstorm. Especially as my brother's house is close by. In spite of the fact that the earl and his wife are away to London for the beginning of the Season, I know he would insist on extending to you his hospitality."

For the first time she noticed that Danforth's hair beneath the curly brimmed beaver was raven black and that his eyes were of a singularly spellbinding blue. The latter, greatly to her discomfort, seemed to pierce her through.

"Are you quite sure?" he demanded quizzingly. "Rather than have us close by, I should have thought you might be wishing us at Jericho."

"But how can you say so," she retorted in bitter accents. "My feelings, however, whatever they might be, hardly signify. You will stay at Oaks. It is the only sensible thing in the circumstances."

"And you, of course, are a very sensible young woman, are you not?" drawled his lordship, his glance seeming to bore holes through her.

Well aware of the light in which he held her recent excursion into a raging snowstorm, Lady Jane blushed.

"In spite of what you may think of me," she said, stubbornly returning his look, "I believe I am capable of making perfectly rational decisions upon occasion."

"I shouldn't doubt it at all, Miss Ashely," he countered smoothly, though she could not but note the suspicious twitch at the corners of the handsome lips. "Very well. On behalf of Mr. Bartholomew and myself, I accept the offer of your brother's house."

Lady Jane, who wished only to be left alone to sort out her own tumultuous thoughts, smiled perfunctorily.

"It is settled then. Jeremy will accompany you to Oaks in order to make you known to the staff. And now, my lord," she added, making no attempt to hide the weariness in her voice, "you will be pleased to either carry me upstairs or set me down. I care not which, so long as you do it at once."

It soon transpired that the marquess was not disposed to relinquish his burden just yet. Instructing Mrs. Bledsoe to send up hot water for her mistress's bath, he carried Lady Jane upstairs and deposited her with great care on the settee in her sitting room, after which, he straightened and regarded her appraisingly.

"You look worn to the nub," he observed with what seemed a characteristic abruptness.

"How very kind of you to notice," she retorted crossly. Untying the bow at her throat, she flung the hood back to reveal her guinea-gold locks. Upon which, she became acutely aware that the troublesome marquess showed no discernible inclination to leave her. Irritated, she arched a brow significantly up at him.

"My lord?" she queried coolly.

His response was hardly what she expected.

"You are a beautiful woman, Miss Ashely. I find it inconceivable that a female of your undeniable wit and charm should choose to hide herself away in the country. Why the devil are you not in London with your brother and his wife?"

"I-I beg your pardon," she stammered, amazed at the effrontery of the man. "It is hardly any business of yours what I do. Nor can I conceive of any reason why you should concern yourself one way or the other."

"I am shockingly ill-mannered. I told you that. I ask because it occurs to me that I have played no small part in this desire of yours to stay in the shade. It has been six—nearly seven—years since Geoffrey Bartlett and I set out for Newmarket on that damnably ill-fated night. Do you not think it is time you ceased to shut yourself away from the world?"

For the length of three full heartbeats Lady Jane was rendered speechless at the nobleman's total disregard for her probable feelings in the matter. How dare he, of all people, presume to dictate to her the acceptable span of her mourning!

"Perhaps it is only that the world holds no appeal for me, my lord," she offered coldly, when she had got her tongue back again. "Or at least the world as you mean it. I am perfectly content with my small part of it and have neither the need nor the inclination to expand it."

"Gammon," he said. "Next you will be trying to convince me you were meant for a nunnery."

"On the contrary," she replied heatedly. "I have not the least desire to convince you of anything. Except, perhaps, my wish to be left alone. Now if there is nothing else—?"

The stern lips curled in a smile, distinctly ironic.

"As a matter of fact there is a great deal more I wish to discuss with you. However, I shall leave it for a later time, Miss Ashely." Bowing at the waist, he made as if to withdraw, only to pause and turn back again at the door. "By your leave, I shall call on you first thing in the morning."

"Oh, by all means, my lord," she returned acerbically. "Indeed, I shall look for you and Mr. Bartholomew to join us for breakfast. Shall we say at nine?"

A gleam of amusement leaped in the remarkable orbs.

"Make it ten," he said without hesitation. "I shall make sure my half-sister is not allowed to disturb you before then. I want you perfectly recovered from your recent adventures."

It was on her lips to inform him that she was an early riser and did not require his intervention on her behalf, but he had already turned and left her, closing the door firmly behind him.

"The devil!" she exclaimed, hurtling a small cushion at the inoffensive oak barrier—practically in the face of Mrs. Bledsoe, who was just entering.

Three

Morning came much sooner than Lady Jane could have wished. Indeed, it seemed she had hardly fallen asleep before Daisy, the upstairs maid, arrived at her door bearing the cup of hot chocolate with which she customarily greeted each new day. In no mood either for company or hot chocolate, she accepted the tray with something less than her usual good cheer and, dismissing the servant girl, said she would be down shortly. Then with a sigh, she fell back once more against her pillows, filled with an unwonted reluctance to rise.

And little wonder, she mused wryly to herself, when she had spent nearly the entire night fighting her pillows. And all because the Marquess of Danforth had come barging into her life, dredging up all the memories she had thought long since laid to rest. No, not just the memories, she mused, frowning, but rather the doubts and uncertainties that always came with the memories, the terrible conviction that she somehow was to blame for what had happened. It was not an easy thing to accept that, far from having come to terms with Geoffrey's death, she had only managed to bury that part of her life for a while in some deep dark corner of her mind, but the truth was, she had not allowed herself to think of Geoffrey and the short time they had shared together for longer than she cared to remember.

Faith, was she really such a coward? she groaned, suddenly not liking herself very much. Surely, she, who had always prided herself on being in control of her life, could bear the memories of the man she had loved!

As if in answer, an image sprang to mind of the young viscount as he had appeared the first time she had laid eyes on him. He had been tooling his curricle through Hyde Park, and she remembered thinking she had never seen anyone quite so dashing. Wearing a many-caped driving coat, his curly brimmed beaver cocked jauntily to one side, he was the handsomest creature she had ever seen. And apparently he had been taken with her as well, for he had wasted little time in persuading Wilfred to present him to her. She had lost her heart to him the very first time he had smiled down at her, his eyes brimful of laughter.

Suddenly she frowned. But how absurd. She could not remember whether they had been green or hazel. Indeed, her recollection of his face was peculiarly hazy, rather like viewing an image through a clouded glass. She experienced a sudden rending pang. Flinging aside the bedclothes, she crossed agitatedly to her dressing table.

"It *must* be here somewhere," she muttered to herself, as she emptied one drawer after another, little caring at the havoc worked on her fine silk scarves and lace underthings, which she flung heedlessly to the floor. Then at last her fingers found at the back of the bottom drawer that for which she had been so frantically searching. Releasing a long, tremulous breath, she drew forth a small black velvet box and laid it on her dressing table.

For a moment she stared at it, reluctant, somehow, now that she had found it, to open it and view the contents inside. At last realizing she was behaving in a perfectly idiotic manner, she took herself firmly in hand. Nevertheless, her fingers trembled slightly as she reached for the box and lifted the lid.

The miniature of Geoffrey Charles Bartlett, Viscount Castlebridge, stared back at her. The blond hair was rather darker than she remembered, and perhaps not quite so curly, she mused whimsically. It had always seemed as rebellious as the man himself. Man? she reflected wonderingly. How very young he looked! And yet he had been two and twenty. Strange that she had always thought of him as being so much older, a man about town, one upon whom she could depend to guide her through the pitfalls of her first Season in London. And he had, of course, but now, in retrospect, she suddenly realized that perhaps he had not been quite so sure of himself as he had wanted her to believe. Not for the first time it came to her to wonder exactly what had driven him to accept so reckless a wager practically on the eve of their wedding day.

Had he been afraid? whispered a small insidious voice. Afraid he might not live up to the expectations of a very young and exceedingly romantic girl who had idealized and adored him? Had he needed to prove something to himself? Was that why he had done it?

She jumped as the chime of the mantel clock striking the half hour brought her to the realization not only that she was sitting quite still, staring, unseeing, at her reflection in her dressing mirror, but that it was nine-thirty. Good heavens! she breathed. It was only thirty minutes till the marquess was to arrive and she was not even dressed. Hastily she closed the box and replaced it in the bottom drawer before ringing for Jenny, the young girl who had been recruited to serve as her abigail in the absence of Nanny Twickum.

In light of recent events she could only suppose it was typical of her luck that her old nanny should have been called away this week of all weeks to tend to an ailing sister, leaving her mistress prey to the ministrations of a green girl. Jenny should have made her appearance as soon as she was informed that Lady Jane had received her morning cup of chocolate.

No doubt the child was daydreaming again, she thought, sighing. Ah, well, she had no one to blame but herself. She was the one, after all, who had insisted the girl be brought upstairs from the kitchen, she reminded herself, rummaging through her armoire for something to wear.

Naturally the fact that she had spent a nearly sleepless night twisting in her sheets and batting at her pillows till almost an hour before dawn had not helped either her disposition or her appearance. In her present frame of mind, nothing would seem to suit. Indeed, after picking out, then discarding four gowns in succession, she finally settled out of desperation on a cambric round gown, the newest addition to her wardrobe and one that she had been saving for a special occasion. Hastily she dressed without the aid of her still absent abigail. Then, observing the shadows beneath her eyes, Lady Jane grimaced.

"Drat the man," she muttered to herself, forced to resort to the rouge pot to add a touch of color to abnormally pale cheeks. It was all his fault she appeared the veriest antidote. Indeed, it seemed patently unfair that, with hundreds of miles of perfectly good roads in England, the marquess's half-sister should have chosen that particular bend in which to overturn her carriage. If she did not know better, she could almost believe Mina's parting wish was coming to fruition with a vengeance.

Dismissing any such foolishness from her mind, she ran a comb briskly through her short curls, then, rising from her dressing table, stepped before the cheval glass for a final critical inspection of her appearance.

All in all she was not displeased with the effect of the cambric morning dress of pale rose. Though Mina most likely would have viewed the high neck encircled by delicate lace points lying flat against the bodice with a jaundiced eye, the round gown falling in soft folds from an empire waist was

perfectly suited to her slender build and displayed a quiet
elegance quite in keeping with the image of cool self-com-
posure that she wanted to portray—that morning in particular.
The long sleeves, puffed above the elbows, then hugging the
arms to lace bands about the wrists, gave the dress just the
right touch of femininity, she decided, reaching up to fasten
her grandmama's pearl drops in her earlobes. Indeed, from
the top of her head, her lovely curls parted in the center *à
la* Madonna, to her rose-colored kid Spanish slippers, she
presented the very picture of a female of refinement, past the
first blush of youth, perhaps, but in the flower of womanhood—a woman, in short, to be reckoned with.

Satisfied that she was as ready as she would ever be for
the coming encounter with the Marquess of Danforth, she
straightened slim shoulders and crossed to the door. Opening
it, she found herself unexpectedly face to face with Jenny,
who instantly blushed to the roots of her carrot red hair.

"Miss Jane," gasped the abigail, dipping hastily into a
curtsy. "I'd have been here sooner, only Miss Winter needed
someone to help with her dress. It was the kind with all those
little buttons down the back what nobody can fasten by themselves. Then she was wondering if maybe I could do something with her hair, and the very next thing I know, Mrs.
Bledsoe's knocking on the door wanting to know why I bain't
where I had ought to be. She was awful mad, Miss Jane, and
I'm terrible sorry I—"

"It's all right, Jenny," Lady Jane interrupted the servant's
flurried outburst. "You did just as you should. Indeed, I must
be grateful you were able to render assistance to Miss Winter.
I fear I have been sadly remiss in not having anticipated her
needs." And, indeed, in all the tumult of emotion occasioned
with finding herself suddenly thrust into the presence of the
man who had irrevocably altered her happiness and changed
her life, she had forgotten her responsibilities as a hostess.

She smiled reassuringly at the abigail, who was plucking with nervous fingers at a fold in her pinafore. "Perhaps we should make it a permanent arrangement, permanent, that is, for as long as Miss Winter remains a guest in this house. Would you like that, Jenny?"

"Oh, but I-I couldn't," the girl stammered. "Who would look after you, Miss Jane? Nanny Twickum wouldn't like it was she to learn I had left you with no one to see your clothes was proper took care of and—"

"Nonsense. I am perfectly capable of taking care of myself. And as for Nanny Twickum, you must just leave her to me. I shall make sure she understands you are doing me a very great service."

It was perhaps no small evidence of the awe in which Nanny Twickum was regarded by the other members of the household, thought Lady Jane with a faint smile, that Jenny appeared far from convinced.

"Yes, Miss Jane," mumbled the girl uncertainly. "If you say so."

"I do say so, Jenny," her mistress replied, coming out into the hall and closing the door behind her. "And now perhaps you will be good enough to tell me where you left Miss Winter."

"She's there, Miss Jane, waiting to see you before you go down to breakfast."

Yes, no doubt, thought Lady Jane, espying a slender figure pacing nervously at the far end of the hallway. Indeed, she would have been very surprised if Miss Winter did *not* wish to have a few words with her before the marquess put in his appearance. Stifling a sigh at what promised to be the beginning of a most trying morning, Lady Jane went to meet her guest.

"Ethne," she exclaimed, taking the girl's hands warmly in her own. "How lovely you look. I am glad to see you have apparently suffered no ill effects from last night's unfortunate mishaps. You slept well, I trust?"

It was true. Cleaned up, rested, and dressed to the nines in a morning dress of sprig muslin, Ethne Winter was more than just pretty. She was a diamond of the first water. Furthermore, she was either a consummate actress intent on correcting any erroneous first impressions she might have made the night before, or she was truly what she appeared to be—a young girl, impetuous, perhaps, and lacking in patience, but innocent nonetheless and far less worldly than she would have had others believe—a female, in short, suffering all the throes of finding herself on the threshold of womanhood. Blushing prettily, she dropped into a curtsy.

"Indeed, yes, thank you." She gave a small grimace, which served only to wrinkle her nose most charmingly. "I did—in spite of the fact that I was in dread of what Nicky will most likely have decided to do with me. Which is why I wished so very much for the chance to see you and—well—to explain my side of things before my brother prejudices you against me."

"I see," temporized Lady Jane. Linking arms with the girl, she turned to descend the stairs. "And does my good opinion mean so much to you? I warn you, there is very little that I can do to help you. I hardly know you, after all, and Danforth is, I must presume, your legal guardian."

"Yes, Mama made sure of that after we lost Papa." A dimple, wholly engaging, if somewhat naughty, peeped out. "Mama, you see, claimed she could do nothing with me. And, indeed, she could not, but only because she made it quite plain she had not the least wish to have anything to do with me."

"I seem to recall that you made a similar allegation against your half-brother. And yet he cared enough to brave a snowstorm to come after you. Does it not occur to you that you

might be a trifle hasty in your judgment of those who appear
to be only a great deal concerned about your welfare?" Lady
Jane queried gently as they crossed the foyer and entered the
parlor adjoining the breakfast room.

"Pooh," ejaculated Miss Winter with obvious feeling. "If
Danforth cares a whit about me, he has never made the least
effort to show it. I should not doubt that it was his precious
cattle that brought him riding *ventre a terre* after us. As for
my mother, what would you think of someone who refused
to bring her own daughter out?"

"I think it would depend on what reasons she gave," Lady
Jane replied calmly. Seating herself on the sofa, she motioned
Ethne to sit down beside her. "I can think of any number by
which she might have been motivated. Perhaps she thought
you too young, or too impetuous by far. It is a very serious
thing, making one's first appearance in society. Right or
wrong, one is judged by initial impressions."

"Eighteen is hardly too young. And I know perfectly well
how to conduct myself in polite society," declared the girl,
immediately jumping up again, as if she could not bear to
remain still. The sudden tinge of color in the smooth cheeks,
moreover, would seem to indicate that she had scored a hit,
Lady Jane was quick to note. Obviously, the child had heard
such things before. "No, the truth is, Mama is shockingly
indolent and cannot be bothered to introduce her only daughter into society. It is far too fatiguing, you see. I have no
doubts that had my future remained up to her, I should have
languished at Hargrove until I was at my last prayers."

"So instead, you contrived to have yourself removed from
Hargrove and into your brother's care, is that it?"

Ethne shrugged slim shoulders.

"But of course. What else should I have done? It was remarkably easy, too. I had only to feign having developed a

tendre for our closest neighbor, Mr. Heaton, who, you must know, is considered wholly unacceptable."

"If you mean Gerard Heaton, I must certainly agree," said Lady Jane, recalling to mind an image of a slender figure somewhat carelessly dressed, with a lackadaisical smile and handsome, if dissipated features. He was a dangerous adventurer with an unsavory reputation and hardly a feather to fly with. Seven years ago, he had been on the lookout for an heiress to retrieve his fortunes. Apparently, nothing had changed. He must be every bit of five and thirty, hardly an eligible parti for a young and inexperienced girl, who had yet even to make her come-out. If Ethne had been flinging her cap after *him,* it was little wonder her mama had tossed up her hands in horror.

"It worked like a charm," confided that young lady, obviously pleased with herself. "Mama positively could not ship me off fast enough to Nicky."

"Only he, I must suppose, proved to be a sad disappointment, else you would not find yourself in your present predicament."

"Oh, how well you must know him," Ethne exclaimed, her darkling glance leaving little doubt that Lady Jane had hit upon the truth of the matter.

"On the contrary, I do not know him at all," Lady Jane demurred. "He should be considered extremely remiss in his duties, however, did he not take you in hand. Especially if you had been so foolish as to earn yourself the reputation of one who was unruly and headstrong. Nothing, I assure you, is more damaging to a girl."

Ethne had the grace to look abashed at that pronouncement from one whom she undoubtedly had looked to for understanding.

"He has absolutely refused to have me brought out this season," she admitted ruefully. Then immediately her head came up. "And for no better reason than it does not suit him to do so at this time. I am to be satisfied with remaining in exile at his estate in Bedfordshire, while he takes his pleasure in London." Heatedly, she began to pace. "Had anyone told me, I should never have believed Nicholas Trevant could be so positively Gothic in his treatment of females. I am well acquainted with his reputation, and it hardly seems fair that he has been free to indulge himself in whatever fanciful notion takes him, simply because he is a man and his father's heir, while I must be treated like some absurdly delicate hothouse flower. Oh, do you not wish sometimes that you had been born a boy?"

"No, never," answered Lady Jane, who could not but note that at that moment, with her hands clenched into fists at her sides and her green eyes flashing sparks of resentment, the girl appeared anything but a hothouse flower. Ethne Winter promised to be a rare handful. Indeed, Lady Jane was moved in spite of herself to something approaching sympathy for the marquess.

"Never?" echoed the girl, eyeing her in patent disbelief.

Lady Jane's lips curved in a smile of amusement.

"No doubt I am sorry to disappoint you, but on the contrary, I find I am perfectly suited to be just what I am."

Ethne gave an impatient gesture of the hand.

"But do you never chafe at the restrictions? Do you not find it galling to have someone always telling you what you may or may not do, simply because you are a female?"

"No doubt I should, were that the case. However, I count myself extremely fortunate that I am mistress of my own life. No one tells me what to do, and though I choose to live here with my mother, there is no one who would stop me did I decide to set up housekeeping elsewhere. I think my own thoughts, make my own decisions, and am not averse to speaking my mind if I believe the occasion warrants it. On the other hand, I value my independence far too much ever to behave in such a manner as to jeopardize it. It is one thing to be free to conduct one's affairs without interference and quite another to flout what is acceptable to the society in which one lives. Not even a gentleman, you must agree, may do the latter with impunity. You have only to look to your Mr. Heaton to realize that."

"Yes, perhaps," conceded the girl, frowning as she appeared to think the matter over. "It is true that Mr. Heaton is never invited to the best houses. And though he may be seen at the assembly rooms, he is very often ostracized, though I really cannot see why, when he is ever so much more entertaining than most of the gentlemen of my acquaintance. Is that why you have never married?" she continued, having hardly drawn a breath between sentences. "Because you prefer your independence?"

No sooner were the words out than she appeared instantly to think better of them.

"Forgive me. I know perfectly well I should not have asked."

"No, you shouldn't," agreed Lady Jane, torn between vexation at the girl's impertinence and amusement at her irrepressible candor. "And, no, that is not the reason I have never married. Really, Ethne, I have nothing against marriage or men in general. Indeed, why should I? I have not the least doubt that it is a most satisfactory arrangement, so long as the two people are compatible with each other."

"Which is to say that you might be persuaded to enter into matrimony," Ethne persisted, favoring her hostess with a disturbingly penetrating look, "should the right man come along?"

"That, Miss Winter, is quite enough," Lady Jane answered quietly, but in such a manner as left little doubt that she had no intention of being interrogated further. "What I should or should not do is purely my own concern. I believe *you* were to be the subject of this interview, not I. And I own I find it somewhat incomprehensible why, if you wished so ardently to be brought out, you should have chosen to elope with Mr. Bartholomew. It would not, after all, appear the best solution to your dilemma. Surely you must realize the scandal of being married over the anvil, even had you managed to bring the thing off, would have ruined you in polite circles."

"Of course I do," declared the surprising Miss Winter. "But that's just it, don't you see? Freddy and I were not eloping. Freddy is a dear, but I could never *marry* him. We are far too different ever to suit. Why, we should be at loggerheads over simply everything, which, I cannot but think, would prove disagreeable in the extreme. No, I simply cannot even contemplate the idea of wedding Freddy, which is why it was so imperative that I talk to you this morning. Oh, Miss Jane, you are my only hope. I am in an absolute quake at the thought that Nick will *force* Freddy to make things right."

Lady Jane, who had fully expected the girl to beg her to bring what influence she could to bear on Danforth to *allow* the marriage, took a full ten seconds to digest this startling revelation.

"If what you say is true," she ventured at last, "then what exactly were you and Freddy doing alone on the road north from London? I warn you, if your intent was simply to run away from home, I fear I can have very little sympathy for you."

"Then you must believe me that that was never my intent," Ethne said earnestly. "The fact that we were on the road north from London or that Gretna Green may lie at the other end of it is all purely coincidental. The truth of the matter is, we set out yesterday morning from Brandymere, one of my brother's holdings in Bedford, with the intention of reaching my aunt Celeste outside of Kettering. We should have made it in plenty of time, too, had it not been for the storm, which nobody could have predicted."

"No one, but Melcourt, at any rate," observed Lady Jane drily.

"I beg your pardon?"

"Never mind. More to the point is why you did not inform Danforth of your intentions. He can hardly be blamed, after all, for misconstruing the circumstances."

"You are right, of course," Ethne said grudgingly, hanging her head most effectively. "And I should have left word had I known he would return so soon from London—*and* had I not been certain he would refuse me permission to go. For if you must know, Aunt Celeste, who in spite of the fact that she is not really my aunt, but Nick's, has given me every reason to believe that she would be happy to bring me out when the time came."

"Oh, you may be sure that she would," observed a cynical voice from the doorway. "And how not, when she is saddled with an entire brood of aspiring offspring on whose behalf she would like nothing better than to command my purse strings. Or yours, my dearest Ethne, should she be successful in promoting a match between you and my cousin Edgar."

Inexplicably Lady Jane felt the blood rise to her cheeks as she looked up to espy his lordship, casually elegant in a bottle-green riding coat that hugged indecently broad shoulders and buff unmentionables that seemed molded to muscular thighs above shining brown military long boots. Lounging with one powerful shoulder propped negligently against the door frame, he was undeniably a compelling figure.

"Nick," gasped Ethne, pressing a hand over her breast. "How dare you sneak up on us like that. You frightened me half out of my wits."

"Then no doubt I should apologize," replied the marquess in tones that were meant to be anything but conciliatory. "Perhaps now you have some small inkling of what I was made to feel upon returning home to discover my sister mysteriously vanished, not to mention my curricle and pair. Fortunately you were spotted leaving Bedford, or I might still be combing the county in search of you."

"I, on the other hand, must count it the very worst of luck," Ethne flung bitterly back at him. "No doubt we should have been well on our way to Aunt Celeste's by now had you not interfered. And just what, by the way, have you done with Freddy?"

The nobleman's lip curled in a smile that was distinctly ironic.

"Need you ask?" he murmured, drawing forth an exquisite enameled snuffbox with what must have seemed to Miss Winter a calloused disinterest, but which appeared something quite different to Lady Jane. *She* arched a single, sapient eyebrow as Danforth flicked open the lid and, taking a pinch of his favorite mixture between thumb and forefinger, leisurely inhaled it before answering. "I believe horsewhipping *is* customary in such cases," he reflected whimsically. "Though I confess I found the notion of administering the young whelp a sound beating at fisticuffs far more appealing. He is my cousin, after all, and I rather doubt that Aunt Caroline would view with equanimity having the whip applied to her only son. A messy business all around, but what would you? It was my sister's honor at stake."

"Faith," gasped Ethne, who had gone deathly pale during that cold-blooded recitation. "Not even you could be so monstrous. If you have harmed a single hair on his head, I swear I shall—I shall—"

"Yes? What shall you do?" queried the marquess with apparent interest.

"She, my lord, will sit down at once and cease to behave like a ninnyhammer," pronounced Lady Jane before the girl could conceive of a punishment dire enough to suit the situation. "And, you, sir, will kindly stop roasting the child."

A sardonic smile flashed across the lean, handsome countenance.

"As you wish, Miss Ashely," he drawled, bowing ever so slightly at the waist in what could only be construed as acknowledgment of a palpable hit by the lady. "I beg your pardon if I have in any way offended."

"I beg you will not be absurd," Lady Jane countered testily. "I should hardly be offended by fustian. On the other hand, I find nothing entertaining in frightening children."

"I am not a child," Ethne protested, her color returning to normal with the realization that Freddy was not even then lying somewhere bloodied and broken.

"Then kindly cease to behave like one. It is obvious that Freddy has satisfactorily explained to your brother the circumstances of your ill-fated journey, else he would be here with his lordship. Which leads me to believe he is suffering from nothing more serious than a headache, or possibly a cold, incurred from his unfortunate mishap. Mrs. Quinn, I suppose, has refused to let him leave his bed?" she queried of his lordship, who appeared to be deriving no little enjoyment from her astute observations.

"Your brother's housekeeper was plying the young whelp with a tisane of rosemary and hissop when I left," he supplied reminiscently. "Oh, you needn't look so concerned, little henwit," he added to his sister. "Mrs. Quinn seemed quite taken with him. One look at him, and she had bundled him off to bed almost before we could explain why we had imposed ourselves on her good offices. I daresay she will not let him out of her sight until he has fully recovered, which is no more than he deserves for this harebrained stunt."

Lady Jane was hard put to stifle an unexpected burble of laughter as much at the gleam of wry appreciation in the nobleman's eyes as at his extremely accurate description of her brother's housekeeper.

"Oh, dear, I do hope she does not smother the poor boy with her well-meant attentions," she managed in a surprisingly steady voice. "She has had a hand in the rearing of two generations of Ashelys. I daresay the one bitter draught in her cup is that Wilfred and Mina have yet to set up their nursery."

"Yes, well, at the very least she will prove an admirable gooseberry, which brings us back to the problem at hand. It had been my intention to relieve you of our presence as soon as the curricle could be brought up. However, it now appears that we shall have to impose on your hospitality another day or two. Which places us in a damnable position. Short of claiming the young culprits were abducted by Gypsies, I fear we shall be hard put to explain so lengthy an absence."

"Yes, you are right, of course," replied Lady Jane, who had devoted some thought to the matter as she lay tossing and turning the night before in her bed. "However, I think it should not be too difficult to wrap the whole in clean linen. I am perfectly willing to do whatever I can to help."

"Well, I fail to see why we do not just tell the truth," Ethne broke impatiently in. "We were on our way to visit Freddy's aunt when the storm overtook us and forced us to take refuge at Melcourt. Where is the harm in that?"

"The harm," answered Danforth, "lies in the fact that had you bothered to inquire beforehand, you would have discovered Aunt Celeste and Edgar have already taken up residence in Town for the Season. As incomprehensible as it may seem, it will be said that we made up the whole to conceal what you and Freddy have gone to great lengths to give every appearance of being an elopement."

"Then we shall simply put it about that Freddy has brought Ethne to Melcourt at my invitation," Lady Jane smoothly interjected, before the girl could react to Danforth's biting tone. "I own I am not quite certain where we should have met. Perhaps it was on one of my shopping trips to Bedford. No doubt we share the same modiste or some such thing."

"Oh, no doubt," agreed the marquess with a gleam of cynical amusement, which could not but set Lady Jane's teeth on edge. "The fact, however, that you share something a deal more pertinent than that would seem to put some strain on such a story. You are remarkably green. Do you think for one moment the tattlemongers would not delight in speculating how Lady Jane Ashely should have come to friendly terms with the Marquess of Danforth's only half sister? I doubt very much that anyone could be brought to believe it."

Lady Jane blushed.

"It is true," she replied. Rising from her seat on the sofa, she crossed to the window and pretended to look out at the snow-covered landscape, the sun shining palely through a thin veil of clouds. "I had not considered that particular difficulty."

"I don't understand. What difficulty?" demanded Ethne, glancing bewilderedly from one to the other of her companions. "Whatever should prevent us from being on friendly terms?"

At the note of hurt in the girl's voice, Lady Jane at last drew a deep breath and turned.

"Why, nothing, Ethne," she said, assaying at least the replica of a smile. "Nothing at all."

"Why, nothing indeed," interposed his lordship, "if you do not consider that I am generally held responsible for the untimely demise of the Viscount Castlebridge, who not only had the dubious distinction of being my friend, but was to have wed Miss Ashely hardly a week following his unfortunate accident in a carriage race. And that is not even the greatest tragedy, is it, Miss Ashely? Far worse is that, because of one foolish wager, you have chosen to bury yourself along with Castlebridge. That is the real reason you have never married, is it not? Because you had not the heart to take up your life where you had left it?"

"How dare you presume to judge me," demanded Lady Jane, struggling to keep her voice even. "You know nothing about me."

"I know you are a beautiful woman who prefers to hide herself in the country rather than put her fate to the touch. What a shame that Melcourt has as yet to provide you with a clutch of nephews and nieces to whom you might so admirably play the role of auntie. That is all that is needed to provide the finishing touch, is it not?"

Lady Jane's hands clenched into fists at her side. Never had she met anyone more despicable. Nor did it help that she had been made to see herself as others must see her—a pitiful creature, languishing away from a broken heart. Indeed, she could perceive all this and more reflected in Ethne's huge stricken eyes. But whereas the girl would envision her as a romantic figure, one tormented with bleeding sensibilities, she knew herself to be above such puerile sentimentality. And from the sardonic glint of amusement in Danforth's eyes, she knew perfectly well that he knew it, too!

"Oh, Jane," exclaimed Ethne, sweeping across the room to clasp the older woman's hands in her own, "can you ever forgive me? If only I had known, I should never have mentioned certain—well—subjects, which could not but be painful for you. What an insensitive gadfly you must think me."

"Nonsense. I think you are no such thing. Nor do I find it in the least painful to discuss what happened a very long time ago. In spite of the fact that his lordship has taken great pains to portray me as some wilting heroine of a particularly bad romance novel, I assure you I have long since ceased to wear the willow."

"Then I collect I am mistaken, Miss Ashely," replied the marquess, with a casualness that somehow put Lady Jane in mind of a stalking panther.

"I suggest, my lord, that we remain to the point. It is Ethne's future that should concern us, not my own, which I am perfectly capable of determining for myself."

"On the contrary, my half-sister's future does not concern you in the least," drawled the marquess, insufferably cool. "You, my dear Miss Ashely, have already done quite enough, for which we are grateful. You would be well advised, however, did you not allow yourself to become any further involved."

Unaccountably, Lady Jane felt a prickling of nerve endings at the nape of her neck. And, indeed, she was later to assume that it was some hitherto unsuspected quirk in her nature that compelled her for some unknown reason to do just the opposite of what his lordship recommended.

"I am not," she said, "in the habit of making empty promises, my lord. I have said I would help, and, indeed, I shall, if it is at all in my power."

"Quite so," Danforth murmured, a suspicious twitch at the corners of the handsome lips. "Very well. I did warn you. The fact of the matter is, the solution to all our difficulties is obvious. I merely hesitated to mention it out of a reluctance to take further advantage of your generosity, ma'am."

"But how very kind in you," observed Lady Jane dryly.

"Pray, do not keep us in suspense," broke in Ethne, beside herself with impatience. "What solution?"

"It is quite simple, really. Miss Ashely, my dearest Ethne, has only to accompany you to London for the Season."

Four

"London!" Lady Jane exclaimed, aghast.

"Oh, but that is a capital idea!" Ethne interjected, clasping her hands together in apparent alt. "Merely to say we are on friendly terms is one thing, but to have Lady Jane Ashely as my mentor would be quite another. It would mean I should be accepted without question."

"You astonish me," her brother pronounced with a sardonic lift of an eyebrow. "Your acceptance was never an issue. Or did you think my reputation so black as to ruin your chances? I assure you that even if Winter were not a name to contend with, Danforth carries no little weight in the circles to which you aspire. Had you stayed at Brandymere as you were told, there would have been no need to impose on Miss Ashely's good nature to bail you out of the toil you have made for yourself."

"Oh, but it is not such a *great* imposition—er—is it, Jane?" queried the girl, as if only just recalled to an awareness of the older woman's presence. Her eyes pleading, she turned the full force of her gaze on her hostess. "I promise I shall be on my best behavior. Indeed, you have been so kind, I should rather die than do the least thing to incur your displeasure."

Lady Jane stared from one to the other, unable to believe the turn fate had just taken.

Good God, she groaned to herself. She would feel the veriest ogre to quash the child's hopes now—as his lordship must be perfectly aware, she realized suddenly, her glance having narrowed sharply on Danforth. *He,* she noted, wore the aspect of a man succumbing to an advanced state of ennui. Obviously he had known all along just where all this was leading and now he believed he had her just where he wanted her. The devil to use her so! And yet, perhaps he would find she was not so easily manipulated.

"Ethne, dear." Taking her eyes off Danforth, she smiled at the girl. "Perhaps you would not mind going in to breakfast without us? Before I inform you of my decision, there are a few things I should like to discuss alone with your brother."

Instantly the girl's face fell.

"You are going to say no, aren't you? And I am sure I cannot blame you. You barely know me after all, and what you do know can hardly have endeared me to you. Oh, what a mull I have made of everything! And just when I was beginning to believe at long last I had found a friend—someone in whom I could confide."

In spite of herself, Lady Jane suffered an unexpected pang of sympathy at the longing in the girl's voice. Indeed, she understood very well what it must have been like for Ethne, growing up, for all practical purposes, an only child of middle-aged parents in the relative seclusion of the Cotswolds. Her own case had not been so very different, after all. Wilfred had been away at school most of the time, while she had remained at home under the tutelage of her old governess, Miss Manville. She knew what it was to be lonely.

"Hush," she said. "You have indeed acted unwisely, but I trust you have learned your lesson. Naturally it is my hope you will go on believing I am your friend—"

"Then I shall be forever grateful," broke in the girl before Lady Jane could finish. "For a little while it has been almost like having an older sister, something for which I have always wished." Turning, she crossed obediently to the door. There, she stopped and glanced back almost shyly over her shoulder. "No matter what you decide, I shall always remember you for that."

Lady Jane stood perfectly still as Ethne, stepping through into the breakfast room, carefully pulled the double doors to. Even then it was only after the space of five full heartbeats that she at last drew a deep breath and, turning, impaled the languid figure of his lordship, one elbow propped negligently on top of the mantelpiece, with a look intended to freeze his very soul.

"You, sir, are undoubtedly the most underhanded, conniving, *unscrupulous* person I have ever had the misfortune to meet," she declared in no uncertain terms. "How *could* you put me in such a position? You must know very well that my offer to do whatever I could to help did not extend to sponsoring Ethne's come-out in London. Indeed, I doubt that it would be at all proper."

"Oh, but you are quite right," Danforth agreed without the least hesitation. "It would be highly improper for an unmarried female of your tender years. However, I never suggested that you sponsor her. Only that you accompany her. No doubt your sister-in-law can be brought to take you both around."

"Oh, you may be sure of it," replied Lady Jane in bitter accents. "She has been trying for the past two years to persuade me to it."

"Then," drawled his lordship, arching a single arrogant eyebrow, "I'm afraid I fail to see the problem."

"The problem is, my lord, that you seem uncommonly determined to disrupt my life. I, sir, have not the least desire to go to London. Indeed, I must demand that you release me from a promise, which you know very well was obtained by unscrupulous means."

"On the contrary, Miss Ashely, I know no such thing,"

replied the nobleman with maddening imperturbability. "As I recall, I did advise you—more than once—not to become involved more than you already were. I suggest in future it would be wise to control this propensity of yours to meddle."

Lady Jane was forced to bite her tongue to keep from delivering a wholly unladylike retort. Oh, how very detestable he was! Obviously he was enjoying himself immensely at her expense. Furthermore, while she little doubted that she was only wasting her time trying to reason with the man, it was equally certain that she would gain little by losing her temper, save perhaps to add to his entertainment.

Determined that he should not get the better of her, she deliberately folded her hands before her.

"Yes, that's better," applauded the wholly despicable marquess, eyeing her appreciatively. "Now, what was it that you wished to say to me?"

In spite of herself, Lady Jane choked on an unwitting burble of laughter.

"Oh, how dare you make me laugh," she exclaimed wryly, "when that is the very last thing I should wish to do."

"Perhaps," replied his lordship with a whimsical air, "it is because I enjoy watching you try so hard not to give in to what you obviously consider an unfortunate tendency toward levity."

Taken off guard, Lady Jane favored him with a moue of displeasure.

"Oh, but you are quite off the mark if that is what you think. I enjoy nothing better than to laugh," she answered in bitter accents. "It is only that it is virtually impossible to remain angry at someone who is constantly provoking one to mirth. Especially, as in your case, when it is done quite intentionally."

A gleam of wry amusement leaped in the sleepy eyes.

"Oh, well, then. In that case, you needn't worry. In hardly

any time at all I am bound to do or say something that will further incite your wrath. Or, should I fail in that, inconceivable as it may seem, you can always remind yourself of who I am. That should be enough to tickle your spleen."

This time Lady Jane was not moved to laughter.

"How very detestable you are," she said quite soberly. "Indeed, you put me out of all countenance." Then, mindful of the fact that her hands had clenched into fists at her sides, she turned abruptly away. Thus she did not see the nobleman's long frame go suddenly taut or the shadow of bitter self-mockery flicker momentarily across the hard countenance. "But then, it is true," she added, straightening her slender shoulders before coming about to face him once more. "We cannot but serve as reminders to each other of what is better left forgotten. Which only makes it all the more impossible for me to accompany your sister to London."

"No doubt," he murmured, his face unreadable behind the mask of ennui. "And yet I had not thought you would be the sort to hold my sister responsible for her brother's crimes. She, at least, you will agree, is innocent."

"But of course she is. And how dare you to suggest I should hold her accountable for any of the despicable things you might do."

"I collect that I am mistaken," he replied smoothly. "In which case, I give you my promise that apart from an occasional appearance to see how my sister goes on, I myself shall remain least seen in your affairs. So you see, there can be no real obstacle to your going."

"Oh, but there is every obstacle," exclaimed Lady Jane, who at the moment could not think of one, save only that she most adamantly had no wish to have cut up the peace and contentment, which over the years she had so painstakingly achieved for herself. At last, flinging up her hands in utter frustration, she gazed bewilderedly into the hard glint of his eyes. "Why in heaven's name are you doing this to me? And do not, I pray, tell me that it is the only way to save Ethne's good name. I am not so green that I do not recognize a faradiddle of nonsense when I hear one."

"You are right, of course—there is one other solution," replied his lordship, neatly sidestepping the question. "Freddy and she can be married by special license. And no doubt that would be the better way out. It would relieve you of the onerous task of pursuing a life of gaiety in Town, and it would deliver me from playing nursemaid to a chit of a girl hardly out of the schoolroom. All in all, a far more expedient answer to our dilemma, would you not agree?"

Lady Jane felt her stomach grow suddenly queasy. How very selfish he had made them both sound, and deliberately, too, if she were any judge of his character.

"Oh, indeed," she said bitterly. "And only Ethne and Freddy would be made to suffer, for if you must know, your sister has already confessed that she and your cousin will never suit."

Danforth had the temerity to shrug with every indication of total indifference.

"Then no doubt they shall learn to make do," he drawled coldly, "as does the rest of the world. Love, after all, has very little to do with marriages among those of our kind. I should say you and Geoffrey would have been the exception, rather than the rule."

It was true. She could not deny it. Marriages were business arrangements or matters of convenience. And if the two so joined should in the end learn to love, then all the better. But if they did not, there was always the possibility of secret alliances for the unhappy wife, and for the husband, any number of barques of frailty with whom he might amuse himself. So long as they conducted themselves with discretion, such things were commonly overlooked, even accepted, by the society in which they moved. But to Lady Jane, who had unwillingly conjured up an image of Ethne as she had appeared just moments ago and of Freddy as he had gamely stood up in the young girl's defense, it could only seem tawdry and wrong. Indeed, she knew, to her dismay, that she could not allow such a tragedy to happen.

"Undoubtedly I should follow your advice and wish you well out of my life," she said, wondering if she had taken leave of her senses. "However, you must know very well that I cannot. No doubt you will allow me a few days to make all the arrangements. I shall have to inform my mother, and Mina, of course. And then there is the matter of a suitable wardrobe. If Ethne is to remain here with me until we depart, she will have to have some of her things sent over. Naturally, we will purchase most of what we need once we are settled in Town."

"Naturally," responded his lordship, insufferably cool. "You will buy whatever you need and send the accounting to me. It will not be the first time I have footed the bill for a lady's wardrobe."

Lady Jane was barely able to stifle a gasp of outrage.

"You will make whatever arrangements you please with Ethne concerning her finances," she stated frigidly. "My own are my concern. I should hope that is understood."

At last she was given to glimpse the hard edge of his temper. Indeed, she nearly flinched at the sudden piercing glint of his eyes.

"Did you think I was offering you a carte blanche?" he queried, his voice steely beneath its velvet softness. "What an odd notion you must have of my character. I assure you, however, that I am not in the habit of ruining innocent females. On the contrary, I should be perfectly within acceptable bounds to stand the nonsense of a few dresses. You will allow, will you not, that you will be going to a great deal of expense on my sister's behalf."

"If I am, it is nothing to signify," she countered, determined not to give in an inch on this one point. "I am well able to stand the nonsense."

Their eyes clashed across the distance and held for a seeming eternity. Then without warning, a shutter seemed to drop in place over the hard features, effectively cutting her off from the marquess's innermost thoughts.

Ironically he bowed.

"As you wish, ma'am," he drawled acerbically. "No doubt I should be pleased to have met one woman who, far from having designs on either my title or my fortune, would as soon spit in my eye rather than to accept even so much as a thank you from Danforth. Strangely, I find the experience anything but gratifying."

Inexplicably, Lady Jane felt her stomach give a slight lurch at something she sensed in the look he bent upon her then, though for the life of her she could not have explained what it was. Quelling the instinct to press her hands to hot cheeks, she hastily turned her face away.

"Yes, well, I am glad that we understand each other, my lord," she said, nettled at the strange sort of power he seemed to have to set her off her balance. "And now, if that is settled, perhaps we should join Ethne. She is undoubtedly beside herself, wondering what we have decided."

Breakfast, as it turned out, was anything but the strained affair that Lady Jane had envisioned it would be, which was due only in part to Ethne's exuberant spirits. Danforth, she soon discovered, could be quite engaging when he chose to be.

But then, she supposed that was only to be expected of a member of the Carleton set, one, moreover, whose reputation as a nonpareil and a Corinthian was only slightly more formidable than his renown as a womanizer and a gambler. Whatever the case, the fact of the matter was that by subtle degrees he put her off her guard, so much so that she eventually found herself engaging quite spiritedly in a discussion of any number of topics, ranging from the current fashion in clothes to world events.

Obviously there was a great deal more to the Marquess of Danforth than the dissolute nobleman she had been used to imagining him. Indeed, not for a very long time had she felt so pleasantly stimulated, she realized, when immediately she caught herself.

Good God, she could not possibly be falling for the man! Even if he had not had a part in Geoffrey's tragic accident, she could hardly thank him for having deliberately used and manipulated her to his own ends. And he had all but admitted his entire motive had been to rid himself of the responsibility of his troublesome half-sister, had he not? Yes, but could she believe him? queried a small, insidious voice from somewhere in the back of her head. Or was it all a sham? Somehow, in spite of everything he had done, she could not quite shake the feeling that, despicable as he might be, he would never be moved by anything quite so petty or mean. Oh, the devil take him! The truth was, she did not know what to believe. If nothing else, Danforth was every bit as dangerous as he was reputed to be, she reflected soberly, eyeing him distrustfully from beneath the luxurious veil of her eyelashes. She would be the veriest fool to allow herself to fall victim to his devastating charm.

With breakfast over and the prospect before her of spending an entire day in the marquess's unnerving presence, she was suddenly tempted to plead a headache and escape to the safety of her bedroom. Only then, she caught him watching her with a gleam of sardonic amusement in the compelling eyes and she had the oddest feeling that he had read her mind.

A blush stained her cheeks, and hastily she glanced away. Then instantly her chin came up, a dangerous glitter in the blue-violet eyes. She was dashed if she would show craven before him. Indeed, she would rather perish than let him see how easily he confounded her.

Leaning back in her seat, she smiled ruefully.

"I fear we have not a great deal to offer here in the way of entertainment. If you care to read, we have a goodly supply of books in the study. Or we could try our hand at cards. I suppose," she added doubtfully, "if the weather permits, we might even make the short trek to Oaks to see how Freddy goes on."

"Oh, could we, Nick?" Ethne exclaimed, looking eagerly to her brother. "I feel perfectly awful about Freddy, stuck in bed with only strangers to see that he is not bored to tears."

"It did occur to me that you might wish to see for yourself that the young thatchgallows was all in one piece," Danforth languidly submitted. "Which is why I saw fit to borrow Melcourt's sleigh. If you bundle up, I trust you will both ride snugly enough."

It was on Lady Jane's tongue to protest that she had too many things to do that morning to be able to accompany them, but before she could suggest that the two of them go on without her, Ethne had already turned to grasp her by the hands.

"Do say you will come with us, I beg you, dearest Jane," she blurted, her lovely face alight with excitement. "I do so love a sleigh ride, and we should have ever so much fun cheering Freddy up."

"Well," she hedged, "I do have some things to which I should attend." She could feel the girl draw back in disappointment. And, more tellingly, she could see from Danforth's expression that he was anything but surprised at what appeared her imminent refusal. On the contrary, it was obvious that he had expected it. Annoyed that he apparently found her so predictable, she reacted out of impulse. "However, since we do have use of the sleigh," she continued, giving the girl's hands a squeeze, "and since I should like to go to the village to return some fabric samples, I suppose we *could* make an outing of it."

Thirty minutes later found her bundled in the sleigh between Ethne and the marquess. To her discomfiture, she felt a soft thrill as Danforth's strong slender hands lifted the reins to set the horse in motion to the jangle of sleigh bells. She told herself that, in the circumstances, it was only natural that she should be experiencing a heightened sense of awareness. After all, it was a perfectly glorious day. The clouds having dissipated, the sunlight was dazzling against the snow-covered fields hedged with thorn, rose, and holly. The air was brisk; and yet, snug beneath her fur rug, she could not but delight in the invigorating touch of the breeze against her cheek. All in all, it promised to be a merry outing, she thought as she settled back to listen to Ethne's excited chatter above the steady whish of the runners.

"Look," cried Ethne, as they came to the fateful bend in the road where she and Freddy had come to grief the night before. "The curricle, it's gone. But how—"

"I took the liberty of having Melcourt's stable lads bring it in," offered his lordship, feathering the turn with ease, "when they fetched your luggage to you. Fortunately, it was not greatly damaged. No doubt it will be ready to take us back to Brandymere as soon as the roads are fit for travel."

"And when do you think that might be?" queried Lady Jane, frowning as she tried to gauge how long it would take for the snow to melt and the roads to dry out sufficiently for a carriage to pass over them.

Danforth glanced languidly down at her from his greater height.

"Wearied of us already, Miss Ashely?" he murmured, as they left the main road and entered the oak wood, from which her brother's estate took its name. "And who can blame you? I fear we have proven a sad trial for you."

"No, how can you say so," she retorted, detecting the glint of amusement behind the sleepy eyes. "Actually, I was thinking of all the things that need doing if I am to make the journey to London any time soon."

"Oh, well, in that case, I should judge you will be quit of us in no more than two or three days, if the weather continues to hold. And if the redoubtable Mrs. Quinn allows Freddy to be moved from his bed."

Lady Jane laughed.

"Poor Freddy. After three days, no doubt he would do anything, including steal from the second story on a rope of sheets tied together, to escape Mrs. Quinn's diet of barley water and bitter tisanes."

"Faith," exclaimed Ethne, horrified at the thought of Freddy doing any such thing, "she sounds an absolute dragon."

"On the contrary," Lady Jane said, smiling, "she is no such thing—as you are about to discover for yourself."

The twin towers of Oaks, nestled on the brow of a low hill, appeared to leap out at them as they emerged from the wooded slopes into the broad sweeping drive. Lady Jane's fond glance embraced the terraced lawn, pristine in its new blanket of snow, the knot garden with its topiary figures of deer, swans, and rabbits among which she had used to play as a child, and, finally, the ivy-covered house, the enduring walls of cut stone embracing great bay windows at either end.

"Welcome to Oaks," Lady Jane said as they drew up and stopped before the wide stairway ascending between twin pillars to carved oak doors. A footman in the silver and blue livery of the earls of Melcourt hurried down the stairs to hold the horse's head as Danforth leaped lightly to the ground.

"Oh, but this is lovely," exclaimed Ethne, seeming to take in everything at a glance as her brother helped her to step down. "Indeed, I should judge it is rivaled only by Brandymere. Oh, I do wish you could see Brandymere sometime, Jane. I know you would love it in spite of the fact that it is not so grand or so large as Nick's other houses."

"I am sure it must be perfectly wonderful," Lady Jane answered, unreasonably distracted at finding herself gazing into the marquess's steel blue eyes as he waited to hand her out of the sleigh. "Indeed, you must tell me all about it sometime."

Not having been to her brother's house for some days, she was accorded a hearty welcome from the members of the staff. Indeed, Wimbly, who had served as butler at Oaks for as long as she could remember, unbent enough to offer the opinion that the old house was considerably brightened by her presence.

"How very kind of you to say so," laughed Lady Jane, allowing him to help her off with her mantle. "But you make it sound as if I never come to visit, when you know very well I tend to make a perfect nuisance of myself."

"Nonsense," offered a familiar voice from behind her. "You're no such thing and never could be. The house has never been the same, Miss Jane, since you left it."

"Mrs. Quinn," exclaimed Lady Jane, smiling as she came about to greet the small dab of a woman with blue eyes twinkling at her from behind rimless spectacles. "How good to see you. And how is our patient today? I have brought Miss Ethne Winter, who is staying a few days with me, to cheer him up if she can."

"And very glad he will be that you have come, miss, I am

sure," the housekeeper said, dipping the young lady a curtsy. "The poor lad was a trifle out of frame last eve, what with his head paining him and a cold starting in his chest. But thanks to some good old-fashioned home remedies, I believe I may say he is feeling more the thing this morning." With these last words, the twinkle, if anything, became more pronounced. "In spite of anything I might say, there was nothing for it but that he must leave his bed. I'll take you to him now, if you like. He's to be found in the study."

"Oh, yes, thank you," Ethne replied, turning with an eager step to accompany the housekeeper up the long, curving staircase, Lady Jane and the marquess following in her wake.

It soon proved that Freddy's state of health was indeed quite improved. The white bandage embracing his forehead and a suggestion of pallor about the cheeks were the only evidence that he was something less than his usual self, and these proved only to make him more interesting in the eyes of one young person in particular.

At sight of his callers, Freddy made hastily as if to rise from where he sat before the fire, a rug tucked snugly around him against the chill.

"Pray do not stand on our account," smiled Lady Jane, motioning him to remain as he was. "We have come to see how you go on and perhaps to cheer you in your convalescence."

"Poor Freddy, how very pale you look!" exclaimed Ethne, who rushed sympathetically to his side. "Does your head hurt very much?"

"I beg you will not make more of it than it is, Ethne," Freddy retorted gruffly, his pallor giving away before a blush of embarrassment. "It's nothing to signify, I assure you." His eyes went to his hostess with a hint of shyness, quickly camouflaged behind a firming of his jaw. "It was good of you to come, ma'am. I believe I have never properly thanked you for what you did last night. You very probably saved my life."

"Actually, it is Ethne you should thank," Lady Jane gently reminded him. "It was she who thought to cover you with the carriage rug and then braved the storm on foot to find help. You must own that she showed remarkable presence of mind."

"But it was my fault he was ever in such a fix," Ethne demurred, determined, it seemed, to adopt a course of martyrdom to make reparation. "The whole thing was my idea after all."

"Cut line, Ethne," Freddy retorted, painfully aware of his own shortcomings in the matter. "I'm as much to blame as you, for thinking I was up to handling Danforth's cattle. You were in my protection, and I made a mull of it. Cousin Nick was perfectly right to read me a curtain lecture."

It was immediately apparent that Freddy's attempt to make a clean breast of things did not sit at all well with Ethne, who was equally determined to absolve him of all culpability. "Oh, how very like you, Freddy Bartholomew," she declared, her commiserative mien giving way to a darkling expression. "I swear, if I said the sun came up in the morning, you would take exception to it. It was all my fault that Danforth's cattle were placed at risk and that you were very nearly killed, and that is all there is to it."

"Come, come now," said Lady Jane, noting the dangerous tremor in Ethne's voice and the ominous jut of Freddy's jaw. "We may all be grateful that nothing more serious came from this than the bump on Freddy's head."

"I beg your pardon, ma'am," said Freddy, momentarily shamefaced. "It's just that I know what Ethne is trying to do, and it isn't at all necessary. After all, I am a man of two and twenty, or at least I shall be in a couple of weeks. I should be obliged if she would not try to make excuses for me. I was the one who was in error."

"Oh, naturally," countered Ethne sarcastically. "I am only a female and consequently cannot be held accountable, is that it? No matter that I am the one who instigated it all."

"You are both guilty of becoming dead bores, if that is any consolation to you," drawled the marquess with telling acerbity. "Which is why you will remain here to entertain Freddy, my dearest Ethne, while I take Lady Jane to the village to do her errands. You will not, I trust," he added, taking Lady Jane's arm and steering her toward the door, "do each other in before we return. As much as I might like to be relieved of the responsibility for you both, I should not wish to impose on the earl's hospitality."

Lady Jane, torn between a keen appreciation of the masterful way in which he had quelled the two obstreperous youngsters and consternation at the prospect of finding herself alone with Danforth, soon found herself tucked snugly once more in the sleigh, the marquess beside her.

"Have you had a great deal of experience dealing with young people, my lord?" she queried, when the marquess had set the sleigh in motion. "Other than your half-sister, that is?"

"No, Miss Ashely," he replied, glancing quizzically down at her as the bay settled into its pace. "I am afraid I have not that dubious honor."

"Odd," she replied. "You would seem to have a natural gift for it. I daresay you would make an excellent father."

"You astonish me, Miss Ashely," drawled his lordship, arching a single, bemused eyebrow. "You are not suggesting, are you, that it is time I set up my nursery?"

Lady Jane gave him a quelling look. "I should never be so remiss, my lord," she retorted. "You know very well that I was referring to Freddy and your sister. Besides, your reputation precedes you. Having made it painfully clear to more than a few mamas with marriageable daughters that you have no intention of falling to Parson's Mousetrap, you are considered quite dangerous, my lord marquess."

"You cannot know how relieved I am to hear it, Miss Ashely. I have taken great pains to make it so. I was not, however, aware that I had ceased to be regarded as a Catch of the Marriage Mart. My Cousin Edgar will no doubt be vastly overjoyed at the knowledge. As my heir apparent, he must least like to see me married."

Lady Jane choked on a burble of laughter at the very absurdity of such a notion. "I wish you will not roast me," she answered. "I did not say that you were not an eligible parti, my lord. Only that you are known to be mercilessly blunt to aspiring misses and their plotting mamas. Should you choose to wed, it is doubtless that you would find any number of willing prospects. Though," she added reflectively, "I should not think it at all likely that you are in the least danger of actively seeking to change your bachelor state."

"You would seem to have come to certain definite conclusions regarding my character," observed the marquess in exceedingly dry tones, "for one who has known me less than twenty-four hours. However, you are undoubtedly in the right of it. Very likely I shall never choose to marry. Or perhaps, Miss Ashely, it is only that the right female has yet to set out her lures."

Inexplicably Lady Jane felt her breath catch at the odd little gleam in the look he bent upon her. Good God, flashed through her mind. Surely he could not be intending to set up one of his infamous flirtations with her! He was odiously arrogant and undeniably overbearing, but he was no fool. He must know that he would catch cold at it if he tried any such thing.

They had entered the village high street then, and, thankfully, she was saved from having to make a reply. Nor was she so careless again as to allow the conversation to touch on any subject of a more personal nature than her choice of plush velvet upholstery over camelot for the drawing room.

Directing Danforth first to Mr. Thompson's Haberdashery, she returned her fabric samples and regretfully informed the proprietor he would not be required to send to Kettering for lengths of material, as she was leaving almost immediately for London. Purchasing needles for Mrs. Bledsoe and licorice for Cook and Jeremy, she next turned to the more difficult of her assigned tasks for the day—the procurement of eggs and simila, the fine flour used in making simnel cakes for Mothering Sunday, which was little less than two weeks away.

Daisy, being too shy to approach her mistress on a personal matter, Mrs. Bledsoe had been delegated to ask Lady Jane to fetch what eggs could be found for the girl's simnel cake. Shrovetide, with Egg Saturday, the day the children went from door to door begging for eggs, which had to be eaten before the beginning of Lent (and flinging broken crockery at the doors of any who refused them), had come and passed some three weeks before, along with Pancake Tuesday, the day the rest of the eggs and cooking fat were used up in making savory griddle cakes before the onset of Lent on Ash Wednesday. Lady Jane, who anticipated, in consequence, a dearth in supply, was pleasantly surprised that she had little difficulty in buying a good two dozen.

The marquess, upon observing her final purchases, was moved to inquire if Lady Jane planned to go "a-mothering."

"I fear my mother long ago gave up any notion that I should ever acquire any proficiency at cooking, my lord," Lady Jane replied, chuckling reminiscently. "Or of bringing home a sweetheart, for that matter. My one and only attempt at making a mothering cake was so durable, it had been better used as a footstool. The eggs and simila are for Daisy, who came to us at the New Year Hiring Fair, and, as befits the season, I have promised her a few days off to visit her family."

"Daisy, it would seem, is fortunate to have you as her mistress," observed the marquess, stepping easily up into the sleigh and settling beside her. "Or does everyone in the wilds of Northamptonshire make it a practice to observe the quainter traditions of Easter?"

"Oh, we are no doubt a backward lot," she replied dryly, "clinging, as we do, to the practices of an older, simpler time. But the truth is, the fasting of *Lenctentid* helps the poorer folk stretch their depleted supplies from the fall harvest. Many of the children who beg for eggs on Egg Saturday depend on the griddle cakes of Pancake Tuesday to get them through till spring."

"And this concerns you, does it?" he queried. His gaze, quizzically probing, brought a deeper tinge of color to her already rosy cheeks.

"They are children, my lord," she answered simply. "I cannot like to think that any should go hungry in a land of plenty. And the children here are far better off than so many of those in the cities. Yes, I suppose it does concern me."

On the short drive back to Oaks, the discussion turned as if by tacit agreement to lighter subjects, the marquess entertaining her with on-dits about various members of the *ton*.

The marquess was possessed of a discerning wit and a keen sense of the ridiculous, and in spite of herself Lady Jane soon found that she was enjoying herself immensely. Indeed, her eyes positively danced at Danforth's drawling account of how Mr. Richard Sheridan had at last attained his membership to Brooks's.

A close friend of Prinnie's, it was common knowledge that the dramatist had been persistently blackballed by George Selwyn and the Earl of Bessborough each time his name was brought up for consideration. "It seems, however," drawled the marquess, straight-faced, "that the night of the voting, Bessborough was mysteriously drawn away from the club with the news that his house was in flames. Naturally his lordship assumed he could depend on Selwyn to pill the undesirable Sheridan. You can no doubt imagine his dismay, however, when he returned from discovering that the fire was all a hum only to find that Selwyn had likewise been called away by what he presumed to be a summons from Prinnie. With the result that—"

"Sheridan had been voted in in their absence," Lady Jane finished for him. For an instant her eyes locked with his, then suddenly they both burst into laughter. "Bravo for Mr. Sheridan," Lady Jane gasped when their mirth had subsided enough for her to draw a breath. "In spite of the opinion of him held by Bessborough and Mr. Selwyn, I found the old gentleman a perfect delight."

Not surprisingly, Lady Jane had discovered in the course of the afternoon that Mr. Richard Sheridan was not the only acquaintance she held in common with the marquess. She had, after all, been introduced to a great many people during her one and only Season in London. More surprising was the sudden realization of how exceedingly odd it was that Nicholas Trevant, Marquess of Danforth, had not been one of them.

She glanced up at Danforth to find him looking at her with an oddly arrested expression. She could not know what a charming picture she presented with her cheeks rosy from the cold and her lovely eyes alight with merriment. He himself gave every appearance of a man who had just been dealt a mortal blow, and suddenly she felt her cheeks grow warm and she was overcome with the absurd urge to lower her gaze like the veriest schoolgirl.

"I find it strange that we never met before," she blurted

instead. "Geoffrey was used to mention you often, but you were never in attendance at any of the social functions. I cannot but wonder why, my lord."

It was like watching a shutter fall into place, shutting off the momentary glow of laughter they had shared.

"Suffice it to say that I was indisposed, Miss Ashely," drawled Danforth in tones that left little doubt he meant that as an end to the matter.

Lady Jane, hurt by his brusqueness, quickly averted her gaze. For a brief time she had actually forgotten that he was the odious Danforth, the man who had taken her love from her and altered her life forever. He had deliberately brought her back to reality, erecting the old barriers with a chilling lack of emotion. Why? she wondered, troubled more than she cared to admit by this unpredictable nobleman. Indeed, she was made to realize for the first time that there was a great deal about the marquess that she did not know.

She was suddenly recalled to the fact that seven years before, there had been a deal of speculation about Danforth's habit of disappearing for weeks, even months, at a time. It was generally thought that the dissolute marquess spent his time on one of the outlying islands participating in depraved orgies or that, bored with the humdrum of London, he pursued a course of endless days and nights of gaming in one gambling hell or another. Geoffrey, who had enjoyed a unique intimacy with the nobleman, had only grinned in amusement at such stories and dismissed them, saying, "The truth be known, Danforth is not nearly so black as he likes to be painted, as you will undoubtedly discover for yourself on the day you meet him."

But that day had never come, until now. And Geoffrey was no longer there to explain what he had meant by his cryptic utterances. For the first time in a long while Lady Jane found herself pondering what would motivate a man to seek to deliberately blacken his own reputation. If he had done it out of a perverse pleasure in earning the censure of his peers, he had succeeded admirably. But what if his real motive had been something else entirely? What if he had done it to draw suspicion away from whatever he had really been up to during those prolonged absences? A secret love perhaps? One that was forbidden because the lady was married? Or was it something else, something he could not wish to be known because it might betray a trust or endanger someone else?

Here her imagination failed her, and, angry at herself for indulging in speculations that seemed meant to excuse the bizarre and probably dissolute practices of the man she was sworn to detest, she tried, with only indifferent success, to thrust the entire matter from her mind.

Fortunately, they soon turned into the long drive that led up to her brother's country house.

Though she was relieved for a time by Ethne's bubbling presence of any farther contemplation of the odious Danforth, she nevertheless found her glance straying more than once through the lively supper at Oaks to the stern, enigmatic features of the nobleman, and it was those same bewilderingly unreadable and seemingly contradictory features that attended her thoughts when, once more safely ensconced in the Dowager's House, she at last sought her bed that night.

Five

For the second time in as many days, Lady Jane awoke in the morning feeling as if she had waged and lost a battle. Which was only to be expected, she reflected ill-humoredly, when each time one was on the point of drifting off to sleep, one found one's self, whether one wanted to or not, suddenly contemplating whether a pair of eyes, far more disturbing than they had any right to be, were more nearly the chill azure of a winter sky or the unfathomable clear blue of a still, deep pool on a cloudless day.

The devil fly away with Danforth! All night she had been plagued with conflicting images of the marquess. He could be odiously cynical one moment, his lip curled in that mocking way he had which never failed to set her teeth on edge, and the very next, his dark head would go back, and his vibrant laughter would ring out, banishing the harshness from his face in such a manner as to render him quite human and altogether too fascinating for her own comfort. Nor did it help that in spite of his infuriating arrogance, he could be suddenly kind and disconcertingly solicitous of her comfort when that was very possibly the last thing she would wish him to be. How dare he behave in a manner calculated to make it difficult for her to recall that he was the man she most despised in the world!

Indeed, had it not been for that final, jarring note on the sleigh ride the day before, she might very well have con-

vinced herself that he was every bit the dangerously charming
rogue that he was painted to be. How incongruous, then, that
the very calculation with which he had quashed the camara-
derie that had sprung up between them should have served
to give birth to a growing doubt that he was anything quite
so easily comprehended.

Danforth, she reflected, frowning, was both more and less
than he seemed to be. That he could be utterly ruthless, she
did not doubt for a moment, or that he would be a dangerous
man to cross. But equally certain was that she had heard and
seen his laughter and sensed at odd moments a kindness in
him, a gentleness even, which led her to believe he was not
a man without feelings. It was this human side, oddly enough,
which she most distrusted. Or perhaps it was only that she
distrusted herself and the purely feminine instincts to which
Danforth's hidden, softer side appealed, she thought irritably.

One thing was certain. Both fascinating *and* forbidding,
Danforth was a man women would all too easily love, and
she had no intention of allowing herself to become one more
in his undoubtedly long line of hapless victims.

That decision made, she resolutely flung back the bedcovers and rose from her bed to dress deliberately in a muslin
round gown, which she had not worn for years and which
she had decided to hand down to Jenny. Unfortunately for
her purposes, however, she failed to note that the blue-violet
of the gown not only perfectly matched her eyes, but served
to enhance the creamy perfection of her skin. Furthermore,
having been purchased at a merrier time in her life, it was
more youthful and far more frivolous than the high-necked
gowns she had adopted since her return to Melcourt. If anything, she appeared younger and even more fetchingly lovely
when she made her appearance in the breakfast room that
morning than she had the day before.

The marquess, on the other hand, did *not* fail to notice it with a rancorous conviction that she had dressed just so expressly for the purpose of rendering her unforgettable in his eyes. She was, it was certain, an original, and nothing was more calculated to capture his interest than one who, in digressing from the expected, yet retained an indefinable air of savoir faire. Even were she to present herself in the meanest rags, Miss Jane Ashely, he was convinced, could not have been mistaken for other than what she was—a wholly alluring, eminently attractive female of refinement.

From having his interest piqued by her mere appearance in a dress which, while not shabby by any stretch of the imagination, was, nevertheless, clearly outmoded and hardly of the sort usually worn when receiving guests of his caliber, he came by degrees to regret the estrangement he himself had wrought between them. His hostess was, he noted as the day wore on, exceedingly careful never to allow herself to be alone in his company.

It had been inevitable from the very first, he told himself with sardonic self-detachment as he watched the object of his undivided attention engage in a riotous game of Jackstraws with her two younger guests, that the truce they had briefly enjoyed had to come to an end. He was, after all, Danforth, and she was Geoffrey Bartlett's beloved Lady Jane. He was ironically aware that the circumstances surrounding Geoffrey's untimely demise must always be an insurmountable barrier between them. What he had found surprising and wholly unexpected was the sudden wave of bitterness that had swept over him as he had deliberately quashed the congenial spell wrought by the intimacy of the sleigh ride and their shared moments of laughter.

Not for the first time, he cursed the fates that had brought him to Melcourt and thrust this meddlesome slip of a woman almost beneath his horse's hooves. Even now he had only to close his eyes to summon the image of her standing in the stallion's path, her eyes wide with startled fear and her face white with the terrible expectancy of being trammeled in the snow. It was a moment he could well have done without. And afterward, as he had knelt and found the pulse throbbing in her neck and felt her flesh, warm beneath his fingers—the sharp stab of relief, which had been damnably short-lived. She had lain so cursedly still! He had been filled with the dread certainty that she must be grievously injured. Grimly, he had begun the search for broken bones, when what did the troublesome female do, but bolt from unconsciousness to impale him with wide, startled eyes—eyes, which even in the pale glow of the lamplight had had a damned unnerving effect on his equilibrium. He had, in fact, had the oddest sensation of having just been shot through with a lightning bolt.

Damn the chit! He was no callow youth to fall victim to a pretty face, even one as remarkably lovely as Miss Jane Ashely's. But then, it was not her beauty that had taken him unawares, he acknowledged ruefully to himself. It had been her unexpectedly calm good humor at awakening to find herself stretched out on the snow, a stranger bent over her running his hands along her limbs in what could only be construed as a most damned familiar manner. Far from reacting either with what would have been an understandable outrage or even a purely feminine swoon, she had not been averse to replying to his rudeness with a pertness that did her no discredit in his eyes. Obviously she was pluck to the backbone. And still it was more than that. He had sensed it almost at once, and subsequent exposure to her company had served only to confirm his intuition. She possessed that indefinable something rare and fine that set her apart from so many other women he had known.

The lady was, in short, quality in the truest sense of the word.

How much greater, then, was his astonishment as a result

of that realization to discover that the female he had run down and subsequently rescued was none other than Lady Jane Ashely!

Singular as it was, it was not merely the coincidence of that chance meeting that he found unsettling. The truth was he had not been prepared to discover that Jane Ashely was nothing like the woman he had been led to believe her to be.

It was not an entirely welcome revelation. He had believed the events surrounding Geoffrey's death, along with the circumstances that had resulted in the further blackening of his own already less than sterling reputation, had long since been safely relegated to the past. Now he was not so certain.

He had never heard what became of the young beauty after Geoffrey's accident, nor had he been in the least curious. He had been glad enough that his own concerns had taken him out of the country shortly thereafter; and upon his return, wounded and ill, he had not been in any state to pursue a matter that was fraught with unfelicitous memories. He had been, consequently, more than a little taken aback to find the lady was, seven years later, not only still grieving for her lost love, but living the self-imposed life of a recluse in the country. Far from being the vain, shallow creature he had imagined her, her depth of feeling for Geoffrey was of the sort to inspire him to envy. Suddenly he had been ashamed for having left her to live with the deception he had had no little part in fabricating. It was the sort of feeling he had seldom experienced before and one that he found more than a little distasteful.

Indeed, he was cynically aware that, though he could not regret what he had done in carrying out Geoffrey's dying request, he had suddenly found himself wishing there had been some other way.

Nor had it helped his state of mind to have popping up with annoying frequency the memory of her lissome form cradled in his arms, the subtle scent of her perfume teasing his nostrils, as he had carried her upstairs to her bedroom that first fateful night.

It had occurred to him then, as he laid her upon her bed, that she was too young and far too beautiful to be left to the sterile life of a spinster. She deserved a second chance at a husband and children of her own. He had, consequently, given in to the impulse to jar Lady Jane Ashely out of the cozy little existence that she had made for herself, and it was only afterward, when he found himself in the sleigh staring into her cursed lovely eyes, that it came to him that he had made a serious blunder.

In underestimating the lady's charm, he had allowed himself to drop his defenses, and suddenly he had found himself enjoying an intimacy with the woman who had the most reason to detest him. No doubt it was an instinct of self-preservation which prompted him to quash the moment with a ruthlessness for which he was well-known to his intimates.

It had been immediately apparent the next morning when he and Freddy had driven over to join the ladies for breakfast that he had succeeded all too well in driving a wedge once more between them. She had treated him from that time forward with an icy civility that made him long to seize her by the arms and shake her.

Bloody hell! he cursed savagely to himself. What was done was done. And no doubt it were better so. It had been bad enough having to conduct his affairs with Ethne underfoot. The last thing he wanted or needed was the additional complication of a Lady Jane Ashely in his life. The sooner he was away from her and about his own business, the sooner he could put her out of his mind, he told himself as he stepped into the sleigh that night to drive himself and Freddy back to Oaks. Oddly, he was not comforted by the notion.

It was, nevertheless, with a feeling of relief that he awakened the fourth day of his stay at Melcourt Oaks to discover the road sufficiently dry to allow for traveling. Cynically, he observed when he arrived at the Dowager's House to announce his intention of departing within the hour that a similar relief was reflected in a pair of blue-violet orbs. It was the *only* sign of emotion he read in the serene mask of Lady Jane's face until Ethne, glancing from her brother's impassive features to Lady Jane's, abruptly snatched Freddie by the hand, and saying something to the effect that he simply must see the daffodils that had bloomed seemingly overnight, immediately dragged him, resisting, from their presence.

On the point of finding herself suddenly and unexpectedly alone with the marquess, Lady Jane visibly started. Her lips parted to call the meddlesome child back, only to clamp determinedly shut again. Her head lifted, and, clasping her hands in front of her, she turned resolutely to face her guest.

"Well," she said profoundly.

"Quite so," agreed the nobleman, when it seemed she did not mean to expand on the subject.

Lady Jane flushed and bit her tongue to keep from delivering him a stinging retort. Then mindful of the lengthening silence, she launched peremptorily into a superfluity of inane observations.

"It would appear you shall have a good day for traveling," she ventured, glancing out the great bay window for confirmation of her pronouncement.

"Oh, indisputably," concurred the marquess without the flicker of an eyelash.

"The air might be a trifle brisk," she nevertheless added, compelled, it would seem, to play devil's advocate. "I trust, however, the weather will hold."

"Do you?" drawled Danforth, growing more intrigued by the moment. Miss Ashely, it would seem, was distracted indeed to take recourse to discussing the weather. It was hardly what he had come to expect of her. Indeed, he had sooner anticipate the keen edge of her wit than trite mundanities. That the peculiar lapse was due to his own unsettling presence was perfectly obvious. What was less apparent, and consequently far more interesting, was the nature of his effect upon her. If he did not know better, he would suspect that the lady was behaving very like a female who was not so indifferent to him as she would like him, or herself for that matter, to believe. "You relieve my mind, Miss Ashely," he added, wondering to what scintillating aspect of the elements she would next allude.

"Still, it is far from warm," she forged on. "Very likely Freddy would do well to wrap up in a carriage rug. It would not do, after all, to chance a relapse."

"Perish the thought. I shall tuck the young cub in myself," Danforth assured her. "And now that that is settled, do you not think it is time you told me what is really bothering you? Somehow I cannot think it's the weather, or even Freddy, for that matter."

If he had thought by that to bring her to the crux of the matter, he had far mistaken his subject.

"I'm afraid I haven't the least notion what you mean," she countered, if not with a guileless air, then most certainly with one calculated to relieve him of any misapprehension that she meant to admit him into her confidence. "Other than the fact that I have been manipulated into forsaking my quiet existence for a Season in London, what could possibly be bothering me?"

"Nothing, apparently," Danforth conceded. "I collect I am mistaken. However, if you should ever find yourself in need of a friend, I should like to think you would not be averse to trusting me. I should hope you would believe you can depend on me."

Startled, her eyes flew to his, and for the space of several heartbeats, she met his gaze squarely.

"I do believe you," she said quietly. "Indeed, I have never doubted it. It was the one thing about which Geoffrey was most adamant."

Danforth's expression remained unaltered, save only for the sudden narrowing of his eyes on hers.

Lady Jane drew a sharp breath and turned abruptly away. "My mother should be home the middle of next week," she announced with seeming irrelevance, and, abruptly crossing the room to a Queen Anne secretary, reached distractedly for one of the drawers. "So there is no need to correspond with her regarding my plans," she continued as she tugged ineffectually at the brass handle. Her mind gradually registering the fact that the drawer refused to budge, she tried again, harder, but without success. "She will no doubt be overjoyed at the news that I am at last doing just as she has urged any number of times these past six years." Again she tugged at the handle, this time bracing her freehand against the upper, glassed-in case. "I have, however, written my sister-in-law"—she went suddenly still as Danforth's tall frame loomed over her—"informing her of my intentions of joining her at the end of the month." She glanced up.

Danforth smiled politely. "Quite proper of you," he applauded. Then, "May I?"

Lady Jane stared blankly at him for the barest moment before it at last came to her that he was offering her his aid.

"Yes, of course," she murmured, furious that her heart had begun beating in a most erratic manner. Hastily, she straightened. "The wretched thing is forever sticking." Reluctantly she stepped back, then watched as the marquess ran the blade of his penknife along the crack between the drawer and the frame. Something gave way, and a second later the drawer was open and Danforth was stepping courteously aside.

"Your drawer, my lady," he announced.

Feeling the veriest fool, she murmured a dignified, "Thank you, my lord."

"Think nothing of it," Danforth advised, perfectly soberly.

From which Lady Jane deduced that he was quite obviously laughing at her. The devil! she fumed. Then, extracting from the treacherous drawer a folded missive sealed with wax, she extended it toward the marquess. "Perhaps you would be so kind, my lord, as to post this for me when you pass through the village."

"Since I shall be leaving immediately for London, I shall see it delivered personally no later than tomorrow." Danforth paused, his eyes unreadable behind heavily drooping eyelids. "In return, you may expect my coach a week from Friday, along with a suitable conveyance for your trunks and whatever servants you deem necessary."

At last, Lady Jane appeared to suffer a distinct crack in the cool composure, which she had maintained the past two days like an impenetrable wall between them. "But that is not at all necessary, my lord," she blurted. "Indeed, I—"

Danforth cut her off with an imperious lift of an eyebrow.

"I shall brook no arguments, Miss Ashely," he had the unmitigated gall to inform her. "Ethne is my sister, after all, and the roads are not without their hazards. I shall rest easier knowing you are both traveling under my aegis."

It was on the tip of her tongue to retort that Melcourt was perfectly capable of providing safe transportation, when she was startled into a low choke of laughter by the ironic gleam of expectancy in his eyes.

"I do wish you will stop doing that, my lord," she exclaimed in exasperation, "whenever you decide to bullock me into doing what I haven't the least wish to do. How dare you anticipate my probable feelings in the matter! It is the shabbiest thing, for you know very well that, by your very attitude, you make it impossible for me to refuse your generous offer."

"Indubitably," agreed his lordship, insufferably amused. "That was, after all, my intent." Taking her hand in his, he raised it to his lips. "It is settled, then. A safe journey, Miss Ashely," he murmured, a disconcerting warmth in the look he bent upon her. "By your leave, I shall call on you in London to see how you go on."

"You, my lord, will undoubtedly do exactly as you wish," Lady Jane snapped, nettled by the unwitting leap of her pulse at his touch. Immediately she blushed in consternation at the gross incivility to which her wayward tongue had led her. "Oh, you really are quite the most provoking man I have ever met," she blurted ruefully, withdrawing her hand from his. "Indeed, you have the unfortunate propensity for bringing out the worst in me."

"An imperfection for which you cannot be faulted," he assured her with a gravity, belied by a suspicious twitch at the corners of his lips. "I would seem to have a similar effect on not a few of my acquaintances."

Lady Jane had, perforce, to stifle a gurgle of laughter. The rogue, she thought, to tease her so. "I shouldn't doubt it at all, my lord," she returned, struggling to regain her composure. "Nevertheless, I do beg your pardon for my unseemly outburst. Naturally you must feel free to come and see Ethne whenever you wish. I should not have it any other way."

"On the contrary," drawled the marquess with characteristic brusqueness, "you would vastly prefer never to be forced to endure my company again. And who could blame you? Certainly not I. I shall endeavor, however, to make the ordeal as painless as possible."

Lady Jane stared at him, not so much at a loss for words as bewildered by his bald statement. Indeed, in spite of the incivility in which his words were couched, she sensed in them a sincere wish to spare her any discomfort. It was just the sort of thing that she found most disconcerting in him, she thought acerbically—his unsettling habit of stepping in and out of character.

It was perhaps fortunate that she was saved from having to make a reply just then by the timely arrival of Ethne and a red-faced Freddy.

"I am glad you are leaving today, and I'm sure I could not care less *what* you do while I am in London," declared Ethne with every indication of one in a high dudgeon. "It is, after all, only my come-out. No doubt I shall rub along well enough without your presence."

"Don't talk so, Ethne," expostulated the object of her rancor. "That isn't fair, and you know it. I've been after my grandfather to purchase me a set of colors practically since I was out of short coats. You can't expect me to tell him just when he's finally come around that I've up and changed my mind, especially when I haven't. And especially not now that Wellington has begun his Peninsular Campaign. Very likely the old gentleman would think I had lost my nerve. And, besides—tell her, Nick. It's in time of war that a fellow has the best chance of advancement."

"Oh, pooh. What could Nick possibly know about war," Ethne said, lifting her chin.

"Nothing, to be sure, my dear," murmured the marquess, who appeared to be succumbing to an advanced state of ennui.

He was awarded a scornful glance for his efforts. "It's in times of war that a fellow has the best chance of getting himself killed," retorted Ethne, crossing her arms and turning her back on the hapless Freddy. "And if that's what you want, then I'm sure I wish you godspeed, Freddy Bartholemew."

"Thank you very much, Miss Winter," Freddy said stiffly. "No doubt I shall endeavor not to disappoint you."

"On the contrary," Lady Jane interjected, "you will both cease at once to play the gaby. You know very well Ethne does not mean a word of what she has said, Freddy. And you know, Ethne, that Freddy is not to be held responsible if he cannot make it to your come-out. Just think how very sorry you will both feel if you allow yourselves to part on such terms."

Freddy, whose face had fallen during Lady Jane's quiet scolding, shifted uneasily from one foot to the other. "Lady Jane is right, Ethne," he said at last, jerking his shoulders back. "I truly regret that I shan't be able to see you at your come-out ball. And I shall regret as well missing the Easter Ball. You will undoubtedly be the loveliest female there. Not that you would be apt to notice whether I was there or not," he added a trifle gruffly. "By then you'll very likely be the Reigning Beauty. Which means you will be so surrounded by suitors that, even if I could be there, I shouldn't be able to fight my way near you. Even so, I want you to know I shall be thinking of you." He paused, glancing doubtfully at Ethne, who, apparently unmoved either by his apology or his glowing predictions, remained adamantly with her back to him.

Coughing at last to clear his throat, he turned manfully to Lady Jane. "It has been a pleasure, ma'am," he said, "and I hope we may see each other again. I cannot thank you enough for all you have done. If ever there is anything I can do to return your kindness, I hope you will remember I shall always be at your service."

Lady Jane, who was suddenly reminded of another young man of two and twenty who had displayed a similar gallantry, was moved to take both his hands in hers. "Gallantly spoken, Mr. Bartholomew." She smiled, giving his hands a squeeze before releasing him. "You may be sure that I shall remember. I shall expect you to keep in touch while you are on the Continent and to come see me when you are home. I shall wish to hear all about your adventures."

"Yes, ma'am," Freddy flushed with pleasure. He stood noticeably taller as he addressed the marquess, who had been

observing the exchange with sardonic amusement. "I'm
ready, Cousin Nick," he said. "Whenever you are. I shall just
go and wait at the carriage."

"No!" Ethne came sharply about, a suspicious shimmer in
her eyes. "Don't you dare think you can go, Fredrick
Bartholomew the Fourth, before I have given you leave to
have done." Crossing swiftly to stand before him, she gazed
accusingly up at him. "I'm sure I have never known anyone
more foolish than you. Furthermore, you are stubborn and
pigheaded and quite the most infuriating person I have ever
met, and if you do not swear this minute not to get yourself
killed, I shall quite possibly never speak to you again."

"Don't be a pea-goose, Ethne," protested Freddy, eyeing
her askance. "More than likely I'll never get a scratch. Don't
know why you're going on so about it."

"Stupid," Ethne countered, leaning her hands on his shoulders. Before the unfortunate Freddy could do more than gape
at her, she raised herself on tiptoe and placed a buss on his
cheek. "You know perfectly well no matter how many suitors
I might have, I should always have time for my dearest
friend," she uttered huskily. "You have always been like a
brother to me." Then, brushing impatiently at her cheeks, she
dropped down on her heels.

"Now you may go," she said, half smiling, half frowning
as she shoved Freddy toward the door.

"Another crisis resolved, it would seem," mused the marquess whimsically as he offered Lady Jane his arm and led
her after the two young people. "It is fortunate the old earl
has seen fit to purchase Freddy his colors. Otherwise, you
very likely would be forced to spend your entire time in London playing peacemaker."

"I suppose so." Lady Jane's brow puckered slightly with a
frown. "And yet I cannot but wish he had chosen a less perilous time to launch a career in the military."

"I believe you are actually concerned about the young whelp," drawled Danforth, his eyes unreadable beneath drooping eyelids.

"I should be unfeeling indeed were I not," Lady Jane retorted, bridling with indignation. "He is a fine boy, and I have grown quite fond of him. Naturally I shall worry."

"Boy? You are not so very old yourself. He cannot be more than three years your junior," the nobleman was odiously quick to point out.

Lady Jane gave him a moue of displeasure. "You are right, of course," she answered wryly, "and yet somehow I feel ages older than he." She did not add that Freddy had yet to lose someone close to him or to realize that he was not immune to death. The Peninsular Campaign would all too soon change all that for him.

Still, Danforth must have read in her face much of what had passed through her mind.

"My young cousin will experience a great deal for which he had not bargained," he observed, "which is only as it should be if he is determined to make a soldier of himself." He smiled ironically as he strode out on to the porch, then paused to look down at her with blue, piercing eyes. "He is not, however, without connections." Lifting her hand, he saluted her knuckles. "No doubt there will be someone to look out for him."

Lady Jane glanced quickly up at him, but he had already straightened and, inclining his head, strode lightly down the steps to the curricle. Lady Jane was left to wonder what he could possibly have meant by his final, cryptic utterance as she watched him mount to the driver's seat and call to Freddy to hurry unless he wished to be left behind.

She was still wondering some few moments later, as she stood arm in arm with Ethne, waving as they watched the curricle draw away.

"Well," Lady Jane said with an air of finality when the carriage had passed out of sight round the bend. She turned to enter the house, Ethne following more slowly in her wake. "What shall we do now?"

"I'm not sure," answered the girl, smiling a trifle wanly. "The house seems suddenly so empty now."

"Then I suggest we go to the kitchens and see how Daisy's mothering cake is progressing. Have you ever noticed? There's nothing so comforting as the hustle and bustle of a kitchen when one is feeling a trifle blue-deviled. And while we are at it, I believe I should not be averse to coloring some eggs for the Easter season, especially since I shall miss decorating the house with fresh-cut sprigs of willow catkins and boxwood and hazel. I wonder if Mina's London cook will prepare fig pudding or parched peas to celebrate the occasion," she mused whimsically. "Somehow I cannot think it at all likely."

Ethne, who was just turned eighteen and was, consequently, not yet so worldly as to be above the allure of dying Easter eggs, perceptibly brightened. "I believe I should like that above all things. I had almost forgot it was Easter. When I was young, it was my very favorite time. Egg-rolling, and Spanish licorice in holy water. Not an Easter went by when the villagers did not come to entertain us with Bold Hector, the Black Prince of Paradise, and the Fool."

"Oh, but one must not forget the King of Egypt, Tosspot, or the Doctor," Lady Jane added, recalling with fondness the Easter play that was traditionally performed on Easter Monday. "And Saint George, of course."

"Oh, naturally, one could not forget *him*," Ethne grinned, assuming a theatrical pose. "Just look at Saint George. So brisk and so bold/ While on his right hand/ A sword he doth hold."

"A star on his breast/," Lady Jane took up the rhyme, smiling, "Like silver doth shine;/ I hope you'll remember—"

"It's Pace-Egging time!" they both chimed in together, and, laughing, proceeded downstairs to the kitchens.

There their nostrils were instantly assailed by an assortment of tantalizing aromas, chief of which were cinnamon and lemon peel, ground cloves, and mace.

They quickly discovered that Daisy, having made her crust of flour, rosewater, and saffron and filled it full of figs, mixed plums, apples, and an assortment of other savory things, was in the process of pinking the edges. When she had finished and the top was duly crisscrossed, she put the whole in a cloth to be boiled, after which, Lady Jane knew, she would glaze it with egg and finally put it in the oven to be baked. The result would be a very large, very hard cake meant to delight the heart of any mother.

The rest of the morning passed quickly enough with dying eggs from solutions of onion skins, flowers and leaves of various plants, chips of logwood, cochineal, and whatever else Cook's ingenuity could devise, so that when they had finished, they had a pretty collection of eggs.

Ethne, taking one up to admire its spiral of colors, glanced mischievously at Jane.

"Who's got an egg?" she chanted, enfolding her own in her palm so that the small end only just showed at the top. "Who's got an egg? Who's got a Guinea egg?"

"Oh, no you don't, miss," exclaimed Daisy, scandalized. "Not such lovely eggs, surely."

"Who wants to pick an egg?" Ethne nevertheless demanded, twin imps in her lovely eyes. "One pick. One pick. Who's got an egg?"

"Not I," laughed Lady Jane. "I'm afraid you will have to wait until you see Freddy again to find a partner for 'Egg-Picking.' I worked too hard on these to happily see them broken for your pleasure."

"You're right, of course," Ethne replied, the mirth fading

from her eyes at thought of Freddy. Pensively she set the egg down with its fellows on the table. "You do think he will be all right, don't you?" she queried without looking up. "I mean, I heard what Nicky said, and you do think he was right? Someone will look after him?"

"I shouldn't doubt it at all, Ethne dear," Lady Jane answered, surprised to discover that she did believe it. Somehow Danforth would find a way to protect Freddy, though she hadn't the least notion how he would manage it.

"I am glad," replied the girl, assaying an uncertain smile. "I could never feel about Freddy the way you did about— well, about Viscount Castlebridge. Freddy has been my friend and playmate far too long for me to think of him in any terms other than in those of a brother. Still, I should miss him dreadfully if anything . . ." She stopped and shook her head with sudden determination. "But, no. I shall not think like that. Nothing will happen to him. Nick has given his word."

Lady Jane could only agree and, seeking to distract her young friend, brought up the subject of the gown she would wear for the Easter Walk, which was held annually in Battersea Park.

Six

In the days following Freddy and Danforth's departure from Melcourt, Lady Jane had reason to wish she had not agreed to wait till Friday week to make her own journey to London.

She had thought to spend the interim packing and preparing for her departure and was consequently taken aback to discover she had rather neglected her wardrobe of late. For the truth was that, while she possessed any number of morning gowns, walking dresses, and three quite serviceable riding habits, she had found little need in the country in the nearly sole companionship of her mama to keep more than a bare minimum of evening gowns and only two ball gowns, neither of which, she was quite sure, was of the sort to pass muster at even the least discriminating of social functions. Furthermore, her store of accessories, such as hats and bonnets, gloves, shoes, and scarves, was sadly in need of replenishing.

The dearth made packing simple enough. She required only a single trunk and one or two bandboxes for those things she deemed worthy of a Season in London. The rest of what she needed she would have to purchase in Town. All of which meant, however, that she found she had far less to occupy her days than she had previously anticipated, and far more time than she might have wished to keep her single remaining guest entertained.

After one whole week alone with Ethne, Lady Jane was wishing most emphatically that she had not been coerced into accepting Danforth's offer of his travel coach. Indeed, she was quite sure that, had she not, she would have set out no later than Wednesday, possibly even Tuesday, for London. While Ethne was, for the most part, a delightful companion, she was yet at that awkward between-age in which she found herself poised one moment on the brink of womanhood and the next, bursting with youthful energy in need of an outlet.

Lady Jane was grown used to the more tranquil pace of the country, and for her, the mornings, occupied with discussing menus with Mrs. Bledsoe, making out shopping lists, supervising and helping with housecleaning, and going over the household accounts, and the afternoons, spent tending her garden, reading a book of poetry, or taking leisurely walks along any one of the numerous country tracks, were sufficient to fill her day. Ethne, on the other hand, though she tried valiantly to conceal it, was clearly bored with such blatantly domestic pursuits. With the result that, Lady Jane soon found both her patience and her ingenuity for keeping her young guest amused stretched to the limit. Indeed, she was tempted more than once to toss caution to the wind and head for London at once in spite of her promise to Danforth. At least there she might have kept Ethne occupied with shopping in Bond Street, seen that she was introduced to other young ladies of her peer group, and even suffered to conduct her young charge on a tour of the sights afforded in a leading capital of the world.

She was forced, instead, to endure the natural proclivities of youth to indulge in mercurial changes of mood, chimerical flights of fancy, and an endless stream of questions of a personal nature. Thinking at last to wear the child out, or at the very least to distract her for a few hours from plotting to save her hostess from a supposed case of Melancholia brought on by her Tragic Loss, Lady Jane made the supreme error one afternoon of the second week with Ethne of proposing they go for a ride. Ethne was delighted at the suggestion, even going so far as to admit she used to ride every day that the weather permitted and to confess that she had simply been pining for fresh air and vigorous exercise.

That in itself should have been sufficient warning. Lady Jane, however, relieved at finding something Ethne unequivocally enjoyed and not loath herself to indulge in the sort of outing she normally found quite pleasurable, chose to overlook it.

It was a mistake. One moment Lady Jane was soaking in the sunshine and savoring the perfume of new spring flowers on the air, and the very next, Ethne, declaring the horses were quite warmed up enough and it was far too lovely a day not to see what they could do, brought her riding crop down sharply across her gelding's rump. Startled at being treated in a manner so completely foreign to that to which it was accustomed, the animal bolted.

What had begun as a leisurely ride along picturesque rural lanes was suddenly become a hair-raising gallop cross-country. Ethne, displaying more bottom than brains, sent her mount flying over stone walls that had been better circumvented, plunging headlong down perilous inclines, and tearing haphazardly through spinnies of low-hanging trees. Lady Jane, who was no slouch on a spirited animal, but who had learned a certain caution from experience, was helpless to do more than ride grimly in pursuit, certain at any moment to see horse and rider come to a disastrous end.

That Ethne did not cause the untimely demise either of herself or her companion did little to alleviate Lady Jane's disapprobation when, some twenty minutes later, Ethne, her face glowing with the pure pleasure of the ride, pulled her mount to a walk. Her glow was quickly extinguished at sight of her hostess's white-lipped countenance.

Lady Jane was as close as she had ever been to losing her

temper with the girl. It was not enough that Ethne had placed them both in peril, but she had risked their mounts as well, one of which was Lady Jane's own beloved mare, Nesta, and the other, a particular favorite of Mina's.

Quelling her first instinct to throttle Ethne on the spot, Lady Jane instead ordered the child to turn her mount toward home. She did not say another word until they had given the horses over to Jeremy and then only to suggest that, as she herself was suffering the headache, she meant to remain in her room until the dinner bell sounded and that Ethne would be well advised to do the same. Apparently the inflection in Lady Jane's voice, or perhaps the total lack of it, was enough to convince the girl that it were better not to argue. Ethne went without a protest.

The mutual isolation would seem to have had its desired effect. Lady Jane was no longer contemplating the merits of confining all pubescent females to the colonies until such time as they might be supposed ready to be readmitted into society, and Ethne appeared in the withdrawing room that evening in what gave every indication of a wholly chastened state.

"Good evening, Ethne," said Lady Jane in her normally well-modulated tones, apparently oblivious to her dinner companion's air of dejection, manifested in a certain lackluster about the eyes and a distinct droop at the corners of the rosebud mouth. "You are just in time. I have only just been informed the soup has been poured and the covers laid. I feel certain you must be as hungry as I after our afternoon outing. There is nothing, after all, so conducive to a healthy appetite as fresh air and exercise. Shall we go in?"

All of which had the adverse effect of eliciting a somewhat strangled outburst from Ethne. "I am not in the least hungry," she blurted. "Indeed, I cannot even contemplate food so long as you are angry with me."

"Then you may rest assured," Lady Jane replied quietly. "I am not angry with you, Ethne."

Ethne, who had been forced to spend what she was quite sure was the most miserable two hours of her life waiting until she could make expiation for her misconduct and thus be freed of the sickening sensation in the pit of her stomach, was not prepared to accept Lady Jane at her word.

"Oh, how can you say so after what I-I did? Are you not going to at least read me a curtain lecture decrying how badly I behaved and how foolish I was to risk laming the countess's prized hack?"

"I'm sorry to disappoint you, Ethne, but I am not in the habit of reading curtain lectures to my guests," Lady Jane assured her. "I am not old enough to be your mother, and I fear I have not the least inclination to act as your nursemaid."

"No, naturally you would expect your guests to know how to behave properly. Oh, please say you forgive me, Jane," Ethne blurted at last in low-voiced remorse. "I have been used to riding practically since I was in short coats, and I did so want to impress you with my skill on horseback. And then, I was having such a ripping good time. I-I'm afraid I simply didn't think."

"That much is obvious," Lady Jane agreed, resolved not to give in to the impulse to forgive the girl before she was certain the lesson was brought home. "However, if you choose to conduct yourself in London with a similar disregard for yourself and for those responsible for you, you will soon find yourself at *point non plus*. Not only will you demonstrate that you cannot be trusted, but you will very likely alienate the goodwill of those who most wish for you to succeed."

Unused to being treated with such severity by Lady Jane, Ethne swallowed and ducked her head.

"Yes, I see that now." Almost instantly her head came up again, her eyes pleading. "But, truly, Jane, I never meant to alarm or upset you. Haven't you ever felt that you will simply burst if you cannot run or shout or ride at a neck or nothing pace? I do, and it is the most dreadful thing. But I shan't feel that way in London. I shall be far too busy attending soirees and galas and dancing till all hours of the night." She halted, her glance uncertain on the other woman's face. "Have I lost *your* goodwill, Jane?" she asked miserably.

"Don't be such a pea-goose," Lady Jane said, and, tucking the younger girl's arm in hers, led her toward the dining room. "Of course you have not. Though I should have been hard put to forgive you had you hurt yourself today—or your mount, which happens to be a particular favorite of my sister-in-law's. In future, you will, I trust, *think* before you give in to impulse."

"Oh, but I shall," Ethne replied earnestly, the color only just beginning to return to her face. "Though I cannot promise I shall always come up with the most sensible answer. I'm afraid I have a sad propensity for landing myself in trouble."

"Then at least promise you will come to me before you do anything foolish. Perhaps together we can avert disaster. Now, let us say no more on the subject. I am far too famished to wish to dwell further on the subject."

Dinner and the rest of the evening was passed in a lively discussion of the ball that the countess would undoubtedly give for her protegée's come-out and all the shopping that must be done before Ethne would be ready to be launched into society. By the time Lady Jane, smothering a yawn, suggested they go up to their beds, the unhappy events of the afternoon seemed all but forgotten.

The following day, which was Thursday, was heralded by the arrival home of the dowager countess, who, remarking that she was very glad to see that the sofa in the sitting room had not had time to shed its familiar velvet upholstery, worn as it was, for some new and probably discordant covering, gave her daughter a warm buss on the cheek before turning to greet the unexpected addition to her household with unruffled blue eyes.

"And this, I must presume," she said, allowing Bixley to help her off with her ermine-lined pelisse, "is the reason why my sitting room has not been transformed into something unrecognizable."

"It is." Lady Jane laughed, drawing the girl forward. "This is Miss Ethne Winter, Mama. Ethne, you have the dubious pleasure of meeting my mother, Lady Abigail Ashely, Dowager Countess of Melcourt. Do not, I pray, let her intimidate you. She is a dear when you get to know her."

"Really, Jane. You make me sound some irascible old lady. I'm sure Miss Winter is not in the least intimidated by me. Indeed, why should she be?"

"Certainly not because you are old, Mama," Lady Jane countered, smiling fondly at her mother, who, with her trim figure and guinea-gold hair, could easily have passed for a woman ten years younger than her fifty-five years, "for you are hardly that. I should, perhaps, tell you, however, that Miss Winter has been somewhat nervous at the prospect of making your acquaintance. She is, you see, the Marquess of Danforth's half-sister."

Lady Abigail's suddenly enlightened glance lifted to meet her daughter's.

"Is she indeed," she said, looking back again at the blushing girl. "So you are *that* Winter, my dear. I confess I did wonder. I used to know your mama well. We came out together. But that was a long time ago. I must say you little resemble her."

"I am told I favor my father more," Ethne replied, eyeing

the dowager with a strange uneasiness, which Jane could only attribute to her kinship with Danforth, "and my brother not at all."

"No, *he* is undoubtedly a Trevant. The spitting image of his late father," agreed Lady Abigail with an odd little smile. "A fine-looking man with whom we were all a little in love. I thought it exceedingly unfair that he apparently was taken almost at first sight with your mama." Her smile deepened, quite banishing the whimsical look from her eyes. "Until, of course, Melcourt made himself known to me. After that, there was never any doubt whom *I* should marry. But enough of the past. Jane, dear, I am famished. Ring for the tea tray, if you will. Then you will tell me how it is that I find Loralee Winter's daughter here to greet me upon my arrival home. I confess I am more than a little curious."

"Yes, Mama. But first, perhaps, Ethne, you would not mind leaving me for a while with Lady Abigail. I think it will be better if we are alone when I tell her the news."

"Very well, if you wish it, Jane," Ethne said with an admirable attempt to conceal her disappointment. Very prettily, she made her curtsy. "Lady Abigail, I have been very pleased to make your acquaintance and beg you will excuse me."

"But of course, my dear," replied the dowager, her curiosity growing by leaps and bounds. "I shall look forward later to hearing all about how your mother goes on."

"Now, Jane dear," she said, when a few minutes later she sat down with her daughter over tea and biscuits, "we are quite alone. I think you may safely divulge what I must presume to be a most intriguing account of how you passed your time while I was gone. I promise I am all ears to hear how Danforth's half-sister has come to be at Melcourt."

"You would be, of course," Lady Jane assented with a wry quirk of her lovely lips. "I myself have difficulty believing the fantastic set of events that transpired in your absence. Indeed, I hardly know where to start."

"Would it be too obvious to suggest that you start at the beginning?" Lady Abigail inquired, settling back on the settee and sipping her tea. "It would, after all, seem the most logical place."

"Yes, well," Lady Jane reflected, "I suppose that would be the morning that Mina and Wilfred left for London. Can it only be three weeks ago today that my meddlesome sister-in-law came to call at the unholy hour of eight in the morning? And then to wish that 'something terribly exciting and wonderfully upsetting should happen to change my life forever'? I cannot but wonder what dread flight of fancy put that notion in her head, for that is exactly what did happen. That I was compelled to brave a blizzard to effect the rescue of a young man who should have known better than to embark on the road to Gretna Green with a girl hardly out of the schoolroom, or that I was subsequently run down by the child's enraged guardian as he rode *ventre a terre* in pursuit of the errant miss, who had, by the way, had the audacity to steal his curricle and prized set of bloods, was not exciting or upsetting enough. Oh, no, I must be further made to discover that the odious gentleman is none other than the devious Marquess of Danforth and that, weary of playing nursemaid to his precocious younger sister, what must he do but plot to make me his scapegoat? But now I have got ahead of myself." Lady Jane paused reminiscently. "I suppose it really began when Ethne appeared on my doorstep after dark in the middle of the snowstorm to inform me that she had left her cousin Fredrick Bartholomew the Fourth injured in a carriage accident. It was that which induced me to venture out in the blizzard and which subsequently led me to my disastrous encounter with his lordship."

Rising abruptly from her seat as if she could not bear to

remain still, Lady Jane began to pace as she related the events
of the past week.

The dowager countess was to wish more than once as she
listened to Lady Jane's somewhat convoluted tale unfold that
she had foregone her annual visit to Aunt Biddel's in Oxford.
Three weeks spent in the company of her husband's aging
spinster aunt could hardly compare, after all, to having been
present to see her daughter cross swords with the infamous
Marquess of Danforth. What an encounter *that* must have
been, mused the dowager, noting with interest the sudden
flash of Lady Jane's eyes at the mere mention of Danforth's
name or, more intriguing still, the heightened color in the
lovely cheeks at the casual account of what would seem to
be a rather uneventful sleigh ride to the village. Clearly, the
nobleman had had an unsettling effect on her normally unruffably cool and composed daughter, and for that she could
only be grateful to his lordship.

After the untimely demise of Geoffrey Charles Bartlett,
Lady Abigail had not liked seeing her daughter transformed
from a vibrant, spirited girl into a woman whom it seemed
nothing or no one could ever touch again. It was, therefore,
with the greatest delight that she detected the first distinct
signs that the child's formidable defenses had at last been
made to suffer a breach. Nor was that all or the least of it,
she was to learn as Lady Jane came at last to the crux of
her tale.

"The point is, Mama, that, while Ethne and Freddy were
exceedingly foolish to have set out for his aunt's in Kettering,
they never meant it to be construed as an elopement. Nor do
they have the least wish to be forced into a marriage that
they cannot want."

"But of course they do not," agreed Lady Abigail, beginning to see at last where all this was leading. "Naturally, the
whole must be wrapped in clean linen. I must presume, since

his lordship has seen fit to leave Melcourt, that between the two of you, you have devised some sort of plan for that very thing?"

"As a matter of fact we have," Lady Jane admitted. "We shall put it about that Ethne came to Melcourt at my invitation."

Lady Abigail accepted this pronouncement with admirable fortitude. "But, of course, that was my very thought. But do you think, my dear, that anyone can be brought to believe it? Even I find it stretches the imagination."

"But of course it does," Lady Jane replied. "It is patently out of the question, unless, of course, it can be demonstrated that Ethne and I are actually on quite intimate terms."

"Oh, of course," applauded Lady Abigail. "Why, I wonder, did I not think of that? And how, may I ask, do you propose to carry the thing off? I shouldn't think it at all advisable under the circumstances that you claim to have been school chums. There is the age difference, after all, and it is bound to get out that you never actually attended a girls' school. I daresay we could put it about that *I* was the agent in all of this, since Loralee Winter and I used to be bosom bows."

If Lady Abigail had thought to win her daughter's approbation with so simple and obvious a solution, she was to be disappointed. Lady Jane, far from expressing her gratitude, launched into a colorful discourse concerning the questionable character, morals, and possible origins of the despicable Marquess of Danforth.

"Oh, but this is everything that is marvelous, is it not?" she exclaimed when she had come at last to the end of her diatribe. "To think if I had only waited, I might have been spared the necessity of selling my soul to the devil—or to Danforth, which is very much the same thing. Unfortunately, recriminations at this date are pointless. The deed is done and I have no choice but to follow through."

"No doubt, my dear," concurred the dowager countess, who had had no little difficulty trying to make sense of her daughter's outburst. "Perhaps you will pardon an old woman's curiosity. Am I permitted to know what loathsome deed it is to which his lordship has persuaded you?"

Lady Jane, who had ceased her perambulations about the room and was standing staring blindly out the window, came around at last to face her mama.

"You might well ask," she said in accents that might have daunted a less discerning personage than Lady Abigail. "His lordship is guilty of nothing less than manipulation and coercion. He has, in short, tricked me into promising to accompany Ethne to London for the Season."

"Has he indeed?" remarked the dowager, apparently much struck at the notion. "You, in London for the Season. However did he manage it?"

"He really gave me no choice in the matter. It was either that or stand by and do nothing. And I simply could not do that. Or at least, I could have done, had I realized you would provide a better solution. And now it is too late. Ethne has her heart set on it, and I should be beneath reproach were I to disappoint her. Which, I have no doubt, is exactly the way he planned it. I daresay I have never met a more despicable, conniving, *deceitful* man. I should not be in the least surprised to learn he was perfectly aware that you and Lady Winter are well acquainted. Indeed, I should not be surprised at *anything* he might do."

"He sounds a perfect rogue," Lady Abigail concurred. "A pity I was not in time to make his acquaintance. How very diverting that must have been. Indeed, I believe I am already quite fond of your devious Marquess of Danforth."

"He is *not my* marquess," Lady Jane retorted, clearly incensed at the very notion. "And if you are so fond of him, perhaps you should be the one to take Ethne to London. I daresay it would serve our purpose just as well, if not better."

"Then, my dear, you would be mistaken," said her mother, imperturbably setting her cup in her saucer in one hand in order to reach for one of Cook's prized brandy snaps with the other. "For I am convinced it would not be at all to the purpose. Besides, I should not dream of interfering. You, my dear, are a grown woman of five and twenty and quite used to affirming your independence. You would naturally take exception were your mama to suggest she relieve you of your obligations. No, my dearest Jane. I have not reared two children without learning when it is best not to intrude in their affairs. And, now, I think we should not keep Miss Winter waiting any longer, do you?"

Lady Jane had not lived with Lady Abigail for five and twenty years without learning to recognize when she had been outmaneuvered by her redoubtable parent. Not interfere in her children's affairs indeed! Faith, she did not know whether to laugh or cry at the transparency of her mama's motives. Lady Abigail could not be more pleased that her daughter had been tricked into going to London!

"No, Mama," she said, stifling a wry smile, and, resigning herself to the inevitable, crossed to the door to summon Ethne.

True to the marquess's word, two coaches bearing the Danforth coat of arms arrived promptly at nine the following morning. Lady Abigail, who would have given a great deal to accompany her daughter on what gave every promise of being a most eventful two months in London, but who did not like to thrust herself upon the hospitality of her son and daughter-in-law, wished Ethne the best of good fortune in her new course, gave her daughter a fond buss on the cheek, and sent them on their way.

The weather was particularly lovely in the wake of the earlier, unexpected snowstorm. The warm days had served to melt the blanket of snow, leaving behind burgeoning green pastures and budding hedgerows, which made for a pleasant journey.

They drove at a leisurely pace and at midafternoon halted near a ruined abbey set in the midst of a spinny of sycamores and ash. Perched on the crown of the hill at their backs was the site of an ancient Celtic hill fort, the circular bank clearly defined by thick growths of bramble bushes. Once there had been fenced paddocks and wooden cattle sheds, but they had long ago vanished. Now there were only the grass-covered mound and the two concentric ditches, overgrown with brambles, to mark the place. The abbey itself sprawled at the foot of the hill near the bourne, its twin towers and crumbling walls all that remained of a once thriving religious community.

Spreading a blanket beneath the trees, Lady Jane and her young companion attacked the picnic lunch Cook had insisted they carry with them in lieu of afternoon tea. Ethne devoured three thick slices of bread spread with honey and butter, then washed them down with milk before Lady Jane had finished her first. With her appetite sated, Ethne displayed fresh signs of restlessness, and it was not long before she had induced Lady Jane to restore the remnants of their lunch to the picnic basket and accompany her for a brief excursion to the ruins.

The crumbling abbey perfectly suited Ethne's strong predilection for Gothic romances. In no time she had invented a ghost to inhabit the turrets and roofless corridors. Lady Jane listened in amusement to the lurid tale that must inevitably accompany such a tormented spirit, until the pitiable creature began to assume an unwelcome similarity to herself.

"Enough, Ethne," she said perhaps more sharply than she

had intended. "I have tried to be patient, but I must insist that you cease to regard me as some poor wretch pining away of a broken heart. Nothing, I assure you, could be further from the truth."

"No, of course it could not. I am sorry to always be harping on it. It is only that—" Ethne hesitated, her gaze averted.

Lady Jane sighed. "You cannot keep from thinking about it, is that it?" she queried.

Ethne's eyes lifted to the older woman's. "I keep thinking about Nicky. Wondering what part he played in it. I know what is said of him, the tales of his gambling and his lights of love, the duels that he is supposed to have fought. And heaven knows, he can be arrogant, toplofty, and infuriatingly high in the instep. But I cannot think he could ever do anything that violated a gentleman's code of honor. How is it possible that he betrayed a man who was his friend?"

"I cannot give you the answer to that, Ethne," Lady Jane said quietly. "Only Danforth can do that."

"I know, and I'm sorry I ever brought it up. Only, you may be sure Nicky will never talk about it. He will never talk about anything concerning himself. I have been with him at Brandymere for six months, and I could not even guess where he goes when he disappears for weeks at a time. Or what he does while he is gone. But in his own way, I think he does care about me."

Lady Jane's heart went out to the girl. "You may be sure that he does," she said. Then, after a moment's hesitation, "Ethne, will it help if I tell you what happened seven years ago? Afterward, will you promise never to mention it again?"

Ethne's face lit up. "I swear it, Jane. Cross my heart and hope to die."

Lady Jane laughed and, taking the girl's hand, led her back to the waiting coach. "Come," she said. "It will be a means of passing the time."

* * *

It was an odd sensation, deliberately recalling those happy days in London. After all the years that had passed, the events that had so dramatically shaped Jane's life had taken on a vague unreality, like the lingering aftertaste of a bittersweet wine. Time, she discovered, had distilled her memories of Geoffrey, so that they came to her like separate, disconnected images, some clear-cut and retaining the vestiges of emotions and others blurred and insubstantial, like the half-remembered residue of dreams. Strangely enough, it was the ones filled with sunshine and laughter, the familiar strains of music, or starlit nights that were most distinct. The others, which had once been sharp-edged and bitter with grief, had dulled and faded so, that she found she could talk about them with only a distant sense of regret.

She could not recall who had carried word of Geoffrey's death to Melcourt. Perhaps she never knew. It had fallen to Lady Abigail to break the news to her daughter. To Ethne, Jane related the bare facts, as she herself had learned them.

Danforth, upon returning to London after one of his extended absences and learning that his closest friend was about to succumb to Parson's Mousetrap, had engaged Geoffrey in a private party to celebrate the event. They apparently had imbibed freely during the course of the evening, which ended in a heated debate concerning the relative merits of Danforth's prized chestnuts over Geoffrey's grays. It was perhaps inevitable that they should resort to a wager to settle the matter. She supposed that it did not even occur to them to be deterred by anything so insignificant as a snowstorm. Danforth's pair was to prove, unfortunately, the better of the two. Having reached the Blue Boar's Inn, which was the designated end of their race, Danforth waited a full hour for Geoffrey to put in an appearance before becoming alarmed enough to head back the way he had come in search of his friend. By the time he discovered Geoffrey, the viscount had lain, injured and half frozen, in the snow for better than two hours.

"Geoffrey succumbed to a fatal inflammation of the lungs," Lady Jane said quietly, "and Danforth, without even staying for the funeral, vanished once more. As for me, I remained at Melcourt, where I eventually got over the hurt. I learned to be contented there." She had been staring out the window at the passing countryside, but now she turned to find Ethne regarding her with pensive eyes. "Still," she said, smiling to dispel the somber mood, "perhaps the marquess is right. Maybe it is time I ventured out of my cozy little corner of the world. I shall not mind doing a little shopping and renewing old acquaintances."

Ethne frowned. "I don't believe it," she blurted. "I don't believe any of it."

"I beg your pardon?" said Lady Jane, considerably taken aback at the unexpected outburst.

"I don't believe Danforth was ever so well to live that he would risk his cattle in a snowstorm on a wager," Ethne declared. "He may indeed be a four-bottle man, but I have never heard it said that he has ever been beyond knowing exactly what he was doing at any given moment. Do you not see? It would be totally out of character. And more than that, he is a man who values his prime bloods. You saw how he was when he arrived at Melcourt, looking for Freddy and me. It was hard to say what upset him more—that I had run away or that we had risked his prized pair of bays in a blizzard. You may be sure that *he* would never risk them in such a manner and for such a reason as a wager. It is all a hum, Jane," she summed up, her expression one of utter conviction. "Danforth lied about what happened that night."

"But that is absurd," Lady Jane exclaimed. "Why would he do any such thing?"

Ethne shrugged an eloquent shoulder. "I daresay he is protecting someone," she answered. "It would be just like him. Especially if it concerned a woman's reputation."

Jane stared at the girl, her mind reeling with the unexpected possibilities. A woman, she thought, but what woman? And how had Geoffrey been involved? Surely he had not been afraid for *her* honor, the honor of the woman he was pledged to marry. She had never done anything to place it at risk. Then whose? And why Geoffrey?

It made no sense, and yet neither did Danforth's supposed part in it, now that Ethne had pointed out the flaws. Somehow it did not seem possible that Danforth would have behaved in so totally irresponsible a manner. Perhaps Geoffrey, who had by nature been lighthearted and reprehensibly reckless, could have involved himself in something so heedless, but not Danforth. Ethne was right. It simply did not suit the image she had formed of the man.

All at once, Lady Jane was forced to analyze her impressions of Danforth apart from his supposed part in Geoffrey's accident, and suddenly it was as if she were seeing him for the first time. She could not deny that there was a recklessness about him. It was apparent in the arrogant curl of his lip, the studied indifference of his stance, and the easy, supple grace of his movements. It was, however, a recklessness controlled by what she suspected to be an iron will and an indomitable pride in the man. He wore his cynicism and world-weary exterior like a cloak to conceal a keen intellect and a penetrating wit. She had witnessed that for herself. She had sensed a steely hardness, about him as well, a strength of purpose, which she doubted not had little to do with his role as a society fribble, an arbiter of fashion, or a dangerous rakeshame. And there was a softer side, too, a gentleness, which she had experienced through the touch of his hands and the rich vibrancy of his laughter. He was selfish, arrogant, and cynical, but he could be thoughtful, too, and discerning. And devious, she reminded herself irritably, feeling a headache coming on. Deliberately seeking to put the maddening marquess from her mind, she turned her attention outward to the rolling countryside through which they were passing, but with indifferent success. Her thoughts kept returning to the enigma that was Danforth.

She had always been a good traveler, and the marquess's travel coach was both luxurious and wellsprung. She was, nevertheless, more than a little grateful when they came at last to the White Hart Inn on the outskirts of Luton. The innkeeper had been expecting them and showed them immediately to a cozy room with its own private parlor where they were served a substantial supper of mutton stew. Lady Jane, weary from more than the day's journey, was asleep almost as soon as her head hit the pillow.

The following morning she awakened feeling considerably refreshed and determined to let nothing spoil the day, which had dawned, golden with sunshine and the prospect of continued fair weather. By midmorning, what had promised fair turned foul with a gathering of rain clouds, followed by a pelting rain, which stayed with them throughout the rest of the day.

It was, consequently, well past nightfall when they at last drew up before Melcourt's Town House on Grosvenor Square. They were greeted by Langston, the earl's very proper London butler, who informed them that her brother and the countess were away for the evening. Glad that the interview with Mina and her brother would be postponed at least until the next morning, Lady Jane saw Ethne comfortably settled, after which she partook of a cold collation in her rooms and went straight to bed.

At least the most difficult of her obligations to Ethne was over, she comforted herself as she slipped between the bedsheets and dimmed the lamp. On the morrow, Mina, no doubt ecstatic at the unlooked-for opportunity to play matchmaker, would take Ethne under her wing. The countess had already established her reputation as a hostess, and her soirees, dinners, and other social entertainments were always well-attended. Having a young heiress to present as her protégée, especially one connected to two premier houses of the realm, could only add to her cachet. In which case, Jane was confident, Mina would insist on taking over all the arrangements for Ethne's come-out, leaving Jane herself to do little more than attend the various social events.

Certain that the better part of her worries were over, Lady Jane drifted peacefully to sleep.

She was awakened the next morning from a dead sleep by a frenetic rap on her door, followed almost immediately by Ethne's flurried entrance.

"Jane," Ethne called urgently, flinging open the drapes before crossing quickly to the side of the bed. "Jane, oh, please, Jane. Say you are awake."

Jane, only just managing to stifle a groan, opened one eye and squinted up at the girl's anxious face against the glare of sunlight streaming through her window. "If I wasn't, I most certainly am now," she said with an air of resignation. Struggling to summon her wits about her, she shoved herself up. "Faith, what time is it? It does not feel as if the morning is well advanced."

"It isn't," Ethne confessed, having the grace to look chagrined. "It is only a little past nine. Forgive me, Jane. I promise I should not have dreamed of disturbing you, save only that I did not know to whom else to turn." Abruptly she flung up her hands and began to pace in no little agitation about the room. "Faith, how very like her to call at so uncivil an hour. And on Sunday, too. I blame myself for it. I should have *known* she would put in an appearance as soon as she learned I was coming to London. I simply never dreamed she would hear so soon. I thought I should have a fortnight at least, perhaps even a month. Time enough to be launched. By then I should already have proven myself a success, and it would be too late to do anything about it. But, no. She is here, and very likely she will prevent me from so much as even making my curtsy in polite society. Oh, it really is too much. After all I have done, and at the very moment when I am on the threshold of achieving everything of which I have dreamed for so long. Perhaps now you begin to see the enormity of the situation."

"I'm sure it is quite beyond my imagination," Lady Jane answered dryly, little knowing whether to laugh or be alarmed at the disturbance. "Especially as I haven't the vaguest notion who *she* is or how she can prevent you from doing anything. Perhaps if you would be more explicit, Ethne, and tell me the lady's name?"

"Oh, but I thought I had made it clear," Ethne replied. "Who could it be, but my mother. She is below now, waiting for me to put in an appearance. And she has brought Danforth with her as well. *Danforth!* The one person I believed beyond being influenced by anyone, let alone our mother. And how typical of her to arrive today of all days. I should be thought beneath reproach were I to be less than amenable to her on the one day of the year when we are meant to honor our mothers. It is, after all—"

"Mothering Sunday," Jane finished for her with an unreasonable sense of foreboding. "Faith, I had quite forgot."

Seven

"Do try and collect yourself, Ethne," Lady Jane suggested, dragging herself with something less than enthusiasm from her bed and filling the washbasin from a pitcher. Having decided not to wait for hot water to be brought up, she grimaced, splashed her face with the cold remnants from the night before, and performed her morning ablutions. "Very likely you are only creating a tempest in a teacup."

"You are not acquainted with my mother," Ethne replied in dire accents. "I daresay you have never met anyone quite like her. Oh, Jane, I could not bear it if she ruined everything. And she will. She cannot possibly have changed her mind about—about things."

"I'm sure it is no such thing," said Jane, who was recalling wryly that only the night before she had been foolish enough to suppose the worst of her travails with Ethne were over. Drying her face and hands, she ran a comb through her short curls, pinched her cheeks to give them color, and touched a dab of powder to her nose. "Very likely Lady Winter has decided that she wishes to be the one to present you." Regretfully, she thought of her customary morning cup of hot chocolate that Nanny Twickum had always made sure she received upon rising. She really must see to the hiring of a new temporary abigail, she supposed as she stepped behind the screen to dress. "Or perhaps something totally unrelated to you has brought her to London. That would explain how she happens to be here coincidental with our own arrival. Quite naturally she would wish to see you—especially as it is Mothering Sunday." Having donned the pale lavender morning dress, which she had had the foresight the night before to have pressed and made presentable for the morning, Jane emerged from behind the dressing screen. "I suggest you calm yourself and behave toward Lady Winter as is proper for the occasion. She is, after all, your mother."

"Oh, yes, she is my mother, and I am exceedingly fond of her," admitted Ethne, who did not appear in the least comforted by Jane's advice. "Indeed, one cannot help but love her. And that is the trouble, as you are about to find out for yourself."

On this premonitory note, Ethne opened the door, then stepped aside to allow Lady Jane to precede her into the hall.

Lady Jane was not quite sure what she expected as she approached the withdrawing room door. Certainly it was not the unsettling leap of her pulse at the sound of a low, thrilling voice, one, moreover, which she recognized immediately as belonging to the despicable Marquess of Danforth. But nor was it the small, somewhat plump female, dressed fashionably in a rose beige silk walking dress, her reddish-gold hair cut in youthful curls about her still pretty face and topped by a lovely concoction of straw and silk flowers perched at a fetching angle.

She could not have been a day short of fifty-five, and yet her trim figure and merry blue eyes would seem to exude a youthful exuberance, which was not at all in keeping with the picture of indolence that her daughter had painted her.

"Ethne, dearest," exclaimed Lady Winter, springing with alacrity to her feet at sight of the girl. "How marvelous you look! And how glad I am to see you!"

"Mama," replied Ethne, and crossed dutifully to place a buss on her mama's cheek. "Happy Mothering Day." Her eyes went speculatively to her half-brother, who was standing, one arm propped negligently on the mantelpiece, his handsome features wholly unrevealing of anything more enlightening than an advanced state of ennui, before coming back once more to Lady Winter. "I must say I could not be more surprised. I did not think anything could persuade you to leave your beloved Cotswolds."

"Nor did I," beamed Lady Winter, framing the girl's face with her hands as she reappraised herself of her daughter's features. "But then, I never dreamed how lonely Hargrove could be until you left, dear. Even with Mr. Fenworthy and Gladys Bloomquist and the others of our Society of Liberated Intellectuals, I fear I could no longer bear it. I confess I leaped at the opportunity to attend the Symposium on Spinoza's Philosophy of Immanent Causation, which is to be held in the Royal Academy the day after tomorrow. And then, too, there is to be a discussion the Friday following on Hegel's use of the dialectic in his search for the Absolute. I could not but think it was an example of Spinoza's causality in operation when I discovered from Nicky that you, too, were in London. Is that not so, Nicky?" she asked brightly of her son.

"I should think it closer to Hegel's synthesis of thesis and antithesis," remarked Danforth ironically. Lady Jane, arching an incredulous eyebrow in response to that wholly abstruse observation, was rewarded with a gleam of amusement in the nobleman's heavy-lidded gaze. Then, deliberately, he straightened. "I believe, Mama, you have not been formally introduced to our hostess, Miss Jane Ashely. Miss Ashely has taken an uncommon interest in Ethne. Indeed, it was at her insistence that Ethne is to be brought out this Season." Jane bit her tongue to keep from pointing out the deliberate inaccuracy of that statement, a circumstance which she could see by the twitch at the corners of his lips he had not failed to notice. "Miss Ashely—my mother, Lady Winter."

"Lady Winter," murmured Jane, ignoring the insufferable nobleman. She came forward. "My mother remembers you with great fondness."

"Does she?" Lady Winter exclaimed delightedly as she met Jane's extended hand. "After all these years. But then, I can hardly have forgotten *her*. Had it not been for Abigail, things would have turned out quite differently. It is doubtful Nicky would ever have been Nicky or Ethne Ethne for that matter."

Ethne reacted to that peculiar declaration with every manifestation of one anticipating a mortal blow.

"Have I wished you a happy Mothering Day yet, Mama?" she blurted, which had the effect of earning her a quizzical look from Lady Jane and a distracted flutter of eyelashes from her mama.

"Why, yes, dear, you did. And I'm sure I could not be more pleased," replied Lady Winter, and then, not to be deterred, continued in her former vein. "But as I was saying, it was, after all, Abigail who persuaded me it would be quite impossible to expect a marquess to overlook the conventions. For myself, I could not see why we should have to go through the formalities of a marriage ceremony when we were already joined on a Platonic plane of existence."

"Well," pronounced Ethne, with an air of finality at that startling revelation, *"I* think we should celebrate somehow."

"Celebrate?" queried her mama. "That would hardly be to any purpose, would it, my dear, since we did in the end give into convention?"

"No, I mean Mothering Day. Perhaps a picnic lunch in the park, or a long drive to see the sights," Ethne urged—to no avail. Her mama had already turned back to Lady Jane.

"Had we chosen to live as free spirits," Lady Winter continued unabated, "as I have always wished to have done—in the tradition of Mary Wollstonecraft, you understand—"

"Indeed, ma'am," replied Lady Jane, who was beginning to grasp a great deal concerning Lady Winter, and, more importantly, perhaps, about Ethne. Mary Wollstonecraft, however, had born a child out of wedlock.

"But of course you do. In which case, you can imagine the complications that would have accrued."

"I should think they would be obvious," murmured Danforth, a glitter of amusement in the look he bent upon Jane, who, it was readily apparent, was having her very first encounter with a bluestocking of the first water. "A veritable Pandora's Box as it were."

"Quite so," affirmed Lady Winter. "Certainly Abigail was quick to point them out. A man in Danforth's position, after all, required an indisputable heir to the title. He could hardly have wished his only son to be a—"

"Mama," forcefully interjected her daughter before Lady Winter could specify *what* her son might have been. "Lady Jane is not Mary Wollstonecraft or even Gladys Bloomquist, and I know you cannot wish to put her to the blush by suggesting something that must be construed as improper by persons of delicate sensibilities."

"On the contrary," drawled Danforth with sardonic amusement, "I suspect Miss Ashely would not be at all scandalized at the possibilities. No doubt they have already occurred to her."

Lady Jane, who had with difficulty swallowed a startled choke of laughter at the marquess's sally, awarded his lordship a censorious glance.

"I'm afraid I have not given the matter much thought one way or the other, my lord," she countered dampingly. "I have, however, found your reminiscences about my mother entertaining in the extreme, Lady Winter. Indeed, I can think of nothing I should enjoy more than a comfortable coze some afternoon. Have you come solely for the lectures, or do you plan to remain in London to take in the social events of the Season?"

"Oh, heaven forbid," exclaimed that lady, with perfect candor. "Once was more than enough for me: I daresay I should never have made my own come-out had not my mama made it plain she would perish of grief did I not. *My* inclination was to set up housekeeping on my own in such a manner as to enjoy the company of persons of elevated intellect. Besides which, I have always been a firm believer in Mary Wollstone-craft's school of thought, which advocates that the ideal of marriage is intellectual companionship, not mindless subservience to a lord and master. I have never approved of parading young girls in the manner of prospective broodmares for the sole purpose of marrying them off."

"A parade, is it?" queried the marquess with a bemused arch of a single arrogant eyebrow. "Odd, but a hunt always seemed a more appropriate metaphor. I suppose it all depends on one's perspective, does it not."

"Really, Nicky," Lady Winter scolded. "Your levity is quite reprehensible at times. Obviously, you haven't the slightest notion what it is to feel one's whole life is to be determined by something so absurd as the outcome of a ball, or by whether one receives the approval of a Princess Esterhazy or a Marquess of Danforth, for that matter. You have never suffered the humiliation of finding yourself a wallflower."

"No, but then neither, I daresay, have you," Danforth did not hesitate to point out. "And nor will Ethne. Besides being reasonably well to look upon, she is far too plump in the pocket and well-connected ever to suffer the fate of a wall-flower."

"Please, Mama," exclaimed Ethne, mortified at this new

turn of events. "Must we go over all this again—now, before Lady Jane?"

"Indeed, I think we must," Lady Jane answered quietly for herself. "I should not like to think I have helped you go against your mother's wishes, no matter how unintentionally. You will admit, will you not, that your account of Lady Winter's views on the subject was not entirely accurate?"

"The truth is," Ethne replied baldly, "I am never certain from one moment to the next what my mother's views will be. She does not hesitate to declare she does not believe in the conventions until her daughter shows an interest in someone of whom she cannot approve. Oh, but then how conveniently she changes her views."

"If by that you are referring to Gerard Heaton," interjected the marquess with a decided lack of levity, reprehensible or otherwise, "then our mother stands acquitted. It was I who made certain you were removed from that unsavory sphere of influence."

Ethne furiously blushed. "And I suppose I am to thank you one day for meddling in my affairs," she retorted, bridling with indignation.

"You may thank your mama that you are not even now somewhere in a nunnery," drawled his lordship, the bored mask of the Corinthian descending over his lean features. "That was my first inclination when I learned of what we shall, for want of a better word, call your youthful 'indiscretion.' "

Ethne, who did not appear in the least gratified by this latest revelation, blanched as white as she had before been red. "I might as well *be* in a nunnery if you do not intend ever to let me make my curtsy in society," she declared in a voice that trembled. "Indeed, I might as well be dead."

Lady Jane, who had been watching Lady Winter during the

heated exchange between Ethne and Danforth, chose at that moment to intervene.

"No one has said you are not to come out, Ethne," she called to the girl's attention. "Indeed, I believe you owe your mama an apology. Had you been listening instead of playing the goose, you would know that is very possibly the last thing she would wish to do. Or am I mistaken, Lady Winter?"

"On the contrary. You could not be closer to the truth, Miss Ashely," applauded that worthy, smiling her approval. "It is my conviction that every female should have the right to determine her own life. I may not approve of Ethne's choice, but if it is a Season in London she wants and if Danforth is willing to stand the nonsense, then who am I to place obstacles in her way?"

"Then you have no objections? You mean to let me stay?" Ethne demanded, afraid to believe in her good fortune.

"The truth is that I should be pleased were you to be settled, my dear, and married, if that is what will make you happy. I, after all, have my own life to live, and I have decided I do not wish to live it alone."

"Why, I wonder, am I not surprised?" murmured Danforth, with a peculiar glint in the sleepy eyes.

"If not alone, then with whom, Mama? Or dare I ask?"

This, coming as it did from Ethne, brought an indulgent smile to Lady Winter's lips.

"But of course you dare to ask," answered her mama. "How else are you to learn if you are not prepared to question? If you must know, I have persuaded Mr. Fenworthy to join me in realizing a dream we have shared for some time."

"A dream? Which dream?" Ethne demanded, apparently having taken her mama's admonition to heart.

"We have decided to establish a community for impoverished writers and intellectuals," Lady Winter informed them. "A place where ideas may be exchanged in an atmosphere of tolerance and goodwill. Oh, you needn't look alarmed," she added, noting Ethne's pallor. "I have no intention of creating a scandal, much as I should enjoy it. I daresay you would both feel compelled to scold and read me curtain lectures, and you may be sure I should find that fatiguing in the extreme. Which is why I asked Mr. Fenworthy to marry me."

"Marry you!" Ethne gasped. "Good heavens, Mama, Mr. Fenworthy cannot be above five and forty."

"He is, as a matter of fact, forty-three. Not that that has anything to say to the matter. I have not outlived two husbands without learning I have no wish to outlive a third."

For once, Ethne appeared too stunned to speak, and since Danforth displayed the annoying aspect of a man content with the role of spectator at a farce, it was left to Lady Jane to make the proper rejoinder.

"May I assume that Mr. Fenworthy's answer was everything you would wish?" she ventured, wondering why she had the distinct feeling she did not really want to know the answers to her questions as she felt Danforth's eyes on her, not for the first time that evening, a disturbingly arrested expression in their unfathomable depths. "And that felicitations are in order?"

"Felicitations, Miss Ashely?" drawled the marquess in sardonic amusement. "Oh, you may be sure of it. Mr. Fenworthy is, after all, my mother's gardener. Or was, when last I was at Hargrove. When, may I inquire, Mother, is the happy event to take place?"

"Of course you may inquire, Nicky," his mother replied. "There is little that you can do, however. For, though I have tried to impress upon you both the tenets of tolerance, goodwill, and understanding, I was quite certain you could not approve."

"Were you, madam? You astonish me," drawled his lordship mildly. "What could I possibly find to disapprove in discovering my mother has taken up with her gardener? Indeed, when have I ever questioned any of the things you might do? I must naturally be pleased that you have chosen to announce your upcoming nuptials in the presence of Miss Ashely, whom you have only just met, never mind that it puts her—and us—in a most damned awkward position. But what would you. No doubt you thought by that to make the news more palatable."

"You have not been properly attending, Nicky," his mother admonished. "I was explaining to Miss Ashely why there could be no objection to Ethne's having her Season in London. Mr. Fenworthy and I, you see, were married in a private ceremony in the chapel at Hargrove more than a fortnight past."

"Madam," murmured the marquess, bowing in acknowledgment of a palpable hit, "may you never cease to amaze me."

"Indeed, I should hope not, Nicky, dear. You are far too easily bored. I daresay it does you good to be jarred occasionally from your complacency."

Upon which Ethne, flinging up her hands and sinking down on a sofa as if her legs could no longer bear her, uttered despairingly, "Faith, I am ruined!"

It was perhaps fortuitous that Mina should have chosen that precise moment to burst on the scene, exclaiming, "Jane, dearest!" and her face alight with pleasure at having her sister-in-law with her at long last in London. "I cannot tell you how sorry I am we were out when you . . . arrived . . . last night," she finished haltingly, her voice fading at the discovery that her withdrawing room was crowded with people. "Oh, I beg your pardon," she hastened to apologize, sensing at once from the various frozen attitudes of her unlooked-for guests that her intrusion had come at an inauspicious moment. "I had no idea—"

"No, of course you did not," said Lady Jane, coming to her sister-in-law's rescue. "Indeed, how could you? Perhaps you may begin to understand when I introduce you to every-one present. This is Miss Ethne Winter, who is to be your new protegée, her mother, Lady Winter, and her half-brother, Danforth. My sister-in-law—Lady Wilhemina Ashely, Count-ess of Melcourt."

"Mina, if you please," the countess corrected, extending the requisite two fingers to Lady Winter. "Wilhemina is such a dreadful mouthful."

"Not at all. It is a lovely name," Lady Winter demurred, graciously smiling. "May I say it is a pleasure to meet the woman who has so kindly offered to take my Ethne around."

"The pleasure is all mine, Lady Winter," Mina responded, rising admirably to the occasion. "I'm sure Miss Winter and I shall rub along famously together. I promise I am quite looking forward to all the fun we shall have shopping and going the rounds."

"Lady Winter and Danforth have come to be together with Ethne on Mothering Day," Jane expanded in order to fill in the sudden awkwardness of the moment. "Which reminds me. Mama, having arrived home in good health, sends you her love. Indeed, I suspect she would have left her trunk packed and come with us had she not been reluctant to impose on your hospitality."

"Is that not just like her," exclaimed Mina, favoring Jane with a glance charged with curiosity. "I can never make her believe we adore to have her around."

"A wise mother knows that it is best to play least seen in her grown children's affairs," Ethne's mama observed with the air of a Tibetan monk. "Unfortunately, it is not always easy for her children to see that the same is true as regards their mama."

"In this case, you may be sure of it," Danforth promised sardonically. "Happy Mothering Day, madam. No doubt I wish you well of it. And now I must beg you will excuse me. You and the ladies no doubt have a great deal to discuss, and I, as it happens, have pressing business elsewhere. Countess. Miss Ashely," he said, bowing to each of the women in turn.

For the barest instant as he straightened, his eyes met Lady Jane's and held them. Her breath caught. Indeed, she felt paralyzed by their piercing intensity.

Then the moment was past, and, announcing that his carriage was at his mother's disposal, he turned on his heel and left them.

"Well, that is that." Lady Winter sighed. "I have made a complete mull of things, as usual. A pity, really, for, had Danforth given him half a chance, I believe he would have found Mr. Fenworthy to be one of nature's noblemen. It is even possible that he might have discovered he actually liked Lucius. I know *I* did—enormously."

Lady Jane and Mina exchanged pointed glances, neither knowing quite what to say. It came to Jane that if all her encounters with the marquess and his relatives were to be of a similarly exotic nature, the months ahead promised to be anything but dull.

It was then that Ethne's solemn voice, breaking into the silence, took them all by surprise.

"I did, too, Mama," she said quietly. "Discovered I liked Mr. Fenworthy, that is."

Her mother's head lifted. "Did you, dear?"

Ethne nodded. "I found him to be warmhearted and-and kind. Most of all I remember his laugh. It used to reverberate with merriment. He cannot always have been a gardener, I think. He did not speak in the manner of a common laborer."

"Mr. Fenworthy has been many things. 'Common,' however, has never been one of them," Lady Winter responded, smiling. "He had traveled all over the world when I met him—Asia, Africa, the Americas. He had been a physician, a sailor, a soldier, a teacher, a bullfighter, and most lately, my gardener. I discovered him, you see, in Cheltenham on one of my frequent visits to take the waters. You remember, Ethne."

"I remember you brought him home with you and that he was quite ill," Ethne nodded. "A fever, you said, that he had contracted in India."

"Indeed, yes. I thought he would perish from it, but we managed to pull him through. And then he stayed in the capacity of gardener. Let me see, that was almost two years ago. Since just before your papa's unfortunate demise. Julius used to try to cheer me with flowers from the garden. I believe it was his unfailing kindness that helped me overcome my terrible loss."

"He sounds a most intriguing—er—person," Mina ventured, still in the dark as to why they should be discussing her guest's gardener in what gave every indication of terms of endearment. "Was it a sudden passing?"

Lady Winter blinked. "Lord Winter's? Oh, indeed. He was a bruising rider. No one would ever have believed he could be thrown by a green horse."

"No, very likely not," agreed Mina, confused. "I meant Mr. Fenworthy, however."

"I beg your pardon?" It was Lady Winter's turn to appear bewildered. "I'm afraid I do not understand. What about Mr. Fenworthy?"

"Mr. Fenworthy," Lady Jane interjected kindly, "is not dead, Mina. He is, in fact . . ."

"My husband," Lady Winter supplied before Jane could complete her statement that Mr. Fenworthy was, in fact, very much alive. "We have only just been married."

"Oh, dear, I thought the way you were talking that—but, now, I see, of course, that I was . . . Oh, my, your *husband?*" stammered Mina, only just beginning to grasp the enormity of her misunderstanding. "Oh, I *am* sorry—I mean *happy*—for you. Oh, dear, I am not sure at all what I mean," she confessed at last, hopelessly flustered. "Perhaps you should explain what I should be, for I am sure I cannot," she ended, turning for help to her sister-in-law.

"I think," said Lady Jane, "that we should all feel better able to deal with Lady Winter's announcement were we to fortify ourselves with something to eat. I suggest, therefore, that we all go into breakfast, where, no doubt, everything shall soon be made clear to you, Mina dear."

Things were indeed made clear to Mina over the repast of grilled kidneys, scrambled eggs, and buttered toast, or, in Lady Winter's case, dry toast and coffee, that worthy claiming that a woman of her age must be careful of her figure. Especially, she added, a gleam of mischief in her eye that strongly reminded Lady Jane of a certain reprehensible marquess, as she had a new husband anxiously awaiting her return to the Cotswolds. Mina's response to that thinly veiled reference to the marital bliss to which Lady Winter *cum* Mrs. Fenworthy was obviously looking forward with unlady like enthusiasm was a deal less restrained than had been Lady Jane's.

Choking, Mina dropped her fork.

"There, there, Mina dear," murmured Jane, thumping her sister-in-law sympathetically on the back. "You did wish for something wonderfully upsetting to happen to utterly change my life, did you not? And now that you apparently have your wish, it would seem we must live with it."

"Yes, but to marry a man who has been one's gardener," she blurted. "It simply isn't done, Jane, and you know it. I daresay we shall be at the very least the laughingstock of the Town when the word gets around. I dare not even think what the worst might be. My reputation as a hostess will be ruined, you may be sure of it. And we may forget receiving invitations from anyone of importance, let alone vouchers for Miss Winter to Almack's, for it simply will not happen. Indeed, we might all very well retire to the country in the hopes that one day, twenty or thirty years from now, all this will finally be forgotten."

"Nonsense," Jane chided. "Our credit cannot be so bad that we cannot weather something that is, you will admit, none of our affair. And Ethne, after all, is an heiress and Danforth's half-sister. I cannot think she will be considered any less worthy a match because her mama has chosen to marry a man she obviously loves."

"Then you obviously do not know the *ton,*" Mina countered, pressing her fingertips to her temples in the manner of one who feels the sudden onset of an excruciating headache. "Of course they will hold it against her daughter, and, because we have associated ourselves with her, they will, by extension, hold it against us as well. I am sorry to have to say it, but I fear Lady Winter has become a liability to everyone."

"No, not to everyone," Ethne said, drawing all eyes to herself. "No one knows I have come to Town with Lady Jane, and no one will know—if I return, now, with my mother to Hargrove."

"Oh, my dear," exclaimed Lady Winter, her eyes suddenly bright, "I could not ask more than that my daughter be the sort to think of her friends before herself. But your sacrifice will not be at all necessary." Without warning and to the

PRESENTING AN IRRESISTIBLE OFFERING ON YOUR KIND OF ROMANCE.

Receive 4 Zebra Regency Romance Novels (A $16.47 value)
Free

Journey back to the romantic Regent Era with the world's finest romance authors. Zebra Regency Romance novels place you amongst the English *ton* of a distant past with witty dialogue, and stories of courtship so real, you feel that you're living them!

Experience it all through 4 FREE Zebra Regency Romance novels...yours just for the asking. When you join *the only book club dedicated to Regency Romance readers,* additional Regency Romances can be yours to preview FREE each month, with no obligation to buy anything, ever.

Regency Subscribers Get First-Class Savings.

After your initial package of 4 FREE books, you'll begin to receive monthly shipments of new Zebra Regency titles. These all new novels will be delivered direct to your home as soon as they are published...sometimes even before the bookstores get them! Each monthly shipment of 4 books will be yours to examine for 10 days. Then, if you decide to keep the books, you'll pay the preferred subscriber's price of just $3.30 per title. That's $13.20 for all 4 books...a savings of over $3 off the publisher's price! What's more, $13.20 is your <u>total</u> price...there's no additional charge for shipping and handling.

No Minimum Purchase, and a Generous Return Privilege.

We're so sure that you'll appreciate the money-saving convenience of home delivery that we <u>guarantee</u> your complete satisfaction. You may return any shipment...for any reason...within 10 days and pay nothing that month. And if you want us to stop sending books, just say the word. There is no minimum number of books you must buy.

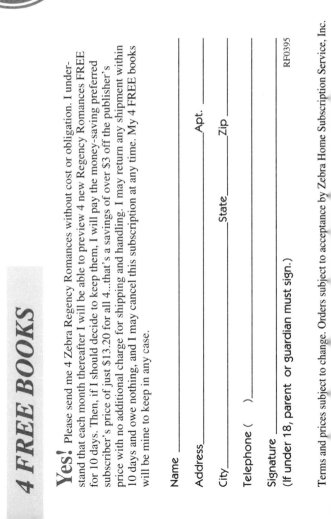

Say Yes to 4 Free Books!

COMPLETE AND RETURN THE ORDER CARD TO RECEIVE THIS $16.47 VALUE. ABSOLUTELY FREE.

(If the certificate is missing below, write to: Zebra Home Subscription Service, Inc., 120 Brighton Road, P.O. Box 5214, Clifton, New Jersey 07015-5214

4 FREE BOOKS

Yes! Please send me 4 Zebra Regency Romances without cost or obligation. I understand that each month thereafter I will be able to preview 4 new Regency Romances FREE for 10 days. Then, if I should decide to keep them, I will pay the money-saving preferred subscriber's price of just $13.20 for all 4...that's a savings of over $3 off the publisher's price with no additional charge for shipping and handling. I may return any shipment within 10 days and owe nothing, and I may cancel this subscription at any time. My 4 FREE books will be mine to keep in any case.

Name _____

Address _____ Apt. _____

City _____ State _____ Zip _____

Telephone ( ) _____

Signature _____

(If under 18, parent or guardian must sign.)

RF0395

Terms and prices subject to change. Orders subject to acceptance by Zebra Home Subscription Service, Inc.

startlement of the others, she came abruptly to her feet to face them with the inspired aspect of a Lord Wellington rallying his troops to battle. "We are all intelligent women here. We have only to put our heads together and study the problem rationally to devise a better solution, I know it. Indeed, we cannot fail." Lifting her cup of coffee on high, for want of something more suitable to the occasion, she evoked the wisdom of Horace: " 'For mortal daring nothing is too high'!"

"Oh, indubitably," murmured Lady Jane, recalling to herself the unfortunate second half of the quotation: "In our blind folly we storm heaven itself."

Mina looked blankly from Jane to Lady Winter, then back to her sister-in-law. "Good God," she groaned, sinking her head in her hands. "We are undone."

It was left to Lady Jane to strike a happy medium between Lady Winter's fervor and Mina's despair. Suggesting that all was not yet lost, she began to assess the true nature of their situation. Indeed, it was not long before breakfast assumed the air of a gathering of generals for the express purpose of formulating plans and strategies for a military campaign.

It was quickly decided that their best defense was to put up a strong offense, and for this they must have recourse to all the weaponry at their command. First and foremost, they must assure that Ethne's coming-out ball should be the event of the Season, second only to that presided over by the Prince Regent himself in celebration of Easter. The discussion of a spring theme for the dance, complete with a profusion of live potted wildflowers set about the ballroom, a fountain with goldfish, and silk butterflies suspended from the ceiling appealed greatly to Ethne, but Mina, glancing sidelong at Jane, was moved to profess the belief that not all the decorations in the world would be enough to insure a *success fou* in and of themselves. For that, they must have someone whose mere presence would be enough to draw even the haughtiest of matrons and the most discerning of mamas. They must have Prinnie himself.

"And you know how that might best be achieved," Mina ended.

"But of course," exclaimed Ethne, her face brightening. "Danforth!"

"Indeed," agreed Mina, glancing from one to the other. "Who better than the one who of all the Carleton set has the greatest influence with the prince?"

It was true. Little as she might like it, Lady Jane was forced to acknowledge that in order to achieve their purpose they could do no better than to enlist Danforth's aid in promoting his sister. Faith, she groaned silently to herself. She might have known from the very beginning that it would be impossible to avoid the nobleman. No doubt *he* had been perfectly aware of it all along. Indeed, she would not have put it past him to have instigated his mother's arrival for that very purpose though she could not for the life of her imagine why he should have wished to have done it. Probably solely for the entertainment it would afford him of annoying her, she thought dourly and immediately vowed that she would not give him that satisfaction. Certainly, there was no point in bemoaning what could not be helped, she told herself firmly, and it looked as if she would unavoidably be seeing a great deal of his lordship.

Once that was settled, in her own mind, at any rate, Lady Jane had perforce to broach a more sensitive subject—the problem of the new Mrs. Fenworthy herself. She did so with all her usual tact, pointing out that Ethne's successful entree into society could be achieved without the slightest difficulty if knowledge of her mother's marriage simply was never to come out.

Asked if she had seen fit to inform anyone other than themselves, Lady Winter replied that, though she could not care less what the members of the *haut ton* might think of her or her actions and, indeed, that she would take no little pleasure from being generally thought a "liberated" female, she was yet not so far removed from reality that she had not recognized that marrying so far beneath her station could not but present obstacles to her daughter's future happiness. She admitted, in short, that she had informed no one as yet and was further amenable, in spite of the fact that it would entail the sacrifice of principle, to keep her marriage a secret until after the Season had ended.

Having won that major concession from her protegée's mama, Lady Jane was next moved to suggest that it would be better for all concerned were Lady Winter to return to Hargrove as soon as was possible. It would never do, after all, she gently pointed out, to misrepresent the facts were she asked any questions of a personal nature. She would have no recourse, as a matter of fact, but to tell the truth about herself, and that, obviously, would never in the circumstances do.

"You are right, of course, my dear," replied that worthy, apparently not in the least offended at being considered something of an embarrassment. "I shall remain only long enough to attend the lectures at the Royal Society, which should occasion no one any great concern. You will agree, will you not, that my chances of running into Sally Jersey, or anyone else of the *Beau Monde,* for that matter, at a lecture on Spinoza are exceedingly slim at best."

Lady Jane did agree, albeit with a peculiar reluctance and an odd sort of queasiness in the pit of her stomach. The former, she attributed to a natural inclination to be cautious, and the latter, she dismissed as a probable reaction to eating grilled kidneys and eggs for breakfast.

Nevertheless, she knew she could not but be relieved when Friday had come and gone at last and, with it, Lady Winter.

Eight

Monday heralded the onset of a whirlwind of activities, chief of which concerned the business of launching Mina's young protegée into polite society. The countess began by finalizing her plans for Ethne's coming out ball.

With Easter falling on the twenty-fifth of April, the Easter Ball would come very nearly at the high point of the Season and was, consequently, expected to be the event to which all others would be compared. Obviously, Mina pointed out, it would be most advantageous to have Ethne's ball before the Easter Fling, but not before all the best people had had time to remove to Town. It was her idea to set the date on the Saturday before Palm Sunday and to add to the decorations sprouting boughs of willow catkins, boxwood, and hazel, which, traditionally gathered in lieu of palms, were believed to bring good luck to a house. Observing dryly that to pull the thing off without Lady Winter's secret being found out they would need all the luck that was available to them, Lady Jane seconded the notion.

That initial decision made, Mina and Lady Jane were left with less than a fortnight in which to draw up the guest lists, make out the invitations and send them out, and arrange for the potted plants, the silk butterflies, and the fountain and goldfish to arrive in time to decorate the halls and ballroom with a spring and Easter theme. Then there were the menus to draw up for the dinner, which was to precede the ball, the

refreshments, which were to be served continuously throughout the dancing, and the supper, which came traditionally at
midnight. Nor were these all or the least of their tasks. They
had also to find time to do their shopping in Bond Street, to
engage a seamstress to make up ball gowns for Ethne, Mina,
and Lady Jane, to make the requisite morning calls to introduce Ethne to a select number of young ladies her own age
and their mamas, and to put in an appearance each evening
at five in Hyde Park, occasionally at the opera, and at least
once or twice at the theater.

Any invitations that might come—and a great many could
be anticipated once it became known that not only had Miss
Jane Ashely chosen to enter her name once more in the marriage lists, but that she was accompanied by a young heiress
who bore the distinction of being both beautiful and well-
connected—could be dealt with as they arrived.

Lady Jane was, consequently, given little time in the week
following her arrival in London either to regret that she was
missing the coming of spring to Melcourt Oaks or to do more
than reflect, albeit with something that suspiciously resembled
pique, that she had apparently been mistaken in believing that
she would be running into Danforth more often than she
might care to have done.

The truth was, she had not laid eyes on the marquess since
Mothering Sunday. Melcourt, who had been commissioned by
his wife to do what he could to discover Danforth's where-
abouts, returned to report without roundaboutation that the
nobleman was, in fact, not to be found anywhere in Town.

Danforth had apparently behaved true to form, mysteriously
vanishing without leaving so much as a clue where he had
gone.

"It can only be hoped that he will turn up in good time,"
said Mina, who, coming in after a particularly trying afternoon spent shopping, had flung herself down on the settee

in her private sitting room and, claiming she was too weary ever to get up again, had begged Jane to ring for tea. "Prinnie will not put in an appearance at Ethne's ball if Danforth is not back in Town, you may depend on it," she continued as Lady Jane crossed to the bellpull. "The prince does not make it a habit to launch young girls into society, even those as well-connected as Ethne. He will come only as a favor to Danforth and then only if the marquess is here to ask it of him."

"I might have known he would do some such thing the moment I came downstairs to find him in our withdrawing room in the company of his mama," bitterly remarked Jane, who having been made to accompany her sister-in-law to practically every shop in Bond Street in search of a grenadine silk shawl to add just the right accent to Mina's marley lace ball gown, was, consequently, not in the mood to be generous. "How very like him to disappear, leaving his mama on our doorstep, so to speak. Not that she proved to be any great difficulty, as it turns out, especially since she is by now safely on her way back to Hargrove, but I cannot but wonder who will show up next."

"I wish you will not make dire predictions," Mina admonished, comically frowning. "Just look what has happened in consequence of my one frivolous remark. Very likely yours will produce Mr. Fenworthy himself, and then what should we do?"

Jane, flopping down on the overstuffed chair and kicking off her patent slippers, wriggled her toes deliciously inside her pink silk stockings as she glanced through the pile of cards and invitations that had accrued in a single day. "I should return to Melcourt and never once look back," she declared heartlessly, "leaving you to explain Mr. Fenworthy to Sally Jersey and Princess Esterhazy. Who, by the way, have honored Ethne with vouchers to Almack's," she appended, waving in the air a letter and the coveted vouchers, which she had just opened. "Apparently, our missing marquess was thoughtful enough to mention to the patronesses before he left for parts unknown that his sister was making her come-out in the company of Miss Jane Ashely. Naturally, they are exceedingly pleased to be able to confer on Miss Winter their unqualified approval and their expectations of seeing us both at the Assembly Rooms."

"How very generous, to be sure," observed Mina in tones laced with irony. "When I casually mentioned to Sally Jersey only last week that I was sponsoring an unexceptional young woman in her first Season in London, what did she do, but coyly suggest that she would have to bring the matter before the other patronesses for their due consideration. And now a single word from Danforth, and the vouchers arrive post-haste."

"There is nothing so irresistible, it would seem, as the charms of a practiced rake," Jane commented philosophically.

"Where, I cannot but wonder, do you come up with such improper notions?" demanded a new, masculine voice from the doorway. "Certainly not from me. Perhaps you would care to tell me, my dearest man-hating sister, what you can possibly know about rakes, charming or otherwise?"

Both women turned to regard the newcomer with varying degrees of affection, Mina's manifesting itself in a sudden glow of warmth that lit up her entire face, and Jane's with a sardonic quirk of an eyebrow.

Just short of six feet in height and slenderly built, he was impeccably attired in a day suit of blue superfine with gray unmentionables tucked into the tops of gleaming brown Hessians. Blond hair, which had begun noticeably to thin, did not detract from his strong, handsome features, which bore a marked resemblance to those of his sister. He was Lord Wilfred Ashely, Earl of Melcourt, and his blue eyes twinkled with amusement at his wife and sister.

"But of course I got them from you, along with boxing cant and how to shoot a gun," Jane asserted shamelessly. "As to rakes, I have met any number of adventurers, fortune hunters, and practiced rogues since my come-out. I was courted for a time, you will remember, by Gerard Heaton, who, though he can be devastatingly charming, is a feckless ne'er-do-well better kept at arm's length."

Melcourt's mouth thinned to a grim line. "I am not likely to forget it," he replied with a marked lack of his former good humor. "The nerve of the fellow to impose on your good nature. I should have done far more than send the bounder packing had you not made me promise not to have done. I daresay he would not have hesitated to carry you off to Gretna Green had you not been wise to him."

"I feel certain that was his intention," Jane admitted, sitting up at the arrival of the tea tray in order to do the honors. "Which is why I sent you in my stead to meet him at what was supposed to be our trysting place. Fortunately the disappointment was enough to convince him I was not in the least interested in being the means of repairing his depleted fortunes."

"Mr. Heaton had a proper understanding of the circumstances before we parted company, you may be sure of it," agreed Melcourt chillingly.

"Which is why nothing ever came of it," Mina pointed out, pulling her husband down beside her on the settee. "Enough about Gerard Heaton. We have been invited to Lady Fitzhugh's tonight. Now, don't you dare say you have already made plans, Wilfred. I have no wish to go without you. Indeed, I should not go at all had Lady Fitzhugh's second daughter, Maria, and Ethne not taken a shine to each other. Having become almost inseparable, they are together even now at Hyde Park with Lady Fitzhugh. I really have no choice but to make an appearance, Wilfred darling, insipid as it promises to be. Do say you will be pleased to go with me."

"For you, my sweet, anything," laughed Melcourt, saluting the back of his wife's knuckles with his lips. "Just so long as you don't make the Fitzhughs a habit. A devilish bore, Colonel Fitzhugh. Always going on about his days in the Carnatic. Are you quite sure you wouldn't rather stay home? I can think of a deal more entertaining ways to spend an evening"

"As can I." Mina, leaning her head against her husband's shoulder, sighed expressively. "Beginning with a long, hot bath. And followed," she added, lifting twinkling eyes to Melcourt, "by a glass or two of champagne with, I think, a bowl of plump, red strawberries."

"Oh, most definitely strawberries," agreed the earl with what could only be construed as an intimate smile. "Shall I order the hot water and champagne immediately sent up?"

Mina snuggled more comfortably in the cradle of her husband's arm. "In a moment, dearest," she answered, closing her eyes. "I find that I am contented just where I am."

Jane, who was suddenly feeling decidedly *de trop,* coughed to clear her throat. "I think," she said, slipping her feet once more into her shoes, "that I shall take myself off to my room. I'm certain I must have a hem to mend or some such thing."

She did not wait for an answer; indeed, she was not certain either of them heard her. Slipping out the door, she circumspectly closed it behind her, but not before she glimpsed her brother lower his head with the unmistakable purpose of kissing his wife.

For a moment Jane stood with her back to the door, a faraway look in her eyes, as it came to her to wonder what her life would have been had she never met and fallen instantly head over ears in love with Geoffrey. Might she not be happily married now to someone else, with a home of her own and children perhaps? Was it not long past the time when she should have ceased to cut herself off from that very possibility?

Not, of course, that she had not had opportunities, she reflected in her own defense. There were eligible bachelors even in the remote fastness of Northamptonshire. She had, not, after all, been a total recluse. She had attended her fair share of house parties and country dances, and Mina had made sure to invite more than one hopeful candidate for her hand to Melcourt every Christmas. It was simply that she had not met anyone in seven years whom she had found to be of even passing interest. No one, that is until Danforth had come barreling into her life. *He,* undeniably, had made a lasting impression, whether she would have wished him to have done or not.

Unbidden, an image came to her of Danforth bending over her as she lay on the snow, his touch gentle as he probed her limbs for broken bones; and again of Danforth, his dark head flung back in laughter, the harsh lines of his face softened with mirth—of Danforth, his expression masked in ennui, but his eyes piercing pinpoints of flame that took her breath away. And suddenly she found herself wondering what it would be like to have him look at her in the way Melcourt was wont to look at Mina.

Instantly, a warm blush stained her cheeks as she realized where her unruly thoughts had led her. Faith, she must be tired indeed if she had begun to think of Danforth in such terms. She might, in light of Ethne's speculations, have decided to reserve judgment concerning the marquess's part, real or fabricated, in Geoffrey's accident; indeed, she might even have come close on occasion to finding she could almost like him; but she could never be *interested* in him, at least not in a romantical way. She was quite certain of that. The notion, in fact, was preposterous.

The hall clock, striking the half hour, jarred her out of her reverie. Brought to an awareness that she must have been standing, staring into space, for a full five minutes or more, she pushed hastily away from the door and proceeded immediately down the hall to her own rooms.

For the first time since she had arrived in London she found herself alone and with nothing more pressing to occupy her for the next three or four hours than an afternoon nap. It should have been a welcome respite from the hurry-scurry of the past week; and, indeed, it was just the sort of interlude to which she had been blissfully looking forward when she slipped away from Mina and Wilfred. Why, then, she asked herself irritably, must she discover herself twenty minutes later unable to settle and roaming like some lost soul from sitting room to boudoir and back again?

But that was not all or the worst of it. Over and over during her perambulations, she had discovered her thoughts irresistibly returning to Danforth.

Faith, surely there were things more worthy of contemplation than a certain marquess's predilection for apparently dropping off the face of the earth without a moment's notice, she fumed, annoyed with herself. Nevertheless, when she should have been emulating her sister-in-law and soaking delectably in a long, hot bath, she had instead been mulling over and over in her mind where Danforth could possibly have gone, and why.

She had little difficulty in imagining any number of places where the insufferable nobleman might have taken himself off to. There were the races at Newmarket, for example, or his hunting box in the Lake Country, or the possibility of a pugilistic bout at some remote country spot. The list was practically endless. Somehow, however, though she could not have explained it to herself, she did not think any of them answered.

Perhaps it was something she had sensed in him just before he took his leave of her on Mothering Sunday. More than once during that rather memorable morning call, she had been acutely aware of Danforth's eyes on her and the unsettling effect it had had on her sensibilities. She had had the oddest feeling that he was committing every minute detail of her face to memory, an impression that had been powerfully re-inforced when she had at last looked into the piercing intensity of those undeniably remarkable orbs.

From out of nowhere had come the bizarre thought that he was behaving in the manner of a man who was not certain when he would see her again.

She had dismissed the notion at the time as being ludicrous in the extreme. It was not, after all, as if he held her in any great affection, or ever could, for that matter. He had made that abundantly clear on the sleigh ride from Melcourt, and nothing he had said or done since had led her to believe any differently. Nothing, that was, save for the peculiarity of that look.

She had completely shut the incident out of her mind until Mina had recalled it that very afternoon by bringing up the subject of Danforth's troublesome disappearance. Then suddenly it had all come back again, and, with it, the inexplicable feeling she had experienced before—that Danforth was somehow in danger.

As if she were a Gypsy or a fortune-teller, able to read people's minds, she chided herself. What danger could possibly threaten the Marquess of Danforth? Somehow, in spite of his less than sterling reputation she could not think that he had got himself involved in a duel. He was arrogant and proud and probably quite capable of defeating any number of persons in a bout of fisticuffs, pistols, or swords, but he was hardly a fool. He was neither so green nor so heedless as to risk exile for a duel.

What, then, could endanger a man like Danforth? She could think of nothing, and still she could not shake the thought that he had been behaving in the manner of a man embarking on a course from which there might be no return.

Oh, the devil fly away with Danforth, she fumed, flinging herself crossly down on the sofa. What could it possibly matter to her one way or the other *what* he did? It was all his fault that she was not even now peacefully riding Nesta along the brook at home or puttering quite happily in her rose garden instead of contemplating the prospect of an insipid evening spent in the company of the Fitzhughs. Indeed, it was his fault that she would miss seeing the men go "a palming" for willow sprigs and fresh cuttings of boxwood and hazel in celebration of Palm Sunday. How dare he lure her to Town on a pretext and then blithely go on his own way, untroubled, she was quite sure, by the fact that he had wrecked her contentment and ruined her habitual tranquillity of mind. Where the devil *was* he?

Jane was to find Lady Fitzhugh's dinner, which was to be followed by a musicale, every bit as flat as Mina had predicted. This, she attributed to the meal, which, consisting of lettuce soup, veal sauté with Duchess potatoes and garden peas, and capped by a *soufflé a la vanille,* was edible, but uninspiring, and to the conversation, which, confined by the dictates of etiquette to Mr. Reginald Fitzhugh on her left and Lord Merriweather on her right, was limited to a discussion of the superiority of the Quorn country over the Border country for riding to hounds on the one hand and to the subject of neckclothitania on the other, and not to the fact that a certain marquess was not in attendance.

By the time the sweetmeats and jellies had been removed and Lady Fitzhugh rose from the table to signal the end of dinner, Lady Jane had as thorough an understanding of "oxer fences" and the unmitigated joy of flinging one's heart over before one when leaping them as she could ever desire. She was equally certain that, far from being in sympathy with Lord Merriweather's abhorrence of the latest trend in fashion for young bloods to ape the manner of coachmen by wearing several whip thongs thrust through the top buttonhole of their driving coats and arranging their neckcloths in the "Mail Coach," she could not have cared less. She was, in fact, hard put not to disgrace herself by giving vent to her amusement by laughing in his face. Nor did it help her state of mind to have found herself wishing, while being forced to listen to an exposition on the relative difficulties of achieving the "Mathematical" versus the "Oriental" or the "Osbaldeston" versus the "Trone a Amour," that Danforth might have been there to share her amusement.

She knew instinctively that he would have done.

The knowledge, however, that the marquess, unlike most of the gentlemen of her acquaintance, understood her keen appreciation of the ridiculous and, further, would have enjoyed the evening's absurdities every bit as much as did she was Dutch comfort. Indeed, it served only to put her unreasonably out of frame.

Danforth, she had begun to realize to her dismay, would seem to be becoming something of an obsession.

It was a fixation, however, which she was determined once and for all to put out of her head. What she needed was a distraction, she decided, as she accompanied the other women into the withdrawing room—something to occupy her thoughts that had nothing to do with Danforth. Perhaps she should indulge in a light flirtation. Not with Reginald Fitzhugh or Lord Merriweather perhaps—indeed, most emphatically not—but with someone who, fully aware of the rules of the game, would provide an entertaining interlude without any complications or misunderstandings.

She allowed her fancy to play with the notion as, smiling and nodding, she attended with only half her mind to a loquacious Mrs. Chadworthy prose on about her daughter's musical talent on the harp, the demonstration of which was to be one of the promised treats of the evening. When Lady Jane came, however, to visualizing the gentleman with whom she would engage in light repartee, only one sprang inevitably to mind—Nicholas Trevant, Marquess of Danforth.

It was perhaps fortunate that Lady Fitzhugh chose that very moment to announce it was time to repair to the music room where the gentlemen would join them directly. Ethne, tearing herself at last away from her new friend, Maria, linked her arm in Jane's.

"Well?" Ethne queried in a thrilling undertone. "What do you think of him? Is he not the handsomest gentleman you have ever seen? And he is ever so charming. I believe I have never been so wonderfully entertained by anyone before."

Jane was taken totally off guard by these observations, which, due to her preoccupation with her own wayward thoughts, assumed the aspect of statements taken out of context. Frantically she tried to remember who had been seated on either side of Ethne at dinner.

She recalled the image of a rather fubsy-faced youth whose sartorial splendor included a profusion of gold fobs strung about his person, sleeves padded at the shoulder seams with buckram wadding to an exorbitant height, and shirt points so prominent as to threaten to pierce his earlobes. Surely *this* could not be the paragon Ethne had described! No, of course not. It must certainly have been the gentleman seated on Ethne's left.

Somewhat above average height, a slender and well-knit

specimen of the male gender with perhaps two and twenty years in his cup, he had been presented to Lady Jane as Lord Phillip Maheux, the Earl of Thaxton's eldest son and heir. She had thought him well enough to look upon, if a trifle young, with unexceptional manners, a winning smile, and blond curls many a female might have gone to great lengths to have for herself. Other than these superficial attributes, she had not formed any great impression of this, the first of what promised to be a long line of Ethne's conquests.

"Am I to assume you are referring to a certain young nobleman who is just now entering?" Lady Jane rejoined, gazing casually over the top of her ivory-handled fan in the direction of Lord Phillip, who gave every indication of one searching the roomful of women for one female in particular.

Ethne's wholly becoming blush would have been answer enough without the sudden nervous flutter of her painted vellum fan. "Do not, I pray, let him see you are looking at him," she whispered back, then, affecting to laugh at a nonexistent remark of Jane's, pretended she were not perfectly aware of the gentleman who, pausing to exchange amenities here and there, was gradually working his way toward her. "Is he not simply divine," she breathed with every indication of one in alt.

"Oh, without question," agreed Jane, feeling suddenly ancient. "He must naturally be considered a *nonpareil* among gentlemen."

"Must he indeed?" queried Mina, coming up behind Jane. "How very exciting. And who is this paragon?"

"Lord Phillip Maheux," Jane answered, smiling. "Who else could it be?"

Ethne, blushing more deeply than before, favored the older women with a comic moue of distaste. "I know perfectly well you are laughing at me. But it does not signify. I think his lordship everything that is pleasing."

"On the contrary, I am exceedingly glad you found something to enjoy in your dinner companions. *I*, on the other hand, cannot say the same," confessed Jane, who had espied Mr. Reginald Fitzhugh enter the room and start immediately toward her. "You will no doubt excuse us, Ethne dear. Maria is waving to you and no doubt wishes you to join her. Come, Mina," she added, smoothly guiding the countess toward a settee at the back of the room, which, in the close proximity of a scroll-backed chair, afforded places for three persons to sit, "I think it is time we found our seats. You, naturally, will wish to have Wilfred beside you," she pointed out, taking the chair, "which means, I am afraid, someone else will have the honor of Mr. Fitzhugh's company."

"Poor Mr. Fitzhugh," Mina crooned soulfully, though her eyes were dancing. "It would seem the colonel's nephew has met with defeat. Indeed, you are being uncommonly hard on the gentleman."

"The gentleman is uncommonly hardheaded," Lady Jane acerbically replied. "Far from viewing his campaign as a failure, he is far more likely to have convinced himself my most ardent wish is to have him living in my pocket. I shall be fortunate if he does not follow me home to Melcourt."

"A fate to be avoided at all costs," Mina said, laughing. "Very likely he would end up a permanent fixture at Oaks, which would not please Wilfred at all. At least Ethne would seem to have had better luck," she added, having observed with satisfaction that young Maheux had reached his objective. "It would seem our young protegée not only demonstrates good taste in her choice of gentlemen, but excellent sense as well. Her new admirer, besides being heir to a title, is assured of a more than respectable income. I daresay she could do a deal worse than Lord Phillip Maheux."

"Counting your chicks before they are hatched, my dear?" queried the Earl of Melcourt, taking his seat on the settee next to his wife. "I wonder what young Mr. Fredrick Bartholomew would have to say to that."

"Why? What should he have to say to it?" demanded Mina in obvious bewilderment.

"Nothing, perhaps," answered her husband, nodding to an acquaintance across the room. "Only, I understand the Earl of Bellamy's grandson was the odds on favorite to win Miss Winter's hand before he left for the Peninsula."

Lady Jane experienced a sudden queasy sensation in the pit of her stomach. "They have known each other since children," she said soberly, "and, though they are quite fond of each other, it is the affection one feels for a brother or sister. Why, Wilfred? What have you heard?"

"Only what I just learned from Colonel Fitzhugh, who is a particular friend of the Earl of Bellamy—that young Bartholomew arrived in time for the siege of Badajoz. Which, you may or may not be aware, fell on the sixth of this month. Word has it that he was posted here as missing in battle on the twenty-ninth of March."

"But this is the eleventh, and the thirtieth was . . ." Mina exclaimed, her glance going to Jane.

"Mothering Sunday," Jane finished for her. "Danforth must have known about Freddie when he brought his mama to see Ethne."

The rest of the evening at the Fitzhughs made little impression on Lady Jane. She was aware of sitting through a seemingly endless array of musical numbers performed by various young beauties on pianoforte, the harp, or the flute and one particularly bad vocal rendition of what presumably was one of Thomas Moore's "Irish Melodies." She managed to applaud at all the appropriate intervals, to smile and nod vacantly in response to any comments made to her, but she could not afterward recall for the life of her who had played or precisely what pieces had been performed. Her thoughts had been entirely on poor, dear Freddie and the sudden, unshakable conviction, no matter how farfetched, that Danforth had gone himself to the Peninsula to search for his cousin.

It was during the first interlude between numbers that Jane bethought herself of the need to convey to Mina and Wilfred the desirability of keeping the disturbing news from Ethne. There was, after all, nothing the child could do for Freddie, save worry herself sick while they waited for further word. In which case, it would seem to make little sense to spoil her first weeks in London. Very likely she would insist on calling the whole thing off, which would serve no good purpose.

While Mina was quick to agree with Jane, Wilfred, ever practical, felt compelled to point out that, if the worst were to happen and it was discovered young Bartholomew had met an untimely end, Ethne might very well find it difficult to forgive them for not having told her the whole from the very beginning. Furthermore, he doubted not that she would be fully justified.

"Then naturally I shall take the blame," Jane replied with a deal more assurance than she actually felt. "I'm only suggesting that we wait a few more days before we tell her. Perhaps by then we shall have happier news."

She did not add that her hopes lay all in Danforth or that these were based on his parting remark, made when he left her at Melcourt. Very likely Mina and Wilfred would see it as a mere grasping at straws, or, worse, as an indication that she had developed a *tendre* for the marquess, and that, besides being preposterous, simply did not bear thinking on. The last thing she could wish would be to have her matchmaking sister-in-law begin making plans to bring her and Danforth together.

Nevertheless, it was to Danforth's promise that there would

be someone to look out for Freddie that Lady Jane clung in the succeeding days of uncertainty and doubt. After all, it was true, she told herself firmly. Fredrick Bartholomew the Fourth did indeed have connections and none more influential than that of the Marquess of Danforth. If anyone could help Freddie, it was his very own cousin.

Nine

As the date for Ethne's ball drew near, Mina and Jane began to believe that luck was indeed on their side. In spite of the fact that it was becoming increasingly unlikely they would be honored by Prinnie's attendance at the gala, it appeared equally probable that they would not require it. Not even so much as a whisper of Lady Winter's marriage to Mr. Fenworthy had thus far been breathed about, and Ethne was already well on her way to taking the *ton* by storm.

Naturally lively and vivacious, she had attracted a deal of notice from her very first rather modest appearances among the *Beau Monde*. These, having been carefully orchestrated by Mina and comprising, as they did, introductions to the daughters of a select number of the *ton*'s leading families, attendance at a few small private parties, and chaperoned strolls along the Broad Walk in Hyde Park at the fashionable hour of five, served to establish Miss Winter as an unassuming, well-brought-up young female of impeccable breeding and unexceptional manners.

With the result that, she had already acquired after almost two weeks in London a sizable gathering of eager admirers who flocked around her wherever she put in an appearance.

Indeed, only Lady Jane herself could boast, had she been so inclined, which she most definitely was not, of having an entourage as impressive as Miss Winter's. It was true it was not so large as Ethne's. What it might have lacked in sheer quantity, however, was more than made up for in quality.

While it was readily noted that the heirs and not a few younger sons of several noble houses clustered around Miss Winter, Lady Jane had attracted the attentions of at least two earls, a viscount and a baron, not to mention Mr. Francis Beauchamp, who, besides being enormously wealthy, was related to half the noble houses in the realm. They were, for the most part, men in their middle thirties to late forties, avowed bachelors and established Men About Town—not the sort to hang out after young misses hardly out of the schoolroom. They gravitated instead to Jane, drawn to her by her undeniable beauty and afterward held, charmed, by her penetrating wit and ready sense of humor.

Mina could not have been more pleased with the manner in which things were progressing, save for one fly in her ointment. In spite of the ease with which Jane had taken up the threads of her life in London and no matter how many eligible gentlemen paid her their attentions, she demonstrated not the smallest sign that any one of them was even close to the point of engaging her interest.

If anything, Mina reflected wryly, observing Jane amid a circle of admirers at Almack's, her sister-in-law seemed distracted, as if, even as she laughed and engaged in light repartee with some of the most attractive men in London, her thoughts were somewhere else. While it was true her air of unattainability quite naturally made her all the more intriguing to the gentlemen, rather like a gauntlet flung down before them that they could not resist taking up, Mina knew Jane too well to suppose it was done deliberately to lure them on. Indeed, she would be better pleased if it were, for then at least she might be assured that Jane took *some* notice of the male contingent, presented to her like a platter of hors d'oeuvres from which she might pick whatever delicacy she pleased. As it was, she could not be certain Jane even knew the Earl of Windhaven from Lord Silverbridge, or Hazleton, for that matter, from Mr. Francis Beauchamp.

The hitherto indefatigable matchmaker was beginning, in short, to believe her sister-in-law's case was quite hopeless.

She might have been somewhat comforted had she known that the cause of Lady Jane's seeming abstraction was the continued absence of a certain eminently eligible marquess. And, in truth, Jane could not still the gnawing voice of anxiety that persisted in tormenting her with an endless array of dire misfortunes which might have befallen the odious nobleman. It would serve him right, she told herself, were he to have fallen prisoner to the French, stopped a musketball, or been made to suffer any of the other thousand and one mishaps that had come to her as she lay sleepless in her bed at night. How dare he go off without a word and leave her to ponder his no doubt ignominious fate! Only the knowledge (and in truth, she had no doubts as to why he had done it) that he had gone to rescue Freddy excused him in some small part. Indeed, it was the waiting without knowing into what dangers he had ridden that was driving her to distraction.

That and the fact that no matter how often she might tell herself it should not matter a whit to her what foolish or reckless thing he might choose to do or what might happen to him as a consequence, at whatever social event she found herself she could not keep from searching among those gathered for a tall masculine figure with raven-black hair, deceptively sleepy blue eyes, and a pair of indecently broad shoulders.

This night had been no different. No sooner had she arrived at the Assembly Rooms and found herself accosted by Mr. Francis Beauchamp, than she experienced a sharp pang of disappointment that it was not someone else bowing elegantly over her hand and paying her the compliment of requesting the first waltz on her dance card. The realization that she had been hoping against hope that it would be Danforth who greeted her made her uncommonly put out with herself—so much so that she failed to notice when sometime later a slender gentleman, somewhat carelessly attired in a loose-fitting coat and less than elegantly tied neckcloth and still handsome in spite of evidence that he was wont to indulge in an excess of drinking and vice, entered.

The newcomer went leisurely to pay his respects to one of the patronesses, to whom he was related, and stood for a time, conversing with her.

But his gaze was on Ethne.

Ethne's thought, as she allowed herself to be led out in the country dance just then forming, was that she had never been happier. Indeed, her first Season in London was proving to be everything that she had hoped it would be, and more, she decided, as she lifted her eyes to meet the compelling smile of Lord Phillip Maheux, her dance partner.

How odd, she reflected bemusedly, dropping into a curtsy as he bowed, that a man could have the power to make her pulse race with a mere touch of the hand or to cause her knees to tremble by his very entrance into a room full of people. She had only to look into a certain pair of hazel gray eyes to feel the peculiar queasy sensation that had even now just invaded the pit of her stomach. Indeed, she might have convinced herself that she was the victim of some bizarre malady, save for the fact that she experienced these peculiarities only when Lord Phillip was nigh.

It must be, then, that only he had this strange power over her, she mused, dazzling him, had she but known it, with her smile as they came together from opposite corners of the square and formed a bridge with their clasped hands. Gracefully, she pirouetted beneath it, acutely aware of the warm blush that had risen to her cheeks at his nearness. She felt a pang of loss as they parted, and her eyes lingered on his as she joined hands with the ladies and moved to the left within the ring of gentlemen, who were proceeding to the right. She lost sight of him as both circles came to a halt and she dropped into her curtsy before the gentleman across from her.

Her face glowed with the pleasure of the dance, and she was wishing the evening might never come to an end as she placed her hand in the gentleman's and rose from her curtsy. Then her eyes lifted to meet his.

The smile froze on her lips, and for the barest instant she thought her heart must fail her. Then, quickly, she recovered her equanimity.

"Mr. Heaton," she exclaimed with at least a semblance of her former gaiety. "I declare. I never thought to see you at Almack's."

"I could hardly stay away, now could I?" Heaton replied. His smile lent his dissolute features a deceptively boyish cast, which not a few females had found, to their subsequent regret, to be devastatingly charming. "After your mama let slip that you were making your come-out? I hear, my dearest Ethne, that you are fast becoming all the rage in London."

"Am I?" Ethne murmured, flashing him a startled look over her shoulder as she slide-stepped around him. When had he seen her mama and what for heaven's sake had passed between them? she wondered with a dreadful sinking feeling.

Having completed a circle around the smiling rogue, Ethne could only be grateful the patterned steps of the dance carried her away from him that she might have time to gather her wits about her. The last person she had wished to encounter at Almack's was Gerard Heaton.

Ethne might have been green, but she was no fool. She had known well enough what Heaton was when she allowed herself to engage in what she had considered to be a light flirtation with him. That, however, had been when she could not see to the day when she would escape the Cotswolds and make her way at last to London. In those days she had been suffering from boredom and acute feelings of dissatisfaction with her life. The knowledge that Gerard Heaton was dangerous had made him all the more appealing. Now, however, she could not but be aware that her credit was not great enough to support having a gazetted fortune hunter hanging out after her. Especially one who might have an inkling of her mama's most recent marriage. He was not above, she knew, using whatever knowledge he might have for his own purposes. Faith, it did not bear thinking on! And yet she had to do more than just think about it. She had to discover what, if anything, he knew about her mama's secret!

"You know you are," Heaton pointed out as they came together again at the center of the square. "Indeed, how could you not, when you are prettier by far than any other female in Town? In that respect, I daresay you take after your mama."

"You flatter me, sir," replied Ethne, lowering her eyelashes to hide the flash of her eyes. Faith, why did he keep bringing up her mama?

"Not at all. It is only the truth, after all. May I call on you? Where are you staying?" Heaton called out as Ethne prepared to rejoin the ladies in the center.

"With the Countess of Melcourt, and, no, you may not, sir," Ethne flung coolly back at him. She saw his face darken with anger. Then she was moving away from him, and moments later she was dropping into a curtsy once more before Maheux.

For the first time since she had met Lord Phillip at Mrs. Fitzhugh's musical soiree, Ethne failed to experience the heady thrill the mere sight of him had always before aroused in her. She had far too many other things on her mind. Indeed, though she tried valiantly to hide it behind a mask of gaiety, she was, in fact, very close to being blue-deviled. A circumstance that Lord Phillip, who was wont to note everything about the lovely Miss Winter, did not fail to observe.

"Is there something amiss, Miss Winter?" he queried as he led her from the floor. "Have I said or-or done anything to put you out of frame with me?"

"Oh, no, my lord," Ethne blurted, her eyes flying to his. "Indeed, how could you, when you have been everything that is kind?" She blushed, aware that she had spoken perhaps too forcefully, and hastily averted her face. Her glance went to the alcove where the refreshments were laid out on a table. "I-I beg your pardon. It is only that I find it a trifle warm. Perhaps if I had some punch—"

Lord Phillip hesitated the barest instant, obviously not convinced that mere thirst was the source of her distress. Then bowing at the waist, he gallantly left her in order to fetch her a cup.

Faith, Ethne groaned to herself as she watched his tall masculine form weave through the mill of people toward the refreshment table, she had made a dreadful mull of things. No doubt he thought her changeable and prone to fits of the sullens. Very likely he had formed a disgust of her just when she had begun to think he might come to like her, even a little.

Oh, *why* had Gerard Heaton to show up, now, when she was on the point of realizing everything of which she had ever dreamed for herself? She was free at last from Hargrove and ready to take her rightful place in society; Lord Phillip Maheux, along with a flattering number of other gentlemen, had done her the honor of paying her their attentions; and the ball to be given in her name was only two days away.

Heaton must not be allowed to ruin it for her, she vowed,

clenching her hands into fists at her sides. And yet, she could not see what she could do to prevent him from it.

She could hardly come straight out and ask him what he knew without revealing that there was something of a damaging nature *to* be known. No, there was only one possible solution to her problem. She must pretend to take up with him where she had left off until she could cajole it out of him—without anyone being the wiser!

She felt sick at the thought of what she meant to do. Somehow she must contrive to meet a notorious rakeshame without the possibility of any witnesses, and then, to allay his suspicions, she must convince him that she was captivated by his charm. It was dangerous and foolhardy, and there was every possibility that she would be ruined in the process. Still, she saw no other solution to her problem.

It was at that point that Lord Phillip returned with her punch and she had, perforce, to laugh and smile when she had much rather be by herself to think. Already a germ of an idea was taking root in her mind.

The next morning Mina was to note that neither of her protegées, it seemed, had enjoyed a restful repose.

Ethne appeared downpin and showed an inclination to mope over her food, while Jane, usually the most congenial of breakfast companions, not only demonstrated a decided lack of appetite, but was moved to declare in no uncertain terms that she would be pleased if her sister-in-law would cease to hover over her like a hen with but one chick. She was, she insisted, not feeling in the least ill. Indeed, she had never been ill a day in her life and did not intend to start now. She simply was not hungry.

Instantly she regretted her unseemly outburst and begged Mina and Wilfred to excuse her hasty words, that, indeed,

she did not mean them. It was only that she was feeling a
trifle homesick and had never wanted to come to London.
Oh, it was all the odious Danforth's fault for tricking her into
doing what she had never wished to do. Then, snatching a
lace handkerchief from her sleeve, she pressed it to her nose
and, mumbling something about having to see to her corre-
spondence, fled from the room.

"Well!" exclaimed Mina in the manner of one on the point
of some momentous illumination. "Of all that is marvelous!"

Wilfred, observing his wife's arrested expression, experienced a sudden shuddering sensation. "Now, Mina," he said,
thinking to divert her before she could reach the conclusion
which, for her, must be inevitable. "No need to make more
of this than it is. Obviously, Jane is not used to participating
in an endless round of social functions. She is tired and could
no doubt use an afternoon and evening off to rest and recoup
her strength."

"Nonsense, it is nothing of the kind," replied his spouse,
then, turning back to the table with the intention, no doubt,
of enlightening him as to the true nature of his sister's un-
wanted display, was recalled to Ethne's presence in the room.
"On the other hand," she hastily amended, "perhaps you are
right. I shall insist that Jane do nothing more strenuous today
than relax and enjoy a good book. Perhaps she would be
pleased to go to the circulating library for that very purpose.
Perhaps it would not hurt you either, Ethne dear, to stay home
today, too. It would never do, after all, to appear wan or the
least hagged tomorrow night at your ball."

"But I am not in the least tired, ma'am," Ethne was quick
to declare. "Indeed, I had hoped that I might spend the day
with Maria Fitzhugh. She suggested that we might enjoy an
al fresco luncheon and an afternoon coze, after which, her
cousin has offered to take us driving in the Park when everyone is there."

"But that sounds delightful, and of course you must go," agreed Mina, who was not in the least averse to having an afternoon free of any obligations. "Perhaps you should send at once to Maria informing her of your intentions."

Ethne, who had not been at all certain she would be able to gain Mina's permission to be absent from the house for the better part of the day, was quick to take advantage of her hostess's suggestion. Begging to be excused, she curtsied prettily and made her exit.

Upon which, the countess, waiting until the child was certain to be out of earshot, turned once more to her husband, her face expressive of triumph. "Oh, my dearest," she exclaimed, "how could I have been so blind as not to have seen it from the very first?"

The earl, recognizing when it is useless to pretend to be absorbed in the morning paper when one's wife insists on his attention, reluctantly folded the London daily and laid it by his plate. "No doubt it is only that you have had a great many other things on your mind, my sweet," he offered in the way of appeasement. "*I* certainly have been equally remiss. I have not the least idea what it is that you have been too blind to perceive."

"No, but then you wouldn't, my dear," his countess was quick to assure him. "Men are always the last to recognize such things, even when they are under their very noses. Oh, Wilfred, it really is too wonderful. Jane, who, if you must know, I had begun to fear was fated never again to lose her heart to another, has at last discovered someone who does not bore her. She has, though I daresay she does not yet know it, fallen head over ears in love with Danforth!"

"Good God, you have gone too far if that is what you are planning," exploded her husband in no little amazement. "Think, Mina, what you are saying. Geoffrey's untimely demise has been laid at Danforth's door. Surely, you cannot think Jane would be willing to simply overlook that pertinent fact."

"*I* think that where the heart is concerned, anything is possible," the countess replied complacently. "It is even possible that Danforth has been misjudged. After all, I cannot think that Jane could feel the way she does did she not know, somewhere deep inside, that he is not the villain he has been painted."

"And I think you are way off the mark, my girl," replied the earl in no uncertain terms. "If you care about Jane, and I know you do, you will do nothing to promote a match that is so patently ill-conceived. Do I make myself clear on the subject?"

"Oh, patently," Mina sniffed, turning her back to the earl. "It is obvious you are grown hard and quite insufferably unfeeling of one whose only fault is that she loves you and yours and wishes all around you to be happy."

"Mina," the earl crooned with a warning inflection.

"It is also clear that you cannot truly love me," Mina continued, ignoring the interruption. "You could not talk to me in that odious manner if you did."

"*Mina.*"

"No, I understand completely. We have been married five years and you quite naturally have grown—comfortable—with me. I have seen it time and again in other marriages. Indeed, it happens all the time. The newness is gone, and you will undoubtedly be forced to look elsewhere for-for whatever it is you are missing. No doubt I shall learn to overlook your coolness in time. Perhaps I shall take up tatting or needlework to fill the hours. Naturally, I shall be forced to obtain a-a cat or a lap pug upon which to lavish my affections, even though it shall no doubt cause me to sneeze. But you needn't worry that I shall be a burden to you. I shall ad-*just*—"

This last was uttered in a squeal, as her sorely beset husband chose just then to sweep her off her feet. "You, my dear, will do nothing of the kind. You know you detest tatting, and you certainly will not replace me in your affections with anything so repugnant as a lap pug. And even if I have grown 'comfortable' with you, my impossible love, I have never once found it necessary to look elsewhere for that with which you so abundantly provide me." Carrying her in his arms, he started purposefully toward the door. "I should hope *that*, at least, will soon be made obvious to you."

"I shall strive," Mina promised, gazing up at him with wide, guileless eyes, "to keep an open mind, dearest."

Ethne, unaware of her half-brother's supposed conquest of Lady Jane's heart or the furor that such a supposition had aroused in the earl's household, wrote to inform Maria Fitzhugh that she hoped she was not too late to accept her very kind invitation to join her for the day. If it was agreeable with all concerned, she would call on her within the hour. In the meantime, she would await her reply. She signed it, "Your very good friend, E.W." Then sealing the missive and requesting a footman to deliver it and return with an answer, she began to pace as she went over the plan she had contrived in the wee hours of the night.

It had been she, Ethne, who suggested to Maria the night before the notion of spending the day together. Mrs. Fitzhugh was amenable on occasion to allowing the girls to go out in the company of Maria's abigail on short excursions, and what could be better or more natural than an al fresco luncheon in the Park? It was the perfect excuse to get away from the house, and Maria's abigail was a deal more biddable than the countess or Lady Fitzhugh. If they were by chance to encounter a certain gentleman while strolling along the Broad Walk, well it would hardly be Ethne's fault. And if, while exchanging pleasantries with that individual, she were accidentally to fall behind Maria and her abigail long enough to try and discover what she wished to know from him, would it not seem an innocent enough occurrence?

It seemed to Ethne that it would. She could not, in fact, discover a single flaw in her plan when, some moments later, the footman arrived with the answer in the affirmative to her message.

Jane could not have been more surprised to discover some time later that she was apparently to have the morning to herself. Indeed, she could not but think it odd that not only had Ethne departed to the Fitzhughs, but Mina had left word neither she nor the earl were to be disturbed for anything short of a major crisis. She had rather expected the house would be in chaos with preparations going forth for the morrow's ball.

Supposing that Mina must have things well in hand, she wandered into the downstairs withdrawing room in search of something other than her own unrewarding thoughts to occupy her.

After leafing desultorily through half a dozen copies of *La Belle Assemblee* and the *Ladies' Monthly Museum,* she almost wished she had not left instructions that she was not to be home to callers. Indeed, more than once she found herself listening for the door knocker or at least for some sound to indicate that Mina had at last emerged from retirement.

It was not, however, until shortly after noon that, having dined from a tray in her room, she had her solitude disturbed.

Mina, wearing a grin of self-satisfaction, sailed into Jane's presence after only the most perfunctory of knocks on the sitting-room door.

"Jane, dear," she cooed, coming to rest with a swirl of silk skirts on the settee upon which Jane was sitting. "I have a wonderful surprise for you. I have only just received a letter from Lady Abigail, and you will never guess who is arriving on the three o'clock mail coach."

Jane indeed was unable to imagine who it might be. Certainly not her mama. The dowager countess was not likely to employ a public conveyance anywhere, let alone all the way to London. "I'm afraid I haven't the slightest idea," she replied when it became apparent Mina, in spite of her pronouncement to the contrary, expected her to offer an array of possibilities.

"Why, Nanny Twickum of course!" the countess beamed. "Apparently her sister has recovered and she could not bear to think of some stranger caring for you. There was nothing for it, but Lady Abigail must put her on the first coach to London."

"Oh, the poor dear," murmured Jane around the lump which had risen unexpectedly in her throat. "You know what a wretched traveler she is. She will undoubtedly be quite knocked out after two whole days in a crowded coach."

"She may be a trifle out of frame," Mina agreed. "Still, seeing you will pluck her up. I shall, of course, send the carriage to meet her."

"And I wish to go with it. Indeed, I shall have it no other way," Jane insisted, glad to have something to occupy her. "If I leave now, I can catch her at the Archway Tavern near Whittington's stone and save her from having to ride further in the discomfort of the mail coach. Indeed, if you will be so kind as to order the carriage brought around, I shall change and be off directly."

Mina offered no objection other than that a footman accompany the coach for her protection, and in less than twenty minutes, Jane had set off north on Albany Street, which took her past Regency Park into Camden and out of the City. Barren and dreary, this was not the loveliest of drives, but it was the most direct. Nevertheless, she vowed they would take the more circuitous and far more picturesque route along Finchley Road on their return trip.

When Jane had made her journey to London seven years before, there had been no recourse but to navigate Highgate Hill, which was renowned for its treacherous incline. Now, however, Nanny Twickum's mail coach would have the advantage of bypassing the steep acclivity by taking the Archway Road. Humorously, Jane wondered how the redoubtable nanny would react to the novelty of finding herself traversing the three-hundred-foot tunnel, which would bring her eventually to the Archway Tavern at the foot of the hill. Very likely, she would not care for it in the least, Jane decided. She would probably consider it a shameful waste of time and labor for something that should never have been. She could almost hear the faithful old dear declare people and coaches were never meant to travel underneath the ground. That sort of thing "were for gophers and moles and other such like vermin, not for the likes of men."

How good it would be to see Nanny Twickum! was her last thought before, settling her head back against the velvet squabs, she succumbed in a light doze to the easy sway of the luxuriously sprung travel carriage.

She was rudely awakened by the sudden lurch and sway of the carriage coming to an abrupt halt. Startled, she gazed out on the familiar landmark of Whittington's stone. Beyond it stood the Archway Tavern at the foot of the hill, a long two-storied house built in a U with an open-air gallery overlooking the inner courtyard. A wooden sign that bore the likeness of the arched entrance to the tunnel swung lazily in the breeze.

Only weeks before, this had been a peaceful way station, but now its yards were choked with wagons and people. Alarmed, she leaned her head out the window.

"What is it?" she called to the coachman above the din of shouts and milling cattle.

"It's the tunnel, m'lady," the coachman shouted back in a voice, gruff with disbelief. "They say it's toppled down wi'out no warnin'. A hundred thirty yards or more of it, buried beneath the hill."

"Good God! But how?" And then the greater horror came to her. "The mail coach! Was it—?"

"It's all right, m'lady," the coachman was quick to assure her. "Nary a soul was so much as hurt. It happened at noon, before the coach ever got so far. They turned it back. Sent it round by the old Highgate Road. Like as not we can still come up wi' it at Kentish Town, was we to drive at a splitting pace."

"Then pray do so. At once, if you please."

As the carriage pulled into the tavern yard to come about, Jane leaned forward to peer out at those who had come to see the wreckage of what had only four years earlier been lauded as a modern-day marvel, the first bypass of its kind. Among the sea of faces were the curious and the stunned, and one other that seemed suddenly to leap out at her.

Danforth! She could not be mistaken. She would have known him anywhere. He was here at the Archway Tavern, stepping up into the waiting travel coach, which bore his coat of arms.

Jane, feeling suddenly and inexplicably weak, sank back against the squabs. With an effort, she quelled her first instinct to order the carriage to halt that she might accost the marquess. The last thing she could wish, she reflected wryly, was to reveal to the odious nobleman that she had noted his lengthy absence or, indeed, that she had been pounding her pillows at night wondering what had happened to him.

Faith, what a fool she had been! In truth she did not know herself anymore, nor could she have explained, even to herself, why her heart should suddenly be hammering beneath her breast at the pound of hooves approaching rapidly from the rear.

It came to her that he, too, must have come upon the tavern ignorant of the catastrophe that had befallen and, barred from proceeding further on the Archway Road, had been forced, like her, to turn back. His coach and four, far swifter than the earl's conveyance, must inevitably seek to pass her.

In moments she would be given to glimpse the stern visage that had wreaked havoc on her tranquillity of mind and robbed her nights of rest. Indeed, her own coachman was already hugging the side of the road to allow room sufficient for the other vehicle to forge ahead.

Instinctively she sat straighter in the carriage, her eyes fixed before her as behooved one who had not the least interest in a passing stranger. Out of the corner of her eye she glimpsed the tapered heads and arched necks of the lead horses as they drew abreast of her, then pulled ahead, followed by the wheel horses and finally the coach. At the last moment before the coach surged past, she gave into the irresistible impulse to turn and look directly across.

Danforth's unmistakable profile, stern-lipped and arrogant beneath the curly brimmed beaver tipped low over his forehead, loomed in her vision. She could see at a glance that he was well and unharmed. For the barest instant she was bewildered by an unexpectedly sharp stab of relief in the vicinity of her breastbone, then an odd sort of queasy sensation swept over her, as she glimpsed beyond him to see that he was not alone.

Stifling a low-uttered gasp, she jerked her head around to

the front, but in that single, swift moment she had gained a definite impression of a woman, both fashionably dressed and exceedingly well to look upon.

Good God, was the thought that swept through her mind, the tales that were told of him were all true. She had seen him with his secret love, and she was obviously a female of refinement. Someone's wife, no doubt, she reflected numbly, which was why the liaison was so carefully guarded.

Faith, how *could* she have been so mistaken in him? To believe he was gone into danger to find and rescue poor Freddy, when all the time he had been in some secluded place in the arms of his illicit love!

Well, she would never be so deceived again. He was selfish and unfeeling, and she was quite certain she gladly wished him to the devil, she told herself, only to be immediately overcome by a perverse and overpowering compulsion to give way to a fit of the vapors.

Ten

Ethne, looking lovely in a walking dress of sprigged muslin topped by a fetching straw cottage hat with a green satin ribbon that tied beneath her chin, would have been grateful had Maria Fitzhugh been rendered suddenly mute.

For what seemed an eternity, but which could not have been above forty-five minutes, Ethne had been made to smile and nod and in general pretend an interest she was far from feeling while the other girl gave vent to a steady stream of gossip concerning everything from Lord Rivingdale's alleged use of buckram wadding to augment lamentably spindly calves to Lady Bellingham's reported overindulgence in spirits at Princess Esterhazy's soiree the night before. Ethne could not have cared less. She had far more important matters to occupy her.

The two girls, in the company of Maria's abigail, had been strolling in the Park since a little after the hour of five and Mr. Gerard Heaton had yet to put in an appearance. It was beginning to occur to Ethne that she might have been wrong to assume he knew anything or that, if he did, that he meant to use it against her. It was even possible, she supposed, that he had absolutely no interest whatsoever in her.

The notion, while not very flattering, was preferable to the alternative, decided Ethne, who was of a practical nature. She could, in fact, think of nothing she would like better than to be totally free of Gerard Heaton's attentions.

No sooner, however, had she convinced herself that she had indeed been worrying about nothing, than the gentleman in question ruined everything by announcing his presence.

"Ah, Miss Winter," drawled Heaton, climbing down from Lord Rivendale's curricle and stopping in front of her. "What a pleasant surprise."

"It is hardly that, sir," replied Ethne. Then, as Heaton's eyebrows swept up in his forehead, "I felt certain you would be here."

"No, did you?" Sweeping his curly brimmed beaver from his head, he sketched an elaborate bow. "I am flattered you thought of me at all."

"You are too modest, sir," Ethne observed with unmistakable irony, that earned her a sardonically amused smile from the gentleman. "I believe, Mr. Heaton, you are not acquainted with my friend Miss Fitzhugh," she added, drawing the other girl forward. "Miss Fitzhugh, allow me to present Mr. Heaton."

"Mr. Heaton, delighted, I am sure," said Maria in the proper manner of a well-brought-up young lady.

"Miss Fitzhugh. It is always a pleasure to meet a beautiful woman." Maria, who was neither beautiful nor used to being referred to as a woman, bridled with pleasure.

Ethne silently groaned and all but rolled her eyes skyward. She had not considered the possibility that Heaton would turn his charm on the gullible Maria, but she should have done.

"Will you be attending Prinnie's Easter Ball, Mr. Heaton?" Maria gushed. "I have heard it said real, live butterflies are to be released during the evening. And that among the potted crocuses and lilies, one might find ceramic Easter eggs filled with coins. It is even rumored there will be live deer on the grounds and perhaps a lamb or two."

"It sounds a positive delight, Miss Fitzhugh," drawled Heaton, who did not bother to mention that, having long ago earned the reputation for being bad *ton*, he was hardly likely to be included on Prinnie's invitation list. "I fear, however, I am engaged elsewhere that night."

"Oh, I do think you should reconsider," pursued Maria, launching into a detailed description of every tidbit of gossip she had heard concerning Prinnie's Easter Ball to be held at Carlton House.

Ethne, who wished only to be rid of Maria's presence, could only feel a growing impatience with these trivialities. It was, in fact, all she could do to maintain a facade of pleasantry. The rumor that there would be an artificial brook running through the ballroom as well as a spinney of potted trees complete with live birds perched in the branches sounded to Ethne patently foolish and ridiculously lavish. Indeed, she could not but wonder where one would find room for a forest at what promised to be an absolute squeeze.

It was, consequently, with an immense feeling of relief that she spotted Lord Featherstone's absurdly high-perched Phaeton swerve out of the stream of curricles, barouches, and landaulets and make way toward the three conversing at the head of the Carriage Drive.

Heir to a title and a fortune, Lord Featherstone prided himself on his sartorial splendor, his horses, and his athletic accomplishments. All of twenty, he was lanky and tall, pleasant-faced instead of handsome, and he had been sent to London by the viscount, his father, to acquire a touch of Town bronze.

Obviously, he had seen her and, being one of her most ardent admirers, could not resist trying to cut a dash before her.

"Miss Winter," he called down from his lofty perch as he pulled his team up with a flourish. "Could not be happier to run into you like this."

Ethne turned upon him the full force of her smile. "You

cannot possibly guess how glad *I* am to see *you,* m'lord. I believe you know Miss Fitzhugh."

Featherstone, wearing the aspect of a man who has just been landed a facer, had perforce to tear his eyes away from the object of his adoration in order to focus on her companion. "Who?" he queried blankly before recognition could save him from sinking himself into ill-repute.

"You know very well who, Chester Featherstone," Maria said indignantly.

"Dashed if it ain't Maria Fitzhugh," he declared, immediately enlightened. "Funny thing if I didn't. Neighbors, after all. Practically grew up together. Though, come to think of it, you look different somehow. Not fubsy-faced anymore. Daresay I mightn't have recognized you. How's Albert? Ain't seen him for a while."

"Albert is rusticating, at Papa's insistence," replied Maria, her cheeks flaming with mortification at being described as "fubsy-faced" in the presence of others. "I am afraid my brother can be shockingly expensive," she added by way of explanation to Ethne and Mr. Heaton.

"On the rocks, is he?" was Lord Featherstone's acute observation. "Nothing to signify. Been there m'self." Upon having summarily dismissed Albert Fitzhugh's unfortunate circumstances as a matter of insignificance, he next turned his attention to the masculine figure lounging beside Miss Winter. Instantly his rather plain, but pleasant, features altered, his normally amiable expression giving way to an only imperfectly concealed dislike.

It was obvious he recognized the gentleman.

"Heaton, isn't it?" he pronounced in clipped accents.

"Indubitably," remarked the gentleman, patently amused. "Lord Featherlight, I believe," he added mockingly, returning the compliment.

"Afraid you've got it wrong," the sprig of fashion returned stiffly. "It's Feather*stone.*"

"No doubt." Heaton shrugged.

Ethne, sensing her young swain on the point of doing something he must certainly regret later, hastily intervened. "You were, m'lord," she said, stepping judiciously between the two men, "about to tell me why you were pleased to see me?"

Featherstone dragged his eyes away from the older man with obvious effort. "Should be honored if you would join me for a turn around the Park," he blurted, hauling back on the reins as the high-spirited team threatened just then to bolt.

"I should naturally be pleased to accept your kind invitation, m'lord," Ethne replied sweetly. "Only I cannot like to leave Miss Fitzhugh, who, you must know, has expressed an admiration for your driving skill." As Maria gasped and parted her lips to utter an indignant denial, Ethne jabbed a well-placed elbow in the other girl's side. "It seems only right, in consequence," she continued blithely, "that you take Miss Fitzhugh up first."

"Oh, but I couldn't!" exclaimed that young lady. "Indeed, I have no wish to—!"

"Pray do not be absurd," Ethne interrupted, firmly shoving her astonished friend toward the carriage. "Of course you want to, you know very well you do. You will have Lord Featherstone believing you doubt his skill if you do not cease to protest, and we shouldn't want that, should we."

"Promise not to put you in a fright," Featherstone assured his reluctant passenger as Heaton obligingly handed her up. "Been driving a team nearly since I left off wearing short coats."

"But I am not in the least afraid," Maria asserted, finding herself on the seat beside him. "Or have you forgot I have seen you drive before any number of times. I daresay you can feather a corner with the best, Chester Featherstone."

Receiving such unequivocal praise from a young lady, who, while not beautiful in the strictest sense, was, he was suddenly moved to note, hardly an antidote, Lord Featherstone visibly expanded. "Right you are, Miss Fitzhugh. Nothin' to be afraid of at all."

"You are to be congratulated, my dear," applauded Mr. Heaton as the Phaeton pulled smartly into the stream of traffic. "I wondered how you meant to rid us of the inestimable Miss Fitzhugh."

Ethne, who could not but resent his insinuating tone, returned his sardonic curl of the lips with a cool disdain. "I was not ridding us of Miss Fitzhugh's presence, inestimable or otherwise. I was providing my friend with an opportunity to engage the interests of a gentleman she admires. Something you, no doubt, would not understand."

"I collect I am mistaken," Mr. Heaton rejoined smoothly, albeit with a suggestive curl of the lips that made Ethne question the wisdom of her being there. "I wonder, however, that you would risk being seen talking with a gentleman without benefit of a female companion."

"But, sir, I should never be so remiss. I have Miss Fitzhugh's abigail to keep me company," she replied archly, glancing pointedly at the lady's maid, standing a respectful distance away. "This, after all, is not Cheltenham."

"No, it is not Cheltenham," Heaton agreed, "but you will admit it has all the makings of a Cheltenham tragedy. Ironic, is it not?"

Ethne's heart gave a leap, and it was all she could do not to betray the sudden trembling in her knees. "I beg your pardon?" she countered with a fine show of indifference. "I haven't the least idea what you mean."

"Do you not?" Heaton's smile inexplicably sent chills down her back. "And I thought you were up to every rig. Perhaps I have misjudged you."

"I should not be in the least surprised, Mr. Heaton," retorted Ethne with a toss of her head. "But not in the way you would have it. If you think I should easily have the wool pulled over my eyes, then you, sir, do not know me at all."

Heaton's sardonic bark of laughter was enough to set Ethne's teeth on edge, but she contrived not to show it. "You, Miss Winter, are a deal more interesting than I remembered," he said, eyeing her with a boldness that made her wish to plant a palm against his smiling face. "You almost make me wish things could be different."

"Things?" lilted Ethne, carelessly twining an end of the green satin ribbon around one finger. "What 'things,' Mr. Heaton?"

If she had hoped to cajole an answer from him, she was to be sadly disappointed. Heaton was far too experienced to be taken in by a green girl, no matter how enticing.

Heaton's lip curled mockingly. "You do that very well, my dear," he had the insufferable gall to inform her. "I regret, however, your curiosity must go unsatisfied for the present. No, don't look so disheartened." Availing himself of her hand, he deliberately lifted it to his lips in a manner that was as insulting as it was meant to appear intimate. "I promise you will learn everything soon enough, and you will naturally be pleased to know you have performed your part to perfection. Anyone observing us might well believe you were flattering me with your attentions. Miss Ethne Winter and the disreputable Mr. Heaton. It should make for an interesting round of gossip, don't you think?"

"How dare you!" Ethne gasped, struck in full by the enormity of his duplicity. He was an opportunist without conscience or scruples, who would stop at nothing. She had been a fool to think she was up to his weight. It would be all over Town by tomorrow morning that Miss Ethne Winter had been seen flinging her bonnet after a gentleman who, while reasonably well connected, was generally acknowledged a loose screw. Good God, he had tricked her!

Then Heaton was doffing his hat and bowing. "It has been delightful, Miss Winter, but I see your friends returning, and much as I should enjoy chatting further, I really think I should be going. You will give my regards to Melcourt and Miss Jane Ashely, will you not? And don't forget your esteemed brother, while you're at it. Danforth and I are such very old friends."

Ethne stilled, her mind whirling. Heaton was lying. Nicky never confided in her anything of a personal nature, but it had been plain as a pikestaff that what he felt for Heaton was anything but congenial. There was bad blood between them, she was sure of it.

"You may be sure I shall," said Ethne, finding her tongue again at last. "No doubt Nicky will find my account of the afternoon vastly entertaining. Goodbye, Mr. Heaton."

She had the dubious satisfaction of seeing a hard gleam of admiration leap in his eyes as, turning on her heel, she coolly walked away. No one observing her greet Maria and Featherstone would ever have dreamed that she felt trembly and weak inside or that her head had begun abominably to ache.

Her one thought as she climbed up to the newly vacated seat beside Featherstone was that she had made a complete and utter mull of things.

"She was seen, I tell you," exclaimed Mina, pacing agitatedly before her husband, who, having just returned home from an afternoon spent at Tattersall's, where he had purchased a riding hack for Jane's use in Town and tripled a cartwheel in a lucky wager on a long shot out of an Irish stable, was feeling particularly well-disposed. "Doubtless the whole world knows by now she was in Hyde Park casting lures at, of all people, Gerard Heaton. Lady Sefton saw them, and she did not hesitate to drive right over to inform me that I should keep a closer watch on my charge. It would never do, after all, to let people believe the girl was as flaunting of the conventions as one other member of her family. What is dreadful is that I haven't the least notion whether she was referring to Lady Winter or Danforth. Surely they cannot all be loose screws in that family."

"Whether they are or not, I cannot see that it is likely to reflect on Miss Winter," said Melcourt, his handsome lips twitching in amusement. "She will be excused a great deal, you will agree, in light of her more than comfortable fortune."

"Oh, indeed," Mina acquiesced bitterly. "By any number of gentlemen without a feather to fly with. Those who have no need of her fortune look for something more in a wife. I cannot think the Earl of Thaxton will look kindly on the prospect of a daughter-in-law who is thought to be reckless and unbiddable. And I had such hopes that Lord Phillip would come up to scratch! I daresay we might as well cancel the ball and remove the knocker from our door. After this, no one who is anyone will darken our threshold, you may depend on it."

"But of course they will. Indeed, why should they not?" queried the earl, striving for a reasonable tenor. "Are you not puffing this all out of consequence, my dear? Naturally, we should be better pleased had the incident never occurred, but now that it has, we must deal with it in a rational manner."

"But I am being rational," insisted his countess, threatening to burst into tears at any moment. "How can you accuse me of being otherwise? Any fool must see what will come as a result of this. We shall be ruined, Wilfred. Not only we, but Jane as well, and that is the unfairest thing of all."

"Unfair, if that were truly the case," Melcourt persisted. "You said yourself, however, that Ethne was not alone with Heaton, that, indeed, she had the good sense to keep Maria Fitzhugh's abigail close by her. And certainly she cannot be blamed if the blackguard chose to impose himself on her. Hyde Park, after all, is a public place."

"And this will become a public scandal because of it," Mina groaned, wringing her hands. "Oh, why was I so foolish as to make that dreadful wish for Jane? Only see what has come of it, and it is all my fault."

"And *I* am sure it is nothing of the kind," said Lady Jane, patting her hair into place after having just removed her hat and laid it on the console table in the receiving hall. She came into the room. "Whatever it is you are talking about."

"Oh, Jane, dear, you are back," exclaimed Mina, rushing toward her sister-in-law as if it had been months instead of only a bare three hours since she had seen her last. "It is dreadful, a total disaster."

"It is, indeed," agreed Jane soberly, marveling that word had traveled so swiftly to London, "but surely you are not blaming yourself for that."

"But whose fault *can* it be?" poignantly demanded Mina, keenly aware that she had failed miserably in her obligations. "I should have foreseen the dangers. I should have insisted she remain at home. At home, she would have been safe, you know she would."

Jane, touched that her sister-in-law should be so distraught over something that she could not possibly have foreseen, let alone diverted, hastened to reassure her. "But she *is* safe. She is not even in the least bit ill after all that she has suffered.

I daresay she is even grateful for what happened, since it means she was spared the necessity of having to go through it. You may be sure the poor dear was not looking forward to the experience with anything less than total dread."

Mina stared at her in astonishment. "But that is absurd. Why, in heaven's name, should she insist on being brought out if she had no wish to have done?"

"But it is perfectly obvious, is it not? You know as well as I that nothing could keep her from it, once she learned I was in London. We can all be grateful she was diverted from her course in time to avoid a tragedy. I am only sorry you were given cause to worry. I never dreamed you would receive word of it so quickly. It must be all over London by now."

"Indeed, you may be sure of it," Mina replied bitterly. "Lady Sefton could not wait to inform us of the news. I suspect she took a great deal of enjoyment in it, for, if you must know, she has always seemed a little jealous of the success I have enjoyed. But that, of course, is all over now."

It was Jane's turn to regard her sister-in-law with no little incredulity. "I beg your pardon," she said, "but I cannot see what the one has to do with the other. And I certainly must find it difficult to believe that Lady Sefton would gain enjoyment from the collapse of the Archway Tunnel. Indeed, why should she?"

Mina blinked, for once robbed of speech.

"Obviously she wouldn't," observed Melcourt, inserting himself into the conversation. "But then, my dearest Jane, it was not news of the Archway Tunnel that brought Lady Sefton here. I doubt anything so insignificant as the ruination of a modern-day marvel of human achievement could compare to the news that your young friend Ethne was seen today in Hyde Park, talking, I might add, to Gerard Heaton."

There was a moment of stunned silence. And then, "Gerard

Heaton!" exclaimed Jane in concert with Mina's, "Good God, what of Nanny Twickum?"

Followed almost immediately by the appearance of Langston, who announced the presence in the receiving hall of his lordship, the Marquess of Danforth, to see Miss Ashely.

"Danforth!" groaned Mina, glancing to Melcourt as she sank weakly down on the sofa. "Faith, it needed only that."

"Very well, Langston," Jane said firmly, when she had recovered from the initial unsettling leap of her pulse. "You may show his lordship into the withdrawing room and inform him I shall be down directly."

No sooner had the door shut behind the retreating butler, than she turned to her brother and sister-in-law. "And, now," she said quietly, "I think you had better tell me. What exactly is it that Ethne has done?"

Some ten minutes later, Jane paused outside the withdrawing-room door to compose herself before entering. It really was too bad, she reflected, steeling herself for the coming interview, that there had not been the opportunity to talk with Ethne before this meeting with the marquess. Ethne might be impulsive and spoiled, but Jane could not believe the child was so foolish as to deliberately fling herself at Gerard Heaton. No, there was something more to this than immediately met the eye, and only Ethne herself could have shed some light on it. The girl, however, had yet to return from Lady Fitzhugh's, and there was no point in procrastinating further.

Unconsciously, Jane straightened her shoulders. Telling herself that she owed the strange, queasy sensation in the pit of her stomach to the fact that she had not eaten anything since breakfast, she turned the door handle and walked into the room.

Danforth, dressed in riding boots and buff unmentionables,

his broad shoulders encased in a tight-fitting coat of blue superfine, stood with his back to her, his gaze apparently fixed on the scene outside the bay window. At the sound of the door opening, he turned.

Jane's heart gave a leap, as his light, piercing glance seemed to impale her. Furthermore, she was furiously aware that a warm rush of blood had invaded her cheeks. She wondered half hysterically if she were cursed to forever feel at a disadvantage with this man. At last, chiding herself for a fool, she drew a steadying breath and forced a smile to her lips.

"My lord," she exclaimed, and came gracefully toward him, her hand extended in welcome. "I fear Ethne is not in at the moment, but no doubt she will be back directly, should you care to wait. I know she would be sorry to miss you." The strong, supple fingers closed lightly about her hand, and she suffered, to her dismay, a disconcerting tingling of nerve endings, rather like a shock of electricity shooting up her arm. It was all she could do not to flinch.

"On the contrary," drawled Danforth, his gaze intent on her face, "she will not be in the least sorry. It was not Ethne, however, whom I came to see. You are troubled, Miss Ashely," he said with his old, familiar brusqueness. "Tell me what has happened."

Startled, Jane's eyes flew to his. It came to her then that he appeared thinner than the last time she had seen him, harder, and there were lines of weariness about his eyes that had not been there before. Still, his tall, compelling figure seemed to fill the room, and in spite of herself, she experienced an unexpected rush of emotions at his nearness, which served only to fluster and bewilder. She tried to free her fingers from his clasp, only to feel his grip tighten, holding her. "I-I beg your pardon?" she stammered. "Whatever do you mean?"

"Do not play the innocent with me, Miss Ashely. I have

come to expect better from you. The truth. What has my bothersome half-sister done to cut up your existence?"

He did not know, flashed through her mind, to be followed almost immediately by the silent query as to why, then, had he come? Not to see Ethne, he had told her. Indeed, he had asked to see her, Jane Ashely. Most annoyingly, she suffered a soft thrill at the thought.

Angry with herself, she firmly disengaged her hand. "I see your manners have not improved in your absence, my lord," she said, her usually calm and well-modulated tones edged with what must have sounded very like petulance to him. Hastily, she moved away from him, as she strove for at least a semblance of composure. "Perhaps you would care to sit down? I should be pleased to ring for the tea tray."

"I, however, should not be pleased. I do not in the least care for tea at the moment." His hard gaze followed her as she seated herself in one of the wing chairs fronting the fireplace. Then, for the first time, the piercing quality of his eyes softened with humor. "What now, Miss Ashely? Would you have me beg pardon for my bluntness? You are obviously not yourself. But then, I have not been in the habit of treating you with kid gloves."

Giving into some irresistible force in him that seemed fated to wreak havoc on her sensibilities, she choked on a gurgle of laughter. "No, you could hardly be accused of that, my lord," she agreed ruefully. "Though there have been times when I have suspected you are not so unfeeling as you would have me believe."

At the end the mirth had faded from her eyes, to be replaced by a compelling intensity that must surely have taken his breath away.

Danforth appeared momentarily checked by the unswerving directness of that gaze. But then the shutter dropped in place, and he straightened, his hand drawing forth an exquisite Sevres snuffbox. "Then you would be mistaken," he drawled, carelessly flicking open the lid with his thumbnail and withdrawing a pinch of snuff between his thumb and forefinger. "I am lamentably lacking in the finer sensibilities." He inhaled and brushed a nonexistent fleck of dust from his sleeve before snapping the lid shut and returning the box to his coat pocket. He looked at her with a singular directness. "Do not, I pray, try and make me something I am not. I should only disappoint you."

"Should you?" she murmured, never taking her eyes from his. "I wonder." She paused, then asked without warning, "Have you had word of Freddy? Is that why you have come?"

A wry gleam of a smile flickered across his lips. "I came to discover how you and my half-sister go on. You, Miss Ashely, have not answered my question."

"Nor, sir, have you answered mine," Jane pointed out. "Tell me he is all right."

"He is alive and in London and proving a damnable nuisance."

"Thank God," Jane breathed fervently. "I was afraid you had come to inform us he had been killed at Badajoz."

"Then you may rest easy. The young cawker was fool enough to catch a sniper's bullet in the arm. He is not, I am reliably informed, likely to perish from it. I have, as a matter of fact, only just this hour returned from fetching his mama to him."

Lady Jane's eyes flew to the nobleman's face. "His mama, but I thought—!" She only just managed to stop herself in time to keep from blurting exactly what she believed of the woman she had seen in the carriage with him.

"You thought what, Miss Ashely?" murmured the marquess, with the arch of a single, arrogant eyebrow. Furiously she blushed.

"It does not matter what I thought," she said, forcing herself to meet his look. "Suffice it to say that I owe you an apology. I saw you today at the Archway Tavern. I-I'm afraid I leaped to conclusions."

She was not sure what reaction she had expected from him. Certainly she was not prepared to have his dark head go suddenly back in laughter. "I'm afraid it is Aunt Caroline to whom you should apologize," he said, his eyes gleaming with amusement. "On the other hand, she might very well be flattered to think she had been mistaken for one of Danforth's inamoratas."

Lady Jane stared speechlessly back at him, hardly knowing whether to laugh or to rail at him for his ungentlemanly display of mirth. In the end, she was not proof against the warm glitter of humor in the look he bent upon her. Her lips gave way to a smile of reluctant amusement.

"How dare you poke fun at me after I have apologized," she said, eyeing him ruefully. "I'm sure I cannot be blamed for thinking the worst, when you are no doubt guilty of any number of reprehensible things."

Danforth's lip curled cynically, spoiling the moment. "You may be sure of it," he drawled, cold again, the mask falling into place. "You would do well not to be seen too much in my company. I have a reputation for being dangerous."

"Have you?" Lady Jane stared at him with an arrested expression in her beautiful eyes. Faith, she had forgotten how laughter transformed him, smoothing out the harsh lines of his face so that he appeared younger and far too attractive for her own peace of mind. Perceptibly, she sobered. "Then I shall not regard it—or your advice."

She had the satisfaction of seeing his eyes narrow sharply on her face, a look of bestartlement darken their piercing intensity. In no little bemusement it came to her then that the impenetrable Danforth was not impregnable. It was possible to breach his formidable defenses. The knowledge infused her with an unfamiliar warmth she was not at all sure she either trusted or liked.

"Besides," she continued, as if her heart had not begun to beat in a most reprehensibly erratic manner, "it is unavoidable. You will have to be a great deal in our company for the next few weeks if you would see Ethne safely settled. For if you must know, she was seen talking with Gerard Heaton."

"The devil she was," exploded Danforth, his lips thinning to a grim line. "And where were you and the countess while your charge was so happily engaged?"

"I told you," she answered, inexplicably hurt at his harshness. "I was at the Archway Tavern to meet the mail coach. And Mina was taking a much needed afternoon off with her husband. Perhaps you are right to fault us for believing she would be safe enough with Maria Fitzhugh. However, it was simply bad luck that Ethne encountered Mr. Heaton at the Park and was subsequently left to exchange pleasantries with him for all of ten minutes. As it happens, she was never truly alone with him. She was never out of the company of Maria's abigail. Still," she conceded, "it was enough to incite a deal of speculation."

"No doubt," Danforth cynically remarked. His expression, however, appeared to imply that he was reserving judgment. "And now that the damage is done, what is it that you expect me to do about it?"

"To begin with," she replied earnestly, determined to test the temper of his mood, "you could demonstrate some concern for Ethne. She is your sister, after all. Perhaps if you would talk to her, instead of playing least seen in her affairs, you might discover she is willing to confide in you. She may be impetuous, but she is not beyond being properly influenced. It is not too late, my lord. She has not been damaged yet, only a trifle bruised."

"Has she not?" His disturbing eyes probed her face. "And

what of you, Miss Ashely? And your sister-in-law. If Ethne has made herself the object of gabblemongers, it cannot but reflect on you."

Jane shrugged. "I trust my credit is great enough to carry me through," she said, smiling a little. "And if it is not, then I shall rely on yours, my lord marquess. You, after all, exert a not inconsiderable influence."

Danforth stared at her. "If I did not know that to be true, Miss Ashely," he said, with a steely edged softness that unwittingly sent a shiver down her back, "Ethne would even now be on her way back to Hargrove, you may be sure of it."

Jane felt a slow heat invade her cheeks at something she sensed in the look he bent upon her then. Confused, she averted her face. "Then we may all be grateful you have decided to return, my lord," she answered, striving for a lightness she was far from feeling. But immediately she looked back at him again. Her eyes searched his. "Why did you go away without leaving word?" she asked. "You must have known I—that we should wonder and—worry."

"No, did you?" he drawled. The mask of ennui descended over his lean, harsh features. "Quite frankly, the thought never occurred to me. I did promise, you will recall, that I should not bother you with my presence."

"You promised, my lord, to call on Ethne," Jane reminded him, nettled at the evasion. Oh, how infuriating he was! Obviously, he had not the least intention of revealing where he had been. "As well you should. As it is, you have arrived in Town only just in time. We depend on you to lead Ethne out tomorrow night. It is her come-out, after all, and you are her closest male relative. You will come, will you not?"

"I naturally shall consider it," he answered smoothly, his eyes behind drooping eyelids odiously unreadable. "I should perhaps be more definite were there some added inducement."

Jane stared at him incredulously. "Inducement, my lord? What inducement do you need beyond assuring your half-sister's success?"

"You assume a great deal, Miss Ashely, if you think for one moment that Ethne's success or failure weighs heavily with me," he drawled insufferably. "The truth is I find little to recommend in debutante balls and much to their detriment. I require something more—your promise for the first waltz, shall we say?"

"You cannot be serious, my lord," Jane stated in dumbfounded amazement. How dared he resort to extortion for what he might have had willingly had he only asked for it like a gentleman!

"On the contrary, I have seldom been more serious," he assured her, his lean, handsome features maddeningly inscrutable.

"But that is quite impossible," she retorted, torn between hurt and resentment at his calloused disregard for her feelings in the matter. "If you must know, the first waltz was to go to Mr. Beauchamp."

"How unfortunate for Mr. Beauchamp. No doubt he will be pleased to sit that one out. Of course, you could refuse me. I daresay my absence will make little difference one way or the other to Ethne's success or failure. There is not the remotest chance she will not be judged a *success fou.*"

Jane's eyes flashed blue sparks of indignation. The rogue, to tease her so! Even if he were right, his failure to present himself could not but hurt Ethne. He was her only brother. What a fool she had been to waste a moment worrying about him. Indeed, she was quite sure that, had it not been for Ethne, she would gladly have wished him to the devil rather than agree to his blackmail.

In her agitation, she had risen from her seat. Now she turned to face him, where he stood, leaning negligently with one arm on the mantelpiece. Jane searched the hard features, trying to see beyond the impenetrable facade of the Corinthian to the man behind it. There was something here that she did not understand.

"Why are you doing this?" she asked, her voice sounding strained in her own ears.

Danforth's lip curled in cynical self-derision, which served only to add to Jane's sense of bafflement. "No doubt because it will amuse me to dance with the incomparable Miss Ashely," he replied, hatefully mocking.

"I don't believe you." Jane frowned in perplexity. "If you wished a place on my dance card, you had only to ask. You must know that."

Deliberately Danforth straightened, his gaze inscrutable on hers. "You are mistaken, surely." Jane froze, her heart leaping wildly beneath her breast, as his hand lifted to brush a stray curl from the side of her face.

"I—I beg your pardon?" stammered Jane, wondering if she had taken leave of her senses.

"The first waltz, Miss Ashely," Danforth answered. "It was already taken."

The next moment he had turned and, crossing with long strides to the door, left Jane to stare in impotent fury after him.

Eleven

Melcourt House on Grosvenor Square bustled with activity throughout the day as all the last-minute preparations for the ball were gotten underway. Jane, looking something less than her usual self after a disturbed night's sleep in which a piercing-eyed nobleman had persisted in inserting himself in her dreams, was ordered to her rooms by Mina immediately after afternoon tea.

"Pray don't be absurd," Mina exclaimed when Jane protested that the countess had already done enough for ten hostesses and must herself be as near to collapse as made no difference. "I have never felt better." *Now that Danforth had returned,* she added silently to herself, *and her dearest Jane was showing all the signs of a woman who no longer knew her own heart. And then, of course, there was the news she had received only yesterday.* She smiled a secret smile to herself. "Go, my dear, and get some rest. I shall have you called in plenty of time for you to dress for dinner."

Jane gave in at last, even going so far as to remove her dress and lie down on her bed, though she was quite certain she would not sleep. Hardly had her head hit the pillow, however, than she fell into a dreamless slumber.

She was awakened a good deal later by Nanny Twickum, who scolded and clucked over her, blaming herself for her darling's wan look. She had ought to've been there to make sure her Jane were properly looked after, the old dear grumbled to herself as she went about the tasks of making her mistress ready for the ball.

Her old nanny's deft and tender care was balm to Jane's overstretched nerves. Indeed, Jane had not realized how greatly she had missed the elderly retainer until she found herself seated before her dressing table while Nanny Twickum ran the brush in long, sure strokes through her mistress's hair. By the time Jane had finished soaking in her bath, she was feeling much more the thing than she had done since a certain nobleman and his relatives had obtruded themselves in her life.

How odd it was, she reflected, when some thirty minutes later she stood staring at her image in the cheval glass, that seven years ago she had stood in this very place, her face lit with excitement, her eyes shimmering with anticipation, because it was her coming-out ball. How young she had been! How eager to grasp the moment! She had been a girl on the verge of blossoming into womanhood.

She was no longer that young, naive girl. She was a woman who had known the dizzying heights of a first, all-consuming love and who had suffered the depths of despair at the loss of it. And she had endured, achieving for herself a triumph of sorts, a knowledge that one does not truly die of a broken heart. Why, then, should she suddenly feel overcome with trepidation at what lay before her?

It was only a ball, she told herself, and not even one given in her honor. All the worries and responsibilities of hostess fell on Mina's capable shoulders, leaving her, Jane, with nothing more exacting to do than laugh and dance and enjoy the evening. And, still, she could not but be aware that her stomach was churning and her mouth was most unaccountably dry. Of what was she afraid?

She could find nothing in the looking glass to account for it. Nanny Twickum, as usual, had worked wonders with her hair, leaving the curls to cluster loosely about her head in a charming disarray a la Titus. Perhaps she was a trifle pale, and there were undoubtedly shadows beneath her eyes, she critically decided. The truth was, however, that she had never looked better. Her skin shone with a pearly translucence, which served to enhance the delicate beauty of her fine bone structure. Likewise, her eyes, made to seem larger in the perfect oval of her face, appeared blue-violet pools, haunted with shadows. They were the eyes of a stranger.

Indeed, she hardly knew herself. Where was the Jane Ashely who had prided herself on her cool unassailability, the poised woman who was always in perfect control of herself and her surroundings? Gone, she thought, or at least certainly in abeyance. Or perhaps she had always been a sham, a pitiable, deluded creature who had comforted herself with the illusion of contentment. Underneath, there had always been a slumbering potentiality for something else, waiting, like dormant coals, for a spark to ignite.

Her mouth curved at the thought, silently deriding her morbid fancies, and deliberately she made her gaze travel down the length of the reflected image of herself.

The gown was both stunning and a deal more daring than she would normally have worn. The overdress of blue gauze shot through with silver threads sparkled in the light, forming a shimmering transparency of fabric over a clinging underlining of violet satin. The exquisite creation left little doubt that she wore next to nothing beneath it, an impression further abetted by ruched sleeves, which revealed shapely arms, and a plunging V neck, which left her shoulders and a creamy expanse of bosom bare.

Faith, what had possessed her to purchase such a dress! It was perilously close to being indecent. Not even the diamond and sapphire necklace about her slender throat or the diamond pendants dangling from her earlobes served to draw attention away from her purely feminine attributes.

A crimson tide swept up her neck to invade her cheeks as it came to her to wonder what *he* would think of her in this gown.

Would he like her? Would he even see her? The answer seemed to strike her like a revelation. He would look, but he would not see. Geoffrey stood between them. To Danforth, she would always be the woman who had loved his best friend and he, the man who had taken that love from her.

She, however, was that woman no longer, she realized with a blinding flash of insight. She had ceased to exist the moment Danforth had come thundering out of the darkness into her life. No longer could she hide within the cocoon of contentment she had spun for herself in the safety of Melcourt's Oaks. Danforth had awakened the sleeping thing inside her, and it was even now beating at the doors of her awareness.

Appalled at where her thoughts had led her, she covered her face with her hands and wheeled away from the disturbing image in the looking glass. Faith, what was happening to her? She felt a terrible truth on the verge of revealing itself to her, a truth she did not want to know, for it might be the end of her. Certainly it would be the end of that other Jane Ashely, that shell of a woman who had wished so desperately never to feel again.

Slowly she dropped her hands and, finding the courage from somewhere, turned to look again at this new creature, this stranger, whose eyes looked out at her, luminous pools of mystery and unplumbed depths.

Whoever she was, whatever she was to become, was inextricably bound with Danforth. He had awakened her to life, to feeling, to the vulnerability of a heart that beat with all a woman's yearning. And if he could not see that now, she would find a way to open his eyes.

Tonight, she thought, when he came to claim his stolen waltz, he would encounter, not the cool composed Lady Jane

Ashely of Melcourt's Oaks, but this new, deeper, more cunning being whom he himself had created. No longer bound by fear and trepidation, she would explore the possibilities of her awakened self and discover once and for all what it was that Danforth had aroused in her.

Taking up her ivory-handled fan and a flat velvet box, she cast a last, fleeting look at her reflection in the looking glass, then with a swirl of diaphanous skirts, turned and left the room.

"Oh, Jane!" breathed Ethne, her eyes wide with unaffected admiration for her friend. "You are magnificent. Breathless. Stunning. I-I almost feel sorry for the poor, unsuspecting men below. You will take them all by storm."

It struck Jane, who had come to bring Ethne a gift of pearls to complement her ivory Russienne silk dress with seed pearls sewn into the bodice, that the girl would break her own share of hearts before this night was over. The child was a vision of loveliness. Her fresh youth and unaffected charm rendered her breathtaking.

"Gammon!" Jane laughed, turning Ethne around to view herself in the looking glass while she herself fastened the pearl necklace about the young slender throat. "You may be sure they will not even see me. They will all be looking at you. This is *your* night, Ethne dearest, and you promise fair to dazzle them all."

"If I succeed in dazzling only *one* gentleman, I shall be happy," Ethne confessed thrillingly, her eyes luminous with barely contained hopes and fears. "Oh, Jane!" she cried, turning suddenly into the other woman's arms. "I shall *die* if he does not come tonight. If-if I have ruined everything with my stupid pride."

Startled and strangely touched, Jane hesitated only briefly

before hugging the girl close. "I must presume you mean Phillip Maheux and that you are referring to the unfortunate incident at the Park."

Ethne, apparently unable to speak, nodded convulsively.

"I see," murmured Jane, stroking the girl's raven hair. "You are afraid he will think less of you because you were seen talking with someone of whom he cannot approve. But do you not see how foolish you are being? If he likes you—and, indeed, how can he not?—then it cannot possibly make any difference to him. He will not credit the tattlemongers. Indeed, he is far more likely to leap to your defense than he is to believe you are something other than you are. And if he does not, then he is not worth spilling a tear over."

Jane waited a few moments more to let her words sink in and to allow Ethne to compose herself before she pushed the girl gently, but firmly, away. "Come, now. Enough. Lift your chin up. Everything is going to be fine. Danforth has assured me that nothing can go wrong."

At that, Ethne did lift her head to fix wide startled eyes on Jane. "Nicky is back? You spoke to him? When, Jane?"

"Yesterday evening. He called to see how you went on and-and to bring us word about Freddy." Here, Jane suffered a pang of conscience. In all the flurry of activity and in the wake of her disturbing meeting with Danforth, she had completely forgotten to tell Ethne about Freddy. "Come," she said, "and sit down for a moment. I have something to tell you."

Ethne, however, appeared not to have heard her. "I must see him, Jane," she declared, nervously gripping the other woman's hands. "I must tell him, now, before it is too late. Oh, I feel it. Indeed, I have thought of nothing else since yesterday. Nicky is in danger, Jane. I know it."

It all came out then, how she had contrived to meet Heaton alone in order to quiz him about her mama, her failure to foresee the trick he had played on her, the things he had said.

"He is dreadful, Jane. At the end, I was frightened of him. He lied, though, when he said he and Nicky were old friends. I could see right through him. He hates Nicky, and he is up to something. He means my brother harm, Jane, I know it."

"I should not put anything past Gerard Heaton," Jane admitted. "I cannot think, however, he is a match for Danforth. You will admit, will you not, your brother is well able to look after himself?"

Ethne faltered, her brow furrowed in a frown. "Yes, I suppose. But—"

"There is only one way a man like Heaton *could* injure Danforth," Jane firmly interrupted. "Through you. You were very foolish to do what you did. You placed yourself in grave danger. Indeed, I am exceedingly disappointed in you, Ethne. You did promise, did you not, that you would come to me before going off half-cocked?"

The girl's face flushed a dusky red, then paled to a pearly white. "I-I did, and I see now that that is what I should have done. I'm sorry, Jane."

"It is a trifle late to be sorry. We can only be glad nothing worse has come of this. Another time, you might have been kidnapped or worse. And that, my child, does not bear thinking on. If anything happened to you, think what it would do to Danforth. To your mama. Think of the scandal. I daresay Danforth would not hesitate to kill Heaton, and then what would become of him? He would be forced into exile at the very least. I do hope you will consider that the next time you decide to pit yourself against a man like Gerard Heaton."

"There will not be a-a next time, I promise," Ethne said, her voice tremulous "Believe me, I have learned my lesson."

Jane nodded, satisfied for the moment. "Good. Then dry your eyes and smile. It is time we went below to greet your guests."

It was not until they were forming the receiving line with

Mina and Melcourt that Jane remembered she had once again failed to inform Ethne of Freddy's condition, and by then it was too late to do more than chide herself for the omission. She could hardly break the news with guests on the point of arriving. And then even the thought of Freddy fled as she glanced around, her cheeks rosy as a result of Wilfred's teasing remark that, in her present gown, she might strike fire even from a certain cold-blooded marquess, and found herself staring into a pair of blue, steely eyes that seemed most unaccountably to pierce her through.

"Danforth!" exclaimed Mina, flashing a fleeting look of triumph over her shoulder at Melcourt. "How good of you to come."

"It is not good of me at all, Lady Ashely," demurred the marquess, saluting Mina's knuckles. "It is rather my pleasure to thank you for your many kindnesses to Ethne."

Mina, whose only other meeting with Danforth had been under less auspicious circumstances, smiled, taken off guard by that gracious speech. "Nonsense," she said. "I have thoroughly enjoyed the experience. I have always dreamed of having a daughter, and now—" Suddenly her cheeks were swept with a becoming tinge of color, and her eyes seemed irresistibly drawn to her husband. "And now it seems there is every chance I may have that dream realized."

Jane stared, startled, from the beaming countess to her brother, who was regarding Mina with every indication of a man who feels his cup is at last full.

"Mina," she exclaimed, ecstatically clasping the other woman's hands, "when? Why did you not tell me?"

"Sometime in November, the doctor assures us," Mina answered, indescribably lovely in her happiness. "We only found out yesterday, while you were gone to fetch Nanny Twickum home."

"Oh, my dear, I could not be happier for you both!"

There was a moment of confusion as Ethne kissed Mina
on the cheek and Danforth shook Melcourt's hand. It seemed
to Jane, watching the two men, that a look passed between
them. Indeed, she had the distinct impression that behind the
two pairs of sleepy eyes, each was gauging the other.

Then the first of the dinner guests had begun to arrive,
and Mina, directing Ethne and Jane and the others to their
places, hastily formed a receiving line with Melcourt at the
head followed by herself and Ethne. As Jane took her place
next to the excited girl, she was keenly aware of Danforth's
looming presence at her other side. More than once as the
arriving guests filed past, she felt his eyes on her, a circumstance, that threatened to disturb her equilibrium.

While three hundred invitations had gone out for the ball,
the dinner party had been limited to what Mina considered
a small select gathering of persons, that numbered no more
than forty guests. They were close friends of the family, for
the most part, or new acquaintances of Ethne's, with a smattering of persons of particular influence and distinction in the
Haut Ton.

In spite of the determinedly cheerful front Mina had maintained throughout the day, she had secretly expected to be
inundated with a host of refusals before the evening had begun. And, indeed, a dozen or so excuses crying off from the
ball had found their way to her door as early as the afternoon
before. Some might have been genuine, but most must certainly be attributed to Heaton's deliberate attempt to discredit
Ethne. It was not until the entirety of her forty guests, including the Fitzhughs and the Earl of Thaxton with his wife
and young Maheux, had traveled the length of the receiving
line that she confided in a gleeful whisper to Jane her belief
that a miracle was about to happen.

Lady Jane, recalling to mind the utter and dispassionate
certainty with which Danforth had declared there was never

a possibility of failure, soon suspected that what gave every evidence of becoming *un fait accompli* had very little to do with supernatural causes. There was an inevitability about the man that augured well for the success of the evening, if not for her peace of mind.

Mr. Francis Beauchamp was one of the last to present himself to those standing in the receiving line, and this proved an unexpectedly awkward moment for Jane.

A man of forty and an avowed bachelor, he was distinguished, witty, and urbane. Believing that he was in little danger of mistaking a light flirtation for anything more serious or, indeed, of losing his head over her, Jane had enjoyed his company as a welcome diversion. She had not expected that he might take exception to discovering Danforth beside her or that he might misconstrue the marquess's presence there. Nevertheless, she was certain she sensed a pointed interest in the manner in which Beauchamp's hooded gaze rested on the marquess before turning to her.

"My dear Miss Ashely," he murmured, "you are a never-ending source of delight. Just when I think you could not look more devastatingly lovely, you appear in the guise of a Helen of Troy. It might be worth the price of a kingdom for the pleasure of waking up to the sight of you at my breakfast table each morning."

"No, how can you say so?" Jane laughed. "Such an extravagance must surely prove a poor bargain, I fear. What did it really ever purchase, after all, but a Trojan Horse?"

"Meaning, I must presume, that my case is as hopeless as was Troy's against Athens," Beauchamp replied, allowing the urbane mask to fall for the briefest instant. "A pity," he murmured. Jane's mirth fled from her eyes with sudden, swift realization. Then Beauchamp was smiling again. "Naturally, however, I must bow to your judgment, my child." Suiting action to words, he straightened and let his sweeping glance travel to Danforth's impassive features.

"Ah, Nick," he drawled. "Back again, are you?"

"As you see." Danforth smiled slightly, his hand going out to meet the other man's. "How are you, Beauchamp?"

"I have nothing of which to complain," replied Beauchamp, idly shaking out his lace cuffs. "However, I have been hearing the oddest things about you, old friend. Something about Badajoz and a rescue performed at no little risk to yourself. A remarkable tale, I must say, if even the half of it is true. How, by the way, is the old earl's grandson?"

"Well enough. I daresay he will recover." The nobleman's eyes glinted between sleepy eyelids. "The question is, will you, however, if you persist in spreading rumors."

Beauchamp laughed. "Longer than you, my dear boy," he said, with unruffled amusement, "do you continue in your present vein. You really must get over this propensity of yours to play the hero. Only think of your reputation."

Chuckling softly to himself, Beauchamp sauntered away to join the other guests in the receiving hall.

"It would seem, Miss Ashely, you have made a conquest," remarked Danforth, his eyes speculative on that slim, retreating back.

"Have I?" murmured Jane with a strange inflection.

Danforth's head came around to find Jane staring at him, her gaze fixed and unfathomable on his face. A single arrogant eyebrow swept upward toward his hairline. "You have just turned down Beauchamp. You cannot wish me to believe you did not know exactly what you were doing?"

Jane did not answer, but took his arm instead. "Mina has given the signal for dinner," she said quietly. "Perhaps, my lord, you would care to escort me in?"

* * *

Moments later, Jane, finding herself seated between Beauchamp on her left and the Earl of Thaxton on her right, could not but be relieved that Mina had seen fit to place Danforth at the seat of honor across from Ethne at the far end of the table. Jane needed distance between herself and the marquess's disquieting presence in order to subdue her riotous pulse and to regather her forces.

Beauchamp's elliptical allusion to Danforth's activities on behalf of Freddy had affected her strangely. Indeed, she had felt hot then cold with the realization that Danforth had placed himself in grave peril to bring Freddy back, but, more than that, had been the sudden, overpowering conviction that there was a great deal about this man that she did not understand.

Perhaps most puzzling of all was what seemed more and more a deliberate attempt to blacken himself in her eyes. Why should he choose to extort a waltz she would willingly have granted him, if not to purposely antagonize her against him? How even more inexplicable that action when set against his earlier unmistakable concern for her! He had made it abundantly clear he would send Ethne home before he allowed the child's impulsive behavior to bring injury to Jane.

What a bewildering mixture of seeming contradictions he was!

The numerous courses came and went, and Jane found to her surprise that she was enjoying herself. Beauchamp was, as ever, both witty and charming. Possessed of any number of *on-dits* concerning the *Beau Monde,* he soon made her forget herself in laughter.

Thaxton, too, proved a cordial dinner companion, and Jane was not loath to take advantage of the situation to subtly bring to his attention Ethne's many amiable attributes. Indeed, she had the satisfaction of discovering that he was a sympathetic father, who had not forgotten what it was to be young. She soon gained the impression that not only did he place little credence in the stories going the rounds about Ethne and Heaton, but that he had long since found the girl to be both likable and charming.

Of greater interest, however, and far more thought-provoking was the discovery that the earl evidently entertained an even higher regard for Danforth.

"I have known the lad since he was a boy. His father and I made the grand tour together." He gazed with a kindly interest at Jane. "At the risk of being thought impertinent, my dear, may I venture to say how greatly I admire your forgiving nature. To do what you have done for Miss Winter in light of certain events cannot but speak well of your generosity of heart. I know how bitterly Nick regretted Geoffrey's loss."

Jane was never sure afterward exactly what reply she might have made to that kindly speech. Having been wholly engrossed in Thaxton's revelations, she was unaware that two footmen had somewhat earlier entered carrying a rather impressively large serving dish. Nor did she realize with what consummate interest the others, and most especially the females, of the dinner party were observing their slow progress around the table. When, having made the entire round of the guests, the footmen came at last to inquire of her if "m'lady" desired a serving from the dish, Thaxton was at the point of confiding in her his opinion that Danforth had been more sinned against than sinning. Jane responded to the servant's interruption with a distracted wave of the hand without taking her attention from Thaxton. Consequently, she did not note the elaborate manner in which the servant, having interpreted her somewhat vague gesture as an assent, scraped the bottom of the dish to retrieve the very last morsel and drop.

Her first awareness that she was the cynosure of attention

came in the form of a chorus of delighted feminine squeals and laughter. "The last pea in the pot! The first maid to marry! It's Lady Jane! The lucky maid, but who's the man she'll wed?"

Only then did she realize the reason for the commotion or remember that it had been her idea to include a pot of carling peas on the dinner menu, purely to add to the entertainment. After all, what could be more appropriate, she remembered reasoning. The dinner was to fall on the day before Carling Sunday. She had hardly wanted or expected that she herself would be singled out as the recipient of the last pea in the pot. Indeed, she had much rather she had not. Mina and Ethne, not to mention Wilfred, would take endless delight in teasing her about it.

Realizing there was nothing for it, but to smile and make the best of the situation, she nodded and laughed at her own expense. No doubt it was purely coincidence that her eyes should alight on Danforth or that she should suddenly be aware of a slow heat pervading her cheeks at sight of him. How very odd, she thought distractedly as she turned her eyes away, that in that single fleeting moment when their glances had suddenly locked, it had seemed that they, two, were alone in the room.

She was still a trifle shaken by that revelation, when Mina rose to signal dinner was at an end. As the ladies withdrew to leave the gentlemen to their cigars and brandy, Ethne came to link her arm in Jane's.

"Jane, you sly puss," the girl whispered. "Indeed, I wonder about you."

"Do not, I pray, accuse me of having anything to do with the way things turned out. You may, I have no doubt, look to my sister-in-law for having arranged it. By all rights, you should have been the last one to be served. You may be sure *I* had no wish for that dubious honor."

"Gammon," Ethne gurgled with laughter. "I saw the way you looked at a certain gentleman, who shall remain nameless. As it happens, however," she hastened to add when Jane halted ominously in her tracks, "it was not the carling peas that I was thinking of. I watched you talking to the Earl of Thaxton. You patched things up for me, Jane, didn't you?"

"It would be just as you deserve had I told him you are incorrigible and impertinent," Jane retorted with mock severity. "As it happens, however, I made sure he was aware of your more admirable characteristics. He responded by way of assuring me that he thought you a delightful young woman with unexceptional manners. Little does he know."

"Thank you, dearest Jane." Ethne beamed, hugging the older woman's arm to her. "I know everything will turn out right now, in spite of-of, well, a certain coolness I sensed in some of the assembled guests. Lady Fitzhugh was most particularly pointed in refusing to allow me even a moment alone with Maria. And then there were some things I overheard Lady Bridgemont saying to the gentleman who sat next to her. She mentioned something about Mama, and Danforth's reputation. I dare not repeat it all."

"Pay no heed to them, Ethne," Jane counseled. "However, I'm afraid we are not out of the briars yet."

The girl's face grew pale. "What if I am given the cold shoulder at the ball? What if I am ignored? I could not bear it, Jane, if I thought I had ruined things for you and Mina— after all she has done for me."

"Then do not think it," Jane said, taking hold of the girl's arm and shaking it a little. "Keep your head up. And whatever happens, smile and be gay. No one must ever guess that you are in the least doubt. To the world you must appear to be confident and self-assured, no matter what happens. Do you hear me?"

Ethne ducked her head, but not before Jane glimpsed a

flash in the green eyes. "I hear you," she whispered back, her head coming up again. "And I shall stand buff. No one, not even Lord Phillip Maheux will ever guess my knees are trembling."

Jane's duties in the receiving line brought her once more in close proximity to Danforth's unsettling presence. He demonstrated his reputation for being capable of a charm, which must have disarmed even the wariest of matrons with a marriageable daughter. As for the male contingent, they treated him, if not always with actual liking, then most certainly with a respect, which Jane attributed as much to his standing as a man, a Corinthian, and a *nonpareil* at swords, pistols, and fisticuffs, as to either his fortune or his title.

He was Danforth, a formidable champion for his sister, and yet, she could not but detect a reserve in the manner in which the arriving guests greeted Ethne, and herself to some degree.

From this she deduced that while Mina's prestige as a hostess had not been done any lasting damage, her own standing in the *ton* and that of Ethne's appeared somewhat in doubt. She well knew the source of Ethne's difficulties. Her own, however, were less certain. Surely, she thought, it was not due solely to her friendship with Ethne. If it were, would not Mina have been made to share in the chill Jane sensed beneath the polite civility of many of those she greeted?

When the time came at last for the receiving line to disband in order that the ball might truly begin, Jane was aware of a growing feeling of oppression beneath her breast. She concealed it behind a cool, gracious exterior. No one, she vowed, would ever know that she had been made to feel the sting of censure. She had done nothing to deserve it, and she would not give into it.

Nevertheless, when she took her place on the sidelines to

wait for Ethne to be led out by Danforth, Jane could not but be moved and grateful to discover Francis Beauchamp making his way leisurely toward her.

"Miss Ashely, I count it my good fortune to be here ahead of the gathering of your admirers," murmured that gentleman, bowing graciously before her. He straightened, and Jane experienced an odd prickling of nerves at the look he bent upon her. "My friends Silverbridge and Hazelton are already coming this way, am I not mistaken. Yes, so they are. And there, of course, is the unavoidable Lethridge. In moments you will be surrounded, and I shall find it difficult to get in so much as a word with you. I should like to take this opportunity, therefore, of requesting the honor of leading you out in the Promenade. I believe I have not quite forgotten how it's done."

Jane smiled, startled and moved by what clearly amounted to a gallant gesture. Francis Beauchamp was one of the most sought-after men in London and the bane of every hostess intent on winning his presence at any social gathering. If he deigned to make an appearance, it would be well after the opening minuet and then only for a few precious moments of his time. It was as unheard of for Beauchamp to attend a dinner *and* a ball given on the same night by the same hostess as it was for him to take part in the Promenade.

"I should be both pleased and honored, sir," she answered gravely. "And grateful," she added, with a level look at the gentleman, "if you would be pleased to tell me why it is that I need the championship of Beauchamp and Silverbridge, not to mention Lethridge."

It was to Beauchamp's credit that he did not pretend to misunderstand her.

"It is nothing to signify, my dear," he murmured. "A small matter of some empty talk. I shouldn't worry about it were I you."

Jane's lips parted in surprise. "I am not worried. Faith, I

have done nothing to make myself the object of gossip. Pray tell me what is being said."

Beauchamp's expression remained maddeningly noncommittal. "Naturally, it could never be my wish to refuse a lady's request. However, I suggest you would do better to ask Danforth."

Jane stared at Beauchamp in speechless astonishment. Danforth! she thought. Good God, surely he could not be the cause of her seeming fall from grace!

She was not given time to question Beauchamp further, as a sudden flurry of movement, followed by an excited buzz of voices, drew her attention to the curving staircase that descended to the ballroom.

At first it seemed that Ethne, standing at the head of the stairs ready to descend with Danforth, had precipitated the disturbance. Then she saw Ethne's face pale and her eyes widen as she was joined by a second gentleman of distinguished bearing.

Jane recognized that portly frame, the florid features. It was Prinnie himself! The pale, slender form of the girl dropped into a deep curtsy, no less graceful for its sudden haste. Beside her, Danforth inclined his head as he accepted the outstretched hand of the newcomer in welcome. Words were exchanged, the content of which Jane could only imagine, but there was no mistaking the genuine warmth in Prinnie's greeting. Then at last, Danforth raised Ethne to her feet and, placing her hand in that of the Prince Regent's, stepped respectfully aside to allow the two to pass before him.

As if on signal, the murmurs ceased, and Jane, along with the rest of the assembled company, paid homage to the prince.

It was the general consensus of opinion that Miss Winter acquitted herself in the minuet with becoming modesty and grace, and even the prince himself was heard to say at the finish of the Promenade that she was a charming little minx very like her mama before her. Then chucking her lightly under the chin, he nodded sagely to Danforth and, accompanied by his usual entourage, expressed his thanks for a delightful evening to the Earl and Countess of Melcourt before he made his departure, leaving little doubt that he had come for the sole purpose of launching Ethne into polite society.

Jane was happy for the girl. It seemed doubtful that anything could tarnish her future in the wake of so impressive a send-off. Hard upon that thought came the realization that with Ethne safely launched, her own presence in London was hardly needed any longer. Indeed, in view of the less than warm accord she had received thus far that evening, she was sorely tempted to pack her trunks and depart for Oaks no later than tomorrow morning.

She suffered a bitter pang at the thought, even as she laughed and summoned a gay rejoinder to Silverbridge's remark that Prinnie must have got his coat without benefit of advice from Beau Brummel. "Damme if it didn't have buttons the size of saucers. Not the thing to wear a coat that draws undue attention to itself. Brummel would fall into a fit of the glooms at the mere sight of it."

"Brummel, notwithstanding, my lord, the prince could not have looked better to me had he appeared in emperor's clothing," Jane offered, smiling. "I confess I was most happy to see him."

"It is most undeniably a coup," agreed Beauchamp, taking Jane's fan and gently waving it before her face. "But then, that is what one has come to expect of Danforth. I daresay his true colors will be found out in the not very distant future."

Jane, feeling rather conspicuous, ensconced on the sidelines surrounded by four of the most eligible bachelors in the realm—rather like a lady in distress surrounded by her guardian knights, she mused sardonically—glanced quickly up at Beauchamp's odd remark. Her lips parted to ask him what he meant by it, when the object of their discussion loomed into her vision.

"Ah, gentlemen," drawled the marquess with his lazy smile. "You present a formidable line of defense. One which I do not hesitate to breach. It would never do to allow you to monopolize all the lady's attentions. I believe, Miss Ashely, this dance was promised to me."

He had addressed his first remarks to Beauchamp, who received them with an unruffled smile and an odd, glittering exchange of glances, which seemed to Jane to convey some sort of silent communication. Then Danforth's gaze, cool and inimitable, came to rest on her. "Miss Ashely?" he murmured, extending a lean strong hand. "Will you do me the honor?"

Jane hesitated only a moment before laying her palm in his. "I beg you will excuse me, gentlemen," she said. Her eyes on Danforth's, she rose gracefully from her chair and allowed herself to be led on to the dance floor.

She had often thought Danforth, with his easy, athletic grace, would be an admirable dancer, and she had not been mistaken. She had not expected, however, to find herself transported, lost in a sublime wordless communication of rhythm and movement. There was only the music, herself and Danforth. She felt as light as thistledown within the circle of his arm.

"You haven't told me yet, Miss Ashely. Are you enjoying your Season in London?"

The words impinged on her unconscious. Only then did she realize she had been dancing with her eyes half closed, her head tilted to one side. She blinked and was brought back to reality.

"The Season," she echoed blankly. Then swiftly recovering, she answered with her usual candor. "Yes, I suppose I have.

More than I thought I should. I never realized how greatly I missed the theater. And the shopping of course. I should be lying if I said I did not enjoy buying the shops out. As for the rest," she shrugged and glanced away from his all too discerning eyes, "I have been entertained, but there is little I shall regret leaving when I return home to Oaks."

Danforth's eyebrow arched ever so slightly. His eyes narrowed on her face. "No, of course," he drawled, "you will have so much, after all, to which to look forward. No doubt the role of auntie will suit you admirably."

Jane's indignant glance flew to his face. "Indeed, sir," she answered, hurt by his sarcasm. "I could not be happier at the prospect."

"Naturally not. I imagine you cannot wait to be home in order to prepare for the happy event. When, Miss Ashely, are you leaving?"

"Tomorrow. Or the next day perhaps." In consternation she bit her lip. She had not meant to tell him that. The devil take him for goading her to it, as he had no doubt meant to do.

The earlier spell of the dance quite vanished, Jane could only be grateful that the strains of the waltz had finally come to an end. Nevertheless, she was conscious of a heaviness in the region of her breastbone as she started to pull away.

Danforth's hand on hers stopped her. Startled and more than a little annoyed, she looked up into his hard impassive features. Something she saw in his eyes, glittery in the candlelight, robbed her of volition. Indeed, she could only stare in wordless amazement as he took both her hands in his.

"It occurs to me, Miss Ashely, that you should reconsider your decision to go," he said, his compelling eyes never leaving hers. With a deliberation that struck her as most singular, he raised her hands to his lips and saluted them. "The Season, after all, has only just begun."

It was only then, when she heard a murmur ripple through

the ballroom and as, bowing, he turned and left her in the company of Beauchamp and Silverbridge and her other stanch admirers, that she realized what he had done. In that single gesture, he had publicly signaled his approval of her—Danforth, in spite of his reputation, the foremost of the Carleton set, the *Nonpareil,* the arbiter of fashion. Whatever talk there had been, he had silenced it, just as effectively as he had silenced any rumors about Ethne.

The realization mortified and inflamed her. How dared he presume so much! She was no green girl in need of his protection. If there had been talk, she was perfectly capable of discovering its source and squelching it in her own way—with unassailable pride and disdain. She cared not a whit what people thought of her. But she cared a great deal what she thought of herself, and Danforth, with his grand gesture, had pulled the rug out from under her, robbing her of her pride of independence and placing her in his debt.

Faith, it was too much—Jane Ashely beholden to Danforth! Indeed, it did not bear thinking on.

Twelve

Jane awakened with a start to golden shafts of sunlight and the cheerful cacophony of birdsong outside her window. It was a new day.

With a groan, she buried her face in the pillows and pulled the bedclothes up over her head. As if by that she might shut out the memories of the previous night, she thought dourly.

Realizing at last the futility of further sleep, she impatiently flung the satin comforter down and flipped over on her back with an effusive sigh, that did not relieve her oppression.

Well, it was over and done, she mused fatalistically, and, thanks to Danforth's masterly stroke, the ball had been a crushing success. Ethne was launched and in such a manner as few could ever have hoped to be launched—by Prinnie himself!

Jane could not but be happy and pleased for the girl. Ethne's success was *un fait accompli,* as was evidenced by the more than flattering attention that had been paid to her by Phillip Maheux, along with a host of other dazzled young bloods. Nor had Jane herself gone without notice. Whatever restraint there had been before Danforth claimed his stolen waltz had dissipated after it was over. She had been swarmed with gentlemen asking for a place on her dance card, which was exactly what he had intended when he coerced her into granting him the first waltz.

No doubt she should be pleased that her standing among

the *ton* had been retrieved, she mused with a grimace. She experienced a warm wash of blood at the memory of Danforth standing over her, insufferably sure of himself, as he paid her the compliment of redeeming her. Faith! Redeemed her from what?

She had not seen Danforth to talk to him again after that one and only dance with him, and though Beauchamp and Silverbridge and the others had remained her nearly constant companions throughout the rest of the evening, they had proven uncommonly reticent on the subject that had been uppermost in her mind. The most she had been able to learn was that there had been vague, unfavorable insinuations made concerning something that had happened seven years before during her first Season in London.

It made no sense. *Nothing* had happened during her first Season. She had met Geoffrey and fallen in love. Nothing could have been more innocent or innocuous.

At last, weary of her own thoughts and unable to remain longer in bed, she rose and rang for a servant to bring her hot water. When several moments later the maid appeared, she was accompanied by Nanny Twickum with Jane's morning cup of hot chocolate.

Jane, seeing the old dear was bursting to talk about the ball, sought to distract her with the one tidbit of news that would mean most to her. Slyly suggesting that it might be more apropos to refurbish the nursery at Oaks than the withdrawing room at the dowager's house, she waited for the old nanny to draw her own conclusions. "So, it be come," breathed that worthy. "And it's glad I am, too, that the earl will have his heir at last. All the same, I'll not be leaving you, Miss Jane, so don't you be askin' me to."

"No, of course I shan't, Nanny," Jane was quick to murmur. "Not if you don't want me to. The truth is, I should be lost without you."

"Well, *someone's* got t'look after ye," said the old woman, her eyes keen on Jane's face in the mirror. "There be strange goings on belowstairs—someone pokin' his nose in where it don't belong. More 'n one has been made up to with the promise of money if they'll tell what bain't no one's business outside these walls. Belike the earl had ought to be told, Miss Jane. The villain were askin' about the young miss and yourself."

Jane started, unable or unwilling to believe her ears. Why should anyone be interested in Ethne and herself?

"Yes, I shall tell Wilfred of course. And the marquess. Miss Winter is his sister, after all. He should be immediately apprised." Turning, she gently squeezed the old servant's hand. "And thank you, Nanny. For everything."

Thoughtfully, Jane dressed in a rose sarcenet morning dress and went below to the breakfast room, intending to approach Melcourt with what Nanny had told her, only to find that he had gone out earlier. With Mina and Ethne still abed, Jane ate a meager breakfast of coffee and dry toast. Before she had finished, Mina appeared, sleepy-eyed and yet wrapped in a glow of happiness, that was only partially due to the success of Ethne's presentation ball.

Perhaps it was only Jane's imagination playing tricks on her, but she thought she detected a subtle change in her sister-in-law, a contentment that had not been there before. It struck a hollow note somewhere deep within Jane, and, unsummoned, Danforth's words returned to mock her: "No doubt the role of auntie will suit you admirably." Oh, the devil fly away him! she fumed.

It was Palm Sunday, and Mina expressed a desire to attend the morning service at St. Paul's. Jane agreed to accompany her.

They found the church crowded. The service was beautiful with its timeless traditions. When it was over, pax cakes bearing the imprint of the Paschal Lamb were handed out with the benediction, "God and Good Neighborhood." Jane returned home, feeling strangely more at peace with herself and the day.

After luncheon, she took Ethne aside and broke the news to her about Freddy.

"He *is* going to be all right?" exclaimed the girl, her face going pearly white. "Oh, why did you not tell me sooner? I must go and see him at once."

Electing to walk the short distance to Danforth's town house on the southeast corner of the square, Jane and Ethne soon found themselves being ushered into a quietly elegant withdrawing-room. There was a vague relief for Jane when the butler announced that his lordship was not within. She had no wish to cross swords with Danforth. Not yet, she told herself, conscious of a vague feeling of disquiet within her breast. Not today.

A small, slender woman with fine, still lovely features that called Freddy to mind, entered with a welcoming smile. Ethne sprang to her feet to embrace her. "Caroline! I only just heard, or I should have been here sooner. Please tell me Freddy is-is not . . ."

"Freddy is no longer in any danger, Ethne. He has been sadly pulled by fever, but that is over now, and I am glad to say that he is recovering. He's asleep and has yet to be allowed visitors, or I should let you see for yourself how well he is doing."

"Oh, but, please, could I not have just a peek? I promise I shan't disturb him. I have brought him some of his favorite chocolates and a book of poetry. Perhaps I could just set them by his bed for when he wakes up?"

Ethne, when she was at her most beguiling, was difficult to resist. Now in earnest, her eyes huge in her white face, she could not be gainsaid.

Freddy's mama relented. "But of course you shall see him—tomorrow. I shall send for you when he is awake and has been prepared to receive visitors, I promise." She turned then to Jane with undisguised interest in her discerning gray eyes. "You are Miss Ashely, are you not? Nicky has told me of your kindness to my son. How can I ever thank you?"

"I shall be thanked by seeing Freddy well again," Jane replied, smiling a little. "I became quite fond of him in the short time he was with us at Melcourt."

"I believe you quite won him over," said Lady Caroline. "He has talked of you often since Danforth brought him home from that terrible Badajoz." Linking her arm in Jane's, she led her two guests to a giltwood sofa flanked by a matching side chair. "He was wounded and taken captive by Spanish deserters—bandits, you know, while carrying dispatches for Wellington. I'm afraid they treated him quite shabbily. It is a wonder he did not lose the arm. Indeed, if it had not been for Danforth, I am sure my son would not be alive today, let alone on the road to recovery. But then, no doubt you have heard how Nick rescued Freddy."

"Indeed, I have not," Jane answered, and Ethne gazed at the other woman with rapt attention. "But I should like to hear it, very much."

"How very like Nick. He is always so closemouthed when it comes to himself. However, I had the impression that with you—" She paused, apparently thinking better of what she had been about to say. "Well, no matter. The truth is, he would tell us nothing of what happened beyond that he found Freddy and, transporting him to Lisbon, carried him home to England on his private yacht. It was Freddy who let slip that Danforth enlisted the aid of Spanish guerrillas to find the bandits and win his release."

Jane was both thrilled and appalled at the tale Lady Caroline related then. Visions of Freddy, wounded, his horse shot out from under him and himself pinned down with no hope of escape, sickened her, even as the thought of that brave boy destroying the dispatches he carried before he was overrun gladdened her heart. How resourceful he was! To have had the presence of mind to convince the leader of the cutthroats that he knew things valuable to the British and therefore how much more so to the French! It had kept the villains from killing him outright. And then, feverish and ill from his wound, to endure the nightmare of days and nights of being forced to hide and flee before the advancing British troops. How terribly he must have suffered!

"But how did Danforth find them?" Jane exclaimed. "You said guerrillas helped him. I don't understand."

"How can I answer you?" Lady Caroline smiled, her fine eyes tired. "All I know is what Freddy told me. There was a man, a Spanish guerrilla captain. Freddy swears this man was no stranger to Danforth. It was through him that Freddy was found."

"Then we must be grateful for such a man and the service he rendered his lordship," murmured Jane and rose. "And, now, I think we must be going. I am glad to have met you, and I could not be more pleased to hear Freddy is mending. Thank you for having us, Lady Caroline."

"Not at all, my dear. Please, do come back again."

The following day saw the house inundated with cards and visitors. Ethne, in spite of her worry about Freddy, held court in the withdrawing-room, and though the girl was gracious and obviously pleased at this proof of her popularity, Jane thought her mind was elsewhere. When a footman arrived shortly after luncheon with a message from Lady Caroline, Ethne hurried to put on her pelisse and accompany him to her brother's house.

She returned half an hour later with tears in her eyes, her smile tremulous, but without the haunted look that she had worn before going to visit Freddy.

"Oh, Jane, he was so changed. Older somehow," she exclaimed, stepping into the other woman's arms. "And yet he was the same sweet Freddy who has always been my friend, even when we were fighting like cats and dogs. Come and sit with me. I want to tell you everything.

"He has suffered, Jane!" she said in a tremulous voice when they had seated themselves on the sofa. "I believe he must have died had it not been for the kindness of a peasant girl, hardly more than a child. She had been stolen from her family and made a slave to those animals. Somehow she managed to steal food for him and to care for him in spite of the danger to herself. Even so, it was low tide for him by the time Danforth was led to the village in which the bandits had taken refuge. They were making arrangements to sell Freddy to the French when Nicky broke in on them. There was a fight, of course." Ethne shuddered. "The leader and two of his men were killed, along with the Frenchman."

Ethne turned huge shimmering eyes on Jane. "The most dreadful thing of all is that poor unhappy girl was carried off again by some of the bandits who managed to escape. You should have seen Freddy's face when he told me that. I believe he fell in love with her, Jane. A-a peasant girl. And now his heart is broken."

That evening Mina and her two protégées were promised to the Earl and Countess of Thaxton for dinner, after which a party had been made up, mostly of the younger set, to go to Vauxhall Gardens for the fireworks. Jane, who had reasons for not wishing to visit Vauxhall Gardens, would have preferred to beg off, but Mina would not hear of it.

"It has taken seven years to get you to London, Jane Ashely," she said ominously. "And now that you are here, you may be sure that I do not intend to allow you to hide out in your room. You are coming tonight, and tomorrow night to the opera, and after that, to an endless round of balls, soirees, and whatever else should happen our way. I shall settle for nothing less, I warn you."

It had not been the warning that persuaded Jane to give into her sister-in-law's blandishments. It was the realization that Mina's sincerest wish was for Jane's happiness, and, to her, that could never mean anything short of marriage, a family, and a home of Jane's own. Jane simply could not bear to quash her expectations.

Vauxhall Gardens had always held a special allure for Jane. The softly glowing light of Chinese lanterns, the painted booths, the strains of music wafting on a perfumed breeze—these and so much more awakened a bursting pang of memory. Indeed, the wandering walks seemed haunted with ghosts of the past.

It was at Vauxhall in the Grecian temple that Geoffrey had first declared his love for her and asked her for her hand in marriage.

But she must not think of that, she told herself as she allowed herself to be seated in a booth in the company of Melcourt, Mina, Ethne, and Lord Phillip. Determined to enjoy herself, or at least to give the impression that she was her usual unruffled self, she turned, smiling, to Melcourt to remark that the gardens were quite as lovely as she remembered them. For the barest instant her smile froze on her lips as she looked beyond her brother's shoulder into the sardonic gaze of the Marquess of Danforth. Ironically, he inclined his head in acknowledgment of her.

To her immediate consternation, she beheld her brother rise and step forward, hand extended, with every indication of one unsurprised by the encounter.

"Danforth," he rumbled. "Good of you to extend to us the hospitality of your booth. Was afraid you had changed your mind and decided not to join us."

"Your worry was misplaced, as you see," murmured the marquess, his handsome lips curving faintly in a smile. "I have taken the prerogative of ordering champagne and a cold collation. I hope that meets with everyone's approval."

Jane cast a meaningful glance at Mina. The deceitful wretch wore an aspect of studied innocence, which did not fool Jane for a moment. The inveterate matchmaker had set her up for this encounter with Danforth, she was sure of it.

Perhaps it was just as well, she thought, remembering her morning's conversation with Nanny Twickum. This would be as good an opportunity as any to acquaint the marquess with what she had learned. With that in mind, she waited until the cold collation of paper-thin slices of roast and ham, servings of green goose, strawberries, and jellies had been sampled and a toast drunk in honor of the impending arrival of Mina and Melcourt's future offspring.

It was then that Ethne expressed a desire to dance, and Phillip, demonstrating that her wish was his command, rose immediately to lead her out of the box toward the rotunda from which came the strains of a Viennese waltz.

Jane smiled somewhat mistily, watching the young couple swallowed up in the crowd. She could not have failed to note Ethne and young Maheux's tendency to engage in long, lingering exchanges of glances or their inability to keep from surreptitiously touching hands beneath the table. How well she remembered what it was like to feel what they were feeling! It was to be intoxicated one moment and in the doldrums the next, and yet how sweet to suffer only to be uplifted again! To her dismay she felt a lump rise in her throat and had hastily to glance away from one pair of discerning eyes.

Faith, what a silly pea-goose she was, she thought, angry at herself for giving into sentiment. She would be in a sad state indeed if she allowed her emotions to run amok at anything so innocuous as the sight of two lovers holding hands.

That, however, was not to be the least or even the worst of her trials that evening. To Jane's mortification, Melcourt, finding himself the object of numerous covert jabs in the ribs from his wife, evinced a sudden, unwonted interest in going the rounds. It was notable that he evaded Jane's eyes as he rose and led a guileless Mina from the box.

Jane, staring after them, was made tinglingly aware that she was alone with Danforth. She could almost have throttled Mina for so baldly abandoning her to him.

Supremely conscious of the silence stretching between them, Jane grasped at the first topic of conversation that came to her mind. "Phillip Maheux seems a fine young man, does he not?" she offered, striving for a lightness of tone. Turning to look at the marquess, she summoned a smile, that felt foolishly awry. "I should be surprised if a declaration were not soon to be forthcoming. They would seem to be lost in a world of their own."

"No more so than you appear to be, Miss Ashely," drawled Danforth, his eyes shadowed in the subdued light of the lanterns. "You seem singularly withdrawn this evening."

"Do I?" Jane blushed, vaguely irritated by his cool insouciance, which had the power to set her off balance. "I beg your pardon if I am poor company."

He laughed. "I did not say you were poor company. Only that you seemed preoccupied."

"No doubt it is only the gardens. They bring back—memories." She stopped and turned her face away. She had not meant to let that slip. Then bowing to the inevitability of the moment, she looked back at him. "Would you care to walk, my lord?"

"Naturally, Miss Ashely, I should be pleased to stroll the grounds." Rising, he offered her his arm.

The night air was cool with the scent of a promised rain carried on the riffle of breeze. In no mood for the boisterousness of the crowd, she linked her arm in his and instinctively guided their steps away from the rotunda.

"Do you come often to Vauxhall?" she queried, as they entered one of the wandering walks. "I'm afraid Mina and Wilfred failed to mention the fact that we were to be your guests tonight."

She sensed the irony of his smile. "Had you known, would you have come?"

"No, I daresay I should have cried off. I do not require any further gestures to ensure my success. Last night was more than enough. I am undoubtedly the second most soughtafter woman in London, thanks to you." Abruptly she stopped and turned to face him. "Why did you do it?"

The cold impassivity of his face baffled her.

"No doubt because I wished to have done. Does it matter?"

"It matters to me. Tell me why it was necessary. Beauchamp hinted that there had been talk. Surely I have a right to know what is being said of me."

To her mounting annoyance, Danforth arched an imperious eyebrow. "But surely you know. You are a diamond of the first water, an incomparable, with unexceptional manners. What more would you like to hear? That the betting books have Hazleton running a close second to Beauchamp as candidates for your hand in marriage? No doubt you will be amused to hear that my name has been entered in the lists as well. Pray don't look apprehensive. I have the distinction of being a dark horse, due to my lamentable reputation."

"Yes, your reputation," she said, bitter with disappointment.

How dared he try to lead her away from the subject! "Shall I tell you what your reputation is, my lord?" she demanded, driven by some devil she did not know she possessed to break through his cool unassailability. "Thaxton believes you are more sinned against than sinning. And Beauchamp assures me your true colors will one day be made known. To Freddy, you are a hero. It would seem the Prince Regent places no little value on your friendship. Indeed, I should say *that,* at least, has been demonstrated beyond a doubt. Therefore, I beg you, do not fling your reputation at my head. I tell you straightly, I do not credit it."

"Then you are as stubborn as you are misguided," he assured her coldly. "Believe it, Miss Ashely. I have taken great pains to make it so."

"That, I *can* believe, my lord," Jane retorted, at last turning the full force of her eyes on him. "What are they saying, Danforth? Tell me, please. I will know sooner or later."

He did not answer for a moment, and she became acutely aware of his eyes piercing the darkness to study her face. At last his voice cut through the stillness with a steel-edged softness. "They are rumors that were dead and should have been buried long ago. Unfortunately, someone has dredged them up again."

"What rumors?" Jane prodded when it seemed he would not go on. "Who has dredged them up? I am not a green girl, my lord, or a hothouse flower in danger of wilting before unfounded gossip. I do not require your protection, or any man's, for that matter."

"Do you not?" he uttered strangely, and it was all she could do not to glance away from the bitter mockery in his gaze. "Then I collect that I am mistaken. My apologies, Miss Ashely."

"Don't!" Jane flushed. "Do not make me ashamed. It is

not an apology I want, my lord. Only your confidence and trust. Why can you not tell me what I wish to know?"

For the first time she was given to see a break in his formidable reserve. A flash, like pain, darkened his eyes, instantly to be hidden behind the bored mask of the Corinthian.

"Careful, Miss Ashely," he drawled, "you will have me believing you are not indifferent to me. And that would never do. Surely you have not forgotten who I am? Or that Geoffrey is dead because of me."

"I have forgotten nothing. I had thought . . . But it does not matter now," Jane answered. Defeated, she turned away. Consequently, she did not see his hand go out to her or the look of bitter self-mockery sweep his stern countenance. When she looked again, the lean face was maddeningly inscrutable. "What does matter is that Ethne may be the object of-of unwelcome attention. Someone, a stranger, has been quizzing my brother's servants. He offered to buy their confidence. He was asking about Ethne."

"Was he?" murmured Danforth, his only show of emotion the leap of muscle along the hard line of his jaw. "Only Ethne. Nothing about you, Miss Ashely?"

"Well, yes. Perhaps he was curious about my comings and goings. But I cannot think I am in any danger. I am well able to look after myself."

"Yes, so you have informed me on more than one occasion," observed Danforth acerbically. "Has Melcourt been made aware of these happenings?"

"No." Jane made a helpless gesture. "You will no doubt think me foolish, but I could not bring myself to bother Wilfred with this. Not now, when he has been so happy. Very likely it will not amount to anything."

"You, my dear, are foolish beyond permission if that is what you think." Jane nearly winced as strong supple fingers closed about her arms. Danforth bent over her to peer into her face. "It occurs to me that it would be unwise for you ever to leave your brother's house unattended. Promise me you will take a footman or a gentleman companion. No doubt any one of your four loyal swains will be more than happy to oblige you."

"Pray do not be absurd, my lord," Jane gasped, prey to a host of unfamiliar sensations at his touch. She felt herself sway toward him without conscious volition and was dismayed to find herself wondering what it would be like to have his arms go around her, to have him hold her as only one other had ever done. Faith, could she truly be so lost to all sense of decency as to wish with all her heart that he might kiss her?

Hastily she drew back, her heart pounding wildly beneath her breast. "I-I should not dream of imposing on others," she finished lamely, wondering if she had so lost all sense of self as to be falling in love with Danforth? She recoiled from the thought. No, surely not. It was only the garden, she told herself. The garden fraught with memories.

"Quite so," Danforth drawled in tones laced with irony. Jane had to catch herself to keep from falling as he released her. "At least promise me you will inform Melcourt," she heard him say as from a great distance.

"Yes, of-of course. If you think it advisable. Certainly we shall have a care for Ethne. As for myself, you need not concern yourself."

"Rest assured," murmured Danforth harshly. "I should not dream of imposing myself on you. You will agree, however, that Ethne's welfare is of some concern to me."

"Of-of course, my lord. You must naturally do whatever you think necessary to protect her." Jane turned away, unreasonably shaken and wishing only to be safely away from there, away from him. "And now, I should like to go back. No doubt Mina and the others will be wondering about us."

He made no comment as he offered her his arm once more and led her back to the booth.

Jane awakened the next morning prey to a headache and would have returned to her room immediately after breakfast had not Mina herself shown distinct signs of being under the weather.

"No doubt it will pass before the morning is out," said the countess, smiling wanly at Jane over dry toast at which she nibbled desultorily. "Unfortunately, I promised Ethne I should take her shopping in Bond Street for shoes to wear with her Easter ball gown. No doubt we shall have to have them dyed to match the dress, which means we dare not put it off till later. Would you mind terribly, dear, doing this one little thing for me?"

"Of course I should not mind," Jane exclaimed solicitously. "Pray do not worry yourself over it. I have some shopping to do myself. Indeed, I believe I shall take Rupert with us to carry packages if you can spare him," she added, mindful of her promise to Danforth to have a special care for his sister's safety.

She had as yet to speak to Melcourt, who was out for his morning gallop in the Park and would not return until after his daily exercise at Gentleman Jackson's private boxing club. Instantly, she discarded the notion of confiding in Mina. She could not like to cause her sister-in-law any distress which was certain to be occasioned by the knowledge that someone was prying into their private affairs.

Giving Mina a buss on the cheek, Jane went upstairs to rouse Ethne from her bed and then repaired to her own room to dress.

On an impulse she could not fully explain even to herself, she changed her dress for a new, far prettier one, a pastel blue jaconet round gown with long sleeves, puffed at the shoulders and snug-fitting down the arm to the wrist, and pearl embroidery about the wrist bands and square neck. Over this she slipped on a pelisse of white sarcenet trimmed with swansdown, worn open at the front and reaching to the ankles. She knew she had seldom looked better as she took a peep at herself in the mirror, and then, when the thought came whispering insidiously to her that she had dressed thus intentionally on the chance that she might run into a certain stern-featured nobleman with piercing blue eyes, she furiously blushed and fled the room.

Ten minutes later she was seated beside Ethne in the carriage bound for Bond Street.

Encountering a lovely spring morning with only a smattering of clouds to mar the perfection of an otherwise blue sky, Jane soon found her headache slipping away. Indeed, it would have been difficult to remain in the doldrums in Ethne's ebullient company.

The child was positively radiant, a circumstance which Jane attributed to the aftermath of the evening before. The Earl and Countess of Thaxton had treated Ethne with every indication that she had their wholehearted approval, and there certainly was no doubting the state of Phillip's mind. Jane could not doubt that he was as smitten with Ethne as she was with him. Only Ethne herself seemed to entertain some doubt as to her status with Phillip. Indeed, in spite of the girl's gaiety, Jane seemed at times to detect a forced note in her laughter.

Jane wondered at it, but did not put her thoughts into a query. If there was something troubling Ethne, surely the child would come to her with it when she was ready.

Moments later the carriage drew up before the shoe shop on Bond Street, and the footman, Rupert, stepped to the door to hand his two mistresses down.

"Jane, by all that is marvelous, look who is here," cried Ethne, arriving on the walk. "It's Nicky."

Jane looked up to behold, strolling leisurely toward them, Danforth, elegant in morning walking dress made up of a single-breasted coat of blue superfine with moderately high collar and plated buttons, a jockey waistcoat with vertical stripes, a white linen neckcloth elegantly tied, dove gray pantaloons tucked into the tops of shining brown Hessian boots, and, perched at a jaunty angle, a black top hat. His only jewelry comprised a solitary diamond in the folds of his neckcloth, a signet ring worn on his right hand, and a watch fob across the front of his waistcoat. A gold-handled quizzing glass hung about his neck on a black ribbon. He was in every way the *Nonpareil,* the Corinthian, the arbiter of fashion.

She could not keep her heart from giving a little leap at sight of him.

"Now, what, I wonder brings him here," queried Ethne, glancing slyly at Jane.

"I'm sure I haven't the least idea," Jane lied, blushing at the child's unveiled implication. Indeed, she thought she knew very well why Danforth should be there. No doubt he had gone out of his way to find them.

"Nicky, you sly fox," exclaimed Ethne, wrapping her arm about her half-brother's. "How clever of you to guess I had already exhausted my quarterly allowance and was wondering how I should raise the wind to make a few necessary purchases."

"It is hardly a matter of guesswork," drawled the marquess dryly. "When have you ever been beforehand with the world?"

"Practically never," Ethne admitted without noticeable distress at her lack of financial self-discipline. "But then why should I, when I have always had you to stand the nonsense?"

"Impertinent brat. It occurs to me that I shall look forward to relinquishing that office to the man unfortunate enough to win your hand. Let us hope he has the wherewithal to support you."

That brought a deep flush to the girl's cheeks. "Pray do not count on it, Nicky dear," she uttered in a stifled voice as she released him and turned away. "I shall very likely only disappoint you."

"Ethne!" Jane called after her, but the girl had already disappeared into the shoe shop. She lifted her eyes to Danforth, who wore a studied expression. "I cannot think what has come over the child," declared Jane in perplexity. "She was waxing ecstatic all the way here over Phillip Maheux. She certainly gave no indication there was any sort of rift between them."

"Then I should not refine on it." Danforth shrugged, apparently unmoved at such an eventuality. "Unless she has taken him in aversion, I have every expectation of wishing them both happy before the week is out. Young Maheux has requested an interview at my earliest opportunity."

"No, has he?" exclaimed Jane, brightening. "I was sure he would come up to scratch. What is more, I am convinced they will deal extremely. Indeed, I considered you the only stumbling block to *un fait accompli,* my lord."

"You cannot be serious, surely," replied Danforth, with the arch of a single imperious eyebrow. "If you think I should stand in the way of the man willing to take the impudent little baggage off my hands, then you have a very odd notion of my character."

"No doubt, my lord," smiled Jane, not in the least inclined to believe him. "I, however, have no intention of discussing your character. I have learned from past experience that I should soon be brought to *point-non-plus*. I meant only that not many would choose to beard the lion in his den. You do not deny, sir, that you can be quite intimidating."

Jane could not but thrill to the blue glint of his eyes.

"Deny it? Most emphatically, ma'am," Danforth drawled, apparently much struck at the notion. "I daresay I am not in the least intimidating. I have tried, without any notable success, to impress you that I am dangerous."

"Yes, but then I am a woman." Jane laughed, turning to enter the shop into which Ethne had fled. "You cannot expect to pull the wool over my eyes. Your bark, my lord, is far worse than your bite."

Ethne, it soon proved, was in no mood to be either conciliatory or easily pleased. The satin slippers with Italian heels, which she had previously favored, suddenly were not in the least suitable for a night of dancing. Nor were the French pumps with colored silk embroidery. The silk bottines were insipid, the white kid slippers with flat heels and pointed toes outmoded, and the Roman sandals with crisscross lacing up the front certainly designed to cripple anyone foolish enough to wear them. One after another, every shoe that the harassed proprietor had to present for her inspection was discarded as being too commonplace, too uncomfortable, or too lacking in appeal by far, until they were forced at last to try another shop.

When the second shop similarly failed to provide shoes to meet Ethne's approval, Jane was as close to exasperation with the girl as she had ever been. Fortunately, Danforth had apparently already reached his limit.

"It occurs to me that you have tried Miss Ashely's patience long enough," he observed. "Not to mention mine." Taking the girl's arm in one hand and Jane's in the other, he led them down Bond Street. "I suggest, therefore, that we facilitate your decision by allowing me to make it for you."

"You?" exclaimed Ethne and Jane in unison. "You cannot

be serious," added his sister, her expression one of mingled suspicion and mirth.

"On the contrary, I have seldom been more serious," replied the marquess, opening the door to a shop that, in addition to shoes, displayed a profusion of examples of the millinery art. "You are about to discover that I am not inexperienced in matters of feminine apparel. Nor am I given to indecisiveness, which is an affliction primarily of the female gender."

"Oh, indeed?" queried Jane, who quite naturally took exception to being thought femininely irresolute.

"Yes, Miss Ashely," replied the marquess. "Indeed."

The aroma of leather greeted them as Danforth ushered Jane and Ethne into the shop. Hardly had Jane time to glance curiously about at the orderly array of hats, shoes, and an enticing selection of ladies' reticules than an elderly gentleman hurried forward, his seamed face expressive of welcome.

"My lord marquess," he exclaimed, with obvious recognition. "Come in, my lord, come in. I was remarking to my dear wife only the other day that it had been far too long since you last graced our humble shop. How, my lord, may I serve you?"

"Ah, Mr. Pettigrew," murmured the marquess, acknowledging Jane's dubious glance with a twitch at the corners of his lips. "Miss Winter has need of a pair of dress shoes. Something both tasteful and elegant. Let me see, how was it you described your gown, my dear? I forget. My lamentable memory, you understand."

"Your memory is every bit as good as mine, Nicky," Ethne mirthfully pointed out. "You know very well I have not described it to you."

"Have you not?" replied his lordship with a bemused air. "Odd, I was sure you had. Perhaps, then, you would care to correct that omission."

"Oh, very well. It is a draped tunic of mint green sarcenet with embroidered hem. I believe I have a swatch with me," Ethne added, reaching in her reticule. "Yes, here it is."

Danforth, accepting the piece of fabric, lifted it to the light to study it through his quizzing glass. "Ah, yes. I believe we must have a low shoe—satin with round toes. Yes, most definitely. The sort with a slit in the toecap to reveal a lining to match the dress. And rosettes, to carry out the theme of the embroidered hem. What think you, Mr. Pettigrew?"

"Excellent, as always, my lord. And, indeed, I have just the shoe," beamed that worthy, making toward a small recess at the back of the shop. "Of course the lining will have to be replaced to match the dress. A small matter of three days, no more. Two, if I have a pair already made to fit the young lady."

Mr. Pettigrew, returning, held out a pair of white satin slippers with rosettes and a slit in the toecap, just as the marquess had ordered. "Oh, yes," exclaimed Ethne, her eyes lighting, "they are perfect, but far too large. I can tell by looking."

"Indeed, my lady has a dainty, well-trimmed foot. If you would be so good as to take a seat, I shall soon have the measurements I need."

Danforth, allowing the quizzing glass to drop, met Jane's eyes over Ethne's shoulder. Irresistibly, she smiled, inclining her head in acknowledgment of a masterly stroke. She might have known his was no empty brag, she mused wryly. Danforth was known to be generous with the barques of frailty who had at one time or another enjoyed his protection. The thought that Danforth had kept mistresses did not shock her. She was no green girl. Indeed, she had cut her wisdoms long ago. Still, she could not quite suppress a strange pang disconcertingly like jealousy. Hastily, she turned away from the marquess's sardonic gaze and pretended to admire the various hats on display.

Pretense soon altered to real appreciation. From opera hoods with an exquisite intermingling of garland of roses and lilies of the valley to a turban headdress with semiprecious stones sewn into the fabric, they were all unique and lovely. In delight she wandered among dainty cornettes for indoor wearing, satin fillets and dainty lace caps, turbans, and small hats for dinner parties. There were high-crowned hats, narrow-brimmed hats, and poke-brimmed bonnets. It was the straw creations, however, which drew her, one in particular earning a small gasp of delight from her.

It was ridiculously frivolous, a straw poke bonnet, trimmed in lace and having an elegant profusion of bows and ribbons and spring flowers. It was like nothing she had worn since her girlhood, which in retrospect seemed fatuous and so far away. Indeed, she chided herself for a silly fool to even consider anything so blatantly trifling, sentimental, and gay. She was far too old for it and would no doubt look wholly ridiculous in it, and yet it appealed to that part of her that once had been so vital, a feminine, joyous side to her nature that she had almost forgotten.

Unexpectedly, her vision dimmed and she felt a lump rise in her throat, as it came to her that, in surviving her terrible loss of Geoffrey, she had lost something even more precious—her youth, squandered years when she might have been something other than a confirmed spinster serving as a companion to her widowed mama. How very empty her life suddenly seemed!

Stifling a sob that seemed to burst from her heart, she wheeled blindly away from the bonnet and into a pair of strong, masculine arms.

A startled "Oh!" broke from her lips, and Danforth's hands clasping her arms were all that kept her from falling.

"I beg your pardon, Miss Ashely," murmured the marquess. "It was not my intent to startle you."

"No, of course it was not. How silly," she gasped, placing a hand to her heaving breast. "I-I'm afraid I did not hear you come up behind me."

"No, how could you. You were intent on that bonnet. As well you might be. It is a fetching piece."

"Ye-s, but frivolous, don't you think?"

"Oh, absolutely," he agreed, smiling. "Which is why you shall try it on. Here, let me help you."

"Oh, no, I-I couldn't," Jane gasped in consternation as the nobleman reached to undo the bow beneath her chin. "Indeed I don't want to . . ."

"But of course you can and do. And why should you not? It is traditional, is it not?"

"Traditional, my lord?" queried Jane, ineffectually trying to prevent him from removing her own modest beehive straw bonnet which she usually affected.

"Easter," he explained, straight-faced. "Flowers stand for love, a deer for good health, the sun for good luck, the rooster for wishes that will come true, and a new Easter bonnet . . ."

"For good fortune in love," Jane finished for him.

"Quite so," he applauded, settling the frivolous concoction of ribbons and flowers over her curls and tying the bow beneath her chin. She felt his fingers still when the thing was done and looked up at him to find him staring at her with a singularly fixed expression. Jane's heart seemed momentarily to stop. Then the look was gone. "There," he said, gently turning her with his hands on her shoulders to face an ormolu mirror affixed to the wall.

Jane stared at the reflected image of herself and Danforth, framed in the oval of the looking glass like a portrait, and felt herself held spellbound. Indeed, she had the oddest sensation that she was seeing both of them for the very first time, and suddenly she read in the luminous depths of her eyes the terrible truth that had been so long knocking at the doors to her heart.

She loved him, wholly and irrevocably—Danforth, who had been the instrument in breaking her heart so long ago!

"It-it is lovely," she said, dropping her eyes from that betraying image in the mirror. His hands on her arms held her when she would have turned away, and she nearly gasped. "But I have no interest in that particular tradition." Striving for a humorous note, she added, "In spite of the fact that I received the last carling pea in the pot."

"Then you will wear it because it becomes you," Danforth answered, turning her to face him. A hand beneath her chin, he gently forced her to look at him. "And because it would please me to purchase it for you. No, no, do not plead the proprieties, I beg you. It is, after all, only a bonnet, Miss Ashely. A mere folderol, not an offer of carte blanche."

Stunned into speechlessness at the warm light in his eyes and reeling from the revelation that had come to her as she gazed into the looking glass, Jane could only stare wordlessly back at him.

She could hardly know the entrancing picture she made, her lovely face framed in the lace and silk frills of the bonnet, her eyes huge and luminous against the pallor of her skin. She appeared absurdly young, hardly more than a schoolroom miss, and strangely vulnerable. Danforth caught his breath at sight of her.

"Quite so," he murmured with an odd sort of finality, and, lightly flicking her under the chin with a careless finger, he left her to pay for their purchases.

Thirteen

The afternoon shopping trip to Bond Street marked a sudden, dramatic change in Jane's relationship with Danforth. Jane, carried on an irresistible impulse, dropped the barrier of unswerving politeness, which she had maintained since those first days at Melcourt; and the marquess no longer played least seen in her affairs. On the contrary, it was observed by an interested *Beau Monde* that Danforth gave every appearance of a man on the hunt.

From that day forward, not an afternoon passed that Jane was not to be seen in Hyde Park perched beside Danforth on the seat of his curricle; and in the evenings, it became commonly accepted that at whatever social function Miss Jane Ashely chose to put in an appearance, Danforth was sure to attend. To have the *Nonpareil* appear at a musicale, a soiree, and an impromptu rout on successive nights was remarkable enough, but to have him materialize at Almack's to stand up with Miss Ashely for the waltz was tantamount to a declaration.

The effect on Jane's popularity was twofold. Ambitious hostesses desirous of a *success fou* made it a point to include Miss Ashely on their invitation lists in the knowledge that with her acceptance would come Danforth's as well. With the result that, not a day passed that she was not inundated with invitations. While her popular demand increased dramatically, however, the number of hopefuls for her hand in marriage was reduced in like proportion, until there remained only her four loyal swains and Danforth. Of these, Beauchamp appeared to have formally withdrawn from the lists, although he continued to seek Jane out and to treat her with an unfailingly warm regard. Hazleton, too, dropped steadily in the betting books, Danforth taking the earl's place as the odds-on favorite to win.

Jane, preoccupied with more important concerns, seemed oblivious to her changed status, save in the matter of the marked attention Danforth was paying her. This, she did not interpret as a serious bid for either her heart or her hand. Danforth, she told herself repeatedly as she lay awake at nights prey to her own secret yearnings, had chosen to appear to be paying her court as a means of ensuring Ethne's safety and perhaps in some measure her own.

He did not love her. He could not. He had made it clear that night at Vauxhall Gardens that there would always be the spectre of Geoffrey's death between them.

Consequently, she found herself torn between torment and a strange thrilling happiness at finding herself thrown so much in his company. No matter how often she might tell herself that she must put an end to the charade either by refusing to see him or by returning home to Oaks at once, she could not find the will to do either. Ruefully she acknowledged to herself that she was a coward. She could not deny herself the bittersweet moments spent with him any more than she could stop breathing. They were all she would ever have.

Her own tumultuous heart should have been enough with which to contend without the added worry of Ethne. That, however, was not to be. The child, displaying a sudden perversity of character, seemed determined to wreck her own future and destroy whatever chance she had ever had with Phillip Maheux. Where, before, Phillip had seemed to loom as the only man in her life, she now made eyes at seemingly everyone in masculine attire. She was, in fact, according to an anxious Mina, fast becoming an unconscionable flirt; and, though Maheux remained loyal, he had assumed the aspect of a brooding, unhappy young man.

Jane, sensing some motivating factor behind the girl's reckless behavior, tried talking with her, to no avail, and ended up threatening to return her posthaste to her mama if she did not cease to behave like a complete and utter hoyden. Jane thought she would not soon forget the look on the girl's face when Ethne had flung back that she would just as soon go now as later.

There was a mystery here that did not bode well for Ethne's happiness.

The arrival of Good Friday found Ethne in one of her bewilderingly radiant moods in sharp contrast to the maddeningly haughty, short-tempered young lady she had been only the day before. This swift change in the girl, Jane attributed to the delivery at breakfast of an invitation to attend an impromptu rout that evening at Maria Fitzhugh's. Snatching the written invitation from Jane's hand, she had rushed eagerly from the room presumably to scribble a reply in the affirmative.

Jane stared after her, perplexed and troubled. She did not trust the mood to last. Indeed, she suspected it to be borne of something very like desperation. She had just made up her mind to talk to Ethne again, to plead with the child, if necessary, to confide in her, when Danforth had arrived bearing with him a basket of freshly baked hot cross buns to celebrate the day and an invitation to go riding in the Park.

Instantly all thoughts of Ethne had fled as she hurried upstairs to change into her riding habit; and when she returned later that morning, flushed and feeling ridiculously like singing, Ethne had already left the house with the intention of spending the day with Maria Fitzhugh.

Jane did not see Ethne again until that evening at the Fitzhughs, and then she immediately sensed a brittleness in the girl's gaiety that both troubled and alarmed her. Indeed, not even the glad surprise of seeing Freddy, intriguingly pale and drawn, his left arm in a sling, but somehow marvelous to look upon, could completely allay an uneasy feeling that all was not well with the girl.

Freddy crossed quickly to Jane, his smile erasing the traces of havoc and something of sadness from his face and transforming him into the glad, clear-eyed youth she had remembered at Melcourt.

"Freddy, how *good* to see you," she exclaimed, giving him her hand.

"Not half so good as it is to see you, Miss Jane. Mama said you came to inquire about me. That was kind in you. I'm only sorry I was asleep and missed you."

Jane gave him a long, searching look. "How are you, really, Freddy?"

In answer, he gave a dismissive wave of the hand. "It was bad at first, but I'm nearly over it. I hope to be returning to my regiment in a few weeks."

"So soon?" murmured Jane, experiencing a pang at the thought of the danger to which he would return. "But then of course you must be anxious to take up where you left off. Promise you will come and see me before you go."

"I shall, certainly, Miss Jane. And thank you. I've never forgotten your kindness to Ethne and me at Melcourt."

Jane, watching him stroll away, marveled at something new she had sensed in him. More than his courage had been tried during those terrible weeks in Spain. She remembered what Danforth had said that last day at Melcourt, that Freddy would experience a deal more than he had bargained for. They could not have been truer words. Freddy had been tested and forced to survive and endure. He was a boy no longer, she realized with something like sadness.

Her gaze went to Ethne, laughing up into the handsome features of a dark-haired youth, who wore a stunned look of adoration. Jane sighed. It seemed all too apparent to Jane that Viscount Edgemont had fallen, another victim to Ethne's spell.

It was then, when all the guests had arrived and Maria Fitzhugh, holding hands with Lord Featherstone, blushingly announced their engagement, that Jane glimpsed the torment behind Ethne's determined mask of gaiety. At first she thought in disbelief that it was Lord Featherstone's defection to Maria that had caused that swift blur of pain to cross Ethne's face. But then, the girl's glance had gone to Freddy and young Maheux, standing together on the far side of the room. A blaze of longing flashed in those lovely eyes at sight of Phillip, then altered swiftly to regret, compassion, guilt— what?—at sight of Freddy?

Jane could not think what that look had meant beyond the certainty that the child loved Phillip Maheux. Still, she had a strong premonition that Ethne had every intention of refusing the young nobleman's offer of marriage. Faith, it made no sense.

As the evening progressed, Jane found herself, to her bemusement, settled among the matrons along the sidelines while the younger set amused themselves with a game of charades. Ethne gave every appearance of one who was enjoying herself immensely, save perhaps that she was a trifle too bright.

Still, the rout appeared to be a resounding success, if a little boisterous, until Maria Fitzhugh unfortunately felt it necessary to mention that, due to the marble tournament held at Tinsley Green near Crawley every year on that day, Good Friday was known as Marbles Day in her home county of

Sussex. No doubt it was Lord Featherstone, who prided himself on being top-of-the-trees at any sport or game, who suggested they stage their own tournament in the middle of Lady Fitzhugh's claret-colored Ushak rug.

Almost immediately the idea caught on. The girls laughingly assumed the task of searching the nursery upstairs for Albert Fitzhugh's collection of marbles, while the gentlemen contrived a marble ring six feet in diameter out of yarn.

When the girls returned some few minutes later with a wooden box containing Albert's collection, forty-nine marbles were placed, according to the rules Maria quoted, in the center of the circle. Amidst a great deal of laughter and banter, six gentlemen, including Featherstone and Phillip Maheux, each with a tolley three-eighths of an inch in diameter held between thumb and forefinger, took up positions around the ring to shoot for the order of the turns.

It was at that point that Maria Fitzhugh was overheard to remark to Miss French that the tournament had its inception in Elizabethan days when a local maiden persuaded her suitors to fight for her hand at a game of marbles. "Since then, of course," she added knowledgeably, "a silver cup has always gone to the champions, while the runners-up receive a firkin of ale."

"Why, then, it wouldn't be right not to have a trophy for the winner," declared Featherstone, frowning. "What shall it be?"

Lady Fitzhugh refusing in no uncertain terms to sacrifice her silver-gilt campana-shaped two-handled cup, which had been in the family for four generations, to serve as a trophy, a lively discussion ensued in which various items were suggested and as quickly discarded.

Jane, nodding with a glazed smile as Lady Billingston prosed on about the beneficial properties of mineral waters, especially as regarded putrefaction of the liver and kidneys, did not see who made the fatal suggestion, but she heard it, as well as Lady Fitzhugh's scandalized gasp, accompanied by a murmur of disapproval among the other matrons. She very much feared it was one of Ethne's unfortunate victims, one, moreover, so madly infatuated he dared to do the girl insult in his wish for a token of her favor.

Whatever the case, one of Ethne's raven curls had been proposed as the winner's trophy, a suggestion to which Phillip Maheux took immediate exception.

"I must assume you meant that as a jest, Edgemont," he declared, coolly stepping forward to face the dark-haired, bedazzled-looking youth, whom Jane had noticed earlier. Clearly the youth bridled at the implications in Maheux's tone of voice. "You will admit, however, it was a poor one. Naturally, Miss Winter could never consider anything so preposterous."

Thrilled at the bold front Phillip made, Jane could only be grateful for his manly intervention. There was something noble and compelling in his leap to Ethne's defense.

Edgemont stiffened. "I admit to nothing, Maheux. Certainly I was not in jest. I suggest we leave it to Miss Winter to decide."

"Indeed, how dare you speak for me, Phillip Maheux?" demanded a haughty young voice. Jane's heart sank at the sight of Ethne, white-faced and trembling, her bearing imperious. "I do not think it in the least preposterous. Indeed, I should be pleased to give one of my curls to the victor."

"Ethne, you cannot mean that," spoke up Freddy. His lean countenance, earnest and pale, worked strangely on Ethne. She blushed, then went pearly white, and for the moment could not meet his eyes.

Then her head came up with a defiant toss of her curls. "But I do mean it," she said. "And I'll thank you, Freddy Bartholomew, not to interfere in my affairs."

"Oh!" gasped Lady Fitzhugh, clasping a hand to her generous bosom. "Scandalous."

Jane started to rise from her chair, thinking to drag Ethne away, if need be, to put a halt to the absurd business before it went any further. She was stopped by the sight of a tall, arrogant figure, limned against the open doorway.

"The Marquess of Danforth," intoned the butler, bowing then retreating, as the marquess strode past him into the room.

For a single, breathless moment, a taut, crackling silence fell over the company. Then Mrs. Fitzhugh, overcoming her shock at the unseemly turn events had taken and realizing with a swelling burst of pride the unexpected honor Danforth had bestowed upon her by his mere presence at anything so insignificant as an impromptu rout, surged upright, bosom heaving, to greet the *Nonpareil.*

"My lord marquess," she crooned, sailing forth with billowing skirts. "How kind of you to come."

"No doubt," murmured the nobleman. His thin lips assumed the faintest of smiles. "How kind of you to invite me." Lifting the quizzing glass to his eye, he swept the assembled guests, intriguingly suspended in various and frozen attitudes. "Ah, Ethne," he murmured. "Young Maheux, I believe. And Freddy. I see everyone is present. Pray do not let me disturb you. By all means, continue as you were."

"Oh, but, my Lord Danforth, I cannot think . . ." Here Lady Fitzhugh's voice appeared to fail her, struck silent, no doubt, by Danforth's imperious lift of an eyebrow. By that, and the sudden swift realization that her supreme moment of triumph was on the point of crumbling to dust around her. Clearly she paled at the daunting aspect of the marquess, carelessly swinging the quizzing glass on its ribbon to and fro, while he waited for her to complete the statement that would disgrace his sister and earn for herself the Corinthian's chilling disdain.

At that moment Jane felt almost sorry for her.

"I-I cannot but think you are right, my lord," trilled Lady Fitzhugh at last, giving in to forces clearly greater than herself. "Do go on with your game, gentlemen."

There was a nervous twitter. The Corinthian dropped his quizzing glass to the end of its ribbon. Then, as, nodding here and there to the various seated matrons, he made his way to Jane, the room appeared to spring into motion.

Maheux knelt with singular determination before the playing ring. Freddy, his face grim, shouldered Featherstone aside and took his place among the shooters, while Ethne, clasping her hands tightly before her, looked on with every aspect of a French aristocrat on the way to the guillotine.

"A charming little farce you've chosen," remarked Danforth, draping himself languidly over the arm and back of Jane's overstuffed chair. He raised his quizzing glass, the better to observe the scene of ritualistic combat. "Really, Miss Ashely, we shall have to do something to cure you of this odd preference of yours for low comedy. It can hardly compare, after all, do you think, to Mrs. Siddons's farewell performance as Lady Macbeth?"

"Hardly, my lord," answered Jane, her eyes dancing, "but what might have been tragic has hopefully been rendered harmless by your timely arrival. And for that, sir, I can only be grateful."

At this, his eyes fell speculatively on the clear-cut profile of her face as she watched Freddy kneel to shoot.

"Grateful, Miss Ashely?" he murmured, resting the quizzing glass against his chin. "Does it not occur to you that your gratitude is misplaced?"

Startled, Jane lifted her eyes to his. "I beg your pardon, my lord?"

Danforth smiled mirthlessly.

"Ethne, Miss Ashely," he said. "The little baggage is my

sister. Does it not seem passing strange that you should feel grateful whenever I choose to fulfill my obligations to her?"

Jane flushed, immediately grasping his meaning. "But, my lord, I never meant—"

"Of course you did, as well you might," he drawled, with a glitter of amusement. "You, my dear, have a happy knack for making me feel ashamed, an emotion to which I am ill-accustomed. I should be better pleased if you would refrain from practicing it in the future."

"Would you?" Jane dimpled irresistibly. "No doubt I shall try and remember that, my lord, if ever it is my wish to please you."

"Jade," remarked the nobleman with obvious feeling.

Jane smiled, but did not comment as an excited chorus of female voices and a cheer drew her attention to the marble game that was well in progress.

What had begun half an hour earlier as a lighthearted diversion had changed to something altogether different, Jane realized, noting Phillip Maheux's stern-lipped intensity. How young he was, and yet how quick to come to Ethne's defense! Jane feared the child did not realize her good fortune. Maheux, for all his youth, had a gentleman's instincts and a man's determination to save her from her own folly. Oh, how very like Geoffrey he was—proud and passionate. No doubt Maheux would have been just as quick to fight for Ethne with pistols or swords. And Freddy, too, she thought. Loyal, generous Freddy. He would do anything for Ethne.

It had been bad enough for Ethne to offer a lock of her hair as a trophy to the winner. Doubtlessly she would be called forward and headstrong, but if she actually gave up one of her curls, she would be considered beneath reproach. It simply was not to be thought of. Still, Jane knew Ethne would go through with it. Her pride would not allow for anything else. The only thing that could save her from the toil she had made for herself was for someone to win who would not demand the token of her. And that could only be Phillip or Freddy!

Phillip drove a pair of marbles from the circle with a single shot, then shifted position to shoot again with grim-faced deliberation.

Of the six shooters, he had the largest collection of captured marbles and had yet to lose his tolley. Freddy was running a close second, with Viscount Edgemont not far behind.

Phillip shot. His tolley hit and bounced off a gleaming cat's-eye. Jane stifled a groan as neither marble made it outside the circle. Phillip had lost his tolley and his turn.

Rising, he stood face to face with Edgemont with hardly six inches between them.

"I say, old man," drawled the viscount, "do you mind?"

Phillip, holding Edgemont's eyes a moment longer, inclined his head in stiff formality and stepped back out of the way. Silently Jane groaned. Pray God, it went no further than a duel with marbles.

Only four marbles remained in the ring as Edgemont knelt, aimed and impelled the tolley forward with his thumb. The tolley struck and scored a captured marble, placing him even with Freddy. He shot again and scored. One more placed him even with Phillip.

Jane was watching Ethne's face, as Edgemont knelt to take aim at the winning marble. Consequently, she did not see the tolley shoot into the circle and score the final marble.

Ethne paled perceptibly. Edgemont bounded triumphantly to his feet. Freddy leaped forward.

"HOLD! I cry fudge!"

Edgemont froze. "Say, what do you mean by that?"

"Your hand moved when you shot," Freddy declared.

"Oh, it did, I saw it," cried Miss French.

"That is a fudge," pronounced Maria Fitzhugh. "You lose

your turn and forfeit the marble you hit out, in addition to one other. That makes it Freddy's turn."

"The devil it does!" objected Edgemont, glaring at Maria.

There was a sudden flutter of fans among the matrons, and Mrs. Fitzhugh gasped. "Oh, dear God, I knew no good could come of this. If only the colonel were here."

Upon which, Featherstone stepped forward to shove his face into the viscount's. "Forgetting yourself, ain't you, Edgemont? Bad *ton* to employ language better suited to a stable before the gentler sex. Have a mind to land you a facer."

Edgemont bridled with resentment.

"You are mistaken, Featherstone," he retorted stiffly. "You haven't a mind at all."

Featherstone's face went a dusky red, and he was furiously struggling to rid himself of his coat, when Maheux stepped hastily between the two.

"Egad, Chester," he uttered fiercely in a voice too low for the female contingent to hear. "Think what you are doing. Think of Miss Fitzhugh. You can't draw a man's cork in your future mama-in-law's living room. And you, Edgemont, stand back. You've caused enough trouble this night."

"The hell you say, Maheux," bristled the viscount.

"No, Edgemont," came in slow, cool accents. "*I* say."

Edgemont's head turned, and he paled to a sickly gray at sight of the marquess, lounging negligently a short distance away, absently swinging the quizzing glass to and fro on its ribbon.

"My lord!" breathed Edgemont in a strangled voice.

"Quite so." Danforth smiled faintly. "And you, my young friend, are in grave danger of becoming a dead bore. If you cannot behave as a sportsman, at least remember what is expected of a gentleman. It would be a shame, don't you think, to disrupt Miss Fitzhugh's party?"

Edgemont flushed and then seemed to jerk to attention. "You are right, of course, my lord. I am afraid I forgot myself. It is only that I—" The young nobleman flashed a single eloquent glance at Ethne, then away again. "But no matter." Manfully, he turned to a blushing Maria and stiffly bowed. "Miss Fitzhugh, I apologize for my ungentlemanly behavior. Naturally, I accept your judgment and forfeit the win."

Maheux's hand fell on Edgemont's shoulder. "It was well-played, Edgemont. I call it a draw, if Bartholomew agrees, and suggest we celebrate with a bowl of punch. What say you?"

"I'd say that sounds an excellent notion," agreed the viscount. Obviously relieved for an excuse to remove himself from the *Nonpareil's* unnerving stare, he allowed himself to be escorted to the refreshment table.

The rest of the young people crowded around the two Marbles Day champions—save for Ethne, who had not moved, and Freddy, who stood staring across the marble ring at her.

There was something poignant in the look that passed between them. Then Ethne's head came up, and her eyes flashed with a strange compelling light. She turned away. Freddy, as if spurred into action, went after her and, catching her by the arm, pulled her out on to the terrace.

Jane, concerned, would have gone after them, had not Danforth stopped her, a hand light on her wrist.

"Leave them be. They are not likely to come to any trouble out there, and I have no intention of being abandoned to the sycophantic attentions of our hostess. You will be doing her a kindness by staying. Left to endure her notions of scintillating conversation, I should shortly be moved to throttle her."

Jane gave into a helpless gurgle of laughter. "Oh, how abominable you are."

"Indeed, ma'am," replied the marquess.

Jane stilled, arrested by the light, piercing intensity of his gaze. "Very well, then," she answered. "For Lady Fitzhugh's sake. And then only until Ethne comes back. I had already made up my mind to go home. I have been thinking it was time I had a talk with Ethne. And after tonight, I fear it cannot wait any longer."

Danforth waved a deprecating hand. "Then rest assured. Your fear is unfounded. Very likely it can be put off indefinitely."

"Indefinitely, my lord?" echoed Jane in astonishment. "Surely you cannot have failed to see that the child is not herself? She is obviously unhappy and deeply troubled by something."

"I should think nothing could be *more* obvious, Miss Ashely," agreed the nobleman with a sardonic gleam of amusement. "I have observed in the past six months of my guardianship, however, that that is the normal state for my half-sister. I should not refine on it were I you."

"Oh, how can you say so?" Jane exclaimed. "I am fond of Ethne, and I do refine on what may be driving her to ruin her chances for future happiness."

Danforth smiled cynically. "Yes, Miss Ashely, and how not, when it would not be in your nature to do otherwise. However, there is not the slightest reason for you to concern yourself with Ethne's problems, real or imaginary. If she requires a curtain lecture over this night's foolishness, then leave it to someone like Freddy, who is far more likely to succeed in discovering the source of this latest start of hers. Or to me, Miss Ashely. If I cannot appeal to her better nature, I can at least make certain she does nothing further to draw undue attention to herself."

"You mean you would send her home in disgrace to her mother," Jane said with bitter certainty.

The cool mocking light in Danforth's eyes was Jane's only answer.

"But surely you must realize that would ruin her? It would spoil her chances of ever marrying creditably. She loves Phillip Maheux. If you can be so unfeeling as to wash your hands of her, I, sir, cannot."

Danforth gave every impression of a man fast succumbing to an advanced state of ennui. "Naturally, you will do as you see fit, Miss Ashely. It was never my intention, however, that you play nursemaid to Ethne."

"Was it not? Then perhaps I was mistaken," retorted Jane, hurt and bewildered by his calloused indifference. "I confess your intentions have never been quite clear to me."

Danforth's harsh, enigmatic laugh seemed to flay her sensibilities. "I am well aware of that, but I remain hopeful of one day remedying that situation. In the meantime, you will be glad to know that I have decided to remove Ethne from your brother's house. Now that Aunt Caroline is here, after all, there is hardly need to impose further on you or your sister-in-law."

"I see," Jane said faintly, struggling against a sudden sickening sensation. "You wish to remove her from my influence."

Danforth regarded her with expressionless eyes.

"Yes, Miss Ashely," he admitted baldly, "in a manner of speaking."

Jane stared at him, rendered speechless by something cold and inexplicably hard in his face. Faith, what a fool she had been to believe he might care for her, even a little, that beneath the cynical facade of the Corinthian was something noble and fine. He had made it plain that he did not approve of the manner in which she had influenced Ethne. Good God, he blamed *her* for the girl's inexplicable behavior! Indeed, he had all but ordered her to have nothing more to do with his sister.

Well, he would have his wish. The Easter Ball on the morrow would see the fulfillment of her final obligation to Ethne. Easter Sunday would find her packed and on her way to Melcourt, and the devil fly away with Danforth!

Fourteen

"Removing her from Melcourt House! But why?" demanded Mina of Jane some thirty minutes after that final, disastrous conversation with Danforth. "Surely he cannot blame us for what happened at Lady Fitzhugh's tonight. You did say, did you not, nothing came of it, thanks to Phillip Maheux's intervention?"

Jane, who had arrived in her rooms some fifteen minutes earlier to encounter her sister-in-law waiting up for her, crossed wearily to her dressing table to remove her diamond necklace and earrings before answering. "Yes, he and Freddy between them took care that there will be no slur on Ethne's name. They were quite wonderful, really."

Mina threw up her hands. "Then I do not understand. Unless it was because I elected to stay home. Oh, that must be it. And he is no doubt in the right of it. I simply did not dream that I should be needed. Lady Fitzhugh assured me it would be a small intimate party made up solely of young people."

"And so it was, Mina," Jane hastened to reassure the distraught countess. "Of course he did not hold you responsible. It is only that since Lady Caroline has taken up residence in his town house, he saw no reason to impose on your kindness. And nor do I, especially now that you are increasing. You know very well that you should not be up till all hours of the night in your present condition. It is not good for you or the baby. Danforth was only being thoughtful."

How easily the lie came from her lips, Jane marveled as she stood for Mina to undo the numerous small fastenings at the back of her gown. At last, kissing the other woman fondly on the cheek and assuring her that she was perfectly capable of undressing herself, she sent Mina firmly off to her bed.

Only then, when she was alone at last, did she allow the mask to drop from her face. How glad she was that she had given Nanny Twickum strict orders not to wait up for her. She was equally relieved that Ethne, showing no disposition to confide in her, had gone straight to her room upon arriving at Melcourt House. Jane wanted only to be alone in order to sort out this dreadful thing that had happened to her.

She felt stunned by the realization that she had been living in a fool's paradise, allowing her emotions to overrule her head. But it was over now. Danforth had made it plain that the past week had been only an elaborate charade, his charming front only a deceitful cover—for what? No doubt she had fallen victim to one of his infamous flirtations, and once he had realized her capitulation, he had lost interest, just as he had with all the others before her.

A searing blush swept over her then receded, leaving her feeling sick and cold. Oh, how *could* she have been so naive as to believe there could ever be anything between them! And yet, she knew she had, in spite of all her reasoning to the contrary. Somewhere deep inside her, she had allowed herself to hope. But no more. If she could not kill her love, she would at least smother that last, lingering voice that told her to wait and see, to withhold judgment. Faith, if only she did not feel this terrible rending beneath her breast! She did not see how she could bear it. And yet she had once before. She would not die of it, just as she had not died that other time, no matter how much she might have wished to have done.

She had one final obligation to Ethne, and then she would be free to return home, she told herself, to Oaks, her garden, and long rides on Nesta. There she could hide her hurt and bury herself once more in the healing solitude of the country. There she could dream and learn to forget as she had done before. No doubt it were better so, she told herself. Love was vastly overrated, if this was what it did to one. She would be better off without it, for what had it ever brought her but pain and anguish too dreadful to contemplate?

If only she dared cry off from the ball, she thought. And, indeed, why should she not? Ethne no longer needed her, and she certainly had no wish ever to lay eyes on Danforth again. Faith, she did not see how she could bear the shame of knowing she had lost her heart to a man who so obviously held her beneath contempt. But why? What had she done to make him think she was not fit company for his sister?

Faith, how could she have been so mistaken in him? How could she have allowed him to break down the defenses she had so painstakingly built for herself? How loathsome and vile he was! Had he not hurt her enough long before she had had the misfortune to meet and fall in love with him? No doubt he was enjoying himself immensely at her expense. To think that she had been just one more victim in his long line of conquests was humiliating enough without the realization that she had allowed herself to be convinced he was too fine and honorable to have had anything to do with Geoffrey's death. And, indeed, even now she could not bring herself to believe it.

Oh, it was too much. She loved him, and she could not accept he was not what she had come to believe him to be.

At last, worn out, her emotions spent, she finished dressing for bed and crawled beneath the satin comforter, only to discover she could not sleep. She lay awake long into the night, staring into the darkness, prey to conflicting images of Danforth, until at last she could not endure her sleepless torment any longer.

Flinging aside the bedcovers, she slipped from bed and donned her dressing gown and slippers. If she could not sleep, perhaps she could deaden her unrewarding thoughts with a book from her brother's library. With a candle in hand, she let herself out of her room and closed the door behind her.

A sound or perhaps a subtle movement of shadow along the hall caused her to halt in her footsteps. In the gloom beyond the fragile circle of candlelight, she could make out little beyond what seemed a formless shadow hovering near the door to Ethne's room. Surely it was too late for one of the servants to be about, she thought, even as her heart began most inexplicably to pound.

"Ethne?" she called, lifting the candle high. "Is that you?" She knew as soon as the words were out that it was not. "Who are you? What are you doing there?"

Instantly the intruder bolted, fleeing down the hall to the servants' stairs and vanishing. Jane, nearly sick with fear for Ethne's safety, rushed to the girl's door. Opening it without knocking, she stole inside and made her way to the bed. She went nearly weak with relief at the sight of Ethne peacefully asleep.

Noiselessly she withdrew from the room and, closing the door, leaned against it while she waited for her knees to stop their trembling. What must she do now? she wondered. Surely she must awaken her brother and tell him of the figure in the hall. Whoever it was, that person was still in the house. She shuddered at the thought, then tried to gather her wits and her courage to make that walk through the dark-enshrouded hall to her brother's room.

As she pushed herself away from the door, something on the floor at her feet caught the light of the candle, flashing white. Curiously, she knelt and reached down to retrieve a sheet of paper, folded and sealed with wax. A letter! The intruder had been about to slip it beneath Ethne's door when he had been interrupted. No doubt he had dropped it in his haste to escape.

Setting the candle on a cherrywood occasional table in the hall, Jane broke the seal with only the slightest twinge of conscience and unfolded the paper.

Ethne's name seemed to leap out at her. Hastily she scanned the message, written in a bold hand. A low gasp broke from her lips, and her face paled. Then, trembling, she crumpled the paper in her hand and, taking up the candle again, made her way back to her room. All thought of awakening her brother was forgotten in the greater turmoil of what she had just learned.

A great deal about Ethne's perplexing behavior had been made suddenly and dreadfully clear. Indeed, Jane's heart went out in pity to the girl if in truth this was not, as the letter had hinted, the first such message to have been delivered to her. Unsigned, it was a dreadful, spiteful letter, meant deliberately to frighten and intimidate the child into doing the will of a man who meant her nothing but evil.

Nor was that all or the worst of it. The villain threatened to blacken Freddy's name and ruin his career if Ethne did not follow his instructions. Oh, how dared he pretend to have in his possession documents that would prove Freddy a coward and a traitor! They were false, whatever they were, and full of lies. Freddy was incapable of doing a base or cowardly deed.

Oh, if only Ethne had trusted her, how much heartache might she not have been saved!

Now, however, she must think what to do. The hideous letter directed Ethne to leave the Easter Ball and wait along the carriage drive for a messenger with instructions to take her to a rendezvous. There would be a carriage and the man

waiting to take her up. The devil to plot the ruin of an innocent girl! Jane shivered at the thought of how close he had
come to succeeding in it. The villain must be stopped, and,
more, he must be prevented from ever doing this again to
someone else. But how?

She did not have to look far to find the answer. Little as
she might like it, there was only one possible solution, and
that was to entrust the entire matter to Danforth.

The following morning, Jane rose early after a fitful night
and immediately upon dressing, sent a hurriedly written note
to Danforth, asking him to call at his earliest possible convenience on a matter of no little importance.

When Rupert had departed with her missive, Jane was left
to pace and wring her hands in nervous dread of the coming
interview with Danforth. In vain did she chide herself for a
silly fool, she, who had always prided herself on her steady
nerve and calm composure. Deliberately, she forced herself
to sit down at the breakfast table, though the very last thing
she could countenance was the notion of food. Even the
thought of coffee and toast was repugnant when one's stomach was behaving in a most unsettling fashion.

She was on the point of abandoning even the pretense of
eating, when Rupert returned with the news that his lordship
was out. "I left your message with the butler, m'lady. He
promised he would see his lordship received it as soon as he
returned, though he couldn't say for sure when that would
be, considering his lordship's uncertain habits. I'm sorry,
m'lady."

Assuring the footman that he had done just as he should
and dismissing him, Jane stood for a long moment in an-
guished indecision.

A plague on Danforth! How very like the insufferable nobleman to be gone just when she needed him the most. Faith, what if he had gone, as he had before, not to return for weeks, perhaps months! What was she to do? To whom could she turn?

Not Beauchamp or Hazleton, or her other devoted friends, surely, she thought, pacing as she went over the possibilities. No one must know of the slur on Freddy's name. Even false, it could not but reflect badly on him, raise doubts about his courage and his honor as a gentleman and an officer in the king's army. She could not allow that! Indeed, she was left with only one recourse. She must confide in her brother, and that was possibly the very last thing she wished to do. Not that Melcourt was not perfectly capable of dealing with the situation. Indeed, she did not doubt for a moment that he was. It was only that she could not like to involve him in what might very likely prove dangerous. Mina would never forgive her if something happened to Wilfred. Indeed, Jane would never forgive herself.

Still, she told herself that she ought to trust him to know what was best to do. Reluctantly, she left the breakfast room with the idea of sending Langston upstairs to inquire if the earl had risen yet and to inform him that his sister wished an audience as soon as was possible. She was stopped by the sound of the front door knocker, followed soon after by voices below, one of which was recognizably Langston's and the other's—Danforth! She could not mistake the cool, drawling arrogance of tone.

Immediately all rational thought fled before the arousal of a flood of sensations, chief of which were a swift beating of her heart, followed by the feeling that she had just contracted a fast mounting fever. Faith, it was too much, she thought, furiously wishing the marquess to the devil for having transformed her into a detestable creature, weak-willed and prey to a bewildering array of emotions.

But he was here, and suddenly she was at the head of the stairs without knowing quite how she had gotten there.

"Danforth! Oh, you have come!"

She thought her heart might fail her as those light piercing eyes lifted to impale her. Then heedless of how it might look, she had gathered up her skirts and was running down the stairs to meet him.

"Jane!" Strong hands closed on her arms, kept her from falling. Then he was leading her, half supporting her with his arm around her shoulders. "That will be all, Langston," she heard him say as from a distance. "Oh, and, Langston, Miss Ashely will not be in to callers."

"Very well, m'lord," intoned Langston.

Jane wondered half hysterically what the stone-faced butler must be thinking of her exceedingly odd behavior, as she allowed herself to be led into the downstairs withdrawing-room. She marveled at how low she must have sunk that she could not even bring herself to care what he thought.

No sooner had Danforth closed the door behind them, than she was clinging shamelessly to him. "I-I thought you had gone again. I didn't know to-to whom to turn. When I think of what that poor child has had to endure. And Freddy. Poor dear Freddy. It is so unfair." Her fingers clutched at his lapels, clung there. "Danforth, you were right. You must take her away at once!"

A single piercing look into her face, then Danforth wrapped her in his arms and held her. His strength enfolding her, his strong hand stroking her hair—it was too much for her. With a gasp, she broke into tears and wept unrestrainedly.

"Softly, child. No harm will come to Ethne," said Danforth, grim-faced, his eyes steely points of flame. After a while, when her weeping had subsided, his hands closed on her arms, held her a little away from him. He bent his head to look into her face. "Tell me what has happened."

Jane drew a long shuddering breath and, suddenly keenly aware of the spectacle she had made of herself, she drew back with a nervous laugh.

"What a fool you must think me," she gasped, brushing at her wet cheeks with her fingertips. "I-I am not usually a wet goose. Indeed, I loathe being made a watering pot. It is so detestably feminine!"

"A hideous prospect," Danforth agreed, but his smile was singularly devoid of mirth. He pressed a linen handkerchief into her hand. "Now, tell me."

She laughed shakily and blew her nose. "There was an intruder here last night, or at least that is what I thought at the time, though now I am more inclined to believe he was someone of the household. One of the servants. It was very late. I couldn't sleep. I thought to get a book from the library." She made a fluttering gesture with her hand. "He was hovering at Ethne's door. I called out to him—something. I don't remember what. He ran." She drew from the plaquet pocket in her dress the letter and handed it to Danforth as though she could not bear the touch of it. "It is hideous, vile. He must have dropped it when I startled him."

She turned away while Danforth opened it and read. When she looked back again, he was composed, hard, his face inscrutable. She shuddered.

"What will you do?"

"Find him. Put an end to it." At last he looked at her. "You must not concern yourself with it. Trust me to look after Ethne."

"I-I do . . . trust you." Her gaze faltered, then, suddenly troubled, lifted to his face. Unconsciously she stepped closer to him. "You intend to fight him, kill him in a duel."

It was not a question. She knew what he intended. Her blood ran cold at the utter certainty.

"Danforth, you mustn't," she exclaimed softly. Her hands

going out to him, came to rest on his chest. Earnestly she gazed up into his face. "Think what season it is. Easter. Think what it would mean to you to be involved in another duel. Even Prinnie cannot save you from disgrace. You will be condemned, forced into exile. Danforth, you cannot do it."

She felt a shudder shake his lean, strong frame. His voice, when he spoke, was colorless and cold.

"Do not be foolish, child. It will never go so far. I told you not to concern yourself."

It was a lie, she knew it with utter certainty. His hands closed about her wrists. She clung, refusing to be dislodged.

"But I am concerned. I ask you not to do this. I beg you not to kill him. His life is not worth ruining yours. Think of Ethne. Your mother. Think of-of me."

"You?" He laughed, his composure broken at last. "Surely you forget yourself. Why should I think of you?"

"Because—because I should not wish to have you go. Because I have come to-to depend on you." The truth trembled on her lips, and in another moment she knew she would betray herself. "Because I . . ."

His eyes narrowed on her face, blazed with a blue fire that seared her soul and robbed her of further speech. He bent over her to peer into her face. "Jane Ashely," he uttered strangely. "*You* ask me to spare this man? The villain who plotted to ruin my sister?"

She sank in his grip, suddenly afraid, wondering what she had unloosed. From somewhere she found the strength to answer him.

"Yes, I-I ask it of you!"

Never before had she seen such contempt, such terrible look of condemnation as he turned on her then. With a low cry, she shrank from him.

For a terrible moment she thought he meant to strike her.

Then with a sudden fierce, burning passion, he crushed her to him.

"Then it was true," he whispered hoarsely. His eyes accused her. "All of it! Damn your treacherous heart. Geoffrey died for you, the poor besotted fool. But I was the greater fool. I took the blame to save your precious name."

"Save me from—what?" Jane gasped, stunned with disbelief. "Those stories, the rumors that no one would tell me. But you will tell me now. Of what am I accused? I cannot bear it not to know."

His laugh rang out, terrible in her ears. "Can you bear to hear that you are accused of unfaithfulness? Shall you feel better knowing you were said to hold secret trysts with a lover even after you pledged yourself to Geoffrey? And now you beg me to spare the life of that lover!"

Jane writhed in his clasp, stricken to the soul. "NO! Danforth, what are you saying? Who—!"

His cold, biting tones cut into her. "Come, my dear. Do not play the innocent with me. You know who. The same man who would have ruined my sister. Geoffrey died on his way to meet him, to force him to a duel to save your good name. But nothing will save him this time. This time Heaton will face *me!* And you, my precious jade, will pay the price for your deceit. Did you truly believe you could save him by flinging yourself at me?"

"That is what you believe? That *I* could-could . . ." She could not go on, and for an awful moment, she thought she must swoon at the terrible truth. Then the awakening of a slow, blinding fury saved her. "Oh, how I wish I were a man that I might kill you for that. My brother *will* kill you when he finds out. But I shall not tell him. I-I pray no one ever will. I loved you for what I thought you were, but now I shall loathe you for what you have said, despise you for as long as I live. Let me go! I cannot bear your hands on me!"

In her rage she struck at him with her fists, fought to break from his hold with all of her strength. Danforth, white-faced, his terrible eyes burning, crushed her ruthlessly to him, bent her to his will. His mouth closed over hers in a burning kiss. And still she fought him, fought herself and the unwitting leap of passion that his cruel embrace awakened in her. Until at last she sagged in his clasp, her strength spent, her senses reeling. Then he released her.

Jane's head lolled back against his shoulder, and she stared up at the chiseled hardness of his face. His breath heaved from his exertions, and his eyes yet smoldered. His lips curved in a chilling smile.

"Now, Miss Ashely, you are paid in full," he said huskily. "As am I. I shall not bother you again. The same cannot be said, however, for your lover. Heaton will pay with his life, you may be sure of it."

With cold deliberation, he put her from him and without a backward glance, strode swiftly from the room. Jane was falling, sinking to the floor, even as he slammed the door firmly shut behind him.

The evening promised well to suit Jane's bleak mood as the carriage turned off Piccadilly on to St. James's Street and from there into Pall Mall, which would bring them eventually to Waterloo Place and Carlton House. There was a distinct chill in the night, and the air was heavy with the portent of rain before morning.

Jane sat in the carriage next to Ethne, who gave every appearance of one in a chastened state. And for once, Mina, seated next to Wilfred across from them, seemed to have very little to say. Jane was aware that she was the cause of her sister-in-law's unwonted reticence, but, try as she might, she could not summon either the wit or the will to dispel the gloom that seemed to hang like a pall on her spirits.

She had thought never to feel again such anguish as she had suffered at Danforth's betrayal. It had been like having her heart cut out all over again. And when that first sharp edge of grief and rage had receded, she had been rendered strangely bereft of feeling, like a dead thing, who must go on performing the motions of living.

It had been Wilfred who found her, weeping and incoherent. Poor Wilfred. She had never seen him look quite like that before—stricken, helpless somehow in the face of her grief. He had lifted her up from the floor and held her until the weeping gave way before his low-murmured sympathy. Then he had gently coaxed the story from her. She remembered raving that she would meet Heaton herself to force the truth from him.

Jane stole a peek at her brother's face, impassive now and unreadable. How different from a few hours ago, when, after carrying her to her bed and leaving her to Nanny Twickum's care, he had stalked, from her room, stone-faced, but with eyes that had seemed to burn with a cold, set intensity. She had been consumed with fear that he had gone to Danforth and would not be consoled until he returned to the house an interminable two hours later.

Then she had lain, sleepless and withdrawn into some strange place where nothing could reach through to her, until at last the thought of Ethne wedged itself in her stunned brain. Driven out of her lethargy to rise and wash her face, she had gone in search of the child. It was the one ray of sunshine in all of this, she thought bleakly, that she had been able to dispel Ethne's fears and persuade her that it was not too late to retrieve her chance at happiness with Phillip Maheux. At least Ethne should not be made to suffer for something that had happened seven years in the past.

* * *

The ballroom at Carlton House, in addition to the several drawing rooms, were already filled nearly to capacity when Melcourt's party descended from the carriage before the stately columned front and, presenting the engraved invitation to the doorman, entered.

They found, true to the rumors that had been circulating the rounds for weeks, the interior had been transformed into something resembling a forest of potted trees with caged birds hanging among the branches and live butterflies flitting among the lily blossoms and crocuses. No doubt there would be not a few who would be disappointed to discover the grass-woven nests cunningly displayed among the foliage contained colored hens' eggs instead of the Fabergé creations wrought of gold, silver, and jewels they had been led to expect. Apparently someone had thought better as well of allowing tame deer to wander freely through the foliage, and Ethne was moved to point out that there was not even a single rabbit or lamb to be seen, though she thought it possible that such creatures might have been confined outside to the grounds. At least the ballroom itself had, save for an abundance of greenery draped about the windows and walls, been spared the lavish conceit of a woody bower in springtime. Things were crowded enough without the additional encumbrance of trees.

Linking arms with Ethne, Jane led her on into the reception hall, while Mina and Wilfred paused to check their wraps in at the cloakroom. "Come, now," she said with a false brightness. "Let us see if we can find Phillip."

Jane felt the girl tremble against her. "Oh, it is too late, I know it. He will not want to see me. And I am sure I cannot blame him, after everything I did to try and make him believe I was unworthy."

Jane lightly shook Ethne's arm. "Gammon. Phillip is head over ears in love with you. He has more than proved himself to you. Only show him that your heart has not changed, and he will fall on his knees to you, I promise."

Ethne's cold hand clutched spasmodically at Jane's. "Faith, there is Freddy!" she exclaimed. Jane, following the girl's eyes, saw Freddy, standing beneath a curved rose trellis complete with roses blooming on the vines. How handsome he looked in his dress regimentals, she thought, her smile whimsical at the sight of interested glances he was drawing from more than one pair of feminine eyes. Ethne's breath caught. "He has seen us! Oh, Jane, I shall die if he looks at me the way he did at Lady Fitzhugh's when he forced the truth from me. How hurt he was! How scornful his eyes! He will never forgive me for believing those dreadful things about him. And, indeed, I shall never forgive myself."

"Nonsense," said Jane, driven to comfort the child. "You never believed it. If you had, you would not have been willing to sacrifice your happiness for him. You have always known in your heart he was fine and good. Only give him time, he will realize as soon as he is over the hurt the true depth of your loyalty."

"You are so good to me, Jane," said Ethne with a catch in her voice, "when I do not in the least deserve it. I cannot think what I should have done had you not come to me today and convinced me those letters were only tissues of lies. If only it has not come too late! There is Phillip. He is talking to Freddy. Jane, they are coming. What shall I do?"

"Stand and take your medicine, Ethne dear."

Jane could not but thrill at the sight of Phillip Maheux's slow, purposeful approach. To Ethne, he must clearly have appeared daunting; and, indeed, he made a commanding figure. Tall, slender, and strikingly handsome in dark evening dress, he was the sort to cause palpitations in any young girl's heart. Just now he wore an expression of unsmiling determination, heightened somehow by the keen flash of his eyes behind drooping eyelids.

He bowed to Jane when he came up to them. "Miss Ashely, I believe I am under your obligation. Leftenant Bartholomew has told me how you uncovered the plot against Miss Winter and, further, that you have been kind enough on more than one occasion to champion me with her brother, the marquess. That is why I make bold to ask if you would allow me to address Miss Winter."

"Please do, my lord," Jane murmured, with a gravity to match his own. "Nothing could please me more."

"Traitor!" gasped Ethne in the other woman's ear, then paled as she looked up to find Phillip Maheux, standing, stern and forbidding, over her.

"It is Easter Eve, Miss Winter," he announced as if this were a most pertinent fact.

"Indeed, my lord, it is," replied Ethne sweetly, apparently having recovered her composure with remarkable facility, though Jane could not but note the somewhat rapid rise and fall of the girl's bosom.

"Had things been different, Miss Winter," continued the young nobleman. "Had you not proven most damned fickle, obstinate, and headstrong, I should have been pleased to present you with a pair of gloves this evening."

Ethne's lips trembled and it was noticeable that her pallor deepened to a pearly white. "Should you, my lord?" she queried, with at least a hint of her old, cool disdain. "But then, I have no need of gloves."

Phillip's chin noticeably hardened, and there was a glint in his eyes that Ethne must have found galling to meet.

"No, not gloves, Miss Winter, but rather the need of a man's steadying hand."

At last twin spots of color burned through the pallor of

her cheeks. "Then you presume too much, my lord. I am steady enough to suit me without a man's hand, steady or otherwise," Ethne retorted.

"It would seem your guardian holds a different opinion. It was he who advised against gloves. And I could not but agree with him. I believe I have been patient with you, but my patience does not extend to giving you the pleasure of making me wait until Easter morning to discover if you shall deign to wear my gloves."

Ethne's head lifted. Her eyes shone huge in her face. "Does it not, my lord?" she said. "But, indeed, it is likely your patience would, in any event, go unrewarded."

Phillip's lips curved in a smile that baffled, even as it thrilled Jane, looking on.

"Quite so," he said, "which is why I brought this instead." Drawing forth from an inner pocket a magnificent ring with emeralds interspersed with diamonds, he held it tantalizingly before the pale-faced girl. "It was my grandmother's, and her mother's before her. And now it is yours, Miss Winter, if you will have it—and me."

"Oh, Phillip." Ethne's eyes shimmered and filled with tears.

" 'Oh, Phillip,' what?" demanded Maheux, refusing to abandon his stern front until he had made sure of his troublesome love.

"Oh, Phillip—*darling!*" Ethne cried, laughing. "Yes. Yes, I will marry you."

As Freddy stepped forward to squeeze Ethne's hands and to thump Phillip enthusiastically on the back, none of the young people noticed that Jane, smiling through her tears, slipped quietly away.

Only Melcourt, who had stationed himself in the shadows of a potted hazlewood to watch, saw her go to the cloak room and call for Ethne's cloak. An odd sort of smile played about

the handsome lips, then, turning away, he went to join his
countess, happily congratulating the newly engaged couple.

Some few minutes later, Jane stood in the shadows of the
columned porch, watching the link boys huddled against a
falling curtain of mist. She could only be glad that Ethne had
that evening chosen a hooded taffeta cloak. Falling to the
ankles, it served to conceal not only Jane's fair hair, but her
dress and form as well. When the messenger came for Ethne,
he would find Lady Jane Ashely waiting for him instead.

And then what? she wondered. Face Heaton with the lies
that he had spread about her and denounce him? It all
sounded so fantastic now that she was actually here before
Carlton House waiting to be summoned to Gerard Heaton.
She had been sick and reeling when Danforth left her, stunned
by his violence and the scorn with which he had denounced
her. Clearly she had been half out of her mind when she
conceived the idea of taking Ethne's place at tonight's rendezvous. What could she possibly hope to achieve save to
place herself in danger and probably ruin her own reputation?

She had come to face Heaton, to learn the truth, she reminded herself. Once and for all, she would know why Geoffrey had died and why Heaton had plotted against her. In her
present state, she did not care what happened after that. She
wanted only to know, that it might all be finally laid to rest.

"Be you the lady what's in need of a carriage?" queried
a gruff little voice out of the shadows.

Jane, instinctively pulling the hood further forward to conceal her face, nodded.

"You're to follow me, if yer please, m'lady."

The figure stealing out of the darkness was small and
slightly built—a boy, who could not have been above twelve.
Had she not been suddenly laboring under the conviction that

she was on the point of placing herself in a most untenable situation, she might have thought it odd that he was dressed in blue and silver livery or that he had rather the look of a gentleman's tiger. As it was, she merely caught her lip briefly between her teeth before squaring her shoulders and hurrying after the boy.

She simply would not allow herself to think beyond the coming confrontation with Heaton.

The carriage, waiting at the end of the drive, was surprisingly rich and luxurious for a man who was well known not to have a feather to fly with, the team of matched grays obviously high-steppers. But then, no doubt he had borrowed both horses and carriage from his friend Lord Rivendale, a noted rakeshame and ne'er-do-well. And, indeed, there were telltale markings of a coat of arms on the side, indistinguishable in the darkness.

Steeling herself for the worst, Jane approached. Her eyes strained to see into the darkened interior to a darker form within. Though she could not make out the features, she knew it must be Heaton. She shivered from more than the cold.

It was not too late, she told herself, realizing how very foolish she was to have come. She could still turn and run. What, after all, did Heaton's lies really matter? What did she care what people believed of her? She was Jane Ashely, and she had done nothing of which to be ashamed. And yet, something held her there—stubbornness or pride, or the knowledge, perhaps, that she would never be free of the past until she faced it and knew all the truth. That, and the memory of Danforth's terrible scorn.

Her breath whistled in her throat as the door to the carriage swung open, revealing a lean masculine hand extended and waiting to help her into that gloomy interior.

Jane recoiled from the thought of having to touch that strong, supple-looking member. The boy had vanished somewhere, leaving her alone in the drive. At last, flinging caution to the wind, she straightened her back and stepped forward to take the extended hand.

An odd, unexpected shock went through her as powerful fingers closed over hers. The palm was calloused and hard, no doubt from outdoor pursuits, and the arm to which it was attached lifted her with remarkable ease into the carriage.

Hardly was she inside than there was the crack of a whip. The door slammed shut. The carriage lurched into motion, and Jane was thrown sprawling ignominiously into the seat. Tangled in her twisted cloak, her face and eyes covered by the hood, she struggled to right herself. She gasped as a lean, powerful hand caught her and settled her firmly in the opposite seat.

Furiously, she yanked the hood aside and, eyes glinting blue sparks of indignation, lifted her head to deliver her abductor a stinging rebuke.

"You—!" was the only utterance she managed to get out.

"Quite so, Miss Ashely," murmured the Marquess of Danforth, a faint, chilling smile on the stern, handsome lips.

Fifteen

"Danforth!" Jane uttered loathingly, when she had recovered from her first shock of surprise. "What are you doing here?"

"Odd, Miss Ashely, but I was about to ask you the same question," murmured Danforth, odiously smiling. "Pardon my curiosity, but is it your usual practice to climb into strange carriages while roaming the streets of London, unescorted and at night?"

Jane only just managed to stifle a gasp of outrage at that gently mocking reminder of their first unfortunate encounter. Oh, the beast to tease her so! "You know very well it is not," she retorted. "Just as you know perfectly well why I am here." She blushed furiously, realizing exactly what interpretation he must have put on her being there. Then bitterly reminded that Danforth could not hold her further beneath contempt, she lifted her head in withering disdain. "What reason could there be, after all, for a woman like me—on the streets, alone and at night?" she said and was rewarded with a faint hardening of Danforth's eyes. "No doubt I should, under different circumstances, be pleased to enjoy your company, my lord. Unfortunately, I already have an assignation to keep. However much I may regret it, I'm afraid I really must demand that you set me down at once."

"And I am equally afraid that I cannot oblige you, Miss Ashely," replied his lordship mildly. "It would hardly be to any purpose, do you think, when Mr. Heaton has asked me to tender his sincerest apology. He, regrettably, has been detained elsewhere."

"Detained?" In spite of her utter contempt for the marquess, Jane felt her cheeks blanch. "Pray, sir, what have you done to him?"

"Why nothing very much," Danforth assured her with a reflective air. "I could not but note when last I chanced to run into the poor fellow, that he was looking most particularly under the weather. I should even say he was on the point of going into an exceedingly sharp decline. Naturally, it occurred to me that a sea voyage would be just the thing for what ailed him. I'm afraid I took it upon myself—purely in the spirit of the Season, you understand—to book passage for him on an East Indiaman bound for the Orient." He paused, his gaze most disturbing on her. Then, "Tell me, Miss Ashely," he added quietly, "do you think I acted out of turn?"

Jane, suffering a sudden, hot constriction in her throat, had perforce to swallow before she could attempt an answer to that most intriguing question.

"No, my lord," she said in a voice hardly above a whisper. "No doubt India will suit Mr. Heaton very well."

"Yes, I thought so myself," agreed the marquess, with an odd sort of twisted smile, "although I had a deuced hard time bringing your brother around to my way of thinking. Melcourt, I fear, was not in the least sympathetic to Mr. Heaton's case. It took all my considerable powers of persuasion to convince him a meeting on a hilltop at dawn was not the most felicitous remedy for Heaton's condition."

Jane stared at the nobleman's smooth, baffling features.

"Melcourt was there with you?" she exclaimed in fading accents.

"I'm afraid he insisted," Danforth admitted with an apologetic air. "And after he had gone to the trouble of calling on me with the express purpose of disabusing me of certain erroneous notions I had entertained, I could hardly deny him the pleasure of accompanying me when I paid my respects to Heaton. As it was, I believe he gained considerable satisfaction from the meeting."

In sudden, swift understanding, Jane lowered her gaze from Danforth's light, piercing gaze. In the pale light of the street lamps, she saw his right hand, strong and supple, glimpsed the white gleam of a bandage over the knuckles. Her eyes lifted, wide and searching, to his face, found the telltale mark of a bruise beneath the nobleman's right eye. Heaton had put up a fight, but clearly he had not stood a chance against Danforth. And her brother had watched it all and said nothing to her! She would have some pertinent questions to put to the earl when next she saw him.

The question, that should have been uppermost in her mind at that moment, but that strangely had remained at abeyance, was now brought forcefully to the fore as the carriage swept around a turn, flinging Jane into the corner.

"Yes, no doubt, he did," she said, suddenly unable to meet Danforth's eyes. "And now that you have told me what you came to say, there would seem little reason to continue. I should like to return to Carlton House."

"I'm afraid that is not in my plans, Miss Ashely," replied the marquess, in the slow, cool accents that never ceased to baffle and yet thrill her with their seeming potential. This time they aroused a feeling not unlike the cold clamp of a vise on her vitals.

"Your—plans," she repeated haltingly, looking at him now with suddenly penetrating eyes. "You came to meet me in Heaton's place. Why?" When he did not answer, but only continued to regard her with that faint, mocking smile, that she so thoroughly detested, she felt the blood drain from her face. "Good God! Danforth, you-you mean to-to keep me. To-to . . . Oh, I cannot say it. You have abducted me!"

"It would certainly appear that way, Miss Ashely," drawled the nobleman, inscrutable behind the impenetrable mask of the Corinthian.

"Then you are—what you said you were. Dangerous. A consciousless rakeshame, an adventurer, oh, I know not what all you are. But you cannot be so far removed from all sense of decency as to wish to-to dishonor me?"

Danforth's pale features in the dim light appeared to take on the hardness of cut marble.

"You flatter me, Miss Ashely," he said, in singularly chilling tones. "At least I have never made it a practice to ruin innocent maids."

"But you would ruin me? Carry me off against my will?"

"You are here, Miss Ashely. And there is no way for you to escape."

"Yes, I am here," whispered Jane, feeling sick with bitter realization. His code of honor did not apply to Jane Ashely. He would take her and use her to his own ends because he believed she was neither innocent nor a maid! But, why? If he did not love her? Surely not for revenge for what he believed to be her betrayal of Geoffrey. He had said she was paid in full for that. Then it must be because it was in his nature to do so.

"The-the stories of you are all true?" she queried, her eyes, huge on his face, searching. "You have done this before with other women? Those weeks when you disappear—gambling and orgies. Oh, how despicable you are!"

She winced at his harsh bark of laughter. "You begin to see the light, my dear. I did try to warn you. A pity you did not believe me."

Suddenly she leaned forward, her hand clutching at the sleeve of his coat. "I do not believe you yet," she said passionately. "Whatever you think I am, I do not deserve such treatment at your hands."

His eyes glittered strangely in the shadow cast by the brim of his hat. "Whether you do or not, Miss Ashely, I'm afraid it is too late. I have decided, you see, that I really must have you."

Her eyes widened in disbelief. "You must have me?" she echoed, feeling dangerously close to hysterics. "Was it not punishment enough that you made me fall in love with you?" Then ashamed at her declaration and unable to bear to have him look at her, she bit her lip and turned her face away to stare blindly into the darkness.

Consequently, she did not see Danforth's long frame grow rigid, his eyes piercing in the gloom. Nor was she immediately aware that the carriage had come to a stop.

The carriage door swinging open and Danforth's voice provided her first awareness that they had reached their destination.

"Come, Miss Ashely," drawled the marquess. "I suggest you compose yourself. We are here."

Jane came back to herself to find Danforth standing outside, his hand extended, waiting to help her down, and beyond, the pleasant aspect of a large house draped in ivy and enclosed within the confines of an ironwork fence through which could be seen a neat lawn and well-tended flower beds. In mounting dread, she realized he had brought her to one of his private residences, one he kept, no doubt, for his lights of love.

She felt weary, defeated, and, worse, she knew that, vile as he was, she had not ceased to love him. It was at this bitter certainty that she grasped, like a drowning man grasping at straws. Surely there must be some redeeming quality in him, some small measure of goodness to which she might yet appeal. Else surely she could not have so thoroughly and irrevocably lost her heart to him.

Steeling herself for what must await her within, she placed her hand in Danforth's and allowed herself to be helped to step down.

The door to the house opened before they had mounted the steps to the porch, and Jane was given to see beyond the staid figure of a proper-looking English butler to a large hall lit by a glass chandelier and made pleasant to the eye by tasteful, well-placed furnishings. It hardly looked what Jane, in her overwrought imagination, would have expected of a gentleman's love nest. On the contrary, it gave every appearance of quiet elegance and gentility.

"Good evening, m'lord," the butler intoned, divesting the Marquess of his greatcoat and hat. "Madam has retired for the evening, I'm afraid. She did, however, leave instructions for a fire to be laid, ready for you, in the West Room. And rooms have been prepared for the young lady. She said she will be most pleased to see you and the young lady at breakfast."

Jane's cheeks flamed with the knowledge that the house was currently inhabited. She would have thought Danforth might at least have had the decency to rid himself of one mistress before he got himself another!

"Thank you, Steddings. This is Miss Ashely. I believe she stands in need of something hot to drink. Hot chocolate, perhaps. Or would you prefer warmed milk, my dear?"

"I-I really couldn't say, my lord," Jane said, suddenly aware that she was shivering in her wet clothing. "Anything or nothing. I care not."

"Hot chocolate, then, Steddings," said his lordship, and, taking Jane's arm, led her through a door into a well-appointed withdrawing room in which thankfully a generous fire crackled warmly in the grate. There, to her dismay, he proceeded not only to wrap her in a warm decorative shawl, which had been draped over the back of the sofa, and to draw her to a seat before the fire, but to kneel before her as well and, picking up first one foot and then the other, tenderly divest her of her wet and ruined pink satin slippers.

She could only stare at him in numb disbelief as wordlessly he chafed one foot and then the other between his hands to bring the warmth back into them. He was administering a like service to her chilled hands when Steddings arrived with the promised chocolate for Jane and brandy for his lordship.

"Very good, Steddings. You may go." Danforth himself placed the cup between Jane's hands, then ordered her with characteristic brusqueness to drink it down. He poured himself a brandy and crossed to the fireplace to stand, one elbow propped on the mantelpiece and his gaze brooding on the fire.

Jane, watching him, wondered suddenly if he were having second thoughts. He had ministered to her as if she were a child—with a heart-rending tenderness that was not at all in keeping with the ruthless rakeshame who had forcibly abducted her, presumably with the intention of carrying her to his bed. There was a mystery here that she did not understand.

"Will you answer a question for me, my lord?" she said after a while. "Will you tell me how it was that Geoffrey learned of my—my indiscretion with Mr. Heaton?"

Danforth answered without turning from the fire. "He was anonymously sent the letter you wrote, agreeing to an assignation." At last he raised his head to look at her. "You are deucedly beautiful, my dear. It is little wonder Geoffrey was willing to fight for you or that Heaton was willing to go to any lengths to have you. Perhaps you are unaware that he meant to use Ethne as a pawn to get to you."

"No, I did not know. Indeed, how could I?"

"Indeed, how could you," replied the marquess with an odd sort of harshness. "Nevertheless, it is true. Heaton knew you would never fall for anything so preposterous as the lies about Freddy, and you had already demonstrated you were too clever to allow yourself to be lured into a trap. How galling it must have been for him to find Melcourt waiting for him at your place of rendezvous all those years ago. He never forgave your brother or you for that. Melcourt made sure he was ruined in polite society. And I drove him into exile in the country. He knew, of course, that I would put a period to his existence if ever I laid eyes on him again. And then, by chance, he ran across Ethne in Cheltenham. When he learned she was to make her come-out under the auspices of the Countess of Melcourt, he saw a way to get even with all of us—through Ethne."

Jane stared at Danforth, beginning to see things as Heaton must have seen them, beginning to grasp the enormity of the plot he had woven around all of them. First, the lies about her supposed affair with him seven years before, the lies that had driven Geoffrey to his death and, more recently, had planted the seeds of doubt about her. Then the letters to Ethne, which would soon have driven the girl to do his bidding.

"He meant to use her as a lure to draw me into the trap," Jane said in a voice that was surprisingly calm. "When he had Ethne in his power, what did he mean to do? Implicate me in her abduction?"

"Oh, he was far more ambitious than that. He wanted you at his mercy, and your fortune is, after all, greater than Ethne's. He meant to offer you the opportunity to save Ethne by taking her place."

"Then he was a fool. I should never have done anything so patently lack-witted. Still, how well he planned it. No one would ever be brought to believe I was not his accomplice if it was thought I was already his lover. He would have had me and my fortune, and Ethne would still have been ruined. The scandal would have touched even Mina and my brother." Her eyes lifted, then, to meet Danforth's. "The one thing he apparently failed to consider," she said, slowly, realizing the truth of her words, "was that I should have told you, rather than submit to being blackmailed."

"It was a major flaw in his character," agreed Danforth, his gaze unwavering, strangely unguarded on her face. "He never ceased to underestimate your ability to see to the heart of a matter and do the sensible thing."

Jane quietly set the cup aside, surprised that her hand was not shaking. "Do you think so, my lord?" she said quietly. "I'm afraid I have not felt at all sensible of late. Indeed, I hardly know myself. Do you know my mother has been used to worrying about me because I never allowed anything to upset me? And now I find that I am become a watering pot at the least little thing." She smiled a trifle twistedly, and at last she raised her eyes to look at him. "It was because of Geoffrey, you see." She spoke quite simply, almost matter-of-factly. "I swore I should never let anyone or anything touch me again."

He did not answer her smile. There was a bleakness in his eyes. "He never believed what was in that letter, you must know that. He never once doubted you, not even in those final moments when he made me swear that you would not be harmed by what had happened."

"But you believed it," she said wonderingly. "You believed it, and still you honored your word to him. You took the lie upon yourself. All those years, Danforth."

"It did not weigh heavily with me," he answered, cynical at last. "Do not imagine that it did."

"No, I shall not make that mistake again," she replied, intentionally ambiguous. "Where do you really go when you choose to disappear for weeks at a time? And do not tell me what is usually said, for I warn you, I shan't believe you."

"Shall you not?" He shrugged. "And yet it is as good an answer as any."

She had risen from her seat and allowed the shawl to fall from her shoulders unheeded to the floor. Now she stepped close to him to peer into his face with eyes that suddenly saw through him. "Are you a spy, my lord? Or a soldier. One of Wellington's lieutenants. I have heard of them. All young, fearless, intensely loyal. Is that how you knew your Spanish guerrilla captain?"

Danforth's hand moved ever so slightly where it lay on the mantelpiece. "Now you *are* letting your imagination run away with you. Danforth, a soldier. Good God, how the world would laugh at you!"

He said it with such bitterness that she most certainly would have believed him had she not seen the telltale twitch of that lean, powerful member. She had broken through his formidable guard, she realized with a strange exultation. Swiftly she moved to carry her attack to its inevitable conclusion.

"I do not believe anyone will laugh, my lord, when the truth is made known. And it will, one day, I have no doubt of it. And now, my lord," she said with her level gaze on him, "perhaps you will be so good as to tell me whose house this is and why you have brought me here."

"It is my mother's house, Miss Ashely," answered the marquess. "And Mr. Fenworthy's. It was hardly practicable to think young Maheux's parents could be kept in ignorance indefinitely of Lady Winter's marital status. They have had the pleasure of meeting Mr. Fenworthy, who is, indeed, one of nature's noblemen. And as for you, Miss Ashely, you are here at Melcourt's suggestion. A wise man, your brother. He knew you would bolt to your lovely Oaks before you could be brought to listen to reason."

"Oh, how perfectly dreadful you are," exclaimed Jane, startled into laughter. "You had me firmly believing you had brought me to your secret love nest, complete with your current mistress." Slowly the laughter died from her eyes, to be replaced by a searching light, tinged with a haunting sadness. "How could you allow me to believe the worst of you, when secretly you have always stood my staunchest friend and protector? For that, my dearest lord marquess, I shall not soon forgive you."

Danforth's lips twisted in a mirthless smile. "And shall you forgive me for believing you faithless to Geoffrey?" he said cynically. "My sweet, lovely Jane—a woman with a heart of jade? It was the one thing that drove me nearly mad. My heart told me you were Geoffrey's good angel, while that cursed letter condemned you as a deceitful, conniving wretch. And then to have you plead for Heaton's life!" He looked at her with eyes like death. "For what I believed then, for what I said to you, I shall never forgive myself."

"Hush." Her hand went to the side of his face in a caress that was instinctive and that she would never have been able to do seven years before with Geoffrey. What a child she had been then—loving, impetuous, but shallow and untested. Had she met Danforth before Geoffrey, how different things would have been. Danforth, who even at twenty-five had been reckless and wild, a hardened rakeshame with a reputation for being dangerous. She did not doubt that she would have been drawn to him, perhaps even have fallen in love with him. But she would not have been up to his weight. Not then, not at seventeen, she realized, thrilling to the sudden, swift leap of flame in his eyes.

She had been forged anew out of the flames of her lost love, then awakened from the slumbering remains to a new self—stronger, deeper, more sure of herself. And all this, she owed to Danforth—the rebirth of feeling, of renewed youth, of Easter in springtime.

His hand reached up to catch her wrist and draw it to his lips. "Jane, I do not pretend that I could ever take Geoffrey's place in your affections. But I am arrogant enough to believe I might have forged a place of my own—and driven mad enough to ask you to be my wife."

"I have never doubted your arrogance, my lord," Jane reflected archly, "or your occasionally questionable sanity—only your motives. I cannot possibly venture an answer unless I *know* why you would want me for your wife."

"Jade," growled his lordship feelingly, his arm going with apparent strong purpose around her waist. "Why do you think I should want it?"

"I have never been one to speculate, my lord," murmured Jane, who was not in the least intimidated at finding herself clutched in the arms of a notorious rakeshame.

"Tormentress," supplied Danforth, pulling her inexorably closer.

Jane, apparently inordinately pleased at the prospect of having the breath brutally crushed from her, smiled adoringly up into his dear beloved face. "I'm afraid, my lord, I must have an answer before you can hope to have yours."

Jane felt her senses reel and her heart lift against her breast at the fiercely tender light that shone in the look he bent upon her then.

"Surely, my dearest most exasperating Jane, you know why. I fell in love with you that first night when you lay, shaken and half frozen in my arms, and still had the temerity to answer my rudeness with a pertness that did you no discredit in my eyes. And, afterward, no matter how persistently I reminded myself that you were Geoffrey's beloved Lady Jane and there could never be anything between us, I failed abominably. I have been driven mad with wanting you, and if you do not say immediately you will be my wife, I shall most assuredly throttle you."

"Then, my dearest lord, if you choose to put it that way, I suppose I must confess. Ever since that day in Bond Street when you bought me that wonderfully ridiculous hat and I discovered that I was terribly, hopelessly in love with you, I have been tormented with the fear that you could never bring yourself to come up to scratch. Oh, yes, Nicholas, I will marry you. Pray do not let us wait a moment longer than is necessary!"

Then indeed did his lordship proceed to crush the breath from her. Clasping her roughly to his chest, he bent his head to kiss her with a fervor that must have sent her senses reeling, for it was certain that her arms had stolen around his neck and that she was returning his embrace in such a manner as bore little resemblance to the unruffably calm Lady Jane Ashely, who had sworn her heart would never be touched by anyone or anything again.

About the Author

Sara Blayne lives with her family in Portales, New Mexico. She is the author of four Zebra regency romances: *Passion's Lady, Duel of the Heart, A Nobleman's Bride,* and *An Elusive Guardian.* She is currently working on her next Zebra regency romance, *A Noble Deception,* that will be published in December 1995. Sara loves to hear from her readers and you may write to her c/o Zebra Books, 850 Third Avenue, New York, NY 10022. Please include a self-addressed stamped envelope if you wish a response.

ZEBRA REGENCIES
ARE
THE TALK OF THE TON!

A REFORMED RAKE (4499, $3.99)
by Jeanne Savery
After governess Harriet Cole helped her young charge flee to France—and the designs of a despicable suitor, more trouble soon arrived in the person of a London rake. Sir Frederick Carrington insisted on providing safe escort back to England. Harriet deemed Carrington more dangerous than any band of brigands, but secretly relished matching wits with him. But after being taken in his arms for a tender kiss, she found herself wondering— *could* a lady find love with an irresistible rogue?

A SCANDALOUS PROPOSAL (4504, $4.99)
by Teresa DesJardien
After only two weeks into the London season, Lady Pamela Premington has already received her first offer of marriage. If only it hadn't come from the *ton's* most notorious rake, Lord Marchmont. Pamela had already set her sights on the distinguished Lieutenant Penford, who had the heroism and honor that made him the ideal match. Now she had to keep from falling under the spell of the seductive Lord so she could pursue the man more worthy of her love. Or was he?

A LADY'S CHAMPION (4535, $3.99)
by Janice Bennett
Miss Daphne, art mistress of the Selwood Academy for Young Ladies, greeted the notion of ghosts haunting the academy with skepticism. However, to avoid rumors frightening off students, she found herself turning to Mr. Adrian Carstairs, sent by her uncle to be her "protector" against the "ghosts." Although, Daphne would accept no interference in her life, she *would* accept aid in exposing any spectral spirits. What she never expected was for Adrian to expose the secret wishes of her hidden heart . . .

CHARITY'S GAMBIT (4537, $3.99)
by Marcy Stewart
Charity Abercrombie reluctantly embarks on a London season in hopes of making a suitable match. However she cannot forget the mysterious Dominic Castille—and the kiss they shared—when he fell from a tree as she strolled through the woods. Charity does not know that the dark and dashing captain harbors a dangerous secret that will ensnare them both in its web—leaving Charity to risk certain ruin and losing the man she so passionately loves . . .

Available wherever paperbacks are sold, or order direct from the Publisher. Send cover price plus 50¢ per copy for mailing and handling to Penguin USA, P.O. Box 999, c/o Dept. 17109, Bergenfield, NJ 07621. Residents of New York and Tennessee must include sales tax. DO NOT SEND CASH.

ELEGANT LOVE STILL FLOURISHES —
Wrap yourself in a Zebra Regency Romance.

A MATCHMAKER'S MATCH   (3783, $3.50/$4.50)
by Nina Porter
To save herself from a loveless marriage, Lady Psyche Veringham pretends to be a bluestocking. Resigned to spinsterhood at twenty-three, Psyche sets her keen mind to snaring a husband for her young charge, Amanda. She sets her cap for long-time bachelor, Justin St. James. This man of the world has had his fill of frothy-headed debutantes and turns the tables on Psyche. Can a bluestocking and a man about town find true love?

FIRES IN THE SNOW   (3809, $3.99/$4.99)
by Janis Laden
Because of an unhappy occurrence, Diana Ruskin knew that a secure marriage was not in her future. She was content to assist her physician father and follow in his footsteps . . . until now. After meeting Adam, Duke of Marchmaine, Diana's precise world is shattered. She would simply have to avoid the temptation of his gentle touch and stunning physique — and by doing so break her own heart!

FIRST SEASON   (3810, $3.50/$4.50)
by Anne Baldwin
When country heiress Laetitia Biddle arrives in London for the Season, she harbors dreams of triumph and applause. Instead, she becomes the laughingstock of drawing rooms and ballrooms, alike. This headstrong miss blames the rakish Lord Wakeford for her miserable debut, and she vows to rise above her many faux pas. Vowing to become an Original, Letty proves that she's more than a match for this eligible, seasoned Lord.

AN UNCOMMON INTRIGUE   (3701, $3.99/$4.99)
by Georgina Devon
Miss Mary Elizabeth Sinclair was rather startled when the British Home Office employed her as a spy. Posing as "Tasha," an exotic fortune-teller, she expected to encounter unforeseen dangers. However, nothing could have prepared her for Lord Eric Stewart, her dashing and infuriating partner. Giving her heart to this haughty rogue would be the most reckless hazard of all.

A MADDENING MINX   (3702, $3.50/$4.50)
by Mary Kingsley
After a curricle accident, Miss Sarah Chadwick is literally thrust into the arms of Philip Thornton. While other women shy away from Thornton's eyepatch and aloof exterior, Sarah finds herself drawn to discover why this man is physically and emotionally scarred.

TODAY'S HOTTEST READS
ARE TOMORROW'S SUPERSTARS

VICTORY'S WOMAN   (4484, $4.50)
by Gretchen Genet
Andrew—the carefree soldier who sought glory on the battlefield, and returned a shattered man . . . Niall—the legendary frontiersman and a former Shawnee captive, tormented by his past . . . Roger—the troubled youth, who would rise up to claim a shocking legacy . . . and Clarice—the passionate beauty bound by one man, and hopelessly in love with another. Set against the backdrop of the American revolution, three men fight for their heritage—and one woman is destined to change all their lives forever!

FORBIDDEN   (4488, $4.99)
by Jo Beverley
While fleeing from her brothers, who are attempting to sell her into a loveless marriage, Serena Riverton accepts a carriage ride from a stranger—who is the handsomest man she has ever seen. Lord Middlethorpe, himself, is actually contemplating marriage to a dull daughter of the aristocracy, when he encounters the breathtaking Serena. She arouses him as no woman ever has. And after a night of thrilling intimacy—a forbidden liaison—Serena must choose between a lady's place and a woman's passion!

WINDS OF DESTINY   (4489, $4.99)
by Victoria Thompson
Becky Tate is a half-breed outcast—branded by her Comanche heritage. Then she meets a rugged stranger who awakens her heart to the magic and mystery of passion. Hiding a desperate past, Texas Ranger Clint Masterson has ridden into cattle country to bring peace to a divided land. But a greater battle rages inside him when he dares to desire the beautiful Becky!

WILDEST HEART   (4456, $4.99)
by Virginia Brown
Maggie Malone had come to cattle country to forge her future as a healer. Now she was faced by Devon Conrad, an outlaw wounded body and soul by his shadowy past . . . whose eyes blazed with fury even as his burning caress sent her spiraling with desire. They came together in a Texas town about to explode in sin and scandal. Danger was their destiny—and there was nothing they wouldn't dare for love!

DISCOVER DEANA JAMES!

CAPTIVE ANGEL   (2524, $4.50/$5.50)
Abandoned, penniless, and suddenly responsible for the biggest tobacco plantation in Colleton County, distraught Caroline Gillard had no time to dissolve into tears. By day the willowy redhead labored to exhaustion beside her slaves . . . but each night left her restless with longing for her wayward husband. She'd make the sea captain regret his betrayal until he begged her to take him back!

MASQUE OF SAPPHIRE   (2885, $4.50/$5.50)
Judith Talbot-Harrow left England with a heavy heart. She was going to America to join a father she despised and a sister she distrusted. She was certainly in no mood to put up with the insulting actions of the arrogant Yankee privateer who boarded her ship, ransacked her things, then "apologized" with an indecent, brazen kiss! She vowed that someday he'd pay dearly for the liberties he had taken and the desires he had awakened.

SPEAK ONLY LOVE   (3439, $4.95/$5.95)
Long ago, the shock of her mother's death had robbed Vivian Marleigh of the power of speech. Now she was being forced to marry a bitter man with brandy on his breath. But she could not say what was in her heart. It was up to the viscount to spark the fires that would melt her icy reserve.

WILD TEXAS HEART   (3205, $4.95/$5.95)
Fan Breckenridge was terrified when the stranger found her near-naked and shivering beneath the Texas stars. Unable to remember who she was or what had happened, all she had in the world was the deed to a patch of land that might yield oil . . . and the fierce loving of this wildcatter who called himself Irons.

Available wherever paperbacks are sold, or order direct from the Publisher. Send cover price plus 50¢ per copy for mailing and handling to Penguin USA, P.O. Box 999, c/o Dept. 17109, Bergenfield, NJ 07621. Residents of New York and Tennessee must include sales tax. DO NOT SEND CASH.